Praise for *Opening Belle*

"Wow. This is the inside story we've been waiting for. Wall Street women never talk because their silence has been bought. Not Maureen Sherry. She tells her story of a working mother's battle against outrageous sexism and financial recklessness with laugh-out-loud insight and winning panache."

—Allison Pearson, author of *I Don't Know How She Does It*

"Corporate sexism and the mortgage crisis are a laugh a minute . . . in this delightful comic novel, at least. . . . So much fun."

—*Kirkus Reviews* (starred review)

"Maureen Sherry's comic novel unspools like a movie. . . . I can just hear Cyndi Lauper's version of 'Money Changes Everything' on the soundtrack."

—*The Dallas Morning News*

"*Working Girl* meets *Wolf of Wall Street* in this in-depth, behind-the-pinstripe peek inside a temple of elite finance, navigated by a sharp, smart woman in an old boys' world."

—Jill Kargman, author and creator of *Odd Mom Out*

"Funny and fast."

—*Booklist*

"*Opening Belle* is an irresistibly Zeitgeist-y novel about motherhood, marriage, misogyny, lust, ambition, discovery, disappointment, entitled nannies, and Goldfish crackers on the floor that (and this is big) rings true. But that's not all. Sherry's novel is also a delightfully funny and frequently damning participant-observer's dissection of the secretive codes and practices of an elite, socially antediluvian tribe of men who, in a very real sense, run the world. For them, the bell has sounded."

—Wednesday Martin, author of *Primates of Park Avenue*

"Filled with humor and heart."

—*Library Journal*

"Rooting for our girl banker/mommy/wife Isabelle is not tough; she is so brilliantly breezy. This book reveals the honest reality of a woman working in a man's world and still being treated like she's in an updated version of the cult classic *Nine to Five*."

—Lucy Sykes, author of *The Knockoff*

"Maureen Sherry reveals what it's like to be a woman working in the adrenaline-fueled, complex, exciting, rewarding, and demanding culture of Wall Street. You won't be bored on this roller coaster ride."

—Amy Goodfriend, CEO Goodfriend Partners, former partner, Goldman Sachs

ALSO BY MAUREEN SHERRY

Walls Within Walls

Opening Belle

A Novel

MAUREEN SHERRY

SIMON & SCHUSTER PAPERBACKS

New York London Toronto Sydney New Delhi

Simon & Schuster Paperbacks
An Imprint of Simon & Schuster, Inc.
1230 Avenue of the Americas
New York, NY 10020

First Simon & Schuster trade paperback edition February 2017

SIMON & SCHUSTER PAPERBACKS and colophon are registered trademarks of
Simon & Schuster, Inc.

For information about special discounts for bulk purchases,
please contact Simon & Schuster Special Sales at 1-866-506-1949 or
business@simonandschuster.com.

The Simon & Schuster Speakers Bureau can bring authors to your
live event. For more information or to book an event contact the
Simon & Schuster Speakers Bureau at 1-866-248-3049 or
visit our website at www.simonspeakers.com.

Manufactured in the United States of America

3 5 7 9 10 8 6 4

The Library of Congress has cataloged the hardcover edition as follows:

Sherry, Maureen.
Opening Belle : a novel / Maureen Sherry.—First Simon & Schuster
hardcover edition.
pages ; cm
ISBN 978-1-5011-1062-7 (hardcover)—ISBN 978-1-5011-1063-4
(softcover)—ISBN 978-1-5011-1064-1 (ebook) 1. Working mothers—
Fiction. 2. Women stockbrokers—Fiction. 3. Wall Street
(New York, N.Y.)—Fiction. I. Title.
PS3619.H46954O64 2016
813'.6—dc23
2015024158

ISBN 978-1-5011-1062-7
ISBN 978-1-5011-1063-4 (pbk)
ISBN 978-1-5011-1064-1 (ebook)

This book is dedicated to Ella, Kiera, Cavan, and Owen, who have watched me work on this their entire lives. Someday I will miss you getting peanut butter on my keyboard.

CONTENTS

1   The Trouble with Barbie   *1*

2   When That Was Us   *14*

3   Slipping Out   *20*

4   Herd on the Street   *24*

5   Where the Heart Is   *37*

6   Dais of the Dicks   *42*

7   How Not to Meet Your Husband, Part II   *46*

8   Ex-Change   *54*

9   On the Floor   *65*

10   Ex-Dividend   *72*

11   How Not to Meet Your Husband, Part I   *77*

12   The Day the Market Moved on Me   *83*

13   Gentlemen Prefer Bonds   *91*

14   In the Money   *96*

15   The End That Was the Beginning   *105*

16   Takeover   *115*

17   Pump and Dump   *121*

18   Naked Girl   *129*

19   Trade You   *139*

20   Putting Out Feelers   *145*

Contents

21 Ticker Tantrum   149

22 Inside Information   160

23 Bond Girl   166

24 Women's Issues   180

25 Tribal Knowledge   193

26 Golden Handcuffs   203

27 Standard Deviation   207

28 It's Because You Fit Me   210

29 Short Squeeze   217

30 The Misery Index   231

31 Chasing Returns   235

32 Consumption   243

33 Front Running   246

34 How She Gets By   255

35 Triple Witching Hour   265

36 Crash   287

37 Trade This   299

38 Better Offer   309

39 Dead Cat Bounce   316

40 Yield   320

41 Rational Exuberance   326

    Acknowledgments   337

CHAPTER 1

The Trouble with Barbie

I'VE BEEN to this holiday smackdown nine times. I know the drill: drink one glass of wine and lots of water. It's not the place in 2007 where a thirty-six-year-old should be seen shaking her groove thing. I'll swerve around the room, chat up some partners I don't speak with often, then head for the door and be gone—slipping on home to Bruce and our diaper-clad chaos.

Steps from the entrance I instinctively pause, summoning a more impressive version of me, trying to get her to show up tonight. I stand taller, trying to find inner fabulousness, while I mentally tick off names of men, because they are all men, who will determine my fiscal year–end bonus. Which of the graying white guys on the executive committee have I not spoken with in the last few weeks and how can I casually remind them of my biggest deals?

I rehearse before the curtains rise. I think potential drama through and summon a false calm, just the way I do when my four-year-old's shrieks threaten to shatter glass. I search for that

1

kind of counter-Zen that gets the men to lean forward and listen. Avoiding the hysterical-female role—the stereotype men I work with have of women—is the key. Staying cool and professional and never slipping into some gossiping, pretty-girl mode is a strategy that's gotten me places.

I mentally list the men with whom under any circumstances I shall not, will not, no matter what they can do for my bank account, dance with tonight. The inner caveman comes unleashed when all of us are together with an open bar and a closed stock market. I imagine every place of employment has a list of suspects to avoid at a party, but the problem with Feagin Dixon—or the problem with men making big money anywhere—is that they can get casual with wedding vows. It's not that they don't love their wives—I think they do—but the headiness of that money sucks the scruples right out of them. Any guy who was perhaps a geek in another life, hears the call of his near-celebrity status, and it makes him horny. If ever there was a time of year these men are in heat, it's now, just a few months before bonus season.

Professionals on Wall Street get salaries to envy. Administrators get $50K to $200K a year; vice presidential salaries are about $250K, and mine at the managing director level is $500K. While that's terrific, what comes next is the mind blower. At the end of our fiscal year, in just a few months, commissions will be divvied up and paid out to the people who reined them in: bankers get the commissions on investment banking deals, traders get the cents per share paid to them by the buyers and sellers of stocks and bonds, and nonproducing executives pilfer from every department they ever set foot in. These bonuses put us in the economic stratosphere, usually doubling, quadrupling, or making irrelevant the actual salary. By staying at the top of my game, I hope to work until I never have to work again, cashing in stock options in my wake and being young enough to do something meaningful. I'll take my tribe of three kids and mostly nonemployed husband and go live in some suburb with cul-de-sacs where I will even enjoy using that word. I'll join the PTA, put my kids on a school bus, give sizeable chunks of money to great causes, and learn how to be reverential to my husband and his esoteric interests known to him as "work." But for now, I'm paying for three private school tuitions, a nanny salary, a dog walker, a housekeeper who only shows up on occasion, rental space to park our car, a mortgage on a family-sized apartment, and the rent on a Hamptons house we run to each weekend to exhale, all with after-tax dollars. I need to work the room tonight.

I stand at the top of the restaurant steps, inhaling the crisp December air, catching sight of myself in the glass doors. I'm not exactly a photo-ready hotshot. I'm an expensively dressed bag lady. Everyone else walking up the steps has primped for this moment. They smell good and their faces glow expectantly. If they've Christmas-shopped their way here, they hold elegant, quadruple-weighted shopping bags that scream the worth of the contents: Hermès, Mikimoto, Takashimaya, and Prada. I, on the other hand, have garbage bag–sized Toys "R" Us sacks that contain the plastic Rescue Bots figures, a giant Haircut Barbie head (think CPR mannequin head with blond wig), and oversized Fisher-Price Peek-a-Blocks. The whole spectacle doesn't weigh much, but the bulk destroys my attempt at holiday elegance—the dress code for tonight. To add to my distress, I've managed to knock my Peek-a-Blocks into full song several times. They are possibly the first battery-*included* toy ever sold. Each time the sack bangs against my knee, I hear a rousing electronic rendition of "Open, shut them, open, shut them, give a little clap, clap, clap."

I'm wondering just how far the public walk to the coat check will be when Ballsbridge swoops in behind me.

Marcus Ballsbridge, most often referred to as Ballsy, is a thirty-nine-year-old father of two. He has the sort of thick, dark hair women just want to tousle. Of course, if one of us ever were to do such a thing, it would be interpreted as some call-to-mate move. The news of her flirtation would be broadcast across the trading floor in minutes. A girl can think of tousling but she dare not do it. He has angular features and a southern drawl laced with charm that quiets the cackle of sales assistants and he's probably the closest thing I have to a work friend. Ballsbridge and I sit back to back on the trading floor. We exchange work-related barbs for much of the day in sibling fashion. The second the market closes we don't speak until the following morning. All our conversations occur between the opening bell at 9:30 a.m. and the close at 4 p.m., which makes this moment officially off-limits. Tonight he surprises me.

"Hey, darlin' Isabelle, you and I hitting all the hot spots, huh?" He grins and holds up a sack that looks like mine only with more expensive packaging.

"We're far more evolved," I say, noting he talks more slowly when time isn't money. From all appearances, Marcus is single-handedly keeping FAO Schwarz out of bankruptcy.

"Are you still in that purple dinosaur stage?" Ballsbridge has an unhealthy fascination with Barney the Dinosaur. He draws him into conversation noticeably often. It's weird.

I proceed to reel off my kids' Santa list, as if my life depended on it. "Bionicles, Peek-a-Blocks, Haircut Barbie, Transformers, and *Yu-Gi-Oh!* cards, plus baby books. I know I'm going to forget something and break someone's heart," I say, and I mean this.

"Honey, you're actually reciting that alphabetically."

Ballsy is happy, Christmassy. Usually when I overhear him talking to his wife on the phone he is fuming. His concerns stem from the fact she just bought something unnecessary, or had some enhancement or spa procedure that perhaps was necessary, but costly nonetheless. Tonight he's different; he's light and fun, while I'm feeling a tinge of panic. Tonight is important and I look bedraggled.

"Hide me, Marcus. I look like a mother, for God's sake." I nod toward my bags.

Without missing a beat he grabs my sacks, banging the Peek-a-Blocks hard, and we enter to the tune of "Triangle A-B-C, triangle 1-2-3."

"Thanks," I exhale, and watch his back disappear into the coatroom with our wares, and I wonder why he's proud to carry toys around and why I'm not.

Metronome is a ten-thousand-square-foot restaurant that has been transformed into a dance hall this evening. It's the early side of the party, when people get liquored up for confidence, so most are hanging around the bar. The DJ spins innocent tunes, wedding tunes: "Celebrate good times, come on!"

Will that song ever just curl up and die already?

A few women dance with each other, hoping to get the party started, but nobody is cutting loose just yet. The evening hangs in an awkward state of sobriety.

The trading floor, the place most of us work, sets the stage for a mating dance. Daily. A grid of attached desks sits in a space a quarter the size of a football field. There are no walls and no cubicles to separate us. During work hours, everyone is either on the phone or flirting. A trading floor has everything to keep adrenal glands pumping cortisol: breaking news, tragedy, money, racism, sexism, and a little less overt sex play than in the past. The blow-up dolls that floated around in the early nineties have been deflated, and the deliveries of erotic chocolates have ceased. As my closest friend, Elizabeth, says when she visits me at work, "I feel like you work in a nightclub." She compares us to the technology start-up where she works and says that Wall Street's just in a more evolved stage of lawlessness than her world.

So the holiday party, with its alcohol, low lights, and music, is a show waiting to start, a nostalgic one-night pass back to the old days, and it never disappoints.

I see my first target—Simon Greene, my direct boss. He's a frumpy, oily, bald, hyperactive guy pushing sixty. He never talks to me unless it's bad news. We haven't spoken in ages, which is a positive sign for my pending bonus. But the time to let him know I'm expecting to be remembered is now. It's time to talk to Simon.

"Merry Holiday," I bumble out. I had started to say *Christmas*, did my millisecond correction because Simon is Jewish, and "Merry Holiday" was the result. I'm sure that cost me.

"Hey, Isabelle," Simon says flatly.

"Cheetah Global is voting soon. I'd like to get you in front of them. Any chance we can visit them together?" I ask.

Who would I put my boss out in front of before payday but my best client? I envision the client singing my praises to Simon just as he inks my bonus check. I doubled the commissions Cheetah paid to Feagin this year. I shake Greene's damp hand and head toward King McPherson, head trader and member of the compensation committee.

King is an excellent second choice to rub shoulders with early in the evening. A striking six-foot-four former Duke basketball player, he quickly becomes the center of any party once a woman's inhibitions are numbed. In other words, if I don't talk to him early, I'm not going anywhere near him later.

"Isabelle!" he yells as I make my way over. He is leaning against the bar with Ballsbridge.

"Happy holidays, sweetie," King says while planting a kiss that includes a small lick on my cheek. I choose not to notice the lick. King is the kind of guy I dated before I took up the cause of the underemployed. He's dashing and funny with an intimate manner that sucks people in. It didn't take long to see a shiftiness

I couldn't trust. To compare? When my husband, Bruce, says he didn't come home because an engine fell out of an airplane while he was flying home from a conference in St. Martin, and that he emergency-landed in St. Barths where the *Sports Illustrated* Swimsuit Edition was being shot, and that he didn't call because he was sharing a room with [insert supermodel's name], whom he was just friends with, and that he didn't want to wake her, it is actually *true*. With a guy like King, it's just not true. I knew I could handle being the breadwinner, but I couldn't handle being the lied-to wife. I used to be the lied-to girlfriend and that life wasn't for me.

King shifts his hand to the lower-back part of my skirt and presses into the small of my back while turning me around to face the bar. Marcus reaches over and pulls the hand off me, like some self-appointed big brother. This should make me feel cared for, but I hate it. I know how to take care of myself.

"Check out what Ballsy bought for his kids!" he says, now hanging his thumb on the back of my skirt. It's distracting and infuriating at the same time but I just go with it and am glad that Marcus lets it go too. While I love his support, it sometimes feels patronizing, like he won't let me fight my own fights.

I turn obligingly to face a coveted, hard-to-find, four-part Greybeards Castle. I know because my seven-year-old wanted one and I told him Santa doesn't do $289 toys. I may be wealthy but I'm not spoiling my kids like that. But Ballsbridge does. The men giggle as they insert the batteries and put the giant plastic keys in the fortress doors (oh please, house keys for a castle?) and hear the castle screech, "Intruder! Intruder!" Bells and sirens roar and King's hand heads farther south toward my ass, actually inside my skirt's waistband. Each time the sirens go off he laughs and with each laugh he fans his hand to brush my ass.

I have two thoughts: I'm disgusted at myself for not walking away, for putting up with this stuff just to talk business, and second, I think of me dumping my toys to hide my other life while Marcus wants to show them off. He's boasting that he went toy shopping, while King says, "That Ballsy, such a good family guy."

"Hey, golden girl." I'm pulled away from King, causing his hand to be caught on my skirt for a moment, by one of the guys on my Avoid list. This is the stuff I've rehearsed for.

He's Salvatore Brody, whom everyone calls Sally, co-head of the over-the-counter desk, and right now he's dancing like an Irish/Italian—a man bred from two cultures known for step-dancing and red wine, and from where I stand, he seems to be indulging in both. I try and follow his moronic motions, smiling all the while as I cross, hop, and 1, 2, 3, 4 while keeping my arms firmly at my side.

The song changes to House of Pain's "Jump Around" and jump we do. I briefly entertain the idea of asking him about a block of stock that traded away from me (someone else bought stock my customer was trying to buy) but realize I'd be screaming in his ear while jumping, and I just don't have that sort of energy right now and I don't want to get closer to him. The song is mercifully short, and I bolt for the ladies' room just to have someplace to go. It's there I run into Amy Yapp.

Amy and I sit about five feet from each other but rarely speak. She's slightly my junior and anxious to be promoted. She sneakily sniffs around my turf every time I have a baby so I usually keep my distance from her. Tonight, though, we stand together at the sink, awkwardly washing our hands in sync, and avoiding eye contact in the mirror in front of us. Her super-chic blond hair has been cut tight to her head, her average height raised significantly by tall, pointed heels, and her red cocktail dress tailored to within a millimeter of her skin. Everything about her is tightly wound.

The sound of running water is too quiet and the absence of talk between us too weird. Why are we so uncomfortable with each other when there is no immediate business to discuss? Amy is recently divorced, childless, and seems to have no outside interests beyond work.

The voices of two sales assistants distract us. Sales assistants are support people who spend their day balancing trades. They match, buy, and sell orders for millions of dollars, which until a few years ago were physical tickets illegibly scribbled with account numbers. These assistants balance the piles of money moving around each day and pray they get it right. They are underpaid, abused women, constantly staring at the juicy carrot of a job like mine. It's unclear to me who of us works harder, but they seem to have more fun, and I make more money. That's the real trade between us.

Stall #1: "Did you see King pull me onto his lap?" [sighs.]
Stall #2: "Puh-leeze, those guys already gave me keys to the after-party."

The after-party is a notorious event held in a block of hotel rooms after the official holiday party. Think of the cool kids who went to the Jersey Shore together after the prom, while the rest of us went home. I was never invited to the after-party either. At this moment, Amy nods toward the stalls, where the conversation regarding Flirtation with Men Who Determine Bonuses continues.

Stall #1: "I can't believe how fresh you were out there!"
Stall #2: "They loved it. That King could give my Anthony a run for his money any day."
Stall #1: "Give him a little something tonight . . . Bonus season, ya know?"

Amy turns up the water stream, hard and loud to muffle the sound of their voices and remind them we can hear everything they say. I know her hands are already clean and I wonder why these women make her so mad? The water gushes loudly, but not loudly enough. Their voices just amplify. I expect to see Amy smirking. I expect to see her rolling her eyes in an "aren't-they-pathetic?" way. Instead she looks at me blankly, her piercing blue eyes looking into mine. *What?* I think. "What?" I say.

She seems mad at me. The water stops, the chatting from the stalls stops, and Amy, with one furious motion, snatches too many hand towels from the glass shelf. The extras flutter to the floor, moved by the wind of her anger as she turns on her heels and leaves.

When I reappear in the main room, the mood has changed from caution and anticipation to debauchery. I'm looking at a frat party in good clothes. The bulk of men on the dance floor have their Hermès ties wrapped Indian-headdress style around their heads like preschool boys. They body-slam each other, and sandwich women caught in their paths. The women shriek in mock horror but make no attempt to leave the floor. One could argue they're enjoying this, but maybe not. Maybe they also feel the need to please, the need to be the team player, to hang out with the big guys as they cling precariously to some piece of the banking pie. I might know that to be true if I ever had a real conversation with one of them, but I don't. Nobody ever really talks about this stuff, especially to me, one of the few senior women on the floor. I became a managing director at twenty-eight here, the youngest to ever do so. And now at thirty-six I am really comfortable in the role. It makes me so proud. It makes me so lonely.

The other thing to note about the dancing Injuns is that they're mostly older higher-ups. The younger ones stand timidly on the sidelines, unlearning every politically correct thing ever taught to them. Body-slamming women or removing pieces of clothing while moving in a sexually explicit manner would seem to be a bad choice in a corporate setting. The scene before them is confusing and they don't know how to act. They stand uncomfortably, shifting their weight and their drinks, trying to take in a subconscious lesson on being a big shot on Wall Street.

The professional women all stand at the bar, appearing slightly lost, as if they came upon this party by accident. They look as if they hardly know one another, because they really don't.

I've been visible enough already; I've been checked off the attendance list for the holiday party and it'd be fine for me to slip away now. Anything that will happen after this moment will not be good and the networking window for the evening has closed.

As I'm leaving I stop to notice a peculiar thing happening on the dance floor. The boys are giddy, slapping their hands in unison while tossing something to each other. Like square dancers, they form a fairly impressive circle and enthusiastically hurl the thing back and forth while clapping to the beat of the music. I catch a glimpse of the object they're throwing: a shiny and sort of hairy ball that catches the light for a moment each time it's thrown. I want to leave but am transfixed because something about the object seems familiar. The dancing, jumping, sweaty men cheer, and the circle grows larger. They shout each time someone catches the thing and I can't help but watch.

When I realize what they are throwing, I have a millisecond conversation in my head that goes something like this:

Logical Me: "Take a second. Do you really want to make a scene?"

Hysterical Me: "I'm going to kick King's bony ass."

Logical Me: "If you do this, you lose all respect; just intercept it, put it back in the Toys 'R' Us bag, and elegantly exit left."

Hysterical Me: "This is it, I'm going in."

Logical Me: "Back away, no confrontation, no fight. Status quo keeps your reputation."

Hysterical Me: "They are throwing around Brigid's Haircut Barbie head. My four-year-old's present from Santa, the one I just stood on a Toys 'R' Us line forty-five minutes for, the last one on the shelf."

I leap the two steps down to get to the dance floor. Marcus has the Barbie head pulled to his ear and releases her quarterback-style. I lunge and intercept and can't believe how well I just did that. I hold her by her tousled hair while some guys start whistling and I start shouting.

"You classless boneheads! This is my daughter's Christmas present. How could you? HOW COULD YOU?" I'm almost as loud as the music. The clapping misses the beats and I hear a few "whoa"s.

I look up to see the women at the bar holding their drinks, paused in midair. Stone Dennis, a young investment banker I've been helping train for our sales department, strides up to me. I remember him as a schmoozer: untalented with numbers, but desperate to be accepted. It's pathetic that he has to be the one to set these guys straight. The music blares on, but the dancing stops as everyone waits to see the next move. I want to tell Stone to not even try to apologize. He is new and young and I know he's not responsible. But instead of trying to talk to me, Stone smiles, leans toward my left hand, and in one motion swipes Barbie yet again and I, in turn, lunge for him.

"Dude," he says to me, "chill out."

Did he really just call me "Dude"?

Some foreign energy enters my body and I feel like I'm watching myself move like a crazy lady. I grab Stone by a wrist and twist him toward me, ending the motion only when Stone has turned 180 degrees and is now in a full headlock. Stone, in turn, lifts his arm and pulls his elbow back. Is this twenty-three-year-old guy trying so hard to be accepted that he's actually about to punch me? I feel more amazed than fearful.

"I am very chill," I hiss in his ear.

"WHOA!" shouts Marcus, and steps between us.

A big vein bulges in Stone's neck and his breath smells like pot. He hurls Barbie back to Marcus, who hands her back to me, even straightens her hair a bit as he does this and then goes so far as to straighten my hair too.

"Belle, geez, they're, like, $19.99 or something. I'll buy you a new one tomorrow," he says, and looks truly sorry.

The crowd watching us grows and I feel my throat thicken. It's really time to leave before I get sobby and pathetic. I say nothing more and head to the coat check to gather my coat and whatever remains in my toy bags.

CHAPTER 2

When That Was Us

TORNADOES, ILLNESS, famine, floods, and fires. I'm trying to get some perspective. It's nothing, really, my little world and its little problems. I know I'm stronger than this. Where is my woman of steel hiding? This is not the person I think of as me. I resemble a car crash lately, a sodden, sulky, weepy, empty mess, rumpled and barely standing at the edge of Union Square. Was it children that took away the chicly dressed alpha girl and replaced her with this diminished version of me?

New York University students pass in clusters and some snuggle into each other as they walk. Their lives seem light and optimistic, and I miss that. I should get home to Bruce and the kid, and I will go home but not until I expel this nervous sparking energy. If he's still awake, he'll want to talk; if we talk I will tell him the story and if I tell him what just happened he will want to do some caveman thing, which will be both a satisfying and expensive choice for all of us. He will lapse into some predict-able speech on the evils of Wall Street, which is convenient for a guy with three digits in his paycheck and four digits of personal expenses every month.

I should want to quit, especially after a scene like tonight. But, if I can put on blinders and earplugs each morning, I'll be fine. I love what I do, we need my income, and who are they to get me so upset? I keep telling myself the culture is the price I pay for the thrill of my job and the great paycheck. I keep walking, toy sacks and all.

A young man and woman, in their early twenties, walk in front of me on the west side of Washington Square Park. The lights in the trees reflect down, forming something like a halo around them. Their jackets swing open, oblivious to the piercing cold air. Steam puffs from their mouths as they laugh uncontrollably at something the man just said. Their fingers touch, without holding hands, and their raging hormones are almost visible in the air around them. Her long hair bobs in and out of her coat collar, tangling recklessly the way mine did before I thought it unprofessional and chopped it to my shoulders. ("Damn," Bruce had said.) Her boyfriend wears jeans with unpremeditated holes in them. I love that. I miss that. Bruce wears khakis now and I can't remember when we stopped looking like that couple and became our own version of a couple just trying to get through the day. I trudge on, wondering about tomorrow morning in the office and what people will say about Barbie's head.

Children can make an intolerable job tolerable. Humiliation takes my relatively thick skin and morphs it into full-grain leather, but my kids are worth it. On days when I fancy myself to be some working mother's version of success, someone who does it all with decent capability, I feel pretty happy about everything. I once relayed this thought to Bruce and he responded by drawing me a pie chart, showing me the time I spend with the kids while they're upright and awake versus time spent with them in the horizontal and asleep position. If it were a Weight Watchers chart, the allotted amount of sugar would be equal to my time spent with children not deep in a REM state.

"That's hurtful," I told him. "And you're only working part-time so it's not like they're orphans and don't you think it's decent of me to bring home real money?" It was a harsh thing to say but Bruce's ego was solidly intact.

"Of course I do," he said. "But at least I'm proud of my life and I'm not answering to people like those guys you work with."

I had wanted to point out that he frequently answers to his playmate, the ATM, withdrawing money I work for at a gasp-worthy rate, or that he finances obscure interests in sports equipment, music, and anything to improve himself that he follows with abandon and then drops. He made me wonder if people who grew up rich and didn't stay that way inherit the unfortunate habit of deploring wealth while at the same time remaining unable to live the frugal existence they extol.

A woman who was in Bruce's boarding school class at Choate, a self-proclaimed "scholarship kid" named Aripcy Salinas, liked to take me aside and fill me with her insights on guys like him. She worked at a competing bank and we sometimes found our-selves in the same room. I found myself listening whenever she asked me what he was up to and I told her some inflated lie about his technology business or his unusual hobbies. Ari saw right through it. Because she was surrounded by those bred with wealth while not having it herself, she had insights I didn't have. As she explained once, "By not taking corporate jobs like in retail or accounting and taking up the arts or fitness therapies or being an expert at throwback stuff like vinyl record collecting or retro ski equipment, they seem cool and creative, like they're making their own way in the world. But," she added, "after a decade or so, it seems stupid."

"Bruce helps a lot with the kids," I lied. "Men don't get enough credit for staying at home." But the reality was that the more money I made at work, the more Bruce's spending climbed on just the sort of stuff she described.

Ari, a Mexican-American, self-starting, no-nonsense beauty, sighed like an old sage. "At least you're not telling me he's a Tibetan pastry expert or a champion three-wheeled bike racer or that he plays the lute."

"Can you at least laugh when you say that?" She wasn't even smirking. "Bruce is a great dad," I said truthfully, "and he's trustworthy."

"Look, it's a gender-neutral problem. The girls I knew who grew up rich and never worked became surfers."

"Surfers?"

"All of them."

"I'd think they'd buy jewelry or something."

"The jewelry and fancy car thing is for the new money. No, they surf and sometimes design stuff that they then have someone else make, and then they sell that to each other out of their living rooms. It's all based on insecurity."

"Surfing based on insecurity?" I asked skeptically. At least Ari was entertaining.

"It's because they never had to work and when they realized that life is more fulfilling if you *do* work they felt too old to start at the bottom and too proud to take a regular, schlumpy job, so they make up their own job that nobody competes against. They get to be really good at something and not as boring to hang out with as they would be if they had no job at all. Ask your friend Elizabeth. The start-up world is full of these people."

Months later, I talked to Elizabeth about Bruce's habit of flitting from one big purchase to another. He bought Pinarello Dogma bikes (plural) that cost as much as a small car

($25K for two) and parabolic skis that nobody uses anymore. He takes car services in nice weather when the bus or one of his bikes would have worked just as well. Bruce really likes having money but doesn't want to do what has to be done to earn any. But because he is a loving father and husband, and because I can afford to keep him deep in racing bikes, I bite my cheek and keep silent.

Elizabeth had said to me, "I grew up with these guys. It's textbook and doesn't get truly depressing until they turn forty. That's when they finally get the message that they're never going to be the success their daddy was."

"So what happens then?" I had asked nervously.

"That's when they go for their yoga teaching certification. Some obscure type of yoga, Forrest or Harmonica yoga."

She was joking and I was laughing, but at the same time my heart was sinking. This conversation happened two years ago, and so far it appeared to be a bull's-eye assessment of my husband on his bad days.

"Still, he's cute," I had said as I thought about his good days. He loved nature, and our kids could identify different trees in Central Park. They were adept scooter riders and acted well loved. I wasn't sure what was okay to demand of a lower-earning partner and I didn't want to turn into a chart-lady, one of those women who made chore lists for her husband, which felt as mature to me as the homeroom helper list in preschool.

"Bruce has always been the cute one," Aripcy had said. "He broke a lot of hearts at Choate. You're the only thing he didn't lose interest in once the wrapping paper was torn off."

The walking lovers stop, as one of them has presumably said something brilliant. Their eyes fix on each other's and they do that lingering thing before diving in for some hard-core face mashing.

As I pass them, I hit my Peek-a-Blocks hard and they explode into song, "Open, shut them, open, shut them, give a little clap, clap, clap. Open, shut them, open, shut them, put them in your lap, lap, lap."

I hail a cab.

CHAPTER 3

Slipping Out

W E LIVE on the Upper West Side of Manhattan in a co-op building where the residents think of themselves as socialist, lefty, and caring, but are as Park Avenue stuck-up as they come. Accidental celebrities who once waited tables but became the 0.02 percent financially successful in the arts live here, as do big-name shrinks, the odd attorney, and us. One resident offered to resell the high-end luxury goods that residents were casting aside and give the money to a homeless shelter. Our hearts are in the right place but we can be tone-deaf.

Back when we bought this Central Park West place, as a newly married, childless, and cash-flush couple, Bruce drew elaborate, architecturally interesting plans for how we would renovate. Our eldest, Kevin, came along so soon, followed by Brigid, Owen, and a seventy-five-pound mixed breed but mostly Labrador dog named Woof Woof, so we took our four thousand square feet of space in the sky and made it into a three-bedroom apartment with lots of space for tricycles and without the media room and his-and-her bath solarium that we once imagined. There's a mini-trampoline in what should be our living room, a Little Tikes slide where an ottoman should be, and countless objects with wheels: Rollerblades, fire trucks, dump trucks, strollers, scooters, Bruce's racing bikes, and longboard skateboards. We never carpeted and we never entertain anyone over four feet tall. We have a mortgage that takes my breath away—dollar for dollar the same amount my parents paid for their house in the Bronx, but I pay it every month.

To my neighbors I'm sure I appear to be a stuck-up, negligent mother. I don't take the time to hang out in the lobby with the other moms. The doormen dote on me this holiday time of year, fully aware of who writes their tip check. They are no different from me in a job with a bonus season that could swing either way.

The night doorman now takes my sacks from me—the sacks I'm completely capable of hauling into the elevator on my own. He puts them on the floor of the elevator and pushes the button for floor fourteen. I still can't even remember his name, a fact that fills me with guilt. My own father was a doorman.

When the elevator door opens, the scene in front of me screams, "Fun!" The slide is perched on the sofa, adding a foot to the drop to the floor, and it appears that mini golf was played because I step on a few rogue balls. I pass by the boys' room, saving my day's highlight of seeing their faces like some sweet dessert, before going to the master bedroom, where I pray I can get to sleep without waking Bruce. He'll sense my distress and want to talk, or worse—get busy. But our bed is empty, the house silent, and the crib is empty too. I don't think too much about this, as Bruce and I fall asleep all over the apartment with whichever kid we were trying to get to bed. I jump into the shower to visualize and dress-rehearse my entry to work in the morning.

I'm drying myself off when I hear the phone ring. The phone?

It's almost 11 p.m. I dash to it with my heart pounding, certain of disaster on the other end. It must be Bruce; maybe one of the kids is in the emergency room. I can't believe I didn't scour the place looking for the bodies.

I grab. "Hello?"

"Uh, is this Isabelle?" says a woman whose voice seems familiar—can't place her but I'm thinking preschool mom?

"Yes it is."

"Belle, it's Amy."

Amy. Amy with whom I was just washing hands at a party. Amy who sits next to me, to whom I rarely speak, and have never once spoken to at home, is calling me now?

"Come meet with us. We're at a bar on the Lower East Side. It's a lot of women from work. Izzy, we can't keep working like this."

Did she really just call me "Izzy," like we're close friends?

"I mean, you heard those women in the bathroom tonight. They're basically prostituting themselves to move their careers. It's got to stop."

Silence.

I don't confide in anyone I work with. This conversation catches me off guard. I try to think. What is she really up to?

"Yeah, well, I'm kind of busy?" I say weakly. I want to hear more. The women I know at work only say positive things about the place. It's not some morale-sucking post office. You don't get ahead with disparaging remarks, so we never say what we really think, we say what our bosses want to hear and accomplish big, capitalistic things at great human cost. Countless young MBAs are brought in, given little direction and ample verbal abuse, and most disappear within five years. The survivors—me included—are people who learn to look the other way. I'm not proud of my ability to do this, but I do it and beat myself up about it. I don't need a support group for this.

"Look, the way we all run around, it'll never happen—us getting together. Come. Really, you'll be surprised at who's here," Amy says.

"Who *is* there?"

"Just come. The Ear Inn. In the south Village. I'm hanging up," and with that, she does.

I'm drying my hair. I'm going to bed. What could they be meeting about? *Please*, I think, *now I'm even lying to myself. I have to go. I can't go. I shouldn't go. My family needs me. They need you? They don't even know you're home. I could leave the apartment again and Bruce would never know.*

I slip on low-riding jeans I've just recently starved myself back into, and some boots with a killer three-inch heel. This brings my five-foot-eleven frame up significantly, and I feel slightly charged and something bordering excitement. I keep telling myself I'm not going and yet I keep getting dressed to go, as if I've surrendered to some powerful force. I crack the boys' bedroom door to see Bruce snoring on a chair with a Nate the Great detective story splayed across his chest. Three angelic-looking children breathe in and out simultaneously. Owen, my two-year-old, is facedown on the floor and not even in a bed, but everyone is safe and alive. I should wake Bruce and send him to bed. I should put Owen in his crib but the odds of waking him up are too high, and the idea of having to explain to Bruce where I'm going too complicated.

I tiptoe out of the room, down the hall, ring for the elevator, and reverse my route back into the cold, much to the interest of the late-night doorman.

CHAPTER 4

Herd on the Street

I PUSH PAST a thick group of December sidewalk smokers, to enter a bar full of pool tables and skinny jeans. The women of Feagin Dixon are huddled around a table and an untouched pitcher of beer. In their business suits, they complicate the mood of the room like tourists in a world not their own. Here they look both familiar and strange to me. I pull up a chair and nobody acknowledges me. We don't instinctively make that high-pitched noise of excitement that women make to greet each other. We're cut from the same non-fun cloth; none of us grew up with money. We are scroungers who found a way to grow wealthy without a pedigree. We tend to not be girlfriend girls. We just want to do business and go home.

I tune in to the middle of a story that a usually spunky Michele Lane is relaying in an unusually subdued voice. Michele's a late-twentysomething strawberry blonde who works on the institutional sales desk dealing with large money managers and is barraged with suggestive and even pornographic emails almost every working day. At least that's what she's telling the table.

"Propositions, threats that I better attend client dinners, better be peppy . . . stuff like that," she says with wide, incredulous eyes.

"Do you have copies of them?" asks Alice Harlington, a dour, no-nonsense analyst who always appears to have just tasted something nasty.

"I printed and filed every disgusting email sent to me from the men we work with," Michele replies. "But they make me second-guess myself each morning when I look in my closet. What can I wear that won't get noticed? How will this fabric move if I sweat? I like to think I'm tough, but this is so draining, so distracting from work."

Her voice trails off and heads nod all together. Women at investment banks tend not to make a fuss for very good reasons. On the first day of work, all Wall Street personnel sign their civil rights away with something called a "U4," which states that if they have a bone to pick, it will be in the privacy of the company's own legal offices, and not in front of a judge or on the pages of the *New York Times*. It would be an expensive and life-debilitating move to speak up. The last woman who should ever do such a thing would be one with three kids. What am I doing here?

Michele is still speaking. It turns out that my immediate boss, Simon Greene, wants to get cozy with her, calling her frequently in the evenings to meet for dinner.

"Still, I never feel as though I can turn him down. I mean, he's my boss!" she finishes quietly, without her usual flag twirler enthusiasm.

I know exactly what Michele means; but what Michele *doesn't* know about her boss is worse. Several weeks ago, I got a call from Edward Howe, a guy who used to be my client, but was now Michele's since he had switched firms. He was her first institutional account—her first step into the big leagues. She set up a dinner to meet Edward until Simon got wind of her ambition and invited himself along to "give her pointers." As Edward later explained to me, she was proposing investment ideas while Simon kept quiet and respectful at the table. That is, until Michele went to use the restroom.

While she was away, Simon leaned over to Edward and asked, "So, are you *doing* Michele yet?"

Edward was so bothered, he called me the next day.

"I can't believe you have to work for an ass like that." And then asked me to report his dinner to our human resources manager.

"Are you serious?" I had laughed.

"Doesn't that bother you?" he asked.

"Bother me? Who cares if it bothers me? Any report filed just goes right back to Simon. Michele would be unemployed by Monday."

Michele now tells the table, "He gave me a pair of diamond earrings with my last bonus. I was gracious, because the instant I turn nasty I'm out of a job, but how do I handle this?"

Then came Violette Hawes. "You accepted diamond earrings from Greene? Are you insane?"

"What should I have done?"

"Are you screwing him?" Amy asks point-blank.

"What? No!" Michele says, but blushes.

"You are," Amy continues.

"She's not," I say. "I have great screwdar and Simon doesn't even register on it."

"'Screwdar' meaning?" Alice asks, looking horrified.

"When men get overly joyful, a bell goes off in my head. It usually means they've either nailed a trade, or a woman who is not their wife. Simon isn't happy enough to be getting away with anything. Can we continue, please?"

Michele tosses me a grateful look and the table slips into the silence of some support group waiting for the next person to share. I hate this stuff.

Violette clears her throat and before she speaks I know she's going to undress me in front of the group.

"I'm uncomfortable having Belle here," she says.

Everyone turns to stare at me. While it may be true that I was less than forthcoming about every detail of her future job, I knew Violette, standing five foot four and holding her own in a Wharton School conference room, was the person we needed, and that she was tough. There are some facts about people practically tattooed on their forehead and Violette being great at her job is a fact.

"Back when I interviewed in 2004," Violette continued, "anyone who could read a balance sheet could get a job. The ball was in my court. I had lots of career options but Belle made it sound like FD was full of thriving executive women."

When Violette came to interview in New York, I arranged meetings with six managing directors to evaluate her. I delivered her résumé materials to the interviewers myself, telling each of them this was a woman we should hire:

Me: "Here's the résumé of a woman from Wharton. We're really interested in hiring her."

He: "What does she look like?"

Me: "She spent four years in commercial real estate before going back to business school. She knows how to close a deal."

He: "Single?"

Me: "She aced her accounting classes."

He: "Smart and tough. I like that in a girl."

Me: "I believe she's a fully grown woman and she'll be here at eleven a.m."

Days later, while leading Violette around the trading room, I felt the sweep of eyeballs follow our every move, and when she finished her final interview, I picked up her reviews from the last man to meet with her.

"I'd do her if I had to," a capital markets partner had written as the title of his review. I let my eyes travel from his notes to his bulging, middle-aged, sweaty face to his bald head and back again, hoping to tell him with my eyes that I was sure Violette was hoping for charitable sex from him.

"Your mom would be proud to read this," I said as I walked away.

Violette tells the table, "It was later, after I took the job, that I saw in my file one guy had actually drawn pictures of my breasts on the top of my résumé. It was only then that I confronted Belle."

"You don't know they were your breasts," I cut in. "Maybe they were just random Botero sketches—"

Violette interrupts me. "Enough of the bullshit," she says, running a hand through her curly dark hair and focusing her almond eyes directly on mine. "I asked for the truth and you lied to me."

"I believe I told you," I swallowed, "that it's tougher at Feagin than most places, but that I went from vice president to managing director in four years and that you wouldn't accomplish that in any other business nor at any other bank. You just have to be able to ignore environmental noise. And do you remember what you told me when I told you that?"

"I told you that I knew how to do that," she answered.

"And I said, 'You're hired.'"

"But I put in more hours than any of you. I work every weekend 'cause I have no social life. I haven't been on a date in two years, and still my accounts suck."

Amy came to my defense. "Violette, we know you research stocks with rabid energy, and turn the dog meat accounts you are given into formidable sources of income. But you aren't succeeding because you mouth off too much. Flipping birds back at management is costly. We all need to work within this culture to change this culture."

Violette leans her curly head conspiratorially to the table and says to the group, "I get that some of you have figured out how to get promoted: have a filter, hold your thoughts, and don't speak up, but Belle actually lies to please management."

"We have all sold out in some way," Amy, who's wearing bangle bracelets, says. Each time she motions with her hands to make a point, a jangling noise underscores it. "That's why we're meeting, to learn how to no longer do that while still maintaining our jobs."

"Belle is a good salesperson, but a lousy friend," says Violette with finality.

Six sharp haircuts turn to look at me, and I realize my name has probably come up before. I never knew I was so disliked and I don't even try to defend myself.

"My job includes recruiting good people, and that's what I do, don't I? I mean, I recruited most of you and you're the best there is."

Lily Jay jumps in to change the conversation and take the limelight off me. "Do you know I still have T. Rowe Price as a client but don't get paid on their business anymore?" she says.

Lily goes on to describe how a man on our desk, Brian Butler, a guy famous for reading research to his clients directly from a morning handout, never adding any personal commentary or original thoughts of his own, took over the account.

"He's expecting triplets. Guess management thought he needed income," Violette snarked.

"Your income?"

"Well, he's supposed to be their FD contact, but at the opening bell he's just sitting and stirring packets of Sweet'N Low into his coffee, methodically testing the result, getting it just right. Then he reads aloud that day's investment ideas, word for word. I mean, people at T. Rowe are perfectly capable of reading the same document themselves. Guess they didn't want to be treated like five-year-olds so they don't take his calls. They call me."

"Wait, but doesn't Fletch Buckfire have half that account too?" Amy jangles.

Lily covered this massive account with a man named Fletch, an old-school sales guy stuck in some permanent stage of adolescence. Lily did all the work while Fletch was the relationship guy, the person who took everyone to the strip bar or hunt club.

"He did, but then he killed his client's dog."

"What?"

"Yeah. They went hunting or whatever you call it when you toss dynamite to make ducks get off their feathers and fly into the air. Then the boys shoot the hapless creatures. Anyway, Buckfire tossed the dynamite stick but the poor dog thought he was playing fetch, so he picked it up and tried to run it back to Buckfire and the T. Rowe guy."

"Wait. This is like a cartoon. The dog ran at them with dynamite?" Alice asks, coming the closest to smiling that I've ever seen her. I expect to see her stoic face spring some crack lines.

"So Fletch shot the dog?" I ask.

"You got it. Anyway, the old boys are a bit pissed at Fletch right now, Butler's awful, and without me there's nobody who actually transacts business between Feagin and T. Rowe Price so they've gone back to calling me, which is fine and I'm still doing all the same stuff except Butler and Fletch get paid instead of me."

"Now that would be hard to swallow," Amy says with motionless hands.

"It's hard to swallow," Lily agrees, pushing her chair back in finality. She shrugs like this is all a waste of time, like there isn't anything any of us can do.

"I covered accounts for Belle when she was on maternity leave," Amy says, "and she got them back. Maybe you'll get T. Rowe back."

I sit there thinking of what I did to get my accounts back each time I had a baby, thinking of Marcus warning me to watch out for Amy and how one evening, when she thought I had left for the day, I found her cutting and pasting client contact information from my unlocked computer. She was emailing everything to herself in a traceable way that a sleep-deprived, too-busy mother would never take the time to check. I guess the reason I still trust her is she didn't lie or make excuses for this and our conversation went like this:

"What could I possibly have done to make you steal my accounts?" I had asked. "All I've ever done for your career is help it and this is how you thank me?"

Amy, all business all the time, didn't even look guilty. She hadn't tried to swipe to another screen. She didn't redden, she just looked me in the eye.

"You've been great to me, Belle, but really, how long are you going to keep this kid/job thing going? I'm just getting myself ready for the inevitable. You would do the same thing."

Would I have done the same thing? I'd like to think I wouldn't. At this table here tonight she seems so trustworthy. What is it about our firm that has us doing things the outside world would never understand, things that only a few years ago we would have thought ourselves incapable of?

Michele, Violette, Lily, Amy, and I all work on the trading floor. One floor above us, the rest of the women work in research and investment banking. Though they have doors they can close, and offices with walls, their physical isolation makes unwanted male attention more covert. One of these women is Alice Harlington.

When she graduated from business school, Alice accelerated onto the fast lane at JPMorgan Chase, research department. She had such a client following that Feagin Dixon enticed her to join us. She was a mathematical whiz and fluent in complicated accounting. She married a plumber who balanced out her crazy travel schedule by pampering her when she was home. "He's like a wife," Alice liked to say, "and he fixes stuff." "Nice," the rest of us would sigh. I looked at Alice's soft, rippled body, thick glasses, flat shoes, and felt admiration for her comfort in herself. Alice never tries to be anyone except Alice.

"Well, ladies, it's important to support the people who help you rise in your career. And Amy, Belle's been nothing but a cheerleader for you. Remember that."

"I do," said Amy, and I believe her.

Alice is another one who doesn't mince words. "But I must share the story of my hiring Sook."

Sook Park is her assistant, who came for his Wall Street interviews fresh out of business school. Alice was looking for a meticulous aide who could plow through spreadsheet computations, reconfigure balance sheets, and analyze income statements of public companies. Sook could do all of this.

"You see, when I called the head of research to finalize the offer to Sook and to come by his office for a handshake, I wasn't prepared for the response I got."

"So what was the response?" asked Violette, visibly annoyed by Alice's buildup.

Here, Alice physically imitates answering a phone, looking over our heads, pushing her thick glasses closer to her eyes. "I got a phone call from a research director asking me if I had actually *met* Sook."

Alice sits back in her chair, thoughtfully choosing her next words.

"So I said to him, 'Of course I've met Sook, he's interviewed here six times, he's terrific with the models'," she says, referring to the earnings predictions he would be responsible for creating.

"'Alice, he's Or-i-en-tal,' Mr. Director told me."

Alice holds an imaginary phone away from her, staring at the receiver quizzically. Her focus came back to the women at the table.

"Ladies, I swear, I thought I was being set up."

She puts the phone back to her ear, pretending again to speak with the assistant director. "'I believe the term is *Asian American*,'" she says softly.

"'They're different from us,' I was then told."

"'Different how?'"

"'Well, he'll drink tea and stuff, and keep food in his desk,'" the director told me.

"'Sook is the most talented person I interviewed and I'm hiring him,' I said. Then just as I was hanging up he said, 'Between the fags and chinks in this place, how do I make any progress in the *Institutional Investor* research rankings?' Then, ladies, he hung up."

We all pause, hanging midmovement while the music in the background seems to get louder.

The other research member at our table is a Julia Roberts look-alike: Nancy Hogan, who was begged to join Feagin with an enormous contract. Her drive and natural intelligence were

Street-famous. Nancy gave her boss days and nights for two years, tirelessly completing tasks that she'd drop everything for. One day, however, she shared too much information with her boss, Thomas Toff.

She had a boyfriend and then she didn't. The fact that she was in New York and he was in London had prolonged what should have been a two-week fling into a six-month relationship. But due to some Russian roulette version of birth control, she was expecting his child. When she could no longer walk around with her skirts open in the back, her blouses hanging over them to camouflage her new girth, she went into Toff's office.

"I went in there expecting to be congratulated. I mean, he's a family guy and loves kids. Instead he said to me," and here she took an enormous swallow of beer, "'I know a place where you can get that taken care of.'"

"Take care of what?" asked Alice, someone I knew was desperate to have a baby.

"Have an abortion."

"Wait. You were six months pregnant," Amy said.

"Thomas was upset at the potential disruption of his own work. He started openly complaining about me, telling people that I kept running off for sonograms."

I remember Toff telling me Nancy's timing couldn't be worse, so I asked him if his own wife got sonograms with their children. "My wife had a husband with a job," Toff had told me.

Nancy now tells the table something I knew was coming.

"I'm leaving right after bonuses this year," she says.

Another very educated talent will walk out the door, leaving no record anywhere of what went on. Nancy, like many before her, will simply evaporate.

"I want to go home to Minnesota," she tells the table. "Minds are more open there."

It was Amy's idea to get us together tonight but it is Amanda Mandelbaum who makes things happen. Amanda is like the aunt who remembers everyone's birthday, who always has something in the refrigerator, who gets truly concerned if you're sick, who says the things you think but would never dare say out loud. She has an ambitious side that enabled her to claw her way from sales assistant status to some purgatorial state of almost vice president. She's made the numbers yet hasn't gotten the title due to her rough exterior. Simon, my boss, told me to "get her to quit acting like a dude." She's five feet two inches of dynamic energy that gets easily irritated.

"So my career is going nowhere if the culture doesn't change, and we're the only ones who can do something about that," Amanda says.

"What exactly do you have in mind?" Alice says, pursing her lips together.

"We meet regularly. We do some things to change the culture. Not with lawsuits but with words. We use the right words at the right moments along with purposeful acts that draw attention to men behaving badly."

This all sounds almost sweet to me. Sweet and naïve. Still, if I were to bet on any change coming our way, Amanda would be the one to make something happen.

"We should meet once a month," she says.

"At least," someone responds.

"I'll send out meeting notifications by email, with 'GCC' under the subject line. They will be from an unknown ISP so look in your spam frequently."

Heads nod. Mine does not.

"Meetings will rotate from restaurant to restaurant and not be in Midtown. It would look strange for us all to be seen together."

I finally speak. "What's with the 'GCC'?" A harmless enough question.

"I've just named our group," Amanda says. "The Glass Ceiling Club, the club for women who cannot see what in the hell is invisibly blocking them from moving up. We will work to change this entrenched culture and we're going to do it with manners, without lawsuits or headlines in newspapers."

"Fitting enough," I say, feeling slightly energized, high school–ish, and even a little hopeful before I remember that I shouldn't take part in any of this stuff. I can't afford the financial punishments of hanging with the rebels. I tell myself I'll stay on the sidelines.

The Glass Ceiling Club vows not to be catty or spiteful. They promise to be forward-looking and not gripe about the past. They promise to help nurture and maintain the young women who recycle through our ranks like yesterday's newspaper, and swear to no longer ignore the locker room environment we work in. Without lawsuits or media, we aim to work like grown-ups in breaking up—as a former CEO described it—"the last culturally pure environment in America."

CHAPTER 5

Where the Heart Is

THE NEXT MORNING I'm in a steamy outdoor shower on some tropical island. Not really. I'm home. My head is hurting as if that party were some off-the-hook night to remember, as if that meeting at the Ear Inn were some beer pong, Jell-O shot throwback, but the pain in my head is really just from sleep deprivation. My kids are hollering on the other side of the door, and it smells like fruit on steroids in here. Magic Marjorie's Mango Shampoo, Dumbo's Sweet Strawberry Soap, Slime Lime Body Wash, Power Rangers He-Man Grape-Scented Conditioner. These are the smells of a shower ruled by children. I'm not sure when my salon-worthy soaps, shampoos, and conditioners got taken over by the marketing division of Nick Jr., but the smell is so sweet I can bite it. I used to have face creams from Chanel, plumping gels from La Mer, but at some point, my supply of $90-per-ounce stuff got used as diaper rash cream, and was never replaced. Most days I smell like I will on this one: like a human Scratch 'n Sniff.

Outside the bathroom door, my seven- and four-year-old bounce on the bed. One jumps on either side of the lump in the middle that is their father. Sometimes Bruce does this fake-sleep thing to avoid our programmed conversations of late:

"Who was Kevin's playdate with?" I ask.

"Ya know, that brat from Australia, what's his name?" He lifts the bedcovers up just enough to let himself be heard.

"Digby?"

"Sounds right."

I want to scream that Digby is forbidden here, that he's out of control, a future drug dealer and leader of organized crime, but instead I swallow the screams and say in a chirpy voice, "Isn't it great? The baby slept through the night." When I finally came back home last night Bruce was back in our bed and Owen was in his crib.

"Hmph," the lump replies. "He's not really a baby. He's almost three." With that he lets the covers fall again and I swallow the urge to tear them off and shake him. Is this really the guy I married?

"Owen has had dry Pull-Ups for two weeks now," I say, as if this really excites me. What I really want to say is *I love you so please get up and get a regular job in the world. Please stop being the depressed house daddy because it makes me feel like I'm all alone in this and I'm cracking.*

But even fake, pleasant bathroom talk isn't getting a rise out of him this morning. It'd be so easy to turn into a whistle-blowing drill sergeant commanding the ship that I'm not aboard during the day, but I try hard not to. Still, there's only a few minutes before I head out into the world, and I need to be sure we've both got the information to get us to the next day.

I do it all in my head: Who drops the kids at school? (Bruce.) Who needs what supplies? (Me/Internet.) Order groceries? (Me/

online.) Who will wait for the never-on-time nanny until she enters squawking a myriad of excuses? (Bruce.) I'm trying hard not to succumb to the instinct to holler the orders that sit like exploding Pop Rocks in my mouth, waiting to be spat out.

Baby Owen is still asleep, which selfishly thrills me. By this hour, he's usually clawing at my neck, panic rising from his pores. He knows his mother's time of departure draws near and he hates it when I leave. I tell myself his behavior is age-related. My other two kids did the same until they eventually accepted that I leave each morning, regardless of their efforts, and that I always come back. The fact that Bruce hangs out with them is my comfort. I mean, they have one parent for most of their mornings, and that's as good as it gets. But Baby Owen can sure emit projectile tears better than his siblings ever did, and I'd be lying if I said it didn't break my heart. Everything in his body language screams of mother-abandonment issues. I do hate those days when he's asleep in the morning when I leave, and asleep when I come home at night. I imagine that he'll simply think it's been one long day when he finally sets his eyes on me tomorrow.

I pick out the three outfits the children will wear for the day. This used to be Bruce's job until the teacher of our four-year-old called me to ask why Brigid never wears panties to school, and why on that particular February morning, she was wearing open-toed sandals with no socks. "It's what she chooses," was Bruce's defense. "And I don't wear socks with loafers in February either."

"But she's FOUR!"

"And I'm thirty-nine!" he had screamed back. From that day forward, I have always been the one to leave out their clothes.

When I finally get clothes on myself, Brigid plops her shoe choice for me on the bed. This is our deal: I choose for her and she chooses for me. Today it will be the three-inch stilettos complete with rhinestones across the toes. I put them on and stand back to take it all in.

"Match good," she says, satisfied with her choice.

"Nice and flashy," I reply.

"Snazzy," she continues.

Brigid is having a good time trying out new words. I have no idea where *snazzy* has come from.

"Snazzy," I agree, admiring her blue eyes that seem largest in the morning.

The lump in the bed groans. My newish auto-alert goes off, that one about trying to remain sexy despite my role as the mother ship. As much as I don't want to, it's time to reignite this morning's inner babe. I head to the lump.

"Do you like Brigid's choice?" I ask him, seductively putting one bent leg up on the bed.

I lift the duvet off his head so he can take in the view. My skirt has hiked up just enough for him to catch the top of my thigh-high hose. Brigid sees them too. "Big socks," she says bluntly, pointing at my thighs. His sandy-blond hair is revealed. While it's moplike, I refrain from suggesting a haircut today. In fact I find myself wondering how he still looks so good. There isn't a line on his sleep-deprived face and even with the sun directly on his head, not one gray hair reveals itself. He opens one green eye and arches his eyebrow.

"The stripper shoes really make the outfit," he says, reaching a bare arm out of the covers. He grabs my calf and purrs. Brigid thinks this is fantastic.

"Daddy's a big cat," she shrieks.

"Daddy's a lion," he answers. "He's gonna eat Mommy up."

Brigid runs screaming down the hall and I return my foot to the floor.

"Good day, Big Lion," I say in a fake English accent. Because the thing we do when we're uncomfortable with each other is break out in random foreign accents. I have no idea why.

"Au revoir, Mademoiselle Big Tease," he returns in some Pepé Le Pew voice.

He's right. Nothing can actually occur between us right now and even if we were alone at this exact second, my biggest desire would be to take the damn big socks off and go back to sleep. Bruce pulls the covers back over his head.

Before I leave I try and reach out to each kid, to make eye contact at least once in every twenty-four-hour period. I turn to my eldest, Kevin, who's still standing on the bed.

"I saw a Blue-Eyes White Dragon on a kid's backpack the other day," I say.

Kevin's latest obsession is *Yu-Gi-Oh!* cards.

"Cool," he says, clearly not interested. He has found the remote and is trying to get our childproof television on.

I bend forward to peck his cheek but kiss mostly air because he's started bouncing again. Brigid has returned but no longer jumps simultaneously with him; instead they go one up, one down, and are probably making Bruce nuts. I sweep my wet hair back into a slick bun; I kiss the jumpers, and the lump, and head to the door. I'm not even fully in the elevator when I hear the Cartoon Network come on the television. Bruce's sudden alertness is not lost on me.

In the elevator, I swap the stilettos for the Ferragamos in my briefcase, and I hand the fancy shoes to the doorman in what is our daily routine. I've never explained it to him and he's never asked why I hand him shoes each morning. I like it this way. Each day he gets a flashy pair of hooker shoes that he hands to the nanny when she shows up. The nanny puts them back in my closet, and the next day we do it all over again.

CHAPTER 6

Dais of the Dicks

I PREDICT THE most awkward time to address what went on with Barbie's head last night will be in the afternoon.

And I am right.

If no major earning announcements break after lunch, no wars begin in an oil-laden nation, or no political scandal takes hold of our attention, there is a dull hum that blankets the trading floor in the midafternoon. This is the time of day people run for an extra coffee, a pack of M&M's, a stimulant legal or not, anything to keep the enthusiasm going. It's at this moment I hear King shout to me from his spot on the dais.

"Hey, Belladonna, get over here."

When I say dais, I mean it. Picture a state dinner setup where the heads of state sit at a long table to keep watch over the guests. But on a trading floor, that dais is filled with the "Big Dicks." No, they are not men named Richard, they are the biggest producers, the highest-paid, and for the twelve years I've worked here, nary a woman has ever been seated there. These Dicks are capable of dialing a phone, using the intercom, or even texting me, but King, our most highly esteemed trader, chooses to stand and scream for me to come to the Dick Dais. I'm seated about two hundred feet and seventy people away, so shouting is the way to be certain everyone knows what's up.

All morning long, most of us have been thinking about Barbie. A few of the women have said things like, "Anything yet?" I've been shaking my head and, deep down, filing Barbie into my cabinet of disposable resentment. But since King has announced the time to deal with Barbie is now, a good portion of the floor perks up. They are ready for the show to start.

I point to my headset, indicating to King that he should dial my extension. I want to stay on my own turf but no, he wants me with the Dicks. He shakes his head firmly that he is on the phone and his business is far more important. I stand and march directly toward him, emitting a confidence I'm not really feeling at all.

"I've got Bob on the line," King says loudly.

This confuses me. I think he means Bob, a trader who sits near me. I turn back toward our row to see Bob clearly off the phone. Wrong Bob. The Dicks are perky, and all conveniently off their lines. They have their headsets on and are staring straight ahead, but I see the telephone boards in front of them and instead of the twinkling lights of a busy trading floor, nothing is illuminated. They are all listening to King.

"What's up?" I say as if I have no time for him.

"Belle, I have Bob Eckert on the line," he says. "What in hell kind of doll head was that last night?"

Bob Eckert, as in the CEO of Mattel, as in the manufacturer of everything fantastic and pink and Barbie. He's on the phone with the rainmaking and debonair King McPherson, a guy aching to connect and make Feagin Dixon Mattel's investment bank for whatever stocks or bonds Eckert chooses to sell in the future.

King is using my Barbie head as an excuse to tell Bob the story of the wild-tempered, sleep-deprived working mother who nearly throttled some upstart for destroying her kid's Christmas present. Male bonding over women being ridiculous is the perfect way to forge a banking relationship in the Fortune 500, where 12 CEOs are women and 487 are men. That's why the Dicks are listening. It's a ballsy call to make. And because he has managed to knock my cool off-kilter I mumble.

"Haircut Barbie."

"Bob, ever hear of Haircut Barbie?" he says, and the Dicks snicker.

King stands now, running his hand from his hip to his hair, his hip to his hair, like a 70s disco dancer. He continues to speak into his headset, while never once slowing his dance moves.

"Hottest toy of the season?" he booms. "Feagin bankers really do have good taste."

I can't believe Eckert has the patience to listen to this. I start to wonder if he's even really on the phone when King says to me, "How many do you need?"

And for no reason I can fathom, I mumble, "Two."

I turn, rather than listen to the rest of the conversation, and head back to my seat where Amy's bright-red face is messing with her no-hair-out-of-place persona.

"Can you believe this shit?" she says.

"Who called you in the ten seconds it took me to get back to my desk?" I ask, wondering how she got the details so fast.

"Call? King had the hoot on. Everyone on the floor heard."

The hoot 'n' holler box is a floor-wide intercom. People use it to yell out merchandise, or blocks of stock that Feagin has in inventory, looking for a buyer like a Bluelight special at Kmart. It's also used for breaking corporate news that affects how a stock trades and is a great distribution device for jokes, flatulence noise, and playground-worthy stunts. To be able to talk to the entire floor at once was too tempting this time. King leaving the hoot on during our little conversation showed everyone how to suck up for business from a powerful CEO. It also showed how to crush a woman who acted up last night.

I just shrug at Amy. "Look, the Glass Ceiling whatever meeting last night was all fantasy. In the clarity of the day, I hope we all realize what bullshit it was. Do we really think we can change this place?" My voice is flat and resigned.

"This is our first opportunity," says Amy, and I see she's been writing names, drawing arrows, as if she's masterminding a plan.

"Which means what?"

"Confrontation. Calling them on the bullshit. Publicly demeaning an employee is wrong. Let's start there."

"Okay, Rosa Parks," I say sarcastically. My two phone lines are ringing. I ignore Amy and answer. "Yes?"

"Say something before I say something." It's Amanda. "We have to stop trying to fit in with them. It's wrong. This is our first chance and if I say something I look like some muthfreaker badass from Queens, but you're the one they respect, you're the one they're dumping on. Confront them. Call them on this bullshit."

"Look, you first. I have way too many people depending on me at home. I'm not your groundbreaker."

Amy looks at me with something bordering disgust. Amanda goes silent.

CHAPTER 7

How Not to Meet Your Husband, Part II

F ROM WHERE I sat nine years ago in that Arctic-cold Las Vegas ballroom, the sea of men in dark suits appeared to all have splendid lives. When you're the girl who was left on the literal curb, the climb back to normalcy appears as easy as ascending the sheer side of El Capitán, far off and unattainable. My fiancé had dumped me over a year before, making the trading floor and work my comfort zone and the only place I wanted to be.

I was putting all my former love energy into work and sure, I had a job where complete focus was translating into extra dollars, but I was certain I was the sorriest millionaire there ever was. That's why when the guy working the video and lights that went along with the presentation—a guy so cute I had noticed him at several of these conferences—came up behind me and said, "Hey," I thought for sure he was going to tell me that my giant head was reflecting on the screen and could I please somehow make myself disappear. I turned toward him, ready to comply, ready to vaporize.

"Oh, I'm sorry," I said, not even making eye contact.

"Wait, what?" he asked. "What are you sorry for?"

"For my head being in the way."

He laughed, and that's when I looked up. He was tall and liquidy, with joints that seemed to gush synovial fluid. He shrugged his shoulders and they floated instead of moving the way most thirty-year-old shoulders do. He was a sandy-blond guy with biceps peeking from a simple black button-down shirt that looked natural, rather than steroidally supplemented. This guy looked like it all just came to him so easily.

"Who said your head was in the way?" he asked me sweetly.

"I heard myself think that," I said, letting those stupid words out before being screened by my brain.

Surfer guy laughed and pushed back some of his longish hair. He had beautiful green eyes that looked electrically lit. I hadn't looked a guy in the eyes in a long time.

"No, I, um, just wanted to say that your bag is open and, well, it looks like you may want to shut it," he said, all Boy Scouty.

I bent to look at my bag and saw what he saw: a slightly tattered Speedo bathing suit, goggles, bathing cap, and an envelope of small bills that had opened itself and spread money, like litter, throughout. Dishevelment had become part of my latest look.

"Are you running away from home?" he asked, and when he smiled, my eyes welled up. Nobody had tried to flirt with me since Henry. Nobody had made me laugh since Henry. Nobody. I turned away.

Since Henry dumped me, the only place I felt calm was in water. The YMCA near my apartment opened at 4:45 a.m. and losing myself in a chlorine bath each morning, crying into a pool so big, mixing water with water was my most comforting place. I carried a Speedo suit around like an anxious person carries tranqs. I had the equipment I needed to swim in case things got bad, in case life presented me with a swimming pool in an over-air-conditioned, glitzy hotel in Las Vegas.

"Name is Bruce," the cute audiovisual guy said, not giving up so easily, "as in Wayne."

Leave it to me to find the only penniless guy in a roomful of investment bankers, and a Batman fanatic at that. I tidied my bag, zipped the top, and turned from him.

"This is the last presentation," he continued to my back. "Want me to show you the real Vegas?"

"Yeah, no. It's not my kind of place," I said not unkindly as I imagined shows with high-kicking women wearing rhinestones or smoke-filled gambling halls. "I mean, I have stuff to do."

"Yeah."

Marcus Ballsbridge, sitting in the row in front of me, turned around as if asking if I needed a save. Back then the older guys on the desk treated me like some heartbroken puppy they rescued from the shelter. I turned toward the guy.

"I have things to do," I said weakly.

"Can totally see you have big plans for your afternoon," he murmured, nodding to the swimsuit. "And I bet they don't get a lot of Speedos in the pools here."

"Yeah, well, my thong bikini is in my other bag. The one with the handcuffs and blindfold in it."

He laughed. I made a cute guy laugh.

"Seriously," he said, "I found this cool place near here . . ."

Several minutes later, for some illogical reason, I rose from my seat and followed Batman out the door. He grabbed a messenger bag as we passed the booth he'd been working from. Attached to it was a well-loved skateboard. I left a ballroom of universe masters to hang with some lunatic and only minutes later was standing in my wool navy suit in ninety-degree weather in a skatepark in Las Vegas. I didn't care that I hadn't dressed for the occasion, that I was wearing pumps with heels meant for a woman sitting at a desk or propped against a bar. I didn't care that this guy could be insane. I just liked being my version of irresponsible; away from everyone who knew me, away from people who knew that my fiancé dumped me, that I was unable to eat like a normal person, and that all I did was work and swim. There was nobody at Doc Romeo Park who felt sorry for me.

At first Batman lent me his giant skater sneakers, which were so big my ankles did U-turns in them. Then I tried skateboarding in my heels, which the twelve-year-olds surrounding us, our fellow skaters, all needed to watch. I finally gave up on footwear and rode barefoot and bareheaded, 'cause while Bruce Wayne's feet were big, his helmet was too small. I have a huge head.

"Is all that cash your drug money?" he asked.

"What cash?" I said. Some little kid had lent me his wood, which I had just learned was skater-talk for board, so Bruce and I were then skating side by side, while the sole of my pushing foot burned with the heat of the asphalt and the friction of each push. Self-inflicted pain felt good to me recently, like it was some designer brand of cutting oneself. I knew I had to stop doing things like this to myself, hurting myself, but wasn't sure how.

"Those ten-dollar bills all over your bag."

"Oh"—I shrugged—"it's from lap dancing. Those are my tips."

Bruce pretended to fall off his board. "No, seriously."

"They're tips, but tips for other people. I like to be prepared."

"You mean you carry cash around just to hand to anyone who needs a tip? Someone who is nice to you? I can be nice."

I smiled. "I can't stand how when in a big hotel everyone tips the person who cleans your room or bartends but then you see the bent lady scrubbing down the lobby bathroom and nobody tips her 'cause it's just not the usual point of interaction, or the guy who has to dust all the floorboards or the man who has to separate the garbage."

"Wait, you tip the floorboard-dusting guy?"

"People don't even notice him. It makes me sad."

"Are you from some long line of cleaning people or something?" he joked, and I was silent.

"You are."

"Maybe. Or maybe I just notice people. I see their faces. I think of their stories. Their jobs suck. They don't want to be there. I love my job. You probably love yours too."

"So you think of their stories and then give them money? I don't get it."

I sighed.

"Fuck me, I'm an ass. I do get it. You make a lot of dough and you feel bad about it. That was guilt money I saw."

"The tips are to tell them they aren't invisible and that I appreciate the clean wooden moldings and that they'll get a better job soon. It's nothing more than that." I skated off, leaving him behind.

"Hey, I don't believe you never rode a skateboard before," he yelled after me. "Nobody skates like that her first day out."

I hadn't exactly lied to Bruce, but I hadn't told him I was a decent snowboarder and a lot of the movement is the same. I didn't tell him because some part of me wanted to impress him, wanted to actually flirt with a guy I had absolutely nothing in common with.

I climbed a staircase to get ready to drop into a half-pipe. Something was overpowering me. I felt a ridiculous high from the danger while Bruce just stood with folded hands, either daring me or incredulous that I would do something so stupid. I had no business being on a half-pipe, with no shoes, no helmet, and on a little kid's board, but I felt nothing but brave and something bordering euphoric. Batman wasn't so sure.

"Not sure you should take this your first day out."

The boys had lined up to watch.

"Don't give in to peer pressure," Bruce continued. "Twelve-year-old dudes are not your peers."

"Whatever," I said, "I live in New York," as if this actually meant I was badass or something.

"Well, you want to drop into this one fast and then move horizontally to slow your speed." Batman looked generally concerned. I'd done this in the snow. I was about to blow his mind.

Just as I dropped into it he shouted, "I live in New York too."

There's a terrific difference between hitting snow and hitting cement. With no boots, or any footwear at all, I got a scraping that was a confusing blur of which body part was hurt more. When I stopped spinning, I mostly felt relief, glad that I had movement everywhere and confused that my butt felt like it was smack on the cement with no fabric between us. After the relief of being alive passed, everything started to hurt.

"Did I hit my head?" I asked nobody. "'Cause I don't think I hit my head."

Bruce was everywhere, several Bruces in fact, and it was hard to tell what he was doing to me. He kept telling me I was okay, which I knew. He told the boys to get the fuck away 'cause they kept saying things like "Holy shit" over and over. I said something like "Don't curse at little kids," which made him laugh, but then his dude-who-stands-arms-folded-outside-the-front-door-of-an-Abercrombie-store face crinkled in real concern again, and the shirt that I so admired back in the conference room was off him and getting pulled up my legs.

"What are you doing?" I said while being sharp enough to note the guy had one decent set of abdominals, and "Wooo," because this time I could see his tattoo. It was the face of the Caped Crusader.

"What a girly tat."

"Just try not talking," he said. "You scared the hell out of me and I need a minute."

He pulled me up into his arms and carted me off to his rental car, putting me across the backseat. He got a jug of water from somewhere and moved from cut to cut, dabbing at my wounds.

"Damn, you're really not hurt too badly."

"It must have looked so funny," I said, slightly giggly. I hadn't done anything dangerous in so long. I saw him grin.

"You are so competitive. What the hell was that about?"

"I just thought I could nail it and, you know, impress you."

"Damn," he said, looking at some bump on my forehead, just when I looked down and noticed I had no skirt.

"Where is my skirt?"

"You shredded it, you crazy shredder." But he wasn't laughing. "I think I should take you to the hospital."

"No way. No hospital for me." Having no skirt on seemed like the funniest thing I'd ever heard of. I had no skirt. I laughed and laughed until I stopped seeing Bruces and I was left with only one. "I liked it more when there were four versions of your torso," I said, which made his face crinkle again.

"Definitely taking you to the hospital."

"No hospital!" I shouted, and then laughed again with the sudden thought, *Who doesn't wear a skirt to the hospital?*

"It tore right up the back. Those little kids will remember this as the happiest day of their lives, seeing a woman with your ass in a thong. Holy Mother of God. Good thing I'm gay."

I put my hands down around my bottom; everything was all covered up down there.

My heightened clarity was making me blanch. "Did I really

just moon those boys?" I asked tentatively, thinking that gay guys have the nicest manners and man, did I have Bruce Wayne pegged all wrong.

"My shirt makes a good skirt," he said kindly. "Let's go get you some ice."

The problem with pulling up to the Bellagio Hotel, where the guest rooms number exactly 3,933, is that swooping bellmen and valet parkers need to keep things moving. They don't want to hear the story about how you lost your skirt. It was then that I saw that Bruce, a guy whose real last name was McElroy, didn't care what anyone thought. He hoisted me over his shoulder and carried me through the casino, now conveniently filled with hundreds of fellow bankers and clients—a bare-chested Adonis carrying me in my bloody white blouse, a purple welt across my forehead, a shirt making do as a skirt, and no shoes. It was our oil and gas analyst who started applauding when he saw me, and soon the whole place looked up from their pursuit of money to join in the clapping. That's how Bruce and I made our way to the elevators, to thunderous applause and whistles. These guys had never once seen me behave badly and here I was, after I finally went on a date, a one-hour date, and I returned bloodied and half-naked. They told that story for years.

I remember thinking in my semi-woozy state that the blinging money machines in the background were telling me that this time I had really hit the jackpot, 'cause as the elevator doors closed, Bruce whispered into my ear, "Was only kidding about the gay thing."

CHAPTER 8

Ex-Change

I T IS THURSDAY. Thursday is the new Sunday in our house—as decreed by the higher power at our Park Avenue preschool. Thursday is the dreaded school chapel day.

Chapel goes something like this: children arrive dressed for the *Titanic* crossing—bows, cashmere sweaters, itchy tights, even crinoline. They shuffle with one or both of their parents into the chapel room, where a very talented group of teachers play and sing their heart out to happy God music. The main storyteller relates a sugar-infused Bible story such as David just wrestling Goliath or Moses taking a boating vacation, or my personal favorite—when Adam and Eve eat forbidden fruit, they are punished by having to wear fancy party clothes. Then we all sing songs, while sitting on the floor holding on to our squirming children, and wonder how we can possibly stand up again since our legs have gone to sleep.

There is an order to how the parents and children sit in chapel. The billionaires sit along the front sides of the room. They tend to be cooler than the rest of us and usually have only one parent in attendance. They don't have to care if anyone likes them so they don't show up just to be seen. The billionaires rarely wear business suits and seem to know it's all right to have a wife with a little paunch. They have hired enough help to insulate them from the annoying millionaire parents who are pining for a playdate. Instead they have their kids play with either fellow billionaire offspring or the full-scholarship kids, of which there are three. They seem genuinely enchanted by their children.

In the front of the chapel sit a group that Bruce, who used to hail from this land of exclusion, calls the "PA Ladies," the not-employed-out-of-the-house, Park Avenue mothers. The school thinks PA stands for "parents association." These are the wives of the millionaires who want to hang with the billionaires. They feel the need to have two adults frame their three-foot kid and they work the crowd like a networking slam. They titter back and forth with their grown-up friends while insisting their kids remain quiet, making a low-level noise that's distracting. They give their children the names of expired ancestors such as Baxter, Ford, and Wyeth. Not coincidentally, some are also the names of New York Stock Exchange companies. Their men wear sharp suits and smell good, and their women wear triple-ply cashmere tops tossed over super-tight low-riding jeans. Their abdominals that occasionally peek from beneath their sweaters reveal nothing about having had multiple children because they only stay pregnant for eight months, induce early, have a Victoria's Secret C, which is the cesarean combined with a tummy tuck, before returning to their two-hour daily workouts. Their shoes tend to be expensive, with delicate high heels that rarely hit pavement, and they have jewelry usually purchased from each other. They are the peer group of my coworkers' wives and they look at me either with pity for not marrying one of their tribe or with what I believe is the bad-mother glare, like they know something about

55

my kids that I don't. It doesn't help that my daughter's contri-
bution to the "Whose Mommy Am I?" bulletin board contains a
drawing of a straggly haired lady with text transcribed from her
mouth stating, "My mommy only likes to read the *Wall Street
Journal.*" The other darlings' pictures state, "My mommy reads
Don't Let the Pigeon Drive the Bus!" or "*Goodnight Moon.*" Who is
that sucky mommy who only reads the *Journal*? Needless to say,
we don't socialize too much.

Toward the back of the room are the working schlumps—the
oddballs, including me and three other moms in business wear.
We tote oversized bags with electronic gear all set to silence. We
sit on the carpeted floor with the most difficulty, given the way
we are dressed, and we try our hardest to not check our phones
during chapel time. We don't necessarily want to hang with the
billionaires but wouldn't mind living like them.

The other parent type that sits with us are the one-offs. There's
one jock mom clad in spandex who pushes a double stroller from
somewhere far away and begins each day looking exhausted.
There is the token overweight mother who wears orthopedic
sandals with socks—either a woman completely comfortable in
her own skin, or someone who has totally waved the white flag
of surrender. Who can compete with this crowd? Also with us sit
two former rock stars who aren't aging well, three adopted girls
from China who live on 5th Avenue, and the two African American students of the school: one has a dad who is the CEO of a
media company and one is the son of another student's chauffeur.

Every Thursday, as I did with Kevin and now do with Brigid
and Owen, I commit my skirt-suited bottom to a piece of floor
in the back of the room with the rest of the misfits. We are happy
there.

How the McElroy family ever ended up in such a fancy school,
being neither blue-blooded, famous, nor rich in New York City

terms, is another story. The old adage that it is easier to gain admission to Harvard than to an elite Manhattan preschool is weirdly true.

If your child is to be accepted to a Manhattan private preschool, an application has to materialize first. There is one day of the entire year that this can happen, provided you have access to multiple phone lines and at least one decent secretary, because you have to call and request one of a limited number of applications. I had an able intern work the phones that first Monday after Labor Day, and after seven hours of dialing, he produced nine applications for the McElroy family. This little exercise is just for the new people. Should your uncle Winston or grandma Hitchcock be a legacy, you're in. Our school gives out three hundred applications for thirty-four spots each year; 90 percent are sibling or legacy spots, leaving about three or four openings to compete for about a 1 percent acceptance rate.

Fifth Avenue Preschool is known as the most difficult to get into. We applied, and given I had no connections, I put zero effort into an impossible situation. On the way to the interview, we got caught in traffic moving at the rate of sludge. I jumped out of the cab, ran the remaining twenty blocks, arrived sweaty, panting, and slightly late. Bruce brought up the rear carrying Kevin piggyback. The director made no eye contact with my cute-as-hell Kevin, my non-billionaire husband, or me. Instead she seemed fixated on the V of sweat that was forming at the top of my breasts and showing itself magnificently through the silk of my blouse. In her eyes, I felt we were the urban version of trailer trash and we were shown the door in fifteen minutes. In my haughty, defensive, and naïve way, *Not a problem*, I thought, *Kevin will go to our local YMCA preschool.*

When we received exquisitely worded rejection letters for not only that preschool but also the other eight that Kevin applied to, including the Y, Bruce and I felt like terrible parents. I had panicked ideas about quitting my job and homeschooling my kids but Bruce pointed out that first, we would have very little income, and second, it is a tad early to throw in the towel on the whole education game when a three-year-old gets rejected.

I revisited all the materials and pored over lists of board members at each school. Surely I knew someone in this town. And I did. The president of that fancy-pants Fifth Avenue Preschool board was none other than Henry Thomas Wilkins III. My ex-fiancé, Henry. The guy who left me on the street. I didn't dare call him. No way. I had made a vow never to speak with him again. No way. Well, maybe.

After seven years of being madly in love, we parted and never spoke another word to each other. I never trolled his name on the Internet; I unsubscribed to my college alumni magazine and broke up with all our mutual friends. When I want to clean my slates, I do it with bleach. The months and months in a black pool of hurt seemed long ago now—buried in some cavern of the heart that modern medicine could never find. Had enough time finally passed for me to pick up the phone?

I talked this over with Bruce, the guy who had made me laugh after Henry was gone. Surely he would agree I should never call regardless of what it meant for preschool admission.

"Call him," he said. Bruce had thought of his answer for five milliseconds.

"What?"

"Clearly you can't have any feelings for that guy. He was so awful to you in the end and guys don't change. What's there to lose?"

"How about my pride?"

"How is this losing pride? Your life is a complete success, you're probably one of the thirty most successful women on Wall

Street. You have three fantastically interesting, smart enough children. What exactly is the part that you are ashamed of?"

A weird silence filled the room. We both pondered the question.

"Unless it's me," he said, looking deep into my eyes.

"WHAT?"

"No, really, Belle, I can understand. He was a poor guy with a fancy name who became rich and got what he wanted and you married a formerly rich guy who's now poor. It's questionable you got what you wanted. I get it. You're like the people who don't go back to their high school reunions. They don't go back because they're embarrassed. If you don't call him, you're the girl who won't go to the reunion."

I had to prove my love for Bruce by calling Henry? Fine. I called and didn't let my voice quiver once. In that weak moment I called the guy who cruelly broke my heart and left me for the society girl he was sleeping with when we were engaged (though that's not how the *New York Times* described her in their wedding announcement). I called him and begged to get my sloppy three-year-old kid into a preschool with a chapel day. A school named Fifth Avenue Preschool that isn't even on 5th Avenue.

To his credit, Henry was beyond helpful. His secretary passed me on to him after I meticulously spelled out my name. Twice. Our conversation was short and direct, like business associates who talk every day. He never even acted surprised to hear I was on the phone. Instead of asking me about my life he asked me the spelling of Kevin's name. (Spell *Kevin*? What was up with his office and the human spell-checking?) He asked me for my last name. (He really couldn't *not* know that, right?) "It's Cassidy," I reminded him. "Not sure if you remember me, but I think we used to date?" I joked, but he didn't laugh.

"Belle?"

Here it comes, I thought, the big apology, the one where he admits to being the lowliest crapper on the earth and that now this favor would make us all good. I'd waited a long time for this one.

"Isabelle, it's nice that you still use Cassidy, I guess, but—"

"Well, yes, that is my name, Henry."

"No. I mean you don't seem like the type to change your last name to your husband's, right?"

"I didn't know there was a type or that you had me pegged, but yes, I haven't changed it."

"So maybe for this application we can call you Mrs. ummm..."

"McElroy? I can only apply to your school if I have my husband's last name?"

"Yes. Sounds weird, but okay. Can you spell that for me?"

And that's how my ex-fiancé changed my last name to my husband's.

In three days Kevin gained admission to a preschool so elite it had no name on the door, no website, no listing in the phone book. It was the beginning of a new legacy, allowing my other two kids to eventually go there too. Of course, payment for this favor is very severe. Besides being committed to paying $31,000 per year for a three-hour-per-day school, and fake changing my last name when I wasn't ready to do that, I had just groveled to the guy who left me on the sidewalk holding my wedding gown in the rain. Now I was committed to seeing either Henry or his silicone-enhanced wife each time I dropped a child at school. Snap.

This Thursday morning I'm feeling the love. Bruce took Kevin to his school, leaving enough time for Brigid, Owen, and me to walk to preschool. I feel the postholiday euphoria of not having to buy and wrap gifts, write cards, and drink every night. Even though I don't know what my bonus will be, the numbers are in and I can relax a little. January is my July.

Brigid is on her scooter, Owen in his stroller, and me in mid-sized heels, briefcase slung over the stroller handles, walking, not running, to chapel. The sun is shining and I'm the picture of the woman who has it all, all at the same time—the babies, the job, and the body that can still rock, though in dim light.

We seat ourselves in the back of the chapel room. I silence the electronics, breathe, and consider that all is right with the world. The very fact that we are early is a routine break, and kids like routine. Owen uses this mindful moment to decide he's done sitting in the back and wants to be closer to the music. I try to distract him with some pathetic bribe, murmuring a ridiculous story about the time that God made Superman. He isn't swayed in the least.

"Wanna sit in front," he says, and not in his "inside" voice.

"Let's stay here and wait for your friend Riley," I say. Riley is always ten minutes late and would be the perfect reason for staying put.

"No."

Brigid likes Owen's idea. "Yes, we should sit in the front, Mama. We never go sit in front." She seems to marvel at the fact she has never considered a different spot on the floor. Her brain just trips with the possibilities. "We SHOULD."

With no further discussion Owen bolts for the front, and Brigid follows close behind, excited to do something she has never considered. My two assertive children plant themselves squarely behind the happy family of Henry.

I awkwardly step between tiny hands and crossed legs on high-heeled shoes, excusing my way to the front. Once there, I squat, suit and all, while giving an apologetic shrug to the PA Ladies in back of me. One gives a knowing half smile while the other clearly smirks. She smirks! Henry turns to give me a weirdly cheesy grin. As if to say, *Belle you are clearly overstepping the bounds of our agreement—you know, the unspoken truce where I get your motley family into preschool and you do not bond with my family in any way.*

I've been really good about keeping this agreement we never made, and so has he. Besides Bruce, nobody at this place knows I even went to college with Henry, never mind lived with him. I'm no longer euphoric. Now my heart is seized with the anxiety of keeping two young children contained for forty minutes.

The music begins, a banjo riff, followed by a song about sowing seeds, growing a garden . . .

"Inch by inch, row by row, gonna make this garden grow."

Sitting cross-legged directly in front of Owen and diagonally from me is the Wife. I've never had such a close-up chance to examine the woman who dethroned me. I take this Christian moment to do so. She is pretty in the classic sense. She has a very good colorist, and her shoulder-length hair has four varying shades of blond, equally striped. She looks as though she could use a good meal, though her perky, large breasts defy the smallness of the rest of her frame. She wears the obligatory low-riders and a thong peeks out the top of her jeans, perhaps sending a message of hidden vixen to us sitting behind her. I want to make a judgment call here but refrain, as she is, in fact, cross-legged, which does pull one's pants lower. I have my arm around Owen. Usually he is rapt, hanging on the storyteller's every word, but today he is engrossed with something else. He has his gaze too low to be paying attention. In fact, it is squarely on Henry's wife's ass.

The song continues, "All it takes is a rake and a hoe, and a piece of fertile ground."

Inexplicably, Owen reaches out and begins stroking Wife's soft, tight sweater. The woman who stole Henry from me is getting stroked by my two-year-old. I grab his hand maybe harder than I intended.

"Ow!" he yells.

Wife turns and says, "It's okay," and gives Owen a gentle stroke on his face before turning back. He reaches out again but not before I intercept.

"OWWWW!" This time the entire front row turns to look at us and I'm glad for the loud music.

I whisper in Owen's ear, "We aren't allowed to touch strangers."

There is such a force in my voice that my rambunctious boy, the one who most loves confrontation, improbably sits back on his faded Gap overalls while I caress his back. The story of reaping and sowing goes on and on. The anger he feels radiates as heat coming from the hand I hold.

It happens the millisecond I adjust my grip. Owen senses this is his moment. He reaches forward fast. I swing out instinctively and catch air. It's too late.

With the small motor skills of someone beyond his years, Owen grabs the thong. He wraps his little fingers around that top strap, the one that's been peeking out at him for the past half hour. It was too difficult to resist in its lacy pinkness. He grabs the thong and pulls it toward him, where it seems to stretch beyond possibility. And it is only when Wife yelps "OWW!" that he releases it with an impressive *Snap!* That was not cheap elastic.

Wife turns to me and I'm expecting I don't know what. I mean Wife is one of the most beloved mothers in the school. She runs the library, she heads the benefit committee, and she has just had her thong snapped in front of all her PA friends. She is probably about to snarl at me but I can't tell for she has no lines, no movement in her face, which has been Botoxed into submission.

I anticipate the scolding I deserve but instead see her blank look turn into a stiff smile.

"It's okay, big guy," she says sweetly. She drips honey packed sweetness onto Owen as he attaches himself to my lower leg and she pats his head before turning to talk to someone else. Chapel has abruptly ended. Henry looks not at me but at the floor surrounding me—my slightly rumpled suit, my practical gray everything, and my giant sack of work with assorted technology spilling out. He says nothing but I can see what he's thinking.

All these years without Henry, all this time apart from someone I thought I would never be apart from, I found comfort in the fact that he ended up with this woman. It's not that I didn't like her, despite her seducing my then boyfriend, it's that I knew what Henry liked and she was not that. I had secretly reveled in the fact he married someone who, despite being rich and connected, had never had a grown-up job, who I'm told spent all her time fixing and refixing their apartment and country house, and managing an army of household staff.

Henry was too smart to stay interested in someone like her. I'd given their union one year of success, the sex year, before deep down I was certain he'd be suffering without having someone like me to keep him grounded, to sharpen his mind, to crack him up. But no, watching his eyes now I could see everything I had assumed was wrong. His face bore no recognition of the girl I had been. He simply looked incredulous. It was then that I knew what he knew.

Henry had picked the right girl.

CHAPTER 9

On the Floor

THE SECRET of working mothers everywhere is compart-
mentalizing: the ability to jam into a mental drawer that
which can't be dealt with at the moment. She jams a family
problem into a mental filing cabinet, slams the door shut, and
does her work. When she gets home she reverses the process,
disconnecting her wireless world while reviewing first-grade
spelling words, or reading *Harry the Dirty Dog* for the fifty-seventh
time. As she does this she tries not to think about the fact that her
entire department will be tested on synthetic mortgage products
the following day and that she needs to get a handle on what they
actually are. I'm a world-class compartmentalizer and I wish this
were an Olympic sport so I could stand on the podium with a
gold medal around my neck and get some love for it.

After the chapel drama, I get to the office perilously close to the
market's opening bell of 9:30 a.m. A pink note is stuck onto my
computer screen. It reads, "Call Tim Boylan of Cheetah Global
regarding EBS."

I've only met Tim once. He is not my daily contact at Cheetah; he's the CEO of the entire place. I interpret this message to mean disaster because top guys don't call with good news. I bury the Owen/thong event deep in the filing cabinet of my brain, and I focus on Tim, on work, on the twinkling LCD screens on my desk.

An asterisk sits next to the EBS symbol, indicating news is breaking on Emergent Biosolutions and the stock will have a delayed opening. Whenever there is news that will significantly impact a stock price, trading halts in that stock while buyers and sellers figure out the correct price to begin again. This must be why Boylan wants to talk. I sold Cheetah over a million shares of EBS based on my advice.

I look over at Amy, who is on the phone, tapping her pen on the red underpart of her Christian Louboutin shoes and making some weird contortion of her face. I know she bought EBS for her own account. She raises her eyebrows toward me in a slightly accusing way, but doesn't say a word, listening intently to her caller.

I snap out of my seat and head to King, looking for information on pharmaceutical trading. King is on the phone, massaging his thick black curls. I get within touching distance, and true to form he tugs on my arm, brings me close to him, and now has his hand on the top of my ass. I pull away in what has become a habitual movement, not unlike the sparring of siblings. There are no boundaries and the parents are distracted. He hangs up.

"How much does Cheetah own?" he barks at me.

"Ten total," I say. "EBS just came public last year. It's a great company."

"Ten?" he repeats. "Ten million shares trading at twenty-two dollars per share?"

"Yes, King, I know. A two-hundred-twenty-million-dollar investment."

"Like a quarter-of-a-billion-dollar investment!" he barks at me so the Dicks surrounding him can hear this too.

"Shit. What happened? Are they killing people?" My heart pounds.

"Anthrax happened," King says solemnly before breaking into a smile.

At first I think there's been an Anthrax breakout or that the vaccine is ineffective but no, it's got to be good news. King is smiling.

"Or Anthrax didn't happen if you're vaccinated?" I respond carefully.

"That's right. Just ask the two million service people in the U.S. military that have gotten the shot and don't have Anthrax," he answers. "They're great customers!" He burps.

Gross. "Yes, but I already know that, and EBS investors know that, so what's the news?" I ask, still unsure why the stock stopped trading.

"They pre-announced earnings. They can hardly keep up with demand. This thing is cheap with a low price-to-earnings ratio, only five times earnings. It's gonna rocket today and I know shit about it."

"Anthrax vaccines aren't the big story, King," I say, now so relieved I could possibly even hug his lecherous self. "It's got to be the immunoglobulin they make. That's what will send the stock higher."

"Whoa," King says, grabbing my waistband. "Don't move. All these losers need to hear about whatever it was you just said."

"Gentlemen!" King announces on the hoot 'n' holler. "Belle Cassidy is getting on right now to tell you boneheads about blabba blobbulinz." And he hands the mic to me. I've already read enough on his computer screen now to piece the story together. Emergent Biosolutions got great news about upcoming clinical trials for their new drugs. The stock is about to trade up and I just made my client a wheelbarrow full of money. But before I have a moment to digest that, I'm put on the spot to talk about it in front of over one hundred people.

The trading floor quiets, but not for one second do I turn red or falter or say *um*, because that would be expected. I clear my throat, raise the mic to my mouth, and pull King's hand from my clothing.

"Trading halted this morning on a New York Stock Exchange stock that isn't on our coverage list," I begin, and see King positioning himself as a buyer, typing bids to send out into the universe, "but it looks like we will be making a market in it today. It's called Emergent Biosolutions, symbol EBS. King is trading it today and it's going higher." I look at King's screens. "In fact, it looks like it's up ten dollars on the open, a thirty percent rise. They make an Anthrax vaccine that's in high demand but they also anticipate groundbreaking discoveries in their immunoglobulin research. Immunos assist the body's own immune system to deal with disease. It's the future of cancer therapies if you ask me."

"Who asked you?" someone shouts, but it's a friendly shout and everyone's either making notes or already calling a client.

"Their research pipeline looks pretty full with immune therapies so really, it's exciting stuff. Looking at the chart, it's got an ascending triangle pattern with increased volume. There's over thirty million shares trading. Go sell some of them."

I smugly hand the mic back to King, who grins. "This is why I'm in love with you. What other banana on this floor can spit stats out like that?"

"All I know is that Cheetah's going to get a double on this one."

"And when they're ready to take their profit, you send them right to the King to sell, okay?" he says while making some weird grab for me.

"I wanna kiss your sweet ass right now, Cassidy."

"It's McElroy," I say, "I changed my name almost three years ago. Behave yourself before you end up needing an Anthrax vaccine."

"Was that a threat? You hot, hot gurrll," he pants, and makes another grab for me, but I am gone. Back to my side, my set, my safety zone.

Traders are my partners on these client accounts and we are assigned to each other. While I work with research analysts to get ideas, talk to the clients, wine, dine, travel, and grovel, when the clients finally do decide to either buy or sell a stock, we need a trader. The guy who smacks gum and slaps male and female ass all day in some primate version of high five, who continually belches in post-lunch competitions, who feels powerful enough to publicly humiliate professional women as a hobby. He must also watch screens all day, stay in touch with the stocks our clients care about, and punch numbers into a machine without making errors. For this he is handsomely rewarded with one-half of my commissions. When an investment goes sour, he's never remembered. The salesperson, that would be me, takes the heat, and merciless berating. From my point of view, it's a good deal to be a trader and yet very few women are. The few we have are corralled together into what is called Estrogen Row. One older woman, for reasons nobody remembers, sits totally isolated at a desk the traders refer to as Menopause Manor. But back to EBS.

I get to call a happy client today. Things are looking up not only because of the money Cheetah has made, but because bonus time is looking sweeter and sweeter. I send a quick email to Bruce letting him know his wife is having a great day. While some men find the idea of their partner making a pile of money intimidating, my idealistic yet logical husband gets wildly turned on in the few hours before he starts remembering how toxic he believes money is.

I call back Tim Boylan, and he offers to buy me lunch. He wants to bring along his new chief investment officer, a guy he just hired. We agree to do it the following week.

"What made you so sure about this Emergent company McElroy?" Tim asks me.

"One of my college housemates is now a doctor. She had me read about immunotherapeutics and it just made sense to me. She loved what she saw. They have a manageable research budget, are profitable, and have a stock that was trading softly. It didn't seem that risky, you know?"

"You're so modest," he says.

"I'm so lucky," I say, and really mean it.

I'm the bipolar twin of the meek person sitting in chapel this morning. The dopamine hit of the stock market going my way is a powerful drug. When Cheetah trades out of the stock, which they probably will do in the next few days, and if they were to trade all of it through me, I'll bring to the firm ten times $.06 per share, or $600,000. I'll give 90 percent of that to the firm and the remaining $60,000 will be split between King and me. I'm having a really, really good day, so I call our caregiver the name she likes to be called, and ask her to get those chicken fingers on the table early, bath early, bed. I love the post-big-trade nights with my husband. He becomes the man I married, carefree, optimistic, and juiced on ideas for us. He oozes wife-support and love, which makes his odd spending habits bother me less and makes me feel we will be okay.

It's 9:30 a.m. and the market opens. Marcus has tuned the television on his desk to *Barney*, and the purple dinosaur now sings about someone loving someone and being in a happy family. He thinks Barney's groovy mood brings him good luck, so he tunes in to the show at every opening bell. He holds his hand out to me, inquiring whether I'd like to share his dance (that eavesdropper—I'm sure he heard me recommending EBS and then bought some for his own account). I allow myself to be whipped from my seat and he pulls our cheeks together to whisper, "Did my first CMO trade."

As in a collateralized mortgage obligation. As in those risky things backed by subprime mortgages that are starting to tank? "Wow, Michael, Barney's quite the life coach . . . making you all confident like that."

Amy glares at us over her shoulder. "We are not flirting," I say to her. Michael spins me back to my seat. "This is what happy looks like, Amy. Try it sometime," he says.

Amy says nothing, reaches across our desks, and without looking at me, or pausing her phone conversation, squeezes my hand. I take that to mean congratulations, but no, instead she adheres a sticky note to my screen and turns away.

"GCC to meet for lunch next Thursday: Details to follow 12:30. Agenda: discuss Naked Girl."

I read it and think how odd it will look if we all go to lunch together and can't she give it a rest, ever? I guess we'll shuffle out individually, pretending to meet different clients but still making people curious. She has slightly dimmed my buzz. I watch her crumple the evidence and toss it in a garbage can.

Maybe she sold her EBS stock too soon.

CHAPTER 10

Ex-Dividend

THE WOMEN'S RESTROOM is a veritable crime scene today since it's wafting cigarette smoke like a 1989 nightclub. Most people don't leave the building during the day so noontime finds a pack of women herded into the ladies' room, many sucking on cigarettes in deep, needy gulps. Our nonsmoking bathroom is fogged in.

I have some compassion for the nicotine-addicted, especially since our chairman-emeritus imperiously lights up wherever and whenever. B. Gruss II smokes cigars while on the Dais of the Dicks, and in the comfort of his own office is known to enjoy a broader range of medicine cabinet supplies. Compared to him, people needing a nicotine fix seem pretty benign.

In the hazy mirror I catch sight of my perfectly tailored suit, and my hair that I dried by sticking my wet head out of the taxi window this morning. Miraculously, it has all fallen into place. There aren't many moments like this, so I toss up some grateful- ness to the universe, quiet thanks for all my stars aligning. Today

I'm all woman because today is my lunch with Tim Boylan, a guy known for never having lunch with anyone.

The ladies in the bathroom take note of the more polished, less sleep-deprived me. A showy sales assistant named Tiffany Antinori, the one the others refer to as Naked Girl, walks in wearing red platform shoes with a skintight catsuit. She looks fabulous and out of place, and lets out a low whistle when she sees me. Can she tell that I've been trying hard to locate my inner babe again?

"New boyfriend?" she inquires.

"Maybe."

"Ewwwwwww," says Amanda, layering on mascara and not even looking in my direction. For some reason she does a full makeover at the halfway point of each day—"Fresh face, fresh ideas," is how she describes this.

Clarisse Evenson, the only other woman at my managing director level, enters like the high school principal, killing the buzz of the place. She is tall and birdlike and even flaps her skinny arms when she gets excited. She and I have different ideas about how to manage employees. I go for the friendly-mentor angle, while she seeks to be headmistress. Cigarette butts are flushed down the toilet and conversation vanishes when she enters the bathroom.

"This smoke is unacceptable," Clarisse snaps, waving the cloud from her face. "Disgusting. Filthy. Illegal. Why there is no MD bathroom for women, I cannot understand." She is referring to the fact that men of managing director stature or higher have a private bathroom, while all the women of the firm share.

"Really, Clarisse?" I say. "Who would be in a female MD bathroom besides you and me?"

"Exactly," she says, and slides the lock on her stall shut.

Tiffany smiles at herself in the mirror. She turns and makes some deep hip-sashay on her way out the door. I note that she didn't actually accomplish anything while in the bathroom, just glanced at herself and left.

"Seriously," says Amy, "why are you so together today?"

"Lunch with the CEO of Cheetah," I say, casually applying lipstick that has neither sand nor fingerprints stuck to it—it's hard to find a lipstick that Brigid hasn't tried out on her dolls. "And the new CIO too." I do a sexy swivel of my own hips and Amy and I high-five.

"WHAT?" says Clarisse, in the middle of her business from behind her closed door.

Amy widens her eyes and puts her fingers to her lips to shush me. I cannot be contained.

"You've heard of Tim Boylan, CEO of Cheetah?" I ask innocently.

"Tim Boylan does not do lunch," she snarls, and throws back the stall door to the sound of a swooshing toilet. "He does not travel nor socialize."

Clarisse stands in front of me, stick arms folded across her chest. She is sputtering, "And why exactly wouldn't you have invited the possible future head of sales to this?"

"Umm, because I have a *current* head of sales?" I answer carefully.

"Look, isn't it obvious that Simon will be retiring soon? There's nobody close to his talent level besides me." Clarisse is flushed in the cheeks, fidgety, and upset. She gives every ounce of her soul to this job, so the thought of anyone beating her gets her agitated. I feel a little sorry for her. Hasn't she noticed that no women are in those positions here and that our executive committee is 100 percent male?

Amy turns on the water again and in the mirror I see her eyes roll.

* * *

The Four Seasons Restaurant on East 52nd Street has waiters who dress better than the guys I work with. It's a flower-filled power scene with tables set around what appears to be a small swimming pool. The place is so subliminally seductive that I got engaged here once; to Henry, not to Bruce.

We were having dinner to celebrate his graduation from Columbia Business School when suddenly, there was Henry on bended knee, with a blue box and the flash of jewelry catching the light just right. I had the surreal feeling of being snapped into a bear trap. I didn't see it coming. Something about the fountains, the music, and the headiness of possibility made me tear up, melt down, and say "Yes" to spending the rest of my life with him. For one gigantic leap-of-faith moment, I ignored my list of things I wouldn't do before thirty and started planning a wedding that ultimately never happened.

So why would I ever come back to this place? Because Tim had said to me, "Where would you like to have lunch?" and the one thing I'm certain of is that you don't pass the ball of power away when it's been handed to you. Choosing a location makes you important. The lamest answer would have been, "I dunno, where would you like to eat?" or, "I'll call you back when I think of a place." No, I had two seconds to give a solid answer, and it had to be a nontrendy restaurant with excellent service, so I blurted out, "Four Seasons?" Before I could recoil and say, "On second thought, how about . . ." Tim said, "My favorite. I'll make the reservation." Thus taking the ball of power back. Well played.

So here I sit beside the same pool I sat beside when my life was carefree. When Henry was a guy I was deeply in love with, when children seemed loud, messy, and not for me and the trajectory of my career seemed due north. That day was so very long ago.

I can see the entrance, and promptly at 12:30 p.m. Tim enters, cloaked in the presence of the self-made. He has an aura that causes people surrounding him to stand taller, to want to be nearer, to rub up against a piece of his magic. He stops at another table to shake hands with someone he knows. When he bends forward I catch sight of his new second-in-command, the guy who gave up mortgage trading at Goldman Sachs to manage large portfolios of rich people's money at a hedge fund. The guy Tim is so excited to bring into the firm to analyze investment ideas with people like me, and to take on the burden of the daily decision making.

That guy is none other than Henry.

CHAPTER 11

How Not to Meet Your Husband, Part I

H IS FIRST WORDS to me in 1990 were: "Are these people your friends? No wonder you came looking for me."

I was standing in line to register for freshman anthropology and was surrounded by some earnest, nerdy souls I didn't know. Henry Wilkins had come from behind, lobbing lines at me directly from *Pretty Woman*, a Julia Roberts movie out that past summer. I didn't miss a beat.

"You're late," I said, taking in all six feet four inches of him and the thick, dark hair he constantly adjusted. He was wearing a real alligator belt holding up khaki shorts on his slim, articulated frame. Guys like him didn't exist in my Bronx neighborhood. No boy I grew up with would quote Richard Gere without making a gagging noise.

"You're stunning," he continued.

"You're forgiven." I smiled before turning my back. I was relieved it was my turn to step up to the registration table because

I didn't know how to keep my witty lines going. Quoting the one movie I had seen six times over the summer was not maintainable. What if he switched movies? He didn't.

"When you're not fidgeting, you're very tall," he continued.

Had this guy memorized the entire film? "You forgot the best part," I countered.

He paused, making me look right at him, right into his intense, dark eyes, and making me understand how I had gotten to be eighteen years old without ever having a boyfriend before. Maybe I'd been waiting.

"—and very beautiful," he finished.

Bingo. He did remember that part.

"Excuse me. It's my turn to register," I said, hating the fact that I was the first to break character.

He didn't back down. "You don't really want to take this class," Henry said, nodding his head toward the anthropology sign.

"I don't think that was in the movie." I laughed as I stepped to the desk. "But I do want this class. I need to learn what drives baboon behavior."

"And that's important why?"

I was not about to tell some stranger about my love for the Bronx Zoo or my crazy theories about the human race. "So I can understand people better."

"Then come with me," he said, like he knew I would obey.

We weren't in some dark alley where something bad could happen. I followed him.

"And who is going to hire you because you studied primate behavior?" he continued as we walked across the giant armory where Cornell University holds registration.

"Lots of places—the New York City DA's office, the corporate office of IBM, or maybe some dot-com thingy."

"You didn't really just say 'thingy,' did you?"

"I did but I didn't mean to. I was at a loss for words." I searched the room in hopes one of my new roommates would spot me with such a cute guy.

He laughed; not that polite-response laugh, but a deep, real one, and that laugh got my heart pounding.

"Okay," he said, "this is the class that'll get you somewhere." He stopped at the front of a line filled with good-looking freshmen waiting to register for Wine Tasting 101.

"Everyone," he yelled out as if he already knew them, "this is Isabelle from the Bronx." I had given him exactly zero personal information.

It turned out that wine tasting was offered as an elective in the School of Hotel Administration. According to Henry, knowing about wine was the most useful class the university offered. He, a first-week freshman, had handpicked the students he felt would eventually run the campus and included me, as he told me later, because my face looked so earnest. He had studied our Freshman Faces, a hardcopy book for every new student, showing their picture and listing their studies, interests, and hometown, and then deduced who should, as he said, "hang out together." He had walked through freshman registration finding those very people and amassing them together for wine tasting. Registering for a class as directed by a stranger seemed like the wildest thing I'd ever done.

"Let me guess, you own a vineyard," I joked.

"Not currently."

"And you're from L.A.?" I continued giving his clothing the once-over.

"Close. Rochester, New York, home of Eastman Kodak, generous tax credits, and more than our share of companies in bankruptcy protection."

"So what's with the outfit?" I asked.

"I haven't yet gone to the place where I'll be from but the native outfit there is this. You may wish to revisit your wardrobe too," he said, nodding at my overalls.

Why did this guy who knew what he wanted seem so sexy? The beer-chugging pot smokers bored me, the intellectuals were too intense, the jocks too single-minded, but a funny, social, smart guy who was ambitious without being nerdy got my heart fluttering, and I was not alone. Henry was surrounded by girls who seemed perfect.

I joined the crew team and eventually found a boyfriend, a lightweight rower named Ansel who stood five eight to my five eleven. Rowing brought the intense work ethic out in me. There was something about forgoing pleasure, skipping parties, going for double workouts, and the higher grades, rocking body, and being a part of our often medaled varsity team that felt great to me. Everyone in my life had a place and Henry's place was in the distance. We'd meet for the occasional lunch where my erratic heartbeat would sometimes betray me to myself, but as predicted, Henry switched girlfriends fast.

In the middle of our junior year I began treating Ansel like a previously loved blankie that I still thoughtlessly carried around. One evening I dragged him to a party and ran into Henry, who proceeded to introduce us to yet another girl whose name I instantly deleted. Their names always ended with the "ee" sound—Joanie, Stacy, Tracy, Francie, Annie—and when he introduced me to this one I stopped listening.

Ansel asked me to dance and Henry didn't even wait for me to say no.

"Well, kids, it's time to cut the charade," he said, grinning away.

"Charade?" his girlfriend and I asked together.

The three of us stood expectantly, waiting for Henry to entertain us in the usual way that Henry did.

"Belle and I have been in love since the first week of school," Henry announced.

"We have?" I asked.

"You are?" both Ansel and the dark-haired girl said simultaneously.

The three of us waited expectantly for the punch line. But this time there was none.

Dark-haired Girl turned toward him. "This time it's not funny, Henry."

Ansel just looked hurt.

"I'm serious," Henry said. "I just don't want to have these thoughts and not share them with the three of you. I mean, I'm not an asshole, or I am an asshole but I don't speak behind people's backs and I don't cheat. I speak in front of people and I speak the truth. Am I right, Belle?"

All three of them turned toward me. Was he right? Were we in love? I mean, I thought about him all the time, melted a little when we ate together or took classes together, and had even gotten to know his whole family when they made their frequent trips to campus, but I had resigned myself to a constant state of agitation. "What do you mean by right?" I asked, buying myself time.

"I'm out of here," his girlfriend said just before weakly smacking his face. The three of us watched her go but Henry turned away first. I never forgot how he could move on like that without looking back.

"So what do you think, Amstel?"

"It's Ansel."

"Yes, sorry. What do you think?"

"About my girlfriend cheating on me?" he asked.

"I've been cheating on you?" I asked. The conversation grew weirder by the second. "Ansel, it's not like you and I are even sleeping together—"

"Wait, you haven't had sex yet?" Henry interrupted, making both Ansel and me feel like losers. "Haven't you been together for, like, a year?" he asked.

"Well, we've talked about it," I said weakly.

"I mean, we're going to," Ansel said pathetically.

"Oh my God, you waited for me," he said softly, taking my hand.

"I didn't wait for you." Had I waited for him? I was so confused.

"Look, can we talk, Henry?" I asked.

"No, can *we* talk?" Ansel asked me.

Henry walked me away that night, away from Ansel and the party and everything safe. For the next seven years we were rarely apart, and when he left me, it was in that same way he left the others. Never once looking over his shoulder.

CHAPTER 12

The Day the Market Moved on Me

D URING OUR Four Seasons lunch, Henry acted as though we had never met, like I was some fresh-faced colleague brimming over with investment ideas for him and he was there to listen.

I stood to shake hands, an automatic business response of mine, and felt my knees weaken from the adrenaline overload. Hadn't he been told whom he was meeting? I searched his face for some shrug of irony but Henry wouldn't break character. Why didn't he give me a heads-up phone call? This was much worse than the forced "Hi" we mutter on the preschool steps. This meant I would be calling Henry daily. He would be my largest client and I was going to be subservient to him. I couldn't breathe.

I didn't touch my food as Tim rambled on about the new investment strategy Cheetah would be adopting under Henry's leadership. I could barely keep my water glass steady when I held it in my shaking hand. I usually hit my stride at such moments, but not that time. Henry snapped open his napkin and proceeded to enjoy three courses with a ravenous appetite.

Everyone has someone they will never get over, where closure is not a possibility. Closure is made-up psychobabble. It's not real. You just have to stay away from that person, because no amount of talking will ever resolve a thing. It's not possible to actually work with that person and Henry was my person.

Henry's boss didn't seem to notice. He was enjoying himself so much he ordered a chocolate soufflé for desert. Soufflé. As in an extra-twenty-minute-waiting-time dessert. And wait we did, trading niceties. My hair began to flop into my face, my earring weirdly fell onto the table, I looked down to see an ugly run in my hose; I was melting.

Boylan said things like, "Henry went to Cornell and Columbia Business School."

And I would nod my head with disbelief and answer with things like, "Really? I went to Cornell too."

"I'd ask what year you graduated," he said, "but I can tell it was well after me."

Polite titter from me.

Henry kept the questions rolling. "Where did you go to business school?"

Henry knew I didn't go to business school, first because I couldn't afford it and then for fear I'd never get another job at my level. I happened to work in the place that cared more about performance than degrees. Our chairman wanted employees he called "poor, smart, and determined to get rich," and when I was hired, that described me. Was he trying to embarrass me in front of his boss? Was this retribution for the thong episode? If he was looking for some white flag of surrender, he picked the wrong victim.

"I didn't go to business school," I said with artificial sweetener raising my voice. "I loved my job too much, and knew real life had already taught me more than anything that could be taught in B school."

"Really?" said Henry, seemingly more engaged now that I was finally lobbing back. "I have to say, I'm a fan of formal training, though I do see your point. By the way, I can't believe you've had three kids *and* are the primary breadwinner. How can you possibly juggle it all?"

That did it. If there's one cliché statement that working mothers everywhere despise, it's that one: the "I don't know how you do it" thing. I never thought I could hate Henry Wilkins but I sure was coming close.

"Did I say I was the primary breadwinner? I don't think I did. Also I think I've seen you at Fifth Avenue Preschool."

Just then the man sitting behind Tim took that particular moment to put a hand out and say hello to him, so I added, "Or maybe it's because we've screwed sixteen different ways to Sunday. Yes, maybe that's why we seem to have met." I lifted my linen napkin, dabbed at my lips, and smiled.

"Oh," Henry said, clearing his throat and reddening. I had shut down the "her husband has no job" conversation. "Well, you'd be hard to miss in a crowd," Henry said in some feeble attempt to regain his footing and because Tim had turned back to our table, "but when I'm at that school I'm so focused on my kids, I never notice the adults."

Gag me. Men have no problem impressing their bosses with their family-man rap, while women never dare mention their families at work. "Yes, I'm sure you were just too focused," I said.

Tim continued to look admiringly at his younger protégé, oblivious to the invisible conversation also going on at the table.

Henry came in for the kill. "Such great food. Not sure I've ever eaten here before."

"I think you got engaged here once," I semi-hissed loud enough for both men to hear and soft enough to sound confusing to Tim.

Henry started to cough and I swear I could see the water he was sipping come out his nose.

"You got engaged here?" Tim asked.

Henry would not want Tim to know he has led anything but the perfect life, and yes, a broken engagement in Henry's world would be equivalent to failure. I watched him try to recover. It started with an odd snort.

"We talked about getting married here, but really we got engaged in St. Barths."

Henry brilliantly made Tim think it was his wife we were talking about, and before Tim could ask how I possibly could have known about Henry's personal life, Henry took the floor.

"I was watching those money market options trading down today, and didn't really understand the fears the market has for them. They're so safe. Why do you think that's happening?" Henry was asking me about markets he knew far better than me but he also knew that conversing about drying-up credit markets was a subject infinitely more interesting to Tim than romance. I answered while staring icily at Henry. Had he become even more of a stuck-up wannabe WASP than I imagined? He never could lie and perform the way he is this afternoon. Is that what he's learned from his socialite wife? His dad was a small-town post-master who wanted to be a novelist. His mother sketched stuff and made casseroles. They were nice, real people. Henry wasn't sprung from jerks. Where had he learned this?

"This is money for teasing men," Henry had declared to me one day, as I proudly flashed a bonus check in front of him.

I had wanted to go out and celebrate because it was the first year my bonus hit seven figures. I was in my late twenties and had cleared a million dollars. Henry was still in business school, which made him go from being incredulous at my hours and pay to being downright nasty about it. Resembling the bitter wife left at home, Henry started acting like some portion of his manhood was being questioned by me. It was clear that Henry wanted to be the provider. The fact that I was outearning him made him nuts.

"It's emasculating," he said. "I wish you were a nurse or a teacher."

"Let's just be adults about this," I implored. "I mean, you want to be successful but you don't want *me* to be successful?"

"I want us both to be successful but I don't want to be married to a man."

"Making good money makes me a man?"

Meanwhile my father, now living in Atlanta, had gotten very ill. I was able to work out of the Feagin Dixon Atlanta office, and sleep in his hospital room each night. One stay lasted almost two weeks, fourteen days of being surrounded by people near the end of their lives, people who didn't take as many vacations as they could have, people who wondered about the chances they never took. I knew the universe was forcing me to look up from my spreadsheets and deal making and LCD screens. It was telling me that I needed to get married fast if I wanted my father to walk me down the aisle.

I came back to New York a day earlier than expected, calling Henry from the airport and wanting to tell him my big idea. I thought we should get married really soon, not in six months like we had planned but more like in two weeks when my dad was getting out of the hospital. I had to tell Henry we couldn't wait any longer. I could hear the familiar click of trading room clocks in the background, the noise he was used to hearing behind me.

"Great that you're here," he said, all warm and friendly. "But some lawyers are taking us to see *Rent* on Broadway tonight. We just closed a deal. Closing parties, you know."

"Okay," I replied, while thinking that no closing party I had ever attended consisted of a Broadway show. "I'm picking up the underskirt for my wedding gown," I said in untypical girlish fashion. The wedding stuff was turning me soft. "I'll see you late tonight."

Henry had wanted us to live together for so long. I was going to use the weekend to get the rest of my stuff out of my sublet I never used and into our new apartment. In the hours he was at the play I would put on my whole wedding show: the underskirt, the bustier, the heels, the hair, and the spectacular silk wedding gown. We could have our own pretend wedding that very night when he came home.

Hours later I was on 8th Avenue, rain pelting down outside, while my friend in the Garment District hooked me up into one spectacular bustier-with-skirt device, to boost my everything and ensure wedded bliss. I twirled in front of a mirror in a room of anorexic mannequins. I noted that the upside of stress is the loss of a tummy. Between a very sick father, a long-distance fiancé, and a job that didn't allow for personal problems, I rarely had an appetite. Still, the gown seemed to wash everything away. The gown made me glow.

The Garment District borders the Theater District in Manhattan. It was nearing eight o'clock, and since I was just several blocks from the 41st Street theater where *Rent* was playing, I had an unstoppable urge to see Henry before the show.

There he was, but not with any lawyer. She was a beautiful blond woman, grabbing familiarly at his arm as they walked by me. Me, the wet woman, the loser with the giant shopping bag full of wedding gear. That was when I should have turned and left and never spoken to him again, but my brain was not capable of processing what I saw as fast as my body was moving. I gamely kept a "happy to see you" face frozen on, and instinctively jabbed my hand forward from my soggy wool coat, to meet the hand of an underfed, bony woman.

"I'm back!" I chirped to Henry, putting down the bag and tossing myself toward him.

He held my arms stiffly, controlling my face so that I only brushed his cheek instead of his lips.

"Belle," he said flatly while looking at the girl.

"Oh, sorry, I'm Henry's girlfriend," I said to Thin Girl, thinking he thought I owed her some explanation. I grabbed the bag too quickly, which made the wet brown paper bag filled with lacy, dreamy stuff of the future tear in a slow-motion *cccchhhhhttttt*. I awkwardly picked assorted white clothing off the wet, dirty ground and hugged the pillowy pile to my chest. I wasn't sure why I said "girlfriend" when I'd been using the *fiancé* word for weeks. This wasn't going at all as expected.

Thin Girl laughed strangely while Henry tossed back his head, nervously running his hand through his hair. "You're not my girlfriend," he said.

He looked at me directly, right in the eye. Just like in college when he dumped his last girlfriend, right before he led me away for the rest of my life . . . up until now. Again, I waited for the punch line, but there wasn't any. I stood in shaky stillness, waiting to be saved, and I watched Henry guide the woman into the theater. He went to the "Will Call" window, surrendered a credit card, and never looked back.

I stood on the curb long after the lights went down, holding the wet and white bride paraphernalia to my chest. I took hours to walk back to the sublet apartment, the one I hadn't lived in since moving most of my stuff in with Henry, the one with the mattress on the floor, the dead plants, and the blankets in the oven. I still had the key. I flipped the lights on and threw the obscenely expensive wedding clothes on the table, where they dripped rain and tears onto a dusty floor.

The next time I ever spoke to Henry was as someone's mother, trying to get her kid into preschool. And now my whole family would be dependent on him and me making giant trades together, from the opening to the closing bell of the stock market, every business day.

CHAPTER 13

Gentlemen Prefer Bonds

I T's 2:45 p.m. on a February afternoon and I'm sitting in the back of a chauffeur-driven car. The driver and I are parked in awkward silence while the late-afternoon sun reflects light from the windshield into my eyes. The glare makes it hard to see my phone, to confirm what I already know: that the person I'm supposed to be traveling with, the person I should be at the airport with right now, has gone AWOL.

I watch people come in and out of the Indian restaurant we're parked in front of in the East 20s, but I'm not here for the curry. I'm here to get our star market analyst, Rudolph Gibbs, out of what I'm told is a whorehouse. I need him out within the next five minutes if we're ever to catch our 4 p.m. flight.

Shuttling adults from point to point puts me in a continual state of anxiousness. I can't strap a grown man into a car seat and plug him with Pirate's Booty to get him to where I need him to be. I confirm and reconfirm plans with assistants, have double-booked flights so we have a backup plan, and despite all this, the trip can still explode into nail-biting drama. If Gibbs and I miss today's flight, we'll miss a dinner with one of my biggest clients.

According to my snoops in the Glass Ceiling Club, Gibbs is presumably in one of the apartments over the restaurant, which is in a circa-1970s nondescript white brick building on a block of nail salons and photo shops. Gibbs is a Gatsbyesque character who always wears English hand-sewn suits and a cravat instead of a tie. A married, brilliant, king-of-the-sound-bite guy, he is often an accurate predictor of movement in the U.S. financial markets, which lets him get away with being such a fop. Business news channels can never get enough of Rudolph Gibbs. My largest client in the South, Raymond James, is bringing ten people to meet Gibbs at this dinner tonight. If he doesn't disentangle himself from whatever matter of business is going on in this building fast, if he doesn't get into this car very soon, tonight will fall apart. I can handle the plane reservations, the car service, the dinner reservations, the handouts depicting graphs of dollar/euro relationships, but I can't control Rudolph Gibbs himself.

"So who is his lunch meeting with?" I had asked his secretive assistant an hour ago. She told me it was with a client from Warburg Pincus. She wouldn't tell me the exact who, but I knew enough people at Warburg to sniff around there. My sources came up with nothing. I went back to his assistant.

"Does he have a love shack?" I asked her. I'd be surprised if he did. It's usually the suburban husbands who keep a small apartment in the city and Gibbs is a New Yorker. After a late night at work, the idea is to crash there instead of going home. But these apartments are referred to as love shacks not because the owner loves to work.

"He does not," his loyal assistant had said almost proudly.

"Maybe I'll try the Indian restaurant I hear he likes." I could tell by the snip in her voice she just wanted to keep her job and to keep his secrets. She wanted me to just go away.

"You know about that place?" she asked me cautiously.

"Some other women told me about it," I said. "I'll find him."

I called Amanda on my desk. "Where exactly is this place?" I had asked her.

"Please hold for brothel listing," she said sarcastically. "King is off the desk. Let me try Ballsbridge."

That's how I've come to be outside this supposed whorehouse. Except what do I do now? Is there a secret knock on the door? The restaurant sure looks legitimate. I get out of the car to take a look inside and even pretend to read the menu posted prominently over the counter. Bollywood posters adorn the walls, the obligatory fake potted plants are in the corner, and the smell of turmeric is in the air. But when I wander over to an inside door to the left of the counter, I notice it's slightly more handsome than its surroundings. It contains a panel of buzzers outlined in polished brass. Each buzzer seems to indicate a connection to either an apartment or maybe a room, and one has the name Unique Interiors. Could that be it? I hesitate to begin pushing random buzzers, but Unique Interiors seems like a promising name. The Indian cook behind the counter watches me.

"You want bathroom, you must buy food," he says. He's about to say something further but then doesn't.

A woman pushing a child in a stroller tries to enter the restaurant, just as another woman attempts to leave. They start that doorway shuffle of politeness where the one leaving pushes the door open and then holds it while the lady and baby enter. It's while the leaving lady supports the open door with both her hand and leg that I notice the heavy amounts of jewelry on her fingers, the shapeliness of her legs, and the enormous heels on her feet.

I follow her onto the sidewalk on a hunch. She looks a bit fancy for this place.

"Oh, excuse me," I say. She scowls, furrowing her brow to form a number 11 above her eyes. She's too young to appear so worn.

"I'm looking for, um, my boss," I lie.

"I not know your boss," she says, and keeps walking, or clomping, in the shoes.

"His wife is about to come here to look for him," I say slowly, "so I wanted to get him out of here first."

She takes a long look at me and at my business suit. "I know not nothing that you are saying," she says a little crossly but not convincingly. I continue with my lie and try to decide where she is from. Russia? Definitely somewhere in Eastern Europe.

"The wife of my boss," I say slowly as I start to walk the block with her. "I need him to come with me now. He will get caught here and she's a mean bitch," I add, getting into my story. I've never met Gibbs's wife but I bet she's no bitch.

"You'll lose his business," I add, desperate to strike a chord here.

"Maybe I help you," she says, "but I not know your boss's name."

I start to say *Rudolph* but then don't. Gibbs would never use his real name.

"Oh, um, Mr. er . . ."

"Mr. Dixon or Mr. Lehman?" she asks, knowing exactly what my problem is. She now seems impatient, as if she is on a lunch break and I'm eating away at her precious downtime.

I think about this for a moment. She didn't really just ask that, did she? These guys just use their firm's name as their own handle? Really? Who the hell is in there from Lehman? I suddenly don't feel shy to go inside. I'm crazed with curiosity.

"Oh, it's Mr. Dixon. Has to be him. Maybe I can go get him?" I ask. I've got to see the inside of this place.

Ms. Eastern Bloc has already turned and is trotting into the restaurant. She waves her arm at me, indicating that I'm to wait. So I do, not wanting to make her mad. I climb back into the backseat of the car and in only three minutes Gibbs comes out into the sunshine, not so much as a cuff link out of place, an overnight bag grasped importantly in his hand, a little lift in his step. He looks like a guy just leaving the gym. He pauses for just a moment, looking for me, then heads right to the car, waving to the driver to not bother getting out and opening the door for him. He slips into the backseat next to me, smelling freshly showered.

"Isabelle!" he exclaims. "You look swell, babe. Do you have the handouts for our meeting tonight?"

I'm so mad at him and so relieved for myself that I sound a little incoherent.

"Well, yes, for maybe the past hour or so."

"Good. Also is your account handling the lunch expenses for this trip? I think so, right?"

He pulls out a leather folder and takes out a crisp bill and credit card receipt.

"Lunch for Six—Warburg Pincus" he has written across the top of his expense report. The amount? $1,800.

He or rather I'm about to expense his time with an escort. Can that be right? The bill appears as if the charge was from the restaurant, this restaurant, this place that couldn't possibly cook up that much tamarind and curry on their best day.

"Let's pick up something at the airport," he says. "I'm not eating any airplane food."

CHAPTER 14

In the Money

EXITING THE PLANE, I practically climb over the small children and people blocking my path with their wheelie bags. I have to keep Gibbs in sight. He charmed his way into first class, something our profit-seeking bank doesn't pay for, while I sat back in coach. This gave him the natural exit advantage and the possibility of escaping me when those cabin doors opened.

"Mom, she stepped on my toe," one little boy with a Power Rangers Zeo shirt whines. He glares at me, along with every adult around him.

"Where there is evil, beware," I say, in my best Power Rangery voice, trying to not have him hate me too much. "It's Morphin time!" I continue as I hurdle past him. His face turns to a look of awe.

He raises his arm. "May the power protect you," he shouts as I catch Gibbs. I look back to see him standing with that clenched fist. He thinks he's just seen a superhero and I think, *I miss my Kevin.*

Gibbs has stopped to tap the bottom of a Dunhill cigarette

box and pops one in his mouth in this nonsmoking airport, while checking the emails on his phone.

"Did you read this, Belle?" he asks me, as we start a semi-sprint to the exit. He is desperate to light up.

"Read?" I race after him.

"This girly memo. This thing about girls getting grabbed."

We exit to the outside and I use his lighting-a-cigarette moment to see what he's talking about.

To: All Employees
From: Metis
Subject: Octopus Hands

Please note that touching, hugging, and caressing other employees, unless specifically permitted, is a breach of one's own personal space. Regardless of how things have been done in the past, regardless of this being tribal knowledge, employees need to know that just like in preschool, hands are to stay by one's side until recess.

Who was stupid enough to send this? I'm infuriated. It will be so easy to trace this email to this "Metis" even though the sender is using some obscure ISP that I don't recognize. Who would crash her career like this? I instantly think of Amanda. She means so well but is so naïve.

"About time your girls are getting organized. It's nuts the stuff you put up with," Gibbs says as he saunters ahead of me, and I, because I'm afraid to lose him, toss my phone in my purse and run after him. "So you actually notice this stuff?"

"How could anyone not notice? I mean, it could be worse. You could be in venture cap, where a whopping two percent of directors are women."

I'm practically hyperventilating. "I didn't think men were all that aware."

"People are aware, Belle. I'm an analyst, for Chrissake, I observe stuff, crunch numbers, watch for trends, but I'm not an activist. I don't actually *do* anything about the stuff I observe. Glad to see someone doing something. Clever."

"Wait up." I'm not sure what I want to say first. "Venture cap professionals are ninety-eight percent male?"

"And ninety-two percent of venture cap funds have no professional women working for them at all."

"So assuming most men in the venture cap world are numbers guys, how do you think they justify the fact that the opinion of half the human race simply doesn't matter? That women who probably outshone them in business school, who control eighty-six percent of consumer decisions in this country, have nothing worthwhile to add? It's the same with us. Our board has no women. Compensation committee? Zilch. Risk committee? None."

"Yes, I would say that's a big mistake. But again, I'm a market analyst, not a sociologist, but if I were a sociologist, I'd agree with Metis and call this tribal knowledge. Everyone's aware it goes on but we never address it. It's like a family secret, and maybe this Metis, this memo writer, is trying to have some sort of intervention, so good for her."

I've forgotten how mad I was with Gibbs.

After dinner I slip to the restroom to call Amanda on her home phone.

"Is this Metis?" I ask sarcastically.

"Wasn't that funny?" she responds lightly.

"A little juvenile and not something that won't have retribution," I answer. "Why'd you do that?"

"What? I didn't do it," she says.

"Was it Amy?"

"Belle, it wasn't any of us. We've all spoken to each other. It was someone else. We aren't the only women in the place who are tired of this stuff."

I shut off my phone and head back to the table. I'm so sure it's one of them.

By 11 p.m. I'm finally checking into the Breakers hotel in Palm Beach. The enormous buckets of elaborate flower arrangements make me mentally genuflect. The opulent lobby is filled with what appears to be South American drug lords, Russian tourists who buy clothing right from the runway, and an army of Wall Streeters wearing the casual-Friday uniform of khakis and golf shirts. I just want to get past the bar without someone asking me to get a drink. I want to take a bath in a clean tub.

It's been a full evening with Gibbs as he charmed commission dollars out of every manager we met with. They hung on his charismatic and whip-smart words and then made golfing plans that I know Gibbs won't keep. I supplied all the stock ideas that would benefit from Gibbs's economic and market theories. Lower oil prices? Buy some airline stock. Strong holiday sales of luxury good items? Buy some Tiffany stock. He and I make a great team, yet all evening I mostly focused on not losing him. Each time he went to the bathroom, I watched the front doors. When I filled the car with gas, I locked him inside. Substance abuse rumors swirl about him and I feel like I have a front-row seat to a guy at the tipping point between having it all and crashing and I don't know how to help.

It's here in the hotel lobby that I reluctantly spring Gibbs free, releasing him smack in the middle of the land of temptation. We hug and I sigh and say, "Please take care of yourself."

"It's hard," he says, knowing exactly what I mean, but he's already looking over my shoulder, seeing someone he knows, someone to have a drink with, and I'm not even on the elevator before he's circled by people wanting a piece of his magic.

The hotel is the antithesis of our disordered apartment and its unrelenting smell of spilt milk. I feel a one-second guilt pang for being happy to be away from Bruce and our chaos tonight but I push that into some other place.

Opening the door to my room, I see my message light already flashing, but since my family and office have my cell number, I'm not concerned as I listen. Two calls are from Henry, who is also here for tomorrow's panel, and two are hang-ups.

"Belle, what's the number for your technology analyst?" he asks in some efficient monotone, as if I'm the means to an end. Since our lunch I've been dealing with him curtly. I've convinced myself this relationship will be tolerable because it has to be. In his second call I recognize a sweeter voice, a voice I used to know.

"Hey, Belle, it's getting late here. Would love a chance to talk to both you and your analyst about CeeV-TV. Think I want to do something on the opening bell tomorrow. Okay, hon, when you get a chance, please call or at least text me. By the way, great idea, and why am I not surprised?"

For a minute I try my hardest to remember that I don't like him. Some muscle memory still won't release the good stuff about Henry and I have to actively think of our lunch disaster to remember that I despise him. But I don't and I wonder why I don't. I want to think of him the way he thought of me at our lunch, just a new business associate and not some guy I'm grateful didn't wind up torturing me until death parted us.

I don't return the call.

I glance at the clock—11:20 p.m. The chitchat on the plane, the prep for the panel tomorrow, the weird "Octopus Hands" memo, and the stock-market dinner chatter with Gibbs have worn me out. I'll call Henry tomorrow when I'll have more brain cells firing. Instead, I call Bruce's cell. Even though it's on, nobody answers. I call again. Not only does he pick up, this time I hear the background sound of energy: high-pitched preschool voices that will not wait.

"What?" he snaps.

"You're up?" I begin cautiously.

"Owen had a nightmare and has been hollering for an hour. I almost had him asleep until the phone rang . . . and then rang again."

"Sorry. My dinner ran really late. What happened in the nightmare?" I'm always looking for details of my kids' dreams, seeking clues about their future adult issues. Which child will hate me the most? Who is feeling the most abandoned?

"Like you care," Bruce positively snorts at me. "Monsters, malfunctioning superheroes, the usual. Just go conferencing and enjoy the clean sheets," he says before hanging up, and I remember I didn't confirm the sheets needed changing when the housekeeping service was in our apartment today. It's stuff like that, stuff Bruce is very capable of handling himself, that I take on because he simply will not. It's some pride thing that I know is territory to not unearth. He's the same with playdates. He told me once he can't exactly set up playdates with other moms, that it's weird to be in their apartments all filled with beds and privacy and kids who take naps. If he doesn't meet the moms on the playground or if it's a rainy day, he's on his own. He never talks about his manhood slipping away but I once gave him a *New York Times* article stating that 40 percent of American households with children now have women being the primary breadwinner and that he really isn't alone. He bunched it up without reading it and threw it into the basketball hoop hanging on the back of the kitchen door. It lay on the ground afterward with both of us refusing to touch it.

Self-inflicted guilt is one thing, but guilt thrown my way from Bruce is not allowed, and hanging up on each other is something that Bruce and I just don't do. It's like swearing: it's what I do when I'm not articulate enough to say something clever. So instead of feeling hurt or angry, or even guilty, I feel just a little bit sad.

I dump an entire container of bath salts into the bathwater. I scrape a chair across the floor next to the tub and prop open my computer to flick through my in-box while I soak the lower half of my body. I slip into water that is too hot, loving the punishing heat, and feel a frantic race to relax, wishing I could get that part of my day finished too.

My in-box pings open. I see not the 30 or so expected messages, but 370. And the subject line of each is something about CeeV-TV. I open the first message, something congratulatory, the next asks for some balance sheet information, the next simply a thank-you for the idea . . . and so on. I google, I read, I swallow. Suds are getting up to my shoulders and I lean farther out of the tub. I notice my hands are shaking and I hastily shut off the jets and stop the water. CeeV-TV has an offer on the table to be purchased by YouTube, which is really a part of Google. It must have happened while I was on the airplane, and by late afternoon my BlackBerry was dead and my iPhone sat unchecked at the bottom of my briefcase. CeeV had about a $900 million market valuation when we first had talked of it, which is simply the number of shares outstanding (90MM) multiplied by the stock price of $10 per share. When I mentioned it to a few hedge fund clients, they were able to buy it around that level. The amount agreed upon in this deal is $30/share, meaning clients who bought it when I told them to would have tripled their money in only two months.

And it wasn't a Feagin Dixon deal—it wasn't a banking deal at all—it was an Isabelle McElroy idea: something that made sense back when Bruce told me he liked their platform and thought they were unique. I simply looked up their financials and made just a few phone calls to people in that industry and spoke about it casually to my clients. A few got as excited as I did and bought some. Tomorrow they'll be ecstatic with me.

Even better, since FD wasn't the banker for CeeV, I was able to invest for myself and put quite a bit of our personal savings account into the stock. How much? I can't exactly remember but it was a lot. I can't breathe: it's a big car, it's a different nanny—or it's no nanny, it's sitting with the PA Ladies at preschool chapel, it's something close to $3 million. I redial Bruce. He lifts the phone and hangs up on me again.

I jump from the tub, covered in stealth bubbles, and run naked to my phone. I call Bruce again from a different extension of the hotel phone. When I hear him lift, I scream, "We're rich, we're rich!" but his fingers are too fast, and again I hear dial tone. "Screw you," I mutter, but I'm smiling into an obnoxiously gilded mirror in front of me while soap bubbles slop everywhere off my body.

I dance, I jiggle, and the housekeeping staff that promises to have the worst timing in the world is knocking on the door, probably to turn down my bed and put chocolates that nobody eats on my pillow.

"Not tonight," I yell as I run for the robe, afraid they'll barge in anyway. The knocking continues. I knot up the robe and head to the door.

"Yes?" I fling back the door, ready to tell my tale to the maid, ready to push twenty-dollar bills in her hand to just skip my room. The adrenaline from the last minute has given me super-strength and I open the door so hard it swings open, smacks against the jamb, and shuts itself. In that second of exposing myself, my face flushed, terry robe hanging in some state of openness, there, in friendly bright-colored shorts and a blue shirt turned up at the wrists, with his face more defined and handsome than fifteen years ago and sporting a grin, that same grin that melted me so very long ago, is Henry.

I stare at the closed door with Henry on the other side. I tighten the robe up to my neck and reach to fix my wet hair. I feel a mound of shampoo suds sitting intact like a Bishop Peak up there. My hand reaches for the knob, and pauses as I get hold of myself and wonder what my next move should be.

CHAPTER 15

The End That Was the Beginning

W HEN MY FATHER was in that despair of metastasized cancer and we were getting beyond any thoughts of good news, I would sit in sterile rooms, partly frozen, braced in locked-down position for more bad news. At these moments, when the weight felt so heavy as to push me deeper in the earth, my mind would yearn for a day of nondescription, a day like any other that got bunched and filed in my drawer under "previous life." I yearned for normalcy and monotony, where conversations between my father and me could consist of music and weather. I wondered about times in our past when I was eager to get off the phone to rush to do something as mundane as answering a client's call, or going to get lunch. I couldn't remember those last times, before a chance diagnosis made cancer the only topic in the room. What did we talk about? If only I had known, how I would have savored that chat and stretched it out. I would have concentrated. I would have been present.

It is the same with the kids. When was the last time Brigid had ridden in a stroller? Was I frustrated on that last trip by her increasing size, or the fact her feet dragged on the ground because she had grown so tall? If I knew there was a very last time I was to push her, maybe I would have lingered in Central Park or bought that ice cream she wanted just to commemorate a final stage of infancy? When did Brigid stop saying "Weely, weely wuv wu" when I gave her a lollipop or read a story with energy, or snuggled with her while ignoring a ringing phone? When did it become "Thanks"?

Somewhere in the future, you may reach to remember something in your current everyday. You know there will be a final time you walk your daughter to school, or have the body that can nimbly ride a bike, or comfortably wear a bikini. Most things aren't there for us as long as we think they will be. And that was confusing me these days with Henry oddly in my life again. Last times were supposed to be final.

Henry isn't speaking as he stands in the doorway. I mumble something first, something awkward about being in a bathrobe, being confused about CeeV-TV, since I just heard the news. But he just stands there adjusting his dark hair, shaking his head in an amused, King-of-the-Hedge-Fund way. I know he bought CeeV-TV stock and put it into Cheetah's fund. I know he bought about 2 million shares with us alone, and that the commissions from that will pay for the second-grade tuition for Kevin. Henry is well on his way to being a partner. Hedge fund partner, multimillionaire, father of three—my Henry is the whole package. He must be ecstatic and here to personally thank me, to tell me we're all even on the preschool front, that he will no longer be such a moron in our professional lives. But instead his movements get curious, as if he is confused or about to cry or in a great deal of pain.

His beautiful smile twists, his brow furrows, and his hand

that's holding up his giant frame in the doorway goes to his forehead. I want to say something further, to ask him what's wrong, but I don't because I still know him well. I'm still fluent in his body language, having mastered it long ago. He can say whatever he wants with words but his body says so much more. He can show off in an investment meeting, he can sit looking rapt with his kids in preschool chapel, but still after all this time, I think I know everything he feels.

His silence makes me want to fill it responsibly—I'm the good girl, the enabler, and I should cover this awkward moment and be the leader here. But the leader is tired of being responsible for so many people. I feel some twinge of damsel, and it feels interesting to try to not take charge; it feels almost feminine. I let the awkward pause hang in the air, letting him deal with it.

His left hand reaches out and firmly goes around my neck. He has always liked my neck. It's long but feels small clasped by his large hand and cold fingers.

"What?" I whisper, even though I know what.

He has no right to be touching my neck.

His other hand comes under my soapy hair. I briefly think how thin it must feel. My babies made my hair fall out, and it never returned to me—my follicles, shutting down and exhausted from thirty-six years of pushing out blond hair, and then brown hair that was abused into being blond again. When hormones pushed them out of my head, they surrendered, rolled over, and died. And now I was sure Henry would notice this. But I feel oddly proud. I have so much now, so much to show for my time away from Henry.

He pulls my wet hair away from my face in that way that tells me he doesn't care that my hair is wet or thin or that it's messing up his shirt. I know if I let him kiss me, it'll be that kiss I'll always compare Bruce's to. Henry's are soulful and deep and they take me somewhere otherworldly. For just a small minute I let him do it, telling myself this will only happen once, and then I make him stop.

In the morning he is gone. I wake up and I'm alone with a lingering smell of soap and Henry in the air. I'm certain he slipped out of bed, scrubbed meticulously, and headed to the gym. He showers *before* working out. I'll next see him at the conference, where I will already be in second place. Henry will have exercised; Henry will have read the paper and every news site. Henry will have all the details about CeeV-TV down cold. Henry will be ahead of me.

I rise from the bed to catch my reflection again in the gaudy mirror. There's a gleam in my eye. Is it the money? Is it Henry or CeeV-TV? I don't know. I do know I like being alone as my conscience does some sorting. Shouldn't I feel dirty and wrong? Does kissing qualify as cheating? How could I be a semi-part of this Glass Ceiling Club that hates having to cover for cheating men while I now straddle that line myself?

Feeling his hands on my face again awoke something that never really left me, something close to giddy. After a few knockout kisses, his hands started moving everywhere, and I finally clasped them behind his back and held them firmly with one hand while my other hand pointed directly into his face.

"We both don't want that," I said matter-of-factly. "What we do want is to talk and we're only going to talk about what we get paid to talk about. Okay?"

"You mean to tell me this is now a business meeting?"

"You are correct."

"Is there a punishment for misbehaving?"

"Expulsion. Immediate expulsion. No second chances," I said, retying the bathrobe and jumping under what felt like twenty pounds of eiderdown in the comforter.

Henry stood, watching me until an idea came to him. He brought a hairbrush from the bathroom and began brushing my hair, reminding me of how I loved when he did this. But I took the brush from him. He then brought over the chair I had propped my computer on in the bathroom, sat on it, and sighed. There was total silence for thirty seconds.

"It's very lonely and cold on this chair."

"You'll be okay."

"Permission to lie down? I'm so damn tired."

I laughed and held open the covers. I felt like I was nineteen. "Permission granted, but I meant what I said about the 'no touching' rule."

We were very well behaved in a Florida hotel room frozen by air conditioning. Henry and I talked for hours about subprime mortgage markets, money market options trading, TIPS, the price of gold, and the fluctuations of the Chinese yuan. We steered clear of the spouses and the six children that lived between us, and I never asked why he left me because at that moment I didn't need to know. I've always been attracted to Henry's brain as much as his body and I always learn something from him, even if we're pulling apart investment deals rather than clothing under the sheets. For us, all that talking was sexy.

Henry asked about work and for some reason I told him about the Glass Ceiling Club. He asked thoughtful, caring questions, soft questions, and I found myself telling him much more than I probably should have. I told him how both a part of and apart from the other women I felt, how frustrated I was not being able to get any further in the firm, and then I was quiet.

"But do these women really deserve to take it to the next step?"

"Some, yes."

"And when you were more junior than you are today and men spoke shit to you, what did you do?"

"It bothered me less than it bothers most women. My skin is thicker."

"Why is your skin thicker?"

I think about that. "I had an awesome dad, which I think is a nice vaccination for life. It also didn't hurt to not be rich. When you're scrabbling upward, the big picture is clearer. I didn't get sidetracked by bullshit."

"Interesting. But it's the limitations that bother you. It's not the politically incorrect stuff. Your elevator stops one floor beneath the top, and you want the penthouse."

"I'm mad someone is telling me where my career tops out, not letting me at least have the possibility of getting to the top. It burns my rubber to know I'm smarter than some of the guys in the penthouse and that I could do a better job than them."

Henry smiles. "You really love the markets. That's always what's made this job for you. You love the story of the markets and that's why you stay. For most people the money is why they stay, but for us it's the markets."

"I love the markets. I mean, every day is different in our jobs and we have to really care what the rest of the world is up to because what's going on in Europe matters. Whether or not the governments in the Middle East are getting along is something we need to know about. This job makes me feel connected to the world. I'm not sitting in some cubicle somewhere being isolated and out of touch and wondering how many subscribers my magazine will have this month or how many batteries my firm will need to buy. This job makes me feel alive."

"We love the markets," he said, and we grinned at each other in a total nerd-fest way.

"But look at Ina," he says, referring to Ina Drew, a woman about ten years older than me, whose career seemed unstoppable. Men loved her. Women loved her. She kept getting promoted and managed to have two kids. She switched firms a few times but was now the chief investment officer of JPMorgan Chase & Co. and a member of their risk committee.

"Yeah, it sure looks like it's working out for her. Also Sallie Krawcheck, CFO of Citigroup, the world's largest bank."

"So it can happen."

"I guess. But isn't it pathetic that we all cite the same few names? In an industry that equals eight percent of the gross domestic product of this country. We can only point to two women who have made a total success of it?"

"Yes," Henry said, and landed his hand on my familiar breast, as if he still had claim to it, making me falter for just an instant, because nobody over the age of two had touched that breast in several years. I'm not married to a boob guy. As nice as that may have felt, I removed the hand, hardly missing one beat of my story. I didn't want it there.

"The management is about to enforce its 'one strike' rule," I said.

"You're kicking me out?" he whimpered.

"I'm going to sleep," I said, and rolled away and onto my stomach, and while I held still, Henry fell asleep the way a little kid does, waving a white flag of surrender. I thought about waking him and getting him out of my bed but instead just watched him and his muscled back through his shirt, rising and falling in time with his breath. His form was lit by a dimmed floor lamp, framing the last four hours like the back cover of a book, and for the first time in a very long time, I didn't feel so alone.

Henry has always been the type of man who can take care of things. In that moment of faux moonlight, I realized that's what I missed most in my current life. I'm fully capable of taking care of Bruce and our brood; it's just so much responsibility. It's so lonely. I stared at the indentation in my bed where Henry had slept, the ghost of so much love almost visible.

My cell phone rocks me out of my daze. It's Bruce. For a woman without guilt, my hand shakes badly as I take the call.

"Hi!" My voice is far too chipper.

"Hells Belle," says a very cute Bruce. "I'm sitting here with Owen on my lap. Owen, what do you want to tell your mama?"

"Mommy has some money and Mommy will bring me new toys," Owen informs me.

"Of course I will, but a little toy from the airport," I reply softly, grateful to talk to him and not his father.

"Mommy can buy a BIG toy, she has so much money."

Bruce must have read the business headlines.

"Nothing like teaching your kids all the wrong values," I bellow, and Bruce takes the phone back.

"Okay, Belle, just how much of that CeeV-TV did you take down?"

Whenever Bruce uses Wall Street jargon in all the wrong ways, it warms my heart. It's cute like a child is cute. Moments like these he forgets that he hates Wall Street. "Well, Bruce, we 'took down' enough to, hmmm, buy a tiny house in the Hamptons and dump that moldy rental."

"No way." He pauses long enough for me to imagine a certain genuflection to the gods. "No way. How much?"

"Umm, enough to pay off the mortgage on a certain Central Park West apartment," I say with only a hint of a tremble.

"Belly Belle, my heart is pounding. My dick is stiff. How much?"

"Stop talking like that in front of Owen," I plead, but little gets past a two-year-old.

I hear a chant begin in the background. "Stiff dick, stick shift dick. My shift is dick." I giggle in spite of our awful parenting.

"I don't know. We own about one hundred ten thousand shares with a cost basis of nine dollars. Watch it trade today, we'll see how it opens, and where it settles, and then maybe I can figure out a number. Look, Bruce, the deal can always fall apart."

"Holy mother of macaroni," he says. "Ninety thousand dollars."

I wince and try to love him despite a mathematical education that he should sue his preppy New England boarding school over. How did they ever graduate him with those skills?

"Umm, not really. Our cost basis was well over nine hundred thousand dollars. It looks like it will open around thirty dollars, so figure twenty-one dollars profit on one hundred ten thousand shares."

"What is the NUMBER?" he hollers. He now has me on the speakerphone. I'm sure I've just heard something crash that contained glass, and I hear the scraping noise of him keeping small digits away from death-defying danger, and this of course makes me admire him. Shit, why had I done that kissing last night?

"It could fall apart, Bruce, but on paper, it's at least a two million and three hundred thousand dollar profit"—I pause—"before tax."

"O-boe, we are RICH!!! Your mommy's a genius!"

"Yup, me rich! Yup, smart mommy!" and then I hear more glass break and I try to envision what they are doing and in which room they could possibly be finding so many things to destroy.

"It was really your idea," I say, generously pumping up Bruce's manly hormones, "and we don't deserve to be rich." I giggle. "We're Central Park West's version of trailer trash."

"Who are you kidding?" he says modestly. "I say a lot about a lot. It's another thing to take action. When you get home we're serving you macaroni and cheese on the fine bone china."

"We don't have bone china."

"But we could."

"You grew up with that. You hated it. You hated doilies too."

"I forgot."

"We'll order sushi," I suggest.

"Yeah, and eat with our hands. That's the sort of rich we are."

"Yeah, let's go crazy and maybe even eat in a restaurant," I say while thanking a higher power for reminding me that my husband is funny, and for this unexpected diversion from my sinful ways. I hang up.

CHAPTER 16

Takeover

M Y JOB at this conference, besides swooning in a wet bathrobe and apparently bunking with clients, is to moderate one of the panels. This means I came up with the topic and secured the guest speakers whom I will interview, Katie Couric–style, in front of the attendees. King is now moderating the one before mine and he's chosen a topic getting traction in the press lately, "Do Hedge Fund Managers Deserve Their Current Level of Compensation?"

While we are paid handsomely, the hedge funders make us look like people on a breadline and many of those hedge fund guys are here. King is digging deep and lobbing milquetoasty questions to the panel to justify their nutty compensation. He does this for two reasons: First, Feagin Dixon gets to appear to federal regulators like we too have a scrutinizing eye on overpayment in the industry. We all do everything in our power to not be investigated and this panel topic makes us look critical of the money machine. The second reason is to appease these hedge funders themselves, whose wealth trickles to us in the form of deal and trading fees. If they stop making crazy money, then so will we. In the end, King will summarize for the audience why these guys are worth every penny and they can feel good about themselves and about us.

From my seat I watch a mathematical geek sitting in the front row, James Simon. He's a guy who bases his trades on numerical fluctuations in his portfolio and hedges his bets. Last year he took home $1.7 billion, a number that seems inconceivable, even in Monopoly money terms. Did James Simon really *earn* $1.7 billion? Did he actually *make* something to do that? Since the union pension funds he manages are probably getting a better return on their money than if it were, say, in the bank, does that justify overpaying a few people? I know a free economy will support whatever the market will bear, but since all these funds have the same rates and conditions, aren't they acting like a monopoly? Do the institutions that have to trust them have any ability to pay lower fees if they all charge the same or are they essentially forced to pay these fees? Has Bruce become like a voice inside my head with this stuff? My own panel is about to start so I stop ruminating and get my head in the game.

All anyone really wants to discuss here is the volatile mortgage-backed securities market, but my topic is something far fresher, something I think is the next place to make some home-run investments in and I'm determined to grab the attention of the room. I've entitled it "What's a Fair Price to Pay for a Library of Freely Submitted Content?" In this world where everyone shares their videos, movies, songs, blogs, and ideas, how do we value the company that everyone posts them to? That's my big idea, something I came up with when I was trying to value CeeV-TV.

My three panelists and I sit onstage, behind a table with poly-
ester drapes Velcroed into place. I sweep my eyes across the room
and can tell that Henry isn't here, because even in a sea of white
men wearing polos and khakis, Henry stands out. I thought he'd
come, especially since he has a truckload of CeeV-TV, and I check
my gut and push away the thought that maybe Henry still can't
stand to see me succeed.

Last night proved we could be great business associates focused
on our mutual success and we're into a new chapter in our relationship that does not include kissing.

The news about CeeV-TV will make my panel discussion the
most timely one of the day. Many of the hedge fund investors
here either own property like CeeV-TV, or are short (meaning
they bet the price will fall) the public stocks of similar companies. But when I look at the audience, I see a sea of distraction.
The questions I have readied for the panelists seem vanilla and
the audience catatonic. While my first guest drones about his in-
vesting methodology, my mind drifts to tomorrow, when I have
that Glass Ceiling Club lunch to discuss Naked Girl and when I
return to my family. Will it be hard to face Bruce? Should I tell
Bruce? Would I tell him just to feel less guilty or to make sure I
never do it again?

"CeeV-TV is an excellent example," this panelist is saying, "of
low barriers of entry into this business. It should be worth nothing because competitors will pop up everywhere."

This speaker is a stocky man, a manager from the pension
funds of the State of California. State employees receive about
one grain of the bushel of compensation the others in this room
get. They tend to not like anything and I wonder if some are mad
at themselves for not starting their career on the private rather
than public side. My attention deficit subsides as the conversa-

tion ratchets up. Then I do what I do best—lob a question that is insightful, provocative, and intelligent.

"So, Liam, do you agree?"

I have no idea what Mr. California has just said. The one thing I do know is that by simply asking someone to agree, the discussion will keep moving while I fumble to get my brain in gear.

"I think this CeeV-TV should be worth about one dollar per share," says the Californian guy. He doesn't like all these new, growth-fueled companies. "This thing is a flash in the pan. If content is free and barriers to entry to stream that content are low, I'm not buying the stock. That's a loser's game."

Many state funds are managed more cautiously, preferring value rather than explosive growth. They tend to be more careful with the money entrusted to them so they want to feel something tangible, to touch the bricks and mortar under their feet before they'll invest in a company. They don't buy dreams. People who believe the positive stuff about the CeeV-TV story like growth. They'll pay big multiples for ideas and intangibles about companies with no profit. My third panelist is one of these growth investors and he finally wakes up.

"I disagree," he says while clearing his throat. He's a smartly dressed British guy, about my age though some balding makes me unsure. "If you sell content that is provided free, how can you be anything *but* profitable?"

"Because, young man," growls California State Fund Guy, "every Tom, Dick, and Harry can do the same thing, which makes your company worthless."

But I know they can't. I'm tempted to interrupt, to tell him why, but the Brit is fired up.

"You cannot implore your target market to think you are cool: you either are or you are not. It's called branding. You can't just go get an image or change your image overnight. CeeV-TV has established itself as cool. Like with people, it's hard to become cool when you've been quite uncool your whole life. CeeV-TV is the coolest thing out there."

British Guy seems to be talking about more than stocks here. I think he's just insulted the nerdy, older pension manager and to me, *that* was very uncool. I need to calm things down but he continues to speak. "In fact, I think the multiple that CeeV-TV is worth is about double where this deal talk is. Google is lowballing these guys. Google is getting a bargain and I'm a buyer of both stocks."

I hear the room wake up. This is where I'm supposed to say something, to inflame the conversation and get us to new territory. I lob another killer question.

"Why?" I ask, even though I can answer this question better than anyone in the room.

"Why?" snooty British Guy asks me sarcastically.

He's irritating as hell now. By picking the one stock I know more about than him, he has met his match. I ready my tirade of facts about CeeV-TV, about to bring the house down. I try to let him finish so we aren't speaking over each other. In other words, I am polite, which in business can also be interpreted as being weak.

"Right. Well, for one, Google is getting a deal. And if Google is getting it at a fire sale price, the public stock of Google will trade even higher. This also means that if Google is getting a deal, others will come to play. This means a bidding war for CeeV-TV."

I listen, thinking this means more money for the McElroys, as the stock is sure to go higher. I envision the CeeV-TV spreadsheet in my mind. I'm about to spew the facts I know so well about this company, but then get interrupted.

The voice comes from the audience and it's not even question time. It's a commanding voice, a voice of authority from a person also able to spew the facts, facts that I've given him.

"Liam, we see other content providers paying triple the CeeV-TV bid multiple. Why did Google go in with such a low offer?" It's Henry.

Liam answers with weak details that support Henry but nobody's even listening. They hear the words *low offer*, they think it's cheap, and they want to be buyers. Henry is leading the investors in this room to bid up his position in CeeV-TV and will move the public stock of Google higher too. Henry already owns both.

Some people leave the room to call their trading desks, some start sending trading orders on their BlackBerry. I now also know the reason Henry was so late to the conference discussion this morning: he was setting up his sell orders. Most likely he'll be selling to the very people who just left the room to go buy his stock, locking in his giant gains in both CeeV-TV and Google. Henry's position will be down to zero by the end of the day. He is ahead of everyone. Henry looks brilliant, and even though it was my idea, everyone will remember it as Henry's. My panel is breaking up, and I never got my moment to shine. I waited too long, and Henry, once again, has won.

CHAPTER 17

Pump and Dump

I BUMP ALONG in a pimped-out van going to King's winter vacation house. Each of these conferences is strategically located near one of our executives' second or third home in Anguilla, Provence, Jackson Hole, or any place where they line the driveways with money. One evening's entertainment will be watching an aging rock star perform for rich people in some depressing way—that was last night thanks to Hootie and the Blowfish, which my dinner with Gibbs had me miss—while the second evening includes dinner at the high-ranking investment fund/host's house. That is tonight. King's third home is located on South Ocean Boulevard in Palm Beach, where he will keep us all outside looking in on a breathtakingly beautiful February evening.

Gone are the days when I avoided being the first guest at a party. I'm so rushed to get everything done that self-consciousness isn't a luxury I have. I need to cross commitments off my list at a mind-spinning rate of efficiency, so here I sit in an empty van, the first van to leave the hotel, in an effort to get to the party, speak to whom I need to speak to, and leave.

The young Cuban driver wears a stiff button-down shirt and a black bow tie. I sit directly behind him in awkward silence because I can't think of anything to say to the back of someone's head. This is a moment that Bruce would embrace, letting conversation flow effortlessly from his mouth in his sincere quest to understand what makes the human race tick. As nice as that is, I'd bet anything that right now he's forgotten to pick Kevin up from a dinner playdate I had arranged and he's not answering my texts. I hate managing our home life long-distance and hate that I don't trust Bruce to get everything done. The driver pumps up the volume of a Beyoncé song and wordlessly lets me out of the van.

The dramatic lane to the house is paved with white, shell-like pebbles that crunch under my feet. Champagne-bearing waiters get the signal to stand tall and greet me. This is a grand entrance to pull off alone but my goal is the usual: get in early, talk to the people I need to impress before they have a few drinks, and catch the first van back. I heard that Henry has already gone back to New York and I'm glad to be rid of the distraction. How did I ever let that guy one-up me this morning and did I really sleep in the same bed as him last night? It's hard to recognize this new Henry who has personality swings that seem manic.

Everything about the house is white-on-white; plush white pillows lie atop deep white couches placed perfectly about the green lawn. Lush white flowers drip lazily out of trophy-like silver urns. I gratefully take a glass of champagne and wander to a precarious lookout to watch the perfectly orchestrated surf, bang and retreat, bang and retreat. My thoughts wander to Bruce, to our children, to the weird possibility that we may suddenly have extra money. Not this sort of white-on-white, third-home-on-the-Atlantic money, but breathing-room money: the type of money that takes one's eyes off survival mode, off getting-through-the-day mode. I wonder about the divorce rate among the rich. Is it higher because they can afford to split everything in two and still have a life? Or is it lower because they can purchase escapes, exotic trips, and lots of shrink time? The possibility of having more money is wondrous. A few home runs like CeeV-TV could change everything in our lives and take the pressure off me for a while.

I really miss Bruce right now. I take out my phone to call, to check that Kevin got picked up from his playdate, to see what Caregiver is concocting as a dinner, to make sure the dog walker came, and to see if Owen was able to nap after his hard night. Suddenly a large hand squeezes my hip from behind and stays there. Instinctively, I turn—ready to push one of the usual culprits away, but it's not a usual culprit. It's Tim Boylan, Henry's boss. He looks as shocked as I feel.

"Oh, sorry to grab you like that," he mutters, self-consciously. "I was just happy to find you in this crowd."

We both look out at a very uncrowded party and I think it odd to hear a universe master apologize. I say nothing.

"Isabelle McElroy, right?"

"Uhh, that's right." I fake smile.

The Grand Papi of Cheetah's $35 billion hedge fund never, ever attends conferences like this one. I didn't know he was here and this throws me because Simon will be livid to not be having dinner with him, and B. Gruss II, our chairman, will want to meet him. How did I not know this? Why didn't Henry tell me?

I recover a little. "How are you, Tim?"

"Great, nice to see you. Sorry to show up on you like this, I wanted to hear your panel this morning so I just flew down for the day."

"No problem. Actually it's great to see you here."

And I mean this. He came because of my panel—did he really just say that?

"I heard the CeeV-TV news yesterday and saw how perfect and timely your panel was. I wasn't disappointed."

"And so you stayed for this evening?"

Tim wrinkles his brow and tugs at his French cuffs, a very fancy look for this party.

"Well, I'm one of those types that shows up for cocktails and skips the dinner, if you know what I mean. Been in this business a long time," he says thoughtfully. "But sometimes it's good to get out of the office and shake a few hands. Sitting in the ivory tower too long gives you hemorrhoids."

"I thought that's why you hired Henry—for the hand shaking part, I mean."

"Yesss," he says carefully. "Finally admitted you know each other from college."

"He told you?"

"Honey, I'm a researcher. Takes no detective to feel the energy at our lunch table that day. Wasn't sure what it was till I asked him."

"Yeah. Sorry about that. I think we were both shocked and didn't want to start reminiscing in front of you. I mean, we dated a little."

"Yes, well, Henry is off to a pretty good start," he mutters. "Have you seen him tonight?"

"I think he said he was going home early because, you know, he misses his three kids," I say ironically.

"Oh." Tim looks confused. "Well, really, Ms. McElroy, I want you to know that I do remember my manners. The reason I'm here tonight is to personally thank you for probably the two best ideas in our portfolio, this CeeV and EBS. If this thing works out, you'll have made our year. Let me know when you want to come work for me!" He laughs.

"Oh, I'm pretty happy where I am now," I lie. "Anyway, I thought you would've sold your position by now."

"Henry wanted to but I said to hold on to that stock 'cause this here is a big idea. You know that time we had lunch at the Four Seasons, I wasn't sure you had it in you. Love when the ladies prove me wrong. Anyway, keep Cheetah up to speed with any information you have on those two stocks, do you hear?"

"I hear," I say, standing tall.

"Doing anything in mortgages?" he asks.

I'm a little surprised that Cheetah is yet another hedge fund on the mortgage bandwagon. "I don't totally understand those MBS, CDO, acronym-laden things, so I'm staying with the basics for now. Henry must be a big help there. Isn't that what he was doing at Goldman?"

Tim smiles. "That's why people trust you, Isabelle. Everyone else would just say yes and pretend they knew something just to get my business. I want you to know that I like your honesty. I also want you to know that Henry may be my hand shaker, but he had no business taking your moment from you in that room this morning."

I know exactly what he means but act like I don't. "What do you mean by that?"

"You put that panel together, you were letting the story unfold naturally, letting your clients get to understanding this idea in a macro way. You were about to ask the question, the one that makes a yawn of a conference into a memorable one, the one that lets people remember it was your idea in the first place. Instead Henry beat you to the punch. Damn kid ended that panel early. It was not his place to do that."

"I'm used to men stealing my thunder," I say.

"Well it damn well cheeses me."

"Go easy on Henry," I say. "And he'll make you lots of money."

"There you go being honest again." We both laugh.

"You know that CeeV investment was the first time I took such a gamble with Henry. I mean, he's a new kid who seemed to be pushing it because you were pushing it. He keeps telling me you've got one sharp brain and that you're the one to watch. So far it looks like that boy knows what he's talking about. I'll be damned"—he gazes past my shoulder thoughtfully—"how'd you come up with that idea?"

"Honestly, my husband was telling me how great their content pipeline is and that he likes their software. It's user friendly so it has appeal to everyone, which encourages the uploading of even more content. It's like YouTube, only he thinks it's better. The earnings potential of a huge video pipeline supplied at no cost is nothing to sneeze at. You can't beat it when your content is fresh, made specifically for you, and provided for free. You stream it, and advertisers salivate to touch the viewers you're able to reach."

"I'm getting it now too," he says, while nodding his head. Tim is truly listening to me, respecting me, treating me differently than he did at the Four Seasons. "Say, what's that you said your husband does?"

Here it comes. "I didn't say, but he's in visual communications."

"What in the hell is that? Sounds girly."

"Not girly. He does all the lights and tech stuff for a conference like the one we're at. He produces video clips for corporations, sometimes builds out the platforms to hang lights from. He does lots of different things," I ramble, rewriting Bruce's nonemployment status into something that once was.

"Good Lord, woman. That's a little wimpy, you have to admit."

There it is: the ugly little fact that people on Wall Street tend to think that any job not commanding multiple millions is not worth having. Someone curing pancreatic cancer? Ah, that's nice. Teaching at a girls' school in Rwanda? Sweet. Get a real job.

"Well, it might not be a dream job for him, but he got a little sidetracked. Our kids came along pretty quickly and my job was just more lucrative."

"Oh, sure, no, I don't mean to be patronizing, you just seem more likely to be with a captain-of-industry type. I understand why you're not home with those babies. You have too much to offer the world."

"Um, actually I love those babies," I say, "and I also love this business . . ." I trail off and sigh because I see that Simon has spotted us and is coming up the path in an explosion of energy. He is positively panting as he nears.

Sweat beads at the top of Simon's head as he advances. He's a guy who likes to be indoors in temperature-controlled equilibrium and the air tonight feels sultry. I take the lead before Simon can embarrass me. "Tim, you remember Simon, he heads equities at Feagin?"

I see a trace of annoyance cross Tim's face. I'm sure they've never really met before. "Yes, good to see you," he says flatly. "Was just telling your girl here she's produced excellent work for us. Hope you can hang on to her."

"Yes," Simon says, "she's going to make this year really expensive for me."

We all yuck in that uncomfortable way.

"Well," Tim finishes, "time for me to catch my plane home. I really just wanted to thank you in person, Isabelle. Remember what I said about Henry stealing your thunder. That won't happen again."

Clarisse has now joined our little party, anxious to be seen with both Boylan and Simon. It's a virtual power-fest, and she can sniff opportunity better than seagulls at a fry shop. Though Boylan is trying to leave, she won't let him pass her.

"Tim, I'm Clarisse Evenson, a senior saleswoman at Feagin. Please let me know if you ever need my help."

She slips a card out of the cuff in her blouse with the ease of a magician. Her perfectly manicured nails press a bit as she places it into his hand, and I see a wave of disgust pass briefly over Tim's face. He reaches past Simon, past Clarisse, and grabs my shoulders, planting a big kiss on my cheek. He's making this a show on purpose.

"Like I was saying, brilliant work, Isabelle. Call me back in New York and let's have lunch again!"

He crunches away on the gravel path, putting his empty water glass on a waiter's tray with Clarisse's card, worthy of absorbing his water spot, beneath it; and we all watch him go. His trip down here was all for my benefit. My CeeV-TV idea made his fund millions, which will keep his investors happy. Tim knows that showing up here will keep me happy, and if I'm happy with him I'm likely to show him my next great idea before anyone else.

"How crass," Clarisse sniffs. "He wasn't even registered to be here tonight."

CHAPTER 18

Naked Girl

S HE'S OF average height but always seems tall in her delicate heels. Her ginger-red hair cascades in thick ringlets down to her elbows, and the perfume she wears smells nightclub-appropriate. For all of these reasons, the men on the floor consistently monitor Tiffany Antinori's every move. Maybe it's her fantastic, overchiseled arms, glistening like wet ice in a sleeveless silk shirt, or maybe it's something else.

Seeing Tiffany walk into work at 7:30 a.m. makes women in Armani Collezioni suits feel like librarians. Our clothes, in shades of drab and drabber, have little personality, while hers suggest something wild. One of the most popular bets to make is whether or not she's wearing underwear on a particular day, and while I don't tell anyone this, I often find myself picking what I think is the right answer. This means even *I'm* staring at her bottom. Tiffany is a distraction.

I'm not sure it's wrong for Tiffany to dress the way she does. Working as a sales assistant, supporting the salespeople and making sure that the money owed from a trade equals the money wired in to cover that trade, she rarely comes face-to-face with clients, so she doesn't really have to wear the corporate uniform. Her necklines plunge where mine rise and her clothes are form-fitting, and made of man-made fabrics that can be washed at home. She takes liberties with the dress code, a code vague enough that one could argue she is compliant. The Glass Ceiling Club resents that her clothing amps up the already overjuiced hormones, so when other women on the trading floor complain about her, we listen. It's hard to believe that one woman's clothing is a distraction worth having a meeting over, but here we are.

Since our first meeting at the Ear Inn, I haven't met with the Glass Ceiling Club. They've met while I've been traveling—the best excuse for poor attendance. A lunch to discuss dress codes seems harmless enough, so off I go.

Just before leaving the office I counted three different episodes of men having ridiculous excuses to visit Tiffany while other traders watched. She works with Marcus so sits diagonally across from my back. I get to hear it all:

"I need to take clients to a hot place tonight. Figured you know a good place."

When she rattled off a great suggestion without a pause, he asked her to join them, she said she already had plans. The second guy asked where the shoeshine man went, and the third wanted to know where she got yesterday's outfit 'cause he'd like to get that for his wife. The wife line is used a lot. The mossy gray carpet that leads to her desk is wearing thin.

The Glass Ceiling Club stands divided on the subject of Tiffany and the distraction she causes.

"Look, she is a woman with a gorgeous body," Amy says. "To say something to her is jealous and petty."

We are in the French bistro La Goulue, where the heavy-paned glass doors are thrown open despite the February date. It's warm and the "ladies who lunch" crowd is everywhere, pressing small shopping bags containing thoughtful gifts into each other's hands while air-kissing against a background of winter white flowers. They wear perfectly tailored Chanel suits, which, despite the four-figure price tags, look like uniforms here. I note how differently the Lunch Ladies and the Working Ladies treat their purses. The Lunch Ladies carry expensive-looking, monogrammed, and buckled units that seem to hold very little. They place these bags delicately on their tables, touching handle to handle and forming an almost perfect X for a centerpiece. When the owner needs to retrieve something from the bag she slips a moisturized hand in and behold, the card, lipstick, or cell phone is pulled out effortlessly. Working women treat their purse as baggage. Ours lie on the floor, bulked out with papers, business cards, electronic gadgetry, and in my case the occasional Lego block. When we need something from our bags we heave the bulk of the contents one way or the other and shuffle through it all. If we had placed them on the fine linen tablecloths of La Goulue they would leave dirt marks.

Alice Harlington, the quiet analyst, says, "Tiffany gives women a bad name. Who can take an employee seriously who walks around with a slit like that?" She is referring to today's outfit, a vampy, to-the-floor black dress with three-inch stilettos peeking from below. When she turns sideways the dress reveals a slit cut to within six inches of her panty line, displaying her beautiful legs.

While we summon up that vision, Amanda enters, hollering to us when she is only halfway across the dining floor.

"Great! You're all here."

The Lunch Ladies turn in unison and confer like surprised birds. They have an artful ability to look displeased without contorting skin into unflattering countenances.

"Badoit with gas," Amanda hollers to the waiter, three tables away, meaning she wants carbonated water. Lately she's been stepping up her Brooklyn shtick to practically wave the flag for the new-moneyed set, even though she has yet to share in the spoils. I may have been raised in the Bronx but I learned from the cradle to leave the accent in the borough. Amanda embraces it, for which I adore her.

"That black halter dress?" she says, rolling her eyes while she refers to Tiffany. "What up with that?"

"Bullshit," Amy says. "If we all spent as much time as Tiffany at the gym instead of under fluorescent lights, we'd be proudly strutting it too. I have a real problem with women telling other women how to dress. I guarantee you the one complaining is always the less fair one looking in the mirror—Snow White and all."

"My vote is to turn up the trading floor air conditioning and force her into some survivalist mode of covering up." I say hopefully.

"Okay, but what about the softball game outfits?" Amanda asks. "Aren't we done with them?"

Each year when autumn leaves have almost all fallen, Simon Greene sponsors a softball game pitting the investment bankers (nerds) against the research, sales, and trading group. It's a "mandatory fun" event, meaning your attendance is required. Central Park would be the likely venue to play softball and have a picnic for three hundred people working twenty blocks away, but instead we carpool through Hedgistan, the area between New York City and Greenwich, Connecticut, where most hedge fund managers live. There, everyone can gasp at the sight of Simon's waterfront compound, and imagine the amount of merchandise they need to trade and banking deals they must close before they too can own such a place.

The Greene compound is regal, with probably fifteen acres of manicured lawn overlooking the Long Island Sound. Two ten-thousand-square-foot white-shingled homes bookend the English-country gardens: one for Simon and his mysterious wife, and the other for his mother. Jewish guys take good care of their moms. A swimming pool in the distance, which remains open until the month of October, seems to melt into the water of the Sound. Despite the beauty of the place, the message is purely museum. We have never been invited to go inside these homes. We eat ham and butter sandwiches for hors d'oeuvres and a fried chicken dinner out of Styrofoam boxes.

Female investment bankers wear khakis from Brooks Brothers, cashmere sweater sets, and pearls. They don't play, just stand on the sidelines and sip white wine while chatting with someone strategic. The banker guys always wear the remnants of their suits from the day, no tie or jacket, but their banker slacks and a dress shirt with rolled-up sleeves. They keep their cell phones going, hovering under the magnificent weeping willows, one finger plugged into their free ear to drown out imagined noise. Occasionally they gesture with the plugged finger and we all imagine they're landing us yet another deal to sell.

The traders care nothing about fashion and wear cutoff shorts, golf gear, a Bruce Springsteen T-shirt from the 1980s, anything they have rummaged from their bottom drawer. They bring their own mitts. A few of our traders were professional athletes in a former life so it's never a fair match. While I'm being checked off in the grand attendance book of team players, I miss my children desperately. It's one thing to not be home because you have an important meeting. It's another to not be home because you're playing ball with adults rather than your own seven-year-old.

At the last game, our pitcher, a former NHL great, turned and conferred with the first baseman enough times to signal something was up. The two were bent in giggles, like naughty boys in church. Several times the pitcher would wind up his pitch but inexplicably stop. I finally saw the reason. Tiffany had just joined his team and was assigned to third base. With an earnest face, she stood bent at the waist, shifting from side to side, and waiting for action to come her way. *Interesting,* I thought. *Does she know that nothing is actually happening in the game right now?* But while she was bent over, the skintight Lycra shorts of hers (no question, no underwear) had ridden up her backside. But that was hardly the cause of the giggling. Above these shorts she wore a halter top, casually tied in a bow around her neck and dropping clear to her breastbone. Her astonishing shirt had no back. It simply dropped down, barely covering each breast, hanging teasingly in place. She either had bulk and spring in her chest to keep everything on or there was something hooking it together under her breasts. What nobody could figure out was without a back-tie, how did it not fly away?

"It was two-sided tape," Amanda said.

"Some sort of elastic under the boob flap," Amy guessed matter-of-factly.

From that point on it was impossible to get anyone to concentrate on the game. The pitcher threw Tiffany the ball a few times to try to get the damn shirt to move and nobody could look away. As I watched her positively strut across that compound, I thought about her courage. Tiffany had no self-conscious urge to either keep her chest covered or to pull the wedgie out of her shorts. She appeared to give no thought to the fact that the temperature was in the sixties. Tiffany knew everyone was watching her and she loved it.

By the time the game wound down, some of the wives started showing up, looking like they spent time getting ready to "drop by." Their carefully applied makeup, bouncy-fresh hairdos, and iron creases in their pants acknowledged the pressure of the Y chromosome–charged workplace. They knew they had to look good because the herd would analyze them in the morning. I knew most of them and stood talking with Annika Hebert, the wife of our chemical analyst, Ryan.

"So, is this someone's friend?" she asked, pointing a jeweled finger at Tiffany.

"No, she works with us," I said, noting the concern on Annika's face.

The stay-at-home wives can feel powerless about the vixens thrown into their husbands' paths. I could see it in their faces when they came to visit the trading floor. They'd register the many men penned up together, the proximity with which we sat, and the late nights of entertaining. It was not the ideal equation for even the most solid relationships. While their husbands moved millions of dollars around the globe, these women were driving their late-model SUVs between school, soccer practice, and spin class. It made for a strange balance of power, especially for someone like Annika, who had worked in our world before she exchanged it for that of the suburban housewife. I think the decision still tortured her.

"Don't worry, Annika, she supports the trading desk," I said, referring to Tiffany. "She doesn't work with your husband."

"Does she have a boyfriend?" she asked hopefully.

"Uncertain. She gets a lot of calls from guys, but she seems to be relatively single."

"She has situated herself well," Annika said evenly, squinting into the departing sunlight. She turned toward me and shrugged.

"So my husband works with a woman who is an eleven out of ten. I'm okay with that," she said.

"I work with her too," I said unhelpfully.

"But I shouldn't worry because why?"

"Well, your husband's a nice guy and you're smarter than her, for one."

"That's two."

"It was a compound thought."

"It's not Ryan I'm worried about."

I knew what was coming next. Whenever I'm with the wives, they will eventually plug me for gossip. Their husbands don't tell them who is hooking up with whom and I've never once shared my inside knowledge on infidelity, but I appear to be the most likely person to let the information leak.

"I mean, does she dress like that at work?"

"Not exactly like that." We both looked over to fully appreciate Tiffany's outfit once again.

"She's fine," I said. "Really, um, confident."

Annika shook her head. "Well, I'm confident . . . was confident . . . whatever."

"You were never *that* confident." And again I nodded toward Tiffany, which made Annika laugh, which made me laugh, which led to her saying, "Why are we both here?"

By the end of that evening Tiffany had won for herself the unenviable title of Naked Girl, and by the next day's opening bell this handle had stuck.

"Naked Girl on one!" kept reverberating behind my back.

That meant Tiffany should answer the first of her telephone lines, that there was a call for her. It wasn't meant to be hurtful, this nickname of hers, and Tiffany seemed to relish it. To her it was a title worth having, recognition in this sea of bland.

Amanda and Alice continue to lobby the GCC for intervention

concerning Tiffany. They feel she reaffirms everything the old-boy network thinks about women—that we improve the landscape on the trading floor, but that the real work, the mega-trades and deals, is to be handled by the men. They see her as bait for clients, a tantalizing young thing to have at a client dinner, while the big boys discuss real things. She can sip her wine and toss her long, ring-curled hair from left to right while smiling at their jokes and arranging for their car service to bring them home.

"Can we at least agree to file a complaint with human resources?" Alice asks, visibly annoyed at our circular conversation. "Just some vague thing about enforcing the dress code."

"That's just great. Women filing a complaint against other women," Amy says. "Men love watching a catfight. No way."

Amanda interrupts. "Maybe she deserves her own memo. Maybe she has no clue *how* to dress professionally."

Something about Amanda using the word *memo* sparks a memory with me. "So it was you?" I ask. "You're the memo writer!"

Amanda laughs. "The hell I am. I had almost forgotten that Metis memo, but really, I think it was terrific, so whichever one of you gals here is too fraidy cat to out yourself, just know that your handiwork is fine with me. You should also know that Amanda thinks that—hello?—Naked Girl deserves her own memo."

I look around the table. Violette Hawes, quiet as ever, blushes, but there's no way it's her. Amy is looking around too, so I don't think it's her. Alice is too humorless to tap into the tone of that memo, but sometimes it's the ones we least suspect. I stare at her until I realize that everyone else is staring at me.

"Are you kidding?" I explode. "It wasn't me!" They better be sure it's not me. There's no way I would do such a thing. "Maybe whoever Metis is, she should be the one to file the complaint about Naked Girl."

" 'Metis was a goddess of wise counsel, cunning, craftiness, and wisdom,'" reads Alice, who just searched the Internet for that piece of information. While she speaks she opens an email on her phone. "And the reason I believe Metis isn't one of us is because she's just sent another email." While we're all sitting here getting nothing accomplished, Metis has been working.

Together we grab for our phones and find the Metis memo in our in-boxes. It reads our thoughts so completely, it is as if this Metis person was sitting with us the entire time.

To: All Employees
From: Metis
Subject: Put some clothes on.

Your mother isn't around to tell you to lengthen your skirt or that cleavage is for hoochie mamas, so we will. You will never be taken seriously if you don't dress seriously. Boys and girls, listen up. Socks go with those loafers. Suits come with a jacket for a reason. And if you have an away game, do us all a favor and find yourself a change of clothes. We don't want to see your oversexed butt wearing the same clothes twice in two days.

Amanda laughs. "Consider the complaint filed."

CHAPTER 19

Trade You

C HAPEL? I can't do chapel. I wake up feeling sweaty and sticky because I've slept in black Lycra running tights. I didn't actually run last night but I thought about it, so I dressed the part right before reading to Owen a book so boring it made us both pass out. We spent the night sweating on each other in my marital bed that contained no husband. That means I got nine hours of sweaty sleep while Bruce found another bed in some other room.

It's Environment Day at Kevin's school, so I got assigned religious duty while Bruce will learn about being green. Right now, sticky me thinks that was a bad trade.

I've avoided Henry since Florida and for the first few days, my research calls were directed right into Tim's office. I suppose that was Henry's punishment, Tim taking some of his responsibility away for a bit, reminding him who is boss, reminding him how it's done. The few times I've spoken with Henry our conversations are crisp business downloads. The type that cater to only one side of his personality, the one that doesn't remember us napping together or ever having known each other. Henry may be at chapel and I don't want to see him.

"Bruce, let's switch back. I can't do chapel," I say when I find him on Brigid's floor, partially in her Dora the Explorer sleeping bag, which only comes up to his waist. He grunts but doesn't turn over. He must have been using Mr. Potato Head as a pillow because the ear of the toy is stuck in his cheek. I slide my Lycra body in the half bag next to him so that we fill every centimeter of the thing and Owen sees a good time in front of him.

"Me too," he says, and climbs on top of us.

"Little guy, you are always cutting in on my action," Bruce says, and envelops our baby in his muscled arms.

I position my nose behind his ear and say, "Honey, I woke up being more concerned with the vanishing polar ice caps and less interested in singing about David and Goliath."

Bruce tries to roll over to face me but has to scooch in slight, almost painful movements to get this done. His face touches my face and Owen, outside of the bag now, straddles us. I want to be close to Bruce to say something funny to him, but I can tell he doesn't need a joke.

"What are you saying?"

"Let's switch. I'll go to Environment Day and you go to chapel."

"It's over two hours long," he says. "You'd be so late for work."

"It's okay. I can call in."

"No way. I did all the work on Kevin's green machine. What if it breaks? You won't know how it operates."

I feel a gush of love toward a guy who both invented and really cares about the success of the green machine. I'm a sucker whenever he shows commitment to anything.

"I'm a fast learner," I say with very little resolve. I know that Bruce is right.

"I don't want you there on the phone checking your Crack-Berry 'cause that's not really being there. Chapel is forty minutes. Stick to fire and brimstone, lady, and besides, I told Kevin I was going with him," he says.

Brigid appears in the bedroom, her hair standing on end and her clear, pool-blue eyes screaming, *Love me.* She looks let down by what she sees on the floor, her frumpy family being held captive by Dora and Swiper. She sighs. "Here, chapel shoes for Mama," she says while thrusting the shoes toward me. She stands back and waits to be awed by the magic of my large feet slipping into something so fabulous. The shoes today are red, fire engine red tap dancing shoes done in a shiny patent leather. They are a leftover from my made-in-China Dorothy Halloween costume. I pull myself out of the sleeping bag and slip them on, resigned.

"Okay, Owen, Brigid, it's chapel time." I sigh.

When the cab turns the block in the 60s between Park and Madison, it's stopped by a fleet of black SUVs jockeying for position perilously close to throngs of three-feet-tall people. I fling open the taxi door.

Brigid bolts out first, her cotton tights bunching at her ankles, her American Girl doll tucked under her arm like a newspaper. I think to myself, *If only I took the time to really dress that child, if I detangled her hair and put her in smocked party dresses, I'd be a better mother.* My thirty-seven-pound Owen begs to be carried, and because of how close we are to the front door, I comply. The smell of his morning hair with just a touch of strawberry jam is intoxicating and I feel slightly better about being here. Then I see Henry's Escalade parked directly in front of the door, the place where no parents are supposed to park. I know it's Henry's car from his license plate, "POLO V." Yes, he's a polo player these days.

I command Owen, "Hug Mommy, really tight."

Using my son as camouflage, I pretend to dash after Brigid and past the POLO-mobile, but my timing is off.

"Belle!" I'm passing too close to Henry to pretend not to hear. I turn nonchalantly. "Hey, P. Diddy."

"Nice shoes, Cassidy—er, McElroy."

My heart stops. I know what he means before I even look down. Shoes. The famous doorman shoe-swap. Today I had forgotten the swap part because Brigid was with me. I look right in his eyes and past the dashing suit, the tint of gloss to blacken his hair, and the $25,000 Hollywood smile and try hard to remember when his teeth were crooked.

"Uh, they're not my shoes."

"They *are* your shoes, so pretty," says Brigid.

"Mom!" Owen is whining to get inside.

I have red patent leather shoes on. Bright red, with heels. Henry stands there with his sons, perfectly tailored, blazered, and khakied. One extends his hand to greet me. Are these kids robots?

"Um, I'm not wearing these, you see," I say weakly as I bend forward and shake the tiny hand while lowering Owen to the ground.

Both of his boys are quiet now, both looking at me quizzically.

"I pick out her shoes," Brigid matter-of-factly informs the sons of Henry. My kid is getting street cred.

"Yes, you do." I look right into the eyes of the elder Henry offspring and tell him, "Brigid has the best taste in shoes. These are extra-special. They make me run fast. They keep me from being late for chapel."

I turn decisively, to quickly escape from Henry and bracing myself for the eyeballs of the PA Ladies. Let them feast their damn eyes on shoes that cost $9.99. I think I even used a coupon.

"Belle, see me after chapel," Henry yells after me. "I have shoes for you in the car."

"You have shoes—women's shoes? What are you trying to tell me?"

"Not me, you know, my wife. She keeps supplies in the car."

Henry lifts his finger and points to a coiffed Filipino man sitting in the driver's seat. The driver does something that magically makes the back door of the POLO-mobile lift open. Henry reaches in and lifts up a nubuck leather cover to reveal a virtual micro-mall. In the back underbelly of Henry's car there are clever little custom racks holding about seven pairs of shoes. There are five neatly folded cashmere sweaters, there are slacks, a jewelry box, running shoes, fur collar, hair accessories, makeup kit, yoga mat, and hairbrushes. Brigid, my future retailer, stands in awe and wants to touch. I can't act impressed.

"Is she going on a camping trip?" I ask.

"Nope," he says simply.

I reach forward and touch a pair of the Jimmy Choos that look museum-worthy. They have never been worn. Who spends $700 on a pair of shoes and keeps them like a spare Kleenex box in the car? I flip the shoe over.

"Size seven and a half. You should remember, Prince Diddy, that us size-ten-and-a-half girls resent the seven-and-a-half-ers."

"I remember, ten and a half narrow." He smiles now. It feels so good to still be able to make him laugh and I'm relieved. I turn and proudly march my red-shod feet into chapel, feeling just a bit of my groove coming back and thinking everything is going to finally be okay, but then as I squat myself on the floor and have the extra minute to turn off my phone, I allow myself to open another Metis memo. This is number ten.

To: All Employees
From: Metis
Subject: Equal Pay for Equal Work

As many employees prepare to be showered with money, let us hope that all persons who decide bonuses divvy money in a way commensurate with accomplishment and not according to gender, race, color, creed, time spent on the golf course, or time spent watching acrobatic women on poles.

The second I opened it, I wished I had not. The banjo player began booming out something about someone being his sunshine, his only sunshine, while I seethed at the stupidity of such a memo, so close to bonus season.

CHAPTER 20

Putting Out Feelers

WHY AM I the only one who thinks this Metis is ridiculous? It's setting up a war. The few of us women who are close to the executive floor are going to be seen as the enemy. "I hate divisive tactics like this," I tell the GCC over cold and seasonably inappropriate March margaritas in Grand Central Terminal. I spent the bulk of my day speaking to an MBA class from Dartmouth and a group of Boy Scouts from New Jersey and they left me feeling better about where the human race was headed. "Our old-boy culture may dissolve on its own without any help from Metis memos."

Amy twists up her face. "Sometimes, Belle, I have no idea where your reasoning comes from."

"It comes from her bank account," says Violette. "I can't blame her, though."

"I love when you speak about me as if I'm not here. Hello? Aren't women supposed to talk behind each other's backs?"

"We don't have time to be sneaky," says Violette. "And we certainly don't have time to be Metis."

For whatever reason, the drink order seemed better as an idea than in reality, because nobody is drinking. The GCC, along with every other employee of Feagin, will be informed of their bonuses tomorrow, and the brittle feeling, the edginess of the moment, has us snapping at each other. The timing of the most recent Metis memo couldn't have been worse.

I'm supposed to be touring business schools this spring, recruiting women for the firm by convincing them that I am the perfect trophy of a woman with the whole life package and presenting that as something attainable. The GCC wants me to be more transparent with prospective hires, even if it means embarrassing whichever banker gets sent on these missions with me.

"Look," Amy says, as she re-spikes her hair into place. "When those kids really know what it's like to pay a mortgage, to buy a car, to have kids, their tune will change. Something has to give if they want to make the money they'll need in this town. Maybe Isabelle and the jocks should give more realistic presentations. Not the 'work hard, wind up rich' theme, but the 'work hard, get rich, and be miserable' theme."

"How about the 'golden handcuff' theme?" asks Violette. "You know, where you start to hit six figures and then seven and then you think you're incapable of doing anything else because nothing will ever seem as worthwhile because it pays a tiny fraction of what this job pays?"

"All I know is that today I spoke to young people who asked about ethical things I never even thought about at their age. Maybe future generations have stuff more figured out." I rise from the table.

"Where are you going?" Amy asks, looking like she actually likes me.

"Look, I have three neglected kids and a stack of mortgage products to review for Cheetah tonight. I also have to rehearse for bonus day. This night could be endless, and sipping frosty beach drinks in a train station is not getting things done."

"You don't sell mortgages."

"I know, but I'm tired of being stupid. I'm constantly asked about them, so it's time I had some intelligent answers."

The women look at me like I'm abandoning them and I have a weird déjà vu of leaving my children behind each morning.

I push on the brass-handled door of the restaurant and into the misty air of New York. I walk the many blocks toward home, both west and north, thinking again of Violette's opinion that I need to tell the truth when pitching the firm. If I did, who would ever work at any top investment bank? Speaking the truth would make me look like a traitor.

In just a few hours it'll be bonus day for the McElroys. I'll be paid for the home runs of the year, the Emergent Biosolutions, the CeeV-TV. Bonus day means that the graph I keep on my computer, the one that represents the amount of money we need to live comfortably in some suburb, grows more black than red. We are getting so close to moving somewhere easier. I envision my children attending a decent public school, Bruce working at something he loves to do, once he finally figures out what that is, and me looking back at these years as being the price we paid to land in a deeply secure financial place.

My BlackBerry buzzes with a plunk of emails. I notice Henry's in the mix and feel slightly enraged. I haven't even gotten home and he's probably looking for those mortgage securities recommendations. This will be a very long night.

Henry has asked me for something no investor takes the time to look at. He wants to know exactly which mortgages are in each bundle, the actual bricks and mortar they represent. To get this information I pulled many strings, and now I have to review it. I have to be up to speed on the stuff most clients don't even look at. We have yet to say anything to each other about our night in Palm Beach, and as the weeks pass, my loneliness seems to grow too.

I click open his email as I stand there in Columbus Circle. Blue lights glisten in the trees behind me, giving my screen a hallowed glow. I read:

In my ocean, you were the drop of ink that turned the water blue.

I stand there for many seconds, forgetting to breathe.

CHAPTER 21

Ticker Tantrum

I DON'T ALLOW myself out of bed before the first number on the digital clock is a five. Even though it's bonus day, I stand firm on this rule, so I lie still, inhaling the dried-out air of our home, and jump up when 4:59 turns to 5:00 a.m. Once again, Bruce slept somewhere else in the apartment. On evenings when I'm not out late with clients, he goes to the gym after dinner, stays until I have everyone in bed, and then prefers to shower and sleep in the back maid's room, where he won't wake anyone up. We haven't had sex in a month but I don't have time to worry about that right now.

I studied the mortgage papers until a mere four hours ago, until my eyes seemed to have cotton sticking in them, and the bottle of eye lubricant I was using ran dry. By then I had accomplished enough to email Tim and Henry the ideas I thought best to buy and sell in their portfolio. And that was the only email I sent Henry. All business.

The more I think about Henry's flowery message, the more I

believe it to be misdirected. Maybe his thong-wearing wife was the intended recipient and he misfired? Maybe he has a girlfriend? Still, last night I couldn't stop flipping back to my in-box, reread-ing his message and trying to not let myself remember that he was capable of being a very different person.

Even though it's early, Brigid has delivered my shoes for the day, a sensible pair of brown loafers. My daughter must sense it's a serious day and has chosen to have me dress like a law student. She places them at the foot of the bed and I lean down toward her smell of cotton and fitful sleep. The sweet breath she exhales into my face calms me. She locks herself onto my neck but I don't have time for our lovey nose kisses this morning.

Greene hands out executive bonuses in fancy restaurants and I want to look neat but not showy. I have no time to deal with my daughter's brown loafer delivery. I'm so distracted I don't even bother to pretend to wear them for Brigid's sake. I opt for some cannot-offend-anybody Cole Haan pumps and Brigid's face scrunches up with tears of rejection. I feel a little heartless not indulging my four-year-old as I toss the loafers in the closet but today I have to be cut from stone. For some reason, before closing the bathroom door on her teary face I say, "This is not me. Real Mommy is coming soon." She looks puzzled. I have to believe this is true for both our sakes.

Four hours of sleep is not enough for any human, no matter what anyone says about Einstein or other geniuses who exist on less. My sagging gray face reflects what's going on inside me. I slap on self-tanner, hoping it will make me appear slightly more vital, but the effect is a little orange. I poke conservative pearl earings into my ears, apply light mascara, and select a fitted suit. I look just okay, which is what I want. I pull out my glasses with clear glass in them—I have good eyesight but wearing them makes me look brainier.

Bruce snores away in the back bedroom despite the fact that all three kids are up, and the ransacking and mayhem is well under way. The apartment needs an entire day's worth of picking up and it's only 6 a.m. There's hardly one drawer that doesn't have something hanging out of it. No book ever gets read and returned to its shelf, no jar of food ever seems to be put in the fridge or the garbage. We dwell in a life of half steps, almost getting clothing to the laundry basket, almost getting the plates out of the sink, and almost closing the coat closet door. I bolt for the door before I become enmeshed in diapers, breakfast, voices pleading to be walked to school, or marital bickering. Like a soldier heading to war I can't think of my family, at least not until tonight.

I walk across the off-white sea of Lincoln Center and I rehearse my litany of accomplishments for the year. My speech to Simon rings like my own aria as I cross Central Park to get to the most power-charged breakfast scene in all of Manhattan.

The Loews Regency Hotel on Park Avenue has three doormen to whip the brass doors open. Those at the breakfast tables are seated by status. Private meetings are in the back, gawkers and tourists right in front, midrange power brokers fill the middle, while the real power sits along the sides, where they can be seen but not easily interrupted. The smell of expensive cologne mixed with fresh, dense coffee caffeinates the room. The only other woman I spot here is a *New York Post* gossip reporter, in place to note who is hanging out with whom. It's a testosterone-fest at 7:30 a.m.

Will Markle, an undercover detective, stops me to say hello. He spies for undisclosed hedge fund managers, letting them know if one CEO speaks with another and what if any takeover or deal implications that could have.

I barely acknowledge him because I see Greene, alone in the back and ready to get this bonus discussion going.

Greene likes to talk about money on neutral territory, away from eyes peering into the glass executive offices and yet public enough to avoid the possibility of raised voices and ugly scenes. Greene has managed to secure one of those unapproachable power tables.

Though paunchy, Greene is spry enough to jump up and pull out my chair to seat me. My brain goes on extreme alert. While most women would think this implies Greene has manners, the men I work with act this way when nervous, or trying to get away with something. Manners appear when someone either needs something or is guilty of something. Greene shakes my hand and his is sweaty. Mine is cold, assured, and I'm so glad I had my head-clearing walk. I can already tell I need all my brain synapses to be firing and Greene wastes no time. Before the bow-tied waiter can pour a glass of orange juice so magnificent the pulp threatens to rise up and turn back to a whole fruit again, Greene says, "I've got an opportunity for you."

I'm not at all hungry for the sweet, delicate muffins but to appear relaxed, I push a piece of one into my mouth, where it sits sugary and unappreciated.

I fire back with my best cheerleader face. "An opportunity? Feagin is one big opportunity."

I fake a breezy, light tone as I smooth the starched napkin across my lap. My phone is buzzing and while I lean down to turn it off, I never let myself release eye contact with Greene, which unfortunately allows me to catch his eyes falling to my cleavage. I sit up straight and adjust my blazer jacket.

"You've had a lifestyle change," he begins.

"I have?" I am very cognizant of this common tactic of beginning a tough discussion with a surprise statement. I'm now on high alert.

"I mean, three kids, the demands of this job," he continues.

"I'm terrific at this job and I've had these kids for a while," I say carefully, because I have no idea where his train of thought is going.

"You are good at your job, but think of the suffering of the children."

I'm knocked off my balance beam. This isn't at all what I envisioned. I try to stay calm.

"You mean . . . what?"

I feel my face get hot and for a second I flash back to Brigid's eyes this morning. Was that suffering I saw?

He continues, "Nobody can properly run a household, have three children, be an MD at Feagin, and keep firing on all cylinders. Even me. My wife mostly stays at our Florida home, my kid's at boarding school. That's how I do it. But you can't possibly do it. Not with babies and whatshisname."

"His name is Bruce and he's essentially taken on most of the traditional mother roles," I lie. "I have just as much free time on my hands as you do." Second lie.

"So I'm doing you a favor and giving you a partner," Simon continues.

"A partner?" My voice is very low.

I tell myself to wait, to count to some very big number before firing back, but I can't wait. I'm always waiting. There's no five-second rule here because I'm exploding inside.

"My husband is all the partnership I need," I say evenly. "Giving me a partner on my accounts is a nice way of telling me my income will be cut and it would make no sense for you to cut one of your largest producers because you'd be taking away her motivation to ever produce again. You're too smart to do something like that." Greene tries to interrupt me but I don't let him.

"I came to a place like Feagin Dixon so I could operate alone, work as hard as possible, and reap what I sow. Feagin is a place that allows that, that pays like that. I'm already giving half of everything I make to a trader and some of them pull their weight and many of them do not. If I understand you correctly you're telling me that I'm now to cut my half into yet another half with some . . . some parasite?"

"You don't even know who I'm thinking of. And honestly, Belle, it's someone who will grow your accounts immeasurably."

"Simon, you're a salesman selling an idea to another salesman. Give it a rest and just let me guess which guy it will be because I know it will be a guy and it will also be someone with no relationships and no accounts. Am I right?"

Greene is slightly rattled but remains direct. "Yes, he's a man."

"*Which* man?" I say, but it sounds like a hiss.

My voice has gotten louder all on its own and the waiter scurries away instead of refilling our coffee cups. I'm fighting to find composure, but I just can't do it. I haven't rehearsed this part. I thought I had anticipated every turn this meeting could have taken but I never saw this coming.

"Simon, a partner implies equality and I can't think of any man who's going to bring an account package equal to mine to the table. It'd be one thing if I was not producing, but I am producing. You gave me the worst accounts years ago, you gave me nothing and I've turned them into something and you still haven't told me which partner you're considering."

"Stone Dennis."

The guy who stole Brigid's Barbie head and considered punching me at the office holiday party. I don't think the guy has any accounts or any work ethic and he's been with us long enough to have found both. That is who Simon considers to be my equal.

Our conversation has spun far from the reason we were meeting in the first place, the bonus. It's time for me to take control. I can discuss the partnering idea later. I need the upper hand of this conversation. "Simon, you do realize that I'm your biggest producer over the last twelve months. I expect to get paid as such." I say this with an icy cool that puts out the fire on my face.

"Well, you do have some of the largest accounts so I should hope you would be."

"Yes, but please tell me you remember the important fact that they weren't big accounts when I got them, and that I grew them, and most importantly I can take them wherever I end up working."

Simon and I begin to zing at each other. Like a Ping-Pong ball, our anger flies back and forth over a votive candle weirdly lit for breakfast service. We're very good at the pithy one-liners delivered in civil tones. He tries to make me believe Stone can grow my accounts even more.

"There's no low-hanging fruit that isn't picked off the tree," I say. "Not on any tree I'm responsible for."

"It's the fruit in the higher branches that Stone is going to pick for you," he retorts with his cheek turning from red to white, from sheepish embarrassment of doing something unethical to anger at being challenged.

"Enough with the fruit metaphors," I hiss at him. "Stone will bring nothing and take something. It's that simple."

We sit in silence for a moment while I try to get my heart rate to settle and his face returns to a more neutral pallor.

"You do realize you're cutting my income in half?" I practically whisper. "Nobody gets their income cut like this when they're doing a good job."

"I didn't say it would be a fifty-fifty split."

"What exactly are you saying?"

"Sixty-forty."

"Stone Dennis will get forty percent of my income for doing what?"

"Belle, he will grow the income. You will take sixty percent home of what will be a much larger pot."

"You don't really believe that." My voice quavers like a girl getting dumped.

"I do and you're not alone. Many people on the desk are going to be splitting accounts."

"Name them," I say, knowing there won't be one male named.

"It's not your business. This is your business." Greene plants his fat fingers flat on my spreadsheet of accomplishments, my list of deals and trades executed in the past year and the stuff we've come to talk about.

"Simon, I came to this firm thinking the sky was the limit. Any ambition I had to run a department was slowly chipped away by the reality of the environment I work in. I *replaced* that ambition with another, the desire to use my brain to make money and my energy to do it quickly. I'm hitting the ball out of the park on every basis that is measured and you keep changing the rules on me, moving the boundaries, making things impossible. My job is a one-person job. Unless—"

I interrupt myself with a terrible thought. It's a one-person job unless they want me to teach Stone my accounts before they push me out. They can't fire me because I bring in too much money, but what if someone knew how to do what I do? What if someone also had good relationships with my accounts? What if I were to become more disposable? I freak just a little bit more.

"Look," Simon says, trying to calm me down, "I see Stone being the party boy on the account, the guy willing to take the clients to strip clubs, the guy who'll drink shots with the junior-level analysts who will one day run those firms. How do I justify paying Stone if I don't give him any opportunity? The guy is getting married to a woman who is a shopper. Then he'll have kids and if he sees no place to grow his business, he's gone."

"Yes, that would be a terrible loss," I mutter.

It's time for me to play with Simon's head.

"Have you heard about this class action suit out of Goldman Sachs?" I ask. "Or the one that Merrill Lynch had to settle for fifty million dollars? Or maybe the Morgan Stanley one?"

"Oh, a bunch of secretaries looking for a big payday?" Simon rolls his eyes. "Yes. I've heard of them."

"You do realize we operate in a similar culture at Feagin and that it's a matter of time until we get slapped with something like that." I'm careful to put myself on the "we" side of things, as if his decision is bad for everyone.

Simon doesn't say a thing for a moment before softening his tone, "Those other ladies look up to you. Be a role model for them. Fighting me on this will only come back to hurt you someday."

I think I have just been threatened but I'm not sure. I begin softly, "Who will be Marcus's partner? What about King, doesn't he need a partner?"

"I believe we're here to discuss your bonus," Simon retorts, and waves his hand, indicating the discussion is over, and if I want to get paid I need to get my head back in the game. So I do. But I really don't.

Several hours later I'm doing math at my desk. Simon has paid me for the past year. Every bonus dollar, so carefully recorded in my nightly Excel spreadsheet, will be handed to me in the form of a check a few weeks from now. It's a number just under three million dollars. I will take that check to my bank and hand it to the teller, who could never fathom such a sum. She will wonder if I won the lottery or have a rich husband and I'll feel embarrassed by what is probably a warped sense of what I need or don't need in my bank account. I think all this comes from growing up without ever having anything new or undamaged or having sandwiches wrapped in newspaper instead of being able to buy the school lunch or even Ziploc bags. Or maybe it's because I never know how much Bruce will spend or if he'll ever work again. I don't know exactly why I think we need so much but I do. It's not to buy a yacht or a new house, it's to feel safe with a partner who brings no money to the table.

By the end of the day, three women were partnered with three young men. Simon couldn't use the same excuse he used for me when it came to partnering up the other women. The other two, Amy and Violette, have no kids or husband or anything else Simon could claim would prevent them from bringing in money. Of course Ballsbridge had his opinion about this.

"Girlfriend," he had said, "you're all fertile lassies. Simon doesn't want some bumper crop of equities markets pushing ever higher while he's caught with sowers and reapers who aren't available to harvest the goods. If the reason they're unavailable is because they've been having unprotected sex, he ends up looking like a moron. Can't blame the guy, you gals need backup."

"Boyfriend," I sigh to him, as I know he's only half joking, "I've been proving I can do the mom/banker/sales thing for a while. The others have no kids. And what's the difference between any woman and you? What's to stop you from just walking out the door one day? What would happen to your accounts? Nobody knows your accounts, so why don't you have a partner?"

"Honey, what I lack are two ovaries. You ladies are a pain in the ass to him. He doesn't want to depend on you. It's that simple." Marcus tweaks my cheek. "You're so damn cute and you're rich. Why worry so much about the things that don't really matter?"

When he says this, the image I have of Brigid crying at the door this morning with red, swollen eyes comes into my head.

If I hurry back home, I can grab both our bathing suits and take her out of school. The two of us can swim at the indoor pool on the roof of the Mandarin Hotel, order boxed bento lunches, wear thick robes, and act like we're visiting from Texas. We can try out fake accents and play Marco Polo and splash anyone who dares to come near us. Without telling anyone where I'm headed, I set my lines to voice mail, rise from my desk, and walk out.

CHAPTER 22

Inside Information

THE NEXT WEEK my business slows when Henry takes his family to an island in the Caribbean called Necker. I find myself looking at Internet photos of what appears to be heaven, and learn that guests have to rent the entire island to stay there. I thought it would be a relief to have him off the island of Manhattan, but instead I'm a woman who surfs photos of someone else's vacation. Maybe that's what Bruce, the kids, and I need, some over-the-top vacation with sparkling sunshine, hiking trails, beach beds, and blended drinks.

Ballsbridge is onto my plan of a sexy getaway when he spies what's on my screen.

"That is not a place to take the kids," he says helpfully while hovering behind my chair, "and it's always a welcoming sign when they tell you to inquire about pricing. Isn't the rule that if you have to ask, you can't afford?"

Naked Girl needs to see what he's talking about so she sits on my desk, *on my desk*, and leans in so she can get up close to my screen. She crosses one leg over the other and we're so close that I'm staring at a mole on her thigh.

"You can take kids there," she says confidently, while wrapping her ginger locks into a loose bun. From her recent body language I get the feeling Naked Girl and Ballsbridge are some sort of an item. "But be prepared to bring the nanny. It's not a 'kids club' place, if you know what I mean."

Marcus and I stare at her but she's not done.

"I did receive the massage of my life on Necker. It was on a bed that floated in the water." She sighs dreamily and pulls her hair down again, making Marcus agitated.

"Because you've actually been there?" he asks.

"It was a short trip but yeah, I've been," she says, and rolls her eyes as if it bored her. "I was on a boat trip and we stopped there for two nights."

I choose to ignore who the "we" was. "A boat like a cruise ship?" I ask while thinking no five-thousand-passenger anything is parking near those delicate reefs.

"A boat like a yacht," she says. "And yeah, if you have to ask the price, you can't afford it." She unwinds her legs and saunters away.

The short riffs from Henry have appeared sporadically: sometimes once per day, sometimes not for three days, launched like stealth missiles directly to their target in the middle of the night. I find myself waking from deep sleep, intuitively expecting their arrival, darting my eyes between my sleeping husband, if he has successfully made it to our bed, and my sleeping phone. One in the bed and one next to the bed and only one begs to be touched and lit up, and it isn't Bruce.

When I open my mail, my pulse quickens. I'm a live, hovering heartbeat, a cocktail party paused, existing for a moment between feeling remembered and not. Each message delivers me into a fairy tale, away from my life of tired working person and exhausted mother. I return to being the person I was, not that many years ago.

I know I'm dabbling in a dangerous space, getting the high an addict craves. But the person I pretend Henry to be really doesn't exist so I tell myself I'm still in safe territory. Reading one-way email is not exactly participating in something that feels close to being a cheater.

If Henry and I had stayed together, would I have left this job by now? Would I be drinking something chilled and frothy on an island and be burying our kids up to their necks in the sand?

I'm wasting time. The whole entanglement with Henry has led to a new habit, something entirely foreign to me. I daydream even now while my in-box pings. Message from Henry:

I just found a leg in the sand. It's blue with a black boot. Plastic. I guess we're not the first humans to visit here. The good news is I found the most perfect rock to give to you. The bad news is that I want to give it to you in person.

I remind myself that I have to end his little game, but his email has made me feel instantly better. I feel energized and girly. Am I so starved for attention that these emails make me some version of happy? Even Stone, who is now cutting his fingernails over his wastebasket, isn't bothering me as much as he should. He began our partnership in an unusual way, acting uninterested in everything except the Metis memos. He bets other guys in the office on who the author is and once told me I speak the way Metis writes. The brat is trying to play with my head and I hate that I let him mentally clutter my brain.

Ping! It's another Henry message. I don't breathe as I open it. It reads:

I've been taking a look at swaps, longevity swaps. What can
you tell me about those?

I crash back to earth. Longevity swaps? I know a lot about
currency swaps and helped Tim do a few of those, but longevity
swaps? I think they have something to do with betting on the
length of someone's life. How does a guy go from dreaming
about me while on an island to figuring out how to profit from
speculating on the human life span?

I'm about to call the swaps desk but glance again at Stone snapping his nail clipper. I feel massive irritation at his very existence.
I call him even though he's ten feet away and watch as he lets
it ring five excruciating times. He has caller ID so he knows it's
me. He puts down the clippers when his pinky finger is perfect
and answers.

"Hey, Stone," I say. "Finished with the manicure?"

He says nothing so I continue, "What do you know about
longevity swaps?"

Stone stands, uncurls his massive frame from his rolling chair,
carefully places his clippers inside his drawer, and finally turns to
face me. He's about six foot two and keeps his tailored shirtsleeves
pulled up to his highly developed biceps. Ruffling his unkempt
hair is a favorite pastime of his. He seems aware of the fact that
he's good-looking.

"Ummm, nothing?"

"Right. Well, give me some good ideas on these things. I'm
going home early today."

"Okay, need any help writing memos?"

I stare at him. He stares at me. "I am not, repeat not, writing
those memos and I'm also not sure why you believe it's your
place to even say that."

His second line flashes now and we look at the turret. It's his

163

fiancée. He hasn't called a client yet or researched anything or initiated any sort of trade and it's been weeks. He's an expensive thing to look at. His face appears pained to not be answering her.

"Oh," he said. "It's for Cougar?"

"Cheetah. Stone, the largest account you now cover with me is called Cheetah."

"Yeah, whatever."

Those tranches of subprime mortgages I put together for Henry sparked a deluge of orders from Cheetah. I write orders for CMOs with a Cheetah account number on them several times per day. Marcus, Amy, and King all sit back in awe as I do less with the slow-moving stock market and more with this shiny new toy called subprime mortgage bonds.

Clarisse is seething with jealousy at my commission runs since they're fatter than anyone else's. Ballsbridge eavesdrops on me, trying to understand how I'm selling so much of this stuff. But Ballsbridge and Clarisse don't have what I have, a counterpart on the bond desk who realizes that together we make a great team. Most bond traders would never share the work and wealth with someone like me, from a different department. My counterpart in fixed income is the goddess Kathryn Peterson, the most senior woman on the mortgage desk, who, up until now, hadn't done one trade with Cheetah, and while I trade all day with Cheetah, I'd never traded a bond before.

A few weeks ago, I approached Kathryn and told her I could get her into that account if we split the commissions and that we would then not need to split them with Stone. She loved the idea and we launched our own partnership. I see her as the perfect way to push Simon back on this partnering thing. He never saw a two-woman partnership, hatched from a department he doesn't run, coming.

Feagin Dixon didn't invent this new mortgage vehicle, Goldman Sachs did, and we, like several other Wall Street firms, are in such a desperate race to catch up that Simon and King don't care who sells this stuff, just get it done, and that's why I'm allowed to sell something not even traded on my floor. In my opinion Henry is a visionary and Henry can't get enough of them. Kathryn and I are happy to be his dealer of choice.

There is a group here at Feagin called the Fundamental Strategies Group. They're supposed to evaluate the risk and profit potential of mortgage packages like the ones I sell to Henry. If I ask them to evaluate the risk of the products I sell, they will hand me a neat piece of paper with maybe ten or twenty bundles that would be a good fit for my client's needs. Then I could go home and take my kids ice skating or feed them something not spawned by our microwave oven. But the problem with using this in-house group is that I don't trust them. The Fundamental Strategies guys also advise our in-house traders, the King McPhersons of my world who have investment positions they want and don't want. It's easy for them to suggest their wannabe castoffs to me for my client to buy. That way Kathryn and I hand them their profit while they load Cheetah up with some junk Henry would probably take a loss on. The way to not get suckered by them is to do the work ourselves. Kathryn and I split the pile while I picture my upcoming evening replete with coffee, a calculator, a sex-starved husband, and children who refuse to go to sleep. Still, to me this seems like a good trade.

CHAPTER 23

Bond Girl

T HE COLUMN OF papers stacked on my desk fan at their edges because Marcus Ballsbridge's ball fan is tilted upward. A ball fan is a fan angled to cool a man's private parts, an appliance apparently necessary when the owner is agitated, and Ballsy is agitated.

Naked Girl has limited movements today because her skirt seems sewn onto her body. Still, she shimmies herself into standing position so she can berate Marcus.

"The breeze from that damn fan gets up my skirt and makes me horrr-ny," she practically yells. Heads lift from twenty feet in every direction.

"When you wear such a narrow skirt," Ballsbridge retorts, "no air can possibly squeeze up there, honey. I wouldn't worry about it."

"Combine a wiggle dress with cold blowing air, Ballsy, and this girl is thinking of something more satisfying than balancing your stupid trades."

Marcus and Tiffany seem locked in some sort of domestic spat. It's like she isn't able to distract the man of her choice anymore, so she tries to retaliate by not answering his ringing phone lines or dishing out sexy talk he doesn't respond to.

From the arc of sweat I see spreading beneath Ballsbridge's Thomas Pink shirt, I assume he's losing money. He can't sit still, taps his computer mercilessly, and has several graphs on his screen with dramatic downward slopes.

Marcus is big in every area of his body. His fingers are so wide they mistakenly press two computer keys at once, the necks of his shirts are custom widths, and the thigh areas of his slacks strain from the muscles beneath. He was a defensive lineman at the University of Texas and it shows. While I'm tempted to turn his fan off and tell Naked Girl she wouldn't be so cold if she actually wore clothes to work, I put a hard drive on my papers to protect them from the hurricane behind me and keep my lips together.

My papers are more lists of collateralized debt obligations, the jargon-laden stuff that Henry has been buying. I've been getting Kathryn to tutor me on these things on slow afternoons like this.

My heels clack across the granite lobby to the elevator as I head to the eleventh floor, where the goddess of mortgages works. Kathryn is a senior managing director, an intense, robotic human frightening in her perfection and beauty who generates stratospheric commissions. Bond Girl sits in a central spot amid the chaotic row of attached desks, and exudes an almost ethereal calm. Her nails are never chipped, there's never a paper on her desk, her garbage can has none of the banana-peeled, coffee-cupped, ripped-ticket remnants that most mortals slough off. Kathryn's garbage remains mysteriously nonexistent.

Dressing sensibly in St. John knit suits and low-heeled pumps, she's the most senior woman in bond land and the only person the traders on this rowdy desk seem afraid of.

As I walk toward her, I note that she's the only employee on this floor of 180 people who never removes her blazer. She stares straight at the triply stacked screens on her desk even when I'm within inches of her. I'm still not comfortable just plopping next to her. I wait to be acknowledged.

I'm not.

I roll a chair beside her and sit myself down, busting into her space. She seems to be meditating on the intricate rows of numbers in front of her with the devotion of a nun.

"Hey, Kathryn," I say, and wait.

Each year, Feagin has a meeting for women who are managing directors and senior managing directors. Out of 13,566 employees worldwide, we are a 1 percent club. Kathryn Peterson has met me at these meetings and yet every time I've come to visit her here, and even though we've been having lots of phone time together putting merchandise up for Henry, she still gazes over my shoulder as if she's trying to place me.

I tell her again that I want to speak more intelligently about the mortgage-backed securities market. I tell her that some of these synthetic products that roll across my desk lately make me feel like a three-card monte guy in Times Square. She doesn't smile or laugh or turn. She simply tolerates me because together we're finding a windfall with Cheetah and we need each other to keep this going.

"Tell me what you know, Isabelle," she says deliberately. This is how our sessions always begin. Like a shrink trying to get the conversation going, figuring out where to start, she waits.

"This is what I know," I say. "Everyone who has ever borrowed money has a credit score. The range goes from three hundred to eight-fifty. If someone's late to pay a debt the score falls. Once below six-twenty you're considered a riskier person to lend to, you've become subprime. Any mortgage issued to you is a subprime mortgage."

"Well, yes?" Kathryn murmurs, unimpressed.

I interpret this comment as, "Duhhh."

So I continue, "The interest rate on that mortgage will be less attractive or higher than a rate available to a person with good credit. Most risky mortgages balloon, making their payback more expensive. If the borrower can't pay the inflated amount she'll have to refinance the house or sell it. Even though many banks lend to people who can't possibly pay them back, the banks figure the value of the real estate will rise, so if they stop getting paid back, they foreclose, leaving them with a property that's gone up in value. That makes the banks' risk minimal." I pause for air.

Bond Girl stifles a yawn and keeps her eyes forward so I plug onward, conversing to the side of her head. "To get investors involved and to lower the risk to the banks even further, Freddie Mac designed a type of bond called a CMO, a collateralized mortgage obligation, which is a pooled piece of debt. The mortgages themselves are the collateral. These bonds are put into tranches or categories that are rated based on how risky the underlying debt is."

"Okay," Kathryn says softly, "so thank you for my history lesson. It was a little boring but you're probably one of the only people here who could tell me all that. What else?"

"Here is where I get into muck," I continue. "So then the banks came up with a clever way to have others invest in the mortgage market. They invented CDOs, or collateralized debt obligations. Instead of just bunching mortgages together that were all in the same risk category, the CDOs take actual mortgage *bonds*, the CMOs, pool them together, and add another layer of complexity to an already hard-to-understand market."

"Unclear," Kathryn says simply.

"Well," I sigh, "some yahoo figured out that by taking the *bonds* on crappy mortgages, instead of the mortgages themselves, sending them back to the rating agencies so the same stuff could be rerated more favorably, he could sell them more easily. A lot of deadbeat loans could appear to be as good as AAA and investors who before would never touch them now buy them like they're at the year-end clearance sale at Barneys." I exhale.

Kathryn Peterson turns to me and smirks. "You got it."

Before I started pitching this stuff, I tried to explain it to humans who didn't work on Wall Street. I started with my daughter, Brigid, who initially listened with great intensity, bulging her eyes in concentration while stroking our dog, Woof Woof. Within a minute she was grinning and within two she was giggling and blurting out, "Gobbly gobbly poo poo!" Because that's what it sounded like to her. Woof looked intrigued.

I moved on to Bruce and spoke the mystical, mythical language of Gobbly Gobbly Poo Poo to him. This time I did it with feeling. But he kept looking past me, hoping to catch sight of the television on the wall in the far room. He scratched his middle and yawned. The dog walked out of the room.

Today I'm still not certain what I've been selling. The only thing I see being created is debt and then derivations of that same debt, explained away as somehow more valuable than the original debt. The fact that this market is so far removed from anything tangible isn't lost on me. Cheetah Global had been hungry to own this stuff and now has begun selling. I need to know why. I admit the whole thing feels wrong, but how can it be wrong when so many smart people think it's right?

Kathryn briefs me. "We've got six lots of these ten-year triple-As. Who can we sell them to?" she asks, scanning her screens and comparing them to the papers I've brought upstairs with me. The fact that she is even speaking to me is something to note. She doesn't seem to work with, or be chummy with, any of the guys surrounding her. She's the one who has fewer friends than me.

King must be worried about the mortgage desk too. I see him across the room here on the bond floor away from his usual territory, and sense his curiosity peak when he sees me sitting with Bond Girl. He beelines over and casually looks at the papers in my hand, the tranches I intend to evaluate today for Cheetah. I tense myself, waiting to be touched. Without fail King lowers his head onto my shoulder and sniffs my neck like a dog. He smells like he hasn't had a shower since last night and I'm highly aware I smell like cheap candles. I've used my kid's smelly shampoos again and King finds this intriguing.

"Marjorie's Mango?" he inquires.

"Slime Lime," I correct. "Gets you clean, won't turn you green."

King lifts the tranche papers with one hand and rests the other on my shoulder. I want to slap it away. "Triple-A, my big nose," he mutters as he sees the bond ratings. He tosses the papers on Kathryn's desk and gives my shoulder a squeeze before walking away.

"Guess he doesn't believe these ratings," I say, trying to be as cool as Kathryn but feeling a little panicked.

"He's on the risk committee now," Kathryn says. "And he obviously didn't get this memo."

She turns her screen so it faces me, allowing me to read the latest email from Metis.

To: All Employees
From: Metis
Subject: Appropriate Relationships

While I'm growing tired of being your nanny, please note that one shouldn't sleep with a subordinate. Remember, the only thing that's making you attractive to someone younger and cuter than yourself is your superior position and your bank account. Once you get sued, your position, account balance, and body parts will deflate. Grow up.

There have been eleven memos by now. Still nobody has been caught and nobody has claimed to be Metis. I'm amazed that Kathryn even admits to having opened a Metis memo, never mind openly showing one to me, all girlfriend-like.

"You shouldn't let him touch you like that," she says simply.

"How do I get someone so senior to leave me alone, and not get fired?" I ask. "And besides, if this mortgage stuff is as messed up as it appears to be, we all have bigger problems than lecherous men." I go right back to talking about why I'm at her desk in the first place.

"I hear some guys on the executive board aren't happy with the loads of merchandise we sit with overnight."

Kathryn half smiles, taking note that I'm sticking with the original subject. "It's a mind-blowing liability if those obligations begin to default," she admits. "But the truth is that if we default, the whole United States banking system will be on its head so that won't happen."

"Yeah," I say wearily, thinking of how much Feagin stock I'm forced to hold. Getting wiped out by my own firm would be the ultimate touché. "But as long as they go north, we're okay," I mutter, uncertain as to whom I'm trying to reassure.

"As fast as we invent these mortgage products we sell them," she says almost sadly. "It's only recently that we've seen any blip in them at all. And besides, this is our job. Every other bank is doing it so I guess we should be too."

"To stay competitive," I mutter.

"To stay competitive," she states, and this time we look right at each other.

A trader named Monty interrupts the action on the floor. Monty is a short, overweight maniac who is screaming into the phone.

"Recognize the trade, bitch."

His face is an interesting shade of purple and the girth in his middle heaves when he screams.

"And he is bothered why?" I ask Kathryn, trying to be calm and more like her. I feel like I'm in junior high again, where I tried to be a different person than myself just to make someone like me.

She brushes her elegantly coiffed hair out of her face with one of her perfectly manicured hands.

"Third day. D-day of not having a trade recognized by an account."

"Hmm."

This is when on settlement and payment day an account just won't agree with a trade, disputing the price or the fact that it ever happened. This can be an expensive problem if the trader and account can't figure it out, but Monty has a terrible method of seeking unity.

"Recognize this trade, you lesbian whore, before I come over there and staple your tits together!"

Monty is now wheezing. He hurls the phone at the turret and jumps from his seat. The other men are doubled over in laughter. Kathryn glances over at Monty, then me, and then back at her screen. Her eyes are a deep, sad brown and I wonder if pharmaceuticals are involved.

I know I'm on a speed date but I have to get all my mortgage-backed securities questions addressed. I ignore the guys' noise.

"So how does all this made-up money translate to the guy on the street?" I ask. "If they're making something from nothing, making money from embellished value, how does this affect regular people?"

"To the guy on the sidewalk," Kathryn says, "who sees Wall Street being greedy? That person wants in on the action and is borrowing money at almost negative interest rates. He's not entirely innocent. People who never thought they could own a vacation home are now taking two. The lady buying dinner food at Wal-Mart is throwing an iPad in her cart, and maybe even a dining room set."

These are the longest sentences I've ever heard her speak. "Everyone is just heady with money," she continues, "money that they're borrowing."

"But does that make them bad or greedy people? Someone is giving them the advice that they can afford this stuff. Someone they trust to know more about this than themselves is telling them to go for it," I note.

Kathryn shrugs and taps away at her keyboards, completing small electronic trades with the ambidextrous skill of a concert pianist.

When I return to my seat, Ballsbridge is barking into his phone while some stock of his swan-dives. Naked Girl has found a rerun of *Barney* on television. She sways in her narrow clothes, arms wrapped around herself like a tilting column, sassing Marcus, "I love you, you love me. We're a happy family."

He catches me looking over his shoulder at his crashing investment idea and is pissed.

"Where the hell have you been?" he rants as he entwines his giant fingers around each other. "You have some presentation to do and some trader keeps coming over here looking for you." He picks up the phone at his turret, reconsiders, then hurls the

phone so hard the receiver cracks in half. Yes, he's definitely losing money. And then it hits me: Ballsbridge has been dabbling in
this dicey mortgage market for his own account.

That night I need to keep talking about this. As I speak to Bruce,
he tosses loaded diapers into the Diaper Genie across the room,
nailing that tiny opening every time. He gets some surge of joy
from the act and waits until Owen gives him a pailful of ammo.
He tells me it's like a carnival game to him, one of his surprising
daddy pleasures.

"What are your other daddy pleasures?" I ask. "I mean, you're
so lucky you get to go on playdates and get to see our kids so
much."

"Um, have you seen me go on playdates?" he asks as he thunks
another load in the Genie.

"Well, I mean I know you and Owen go to the park a lot."

"That's right, the park, and then if he's playing with other kids
and all the moms go off to lunch or nap at someone's house, it's
not exactly like they include us."

"What? You aren't included?"

"Belle, think about it." *Thunk.* "Oh, Daddy, come on over to
my apartment where we can be alone while our kids nap. It's
just weird."

I had never thought about this and feel protective of my husband, like he's the excluded kid in the lunchroom. "What do the
other stay-at-home dads do?" I ask.

"That's what I am now? A stay-at-home dad? A SAD dad. I hav-
en't stopped working, Belle, not entirely. I have other stuff going on."

I think about this and wonder about the other stuff but know
not to ask. "Why didn't you ever tell me about the playdate shut-
out thing?" I ask.

"'Cause you hardly ask anything about what goes on here all day."

I sit watching him for a moment, letting it sink in that he sees himself in a different role than I see him in and that probably explains why he still thinks we should split domestic tasks, or that I need to thank him every time he empties a dishwasher with the same enthusiasm he would thank me for an Emergent Biosolutions or CeeV trade.

I start to say something but he puts his diaper-hands on my lips and shushes me. "It's a little lonelier for dads who work out of the home, that's all," he says gruffly, and I think I hear his voice twitch.

I have a sudden urge to bed this man, germ-hands and all. When he starts throwing again, I start to fill the silences, to blab to him, telling him about work, about the finicky mortgage market, and I'm glad the kids are preoccupied with the slide in the living room. When he's finished pitching practice he drops to the floor and begins doing push-ups. Grunting and talking is not sexy business and he only acts like this when he's bothered by the subject matter.

"Belle, I know nothing except this. The guy who cuts my hair?" He exhales. "He has a weekend place in Miami. Our babysitter . . . humph—"

"Childcare provider," I interrupt softly as I watch his undershorts sag below his belly, depressing me slightly. I still haven't replaced those for him and he's too cute to be dressing like this.

"Yeah. Whatever." He does three more push-ups before continuing, "Our childcare provider put a down payment on her own apartment in Brooklyn and we're not overpaying her. Do you know what her down payment was?" He heaves. "Three thousand dollars."

"That's it?"

"A balloon mortgage. She'll pay close to five thousand dollars a month in only one year and I'm not anticipating her getting a massive raise. She just can't afford to buy a place and yet a bank gave her a mortgage. She doesn't know better."

"What the hell kind of bank would make that loan?"

Bruce twists his face in an accusing way. "One that's going to repackage and resell it with a shiny triple-A rating."

Drops of sweat fall onto our cream-colored carpet and I resist the urge to put a towel under him and break his rhythm. I'm not going to Kathryn-ize this moment.

I'm so happy to be connecting with my husband, even if it's just to talk about this stuff, even if it's with someone who doesn't quite understand it. "It feels like everyone is comfortable with debt up to their chins," I say. "They think everything will go up in price and that the home they're buying is an investment. They think they're going to get rich."

"You're not seeing humans as individuals," he tells me. "You're lumping everyone into categories. You keep saying 'they.'"

"I'm not."

"You just said"—he huffs as he does some sort of triceps dip—"*they* think they're going to get rich. 'They' meaning who? The rest of America who wants to buy a house? It's not the fault of the buyer that they want a piece of the dream. They're being told they can afford things they probably can't and it's the *banks'* responsibility to not make the loan in the first place. The guys who went to business school are educated in analyzing that stuff, not the airline pilot, the sanitation worker, the beautician, the dog-walker. They haven't taken mortgage-lending classes. It's up to the banks to be honest. But they don't want to be honest 'cause they get to take the money and eventually the home too."

I'm listening and I'm trying not to agree, trying not to think that my husband is a beautiful and smart human being and that sometimes I marginalize his opinions.

Bruce can't stop talking now. "It's okay to say no, that the reality is a housekeeper probably has insufficient income to buy a big house. It's not okay to say sure she can afford it, knowing she can't. Once they've bankrupted her and she has to surrender the house, her family will get to go live in her car while her bank takes the house, an asset they've made money on. It's a crime." Bruce rolls onto his back.

"The stuff I sell?" I say defensively. "They're put into *pools* of mortgages, Bruce. They're bunched together, good and bad."

"That's what I mean. Stop thinking in sweeping bunches of money and think of the human being, singular, on the other side of the trade, when that trade goes bad. There's a guy who drives a dump truck who can't handle his payments any longer, there's a low-paid teacher in Minnesota struggling to hang on to her house because she lost her job. Little does she know that by borrowing and begging and getting herself whole on her mortgage, she's also buying someone like King more chilled champagne. And if she doesn't get herself whole? It's not gonna hurt King's wine cellar one bit. She's taking all the risk. He's taking all the money."

Bruce entwines his fingers behind his head and starts doing sit-ups. He's done speaking but now it's me who is agitated. There are glimmers of something that deep down I've already known to be true about my line of work. It's something I'd rather not think about and now I have to. I lie next to him and we synchronize our sit-ups. Brigid comes and sits on my middle to help. We go up and down without speaking, just thinking. Woof starts licking the salt off Bruce's face. Together we grunt, contracting our soft bellies in uncomfortable crunches and exhaling with temporary relief. We do this over and over while we both wonder what is real and what is not. Do I have a great job or am I wrecking people's lives? Do we have a great marriage or are we just getting by? We overflow with questions we can neither ask of each other nor answer ourselves.

CHAPTER 24

Women's Issues

T HE NEXT DAY a letter arrives via interoffice mail. Jarrod, a heavily tattooed and improbably lovable ex-con, who with much personal comment delivers mail to the five thousand people in our office, drops it off.

"Belle Bottom!" he shouts. "HELLS BELLE!" he goes on, despite my being on the telephone. "Better open this one . . . FAST!"

I glance down at the ivory-colored envelope he dropped on my desk after he showed it to Marcus. It's Cartier stationery, the heaviest stock they make, with a wax seal that says "BG" on the back. This is no memo and there's only one BG (B. Gruss II), a man so old-school that he handwrites everything. He receives but doesn't send email, doesn't use a cellular phone, and doesn't seem to like having his title of chairman. When he attends a meeting, he sits with the CEO and King McPherson and when he speaks, it's short and fueled by caffeinated drinks. If he isn't the one speaking, he doesn't seem interested. Still, he weighs in heavily on any discussions regarding the direction of the firm or bonus decisions. If any department slacks off, it's Gruss who will address them publicly.

Nobody brings in as much banking business as Gruss, and of the 487 out of 500 male CEOs in the S&P 500, there are hardly any he hasn't played golf or gone drinking with. He has the reputation of printing money for the firm as he sits alone in a glareless black-walled office with no papers visible to those who come to visit. He stabs at a row of twinkling telephone lights, reaching out to his fellow universe masters with a "Well how the hell have YOU been?" which he inevitably follows with "I called you today because the moment has come, my friend, to take some real cash out of that company of yours and put it in your pocket. Let's sell more stock of yours to the public!" Then he will inevitably disappear on some pharmaceutically enhanced bender, usually near some oceanfront golf course.

In his late sixties, BG remains macho-handsome despite a shiny bald head, and a tendency to wear copious amounts of cologne and monogrammed velour slipperlike shoes. He isn't accountable to anyone yet we are all accountable to him. He brings in massive banking deals, takes a piece of the action for himself, and enjoys a first-class life that Feagin Dixon pays for.

To this day I've had only one conversation with him, the day of my last promotion. He sent one of the four beautiful women who administratively assist him to retrieve me from the trading floor and buzz me into his office. There I stood, taking in the screens mounted on every wall, each depicting either a news headline or a financial market somewhere in the world. The only thing on his desk was an ashtray, a deck of cards, a Red Bull, and an unlit cigar. He never got up when I walked in, just creased up his always-in-the sun forehead and appeared to look me up and down while rubbing his head.

"You the one with the high-yield piece?" he asked, referring to the interdepartment investment paper I wrote each week.

"Yes," I said, wondering if I'd made a mistake.

"And you got promoted?"

"Yes."

"Good. You should be."

He stood and raised his arms wide like he wanted to hug me and I didn't know what to do with myself.

"There's a lot of you," he snorted, caught a little off guard by my height and because my body language wasn't in hug position. I awkwardly opened my arms.

"It's good. It's not great but it's really good," he said as he came in for some very stiff, congratulatory body touching. Little bumps of disgust sprang up on my forearms and that was my first interaction with Gruss. This letter now on my desk will be my second.

Marcus picks up where Jarrod left off. "Aww, Mr. Big Guy doesn't write to me," he says. "But of course, I'm not as cute as Mama Belle here."

I put the unopened letter down so I can respond to my twinkling turret lights. All three of my lines are flashing while my new partner, Stone Dennis, chats on the phone with a friend. I roll my eyes at him and point at the phone bank, indicating that maybe answering the phone would be a decent way to further our partnership. Stone looks at me blankly.

Stone resents everything about me even though his commission runs now actually have numbers on them. I resist screaming at him by using my supreme self-control, the same I used when I caught my Kevin unwrapping, aiming, and sailing an entire box of tampons out our fourteenth-story window. With Stone there's no way to give him a time-out, no way to punish him at all.

The first light I hit is from Chungda Dolma, managing director of the subprime mortgage department in Los Angeles. She's a Nepalese workaholic who had a mystery pregnancy, never once hinting at the source of her state. People only realized she was pregnant five weeks before she delivered. Early.

"What's the message here?" she says, without bothering to introduce herself.

"My weekend was fine, thanks," I answer.

"Sorry," she replies, "I know, how rude. How are you?"

"Didn't you just have a baby?" I ask.

"Two weeks ago—"

"Two weeks—?"

And without waiting for us to pretend to be normal people, for me to ask the size, gender, or name of her baby, or for me to comment on the fact that she is in an office after giving birth fourteen days ago, we just get right into it.

"Is someone rocking the boat at Geisha Girl Central?" she asks.

Several months ago Feagin Dixon hired unemployed models to escort moneyed clients from our front doors to the executive dining rooms. *BusinessWeek* magazine ran a story about it, and the models were once again unemployed.

"What do you mean?" I answer.

"The letter, Isabelle, or tell me that you didn't get one?"

"Hold, please."

In one motion I put Chungda on hold, pick up the next line, and tear open the ivory envelope.

"Belle McElroy."

"Isabelle. Kathryn Peterson here from mortgages. I was wondering if you'd gotten the Gruss letter."

In the end, I'm the only member of the GCC who received this thing. It's a summons to some of the most senior women of the firm to discuss "women's issues." It's been cc'd to our legal department, the first red flag. Who sends a formal invitation and mentions a carbon copy on it? Maybe top management is realizing FD could be sued the same way Goldman and Merrill Lynch have, that maybe it's a matter of time before FD is on the front page of the *Wall Street Journal* for all the wrong reasons.

The Glass Ceiling Club members, when they learn of it, become positively electrified and agree to meet for lunch that afternoon at a cavernous downtown place called Buddakan, a festival of hip and beautiful people. When I finally get downtown it looks like every patron in the place is employed in a career involving style. The leggy women around me dress richly but are probably not, while the women at my table, close to the same age, dress for less but really are rich. The dishes are large and the portions are small, artistic affairs. Eating is a weakness to this crowd but not to us. The alcohol starts to flow, the dishes start to arrive, and we start to talk. I've never once seen us drink at lunch but we seem to be celebrating something we can't even describe.

"Maybe," I suggest to the group, "Feagin is forming a diversity committee in this new fiscal year. Maybe we're trying to catch up with other banks."

"Gruss is worried about something, Belle," says Amy. "It's your job to find out what it is."

"I'm sure he's just responding to that letter Amanda sent our CEO, requesting that he meet with us," I say.

"Yeah, I'd agree with you," says Amanda, "if I'd actually sent the letter."

"You didn't send it?"

"Did not."

"Then it's the Metis memos. They're going to everyone, probably even the press," I say.

"Who better to address them than a guy famous for only attending really important meetings, a guy we're all forced to respect? Send the ladies to chat with the chairman. That'll shut them up. It's genius."

★ ★ ★

The GCC decides I should represent all of our concerns at the lunch, and as much as I don't want to be seen as a troublemaker, I'm the only one of us who'll get to ask any questions. Before I do that, I need to talk to Bruce. If our income is about to take another hit, he's really got to know why. I mention this to the table.

"You need your husband's permission?"

"You're as submissive as we're supposed to be."

"Doesn't her husband have, like, an office job or something?"

"She confuses me. I mean, she's so strong in some ways and so wussy in others." That last one was Amanda.

"You guys are like school bullies," I point out. "If I was insecure, you'd actually bother me."

"Ladies, give it a rest," Amy says. "I mean, we don't think like Belle because none of us is part of a decent marriage. Most of us who were married," she says reflectively, "sucked at it."

I sit here stunned to silence, not because of what they want me to do, but because I now understand they see Bruce and me as their finest example of a happy, working marriage.

"Focus on the constructive," I say while Amanda nods and writes. She's listing grievances and thoughts about how to change things going forward. She passes her draft around the table, making certain everything is there.

For us there is no real possibility of a career path, there's just money. I tell myself that I know how to make money now. I have sales skills and an understanding of balance sheets that make me employable. I still believe in the good things that banking can do to help people and help our country. Loans allow growth, business growth means jobs, and jobs mean stability. While I'm not sure about the mortgage market, I do believe in investment and loans and people owning their own shelter. The women talk on and on while I think about my mother, something I don't do enough. She was obsessed with owning the house where we eventually lived and it took years until we saved enough to make that happen. I get that. That's not greed. It's a basic human desire for safety and stability and control over your life. It's knowing your kids have a home that won't ever be taken away. Wanting such a thing did not make my mother greedy. It made her a good mom.

In the end our list looks like this:

- Equal pay for equal work.
- Recruitment of quality female MBAs remains a challenge because of our culture. Candidates have reservations about the arduous hours, lack of female partners, no female representation on the board.
- No flexibility for working mothers even though many of our jobs don't require us to be physically in the office.
- Disallow romantic relationships between employees having direct power over each other.
- Give employees back their civil rights and drop the arbitration clause, letting individual harassers be sued. This will force the firm into a more professional culture.
- Risk management—Women need to be on the risk committee. We aren't comfortable with current portfolio positions.

And that's where we stopped. These items were imperative to the survival of our firm and I couldn't imagine any employee being against them.

I leave Buddakan and any thoughts I had about returning to the office. Instead I head toward home. I stop at a Whole Foods and load up a cart for a family twice our size. Our cupboards are always ridiculously empty and while Bruce never complains or takes care of this problem, our kids' penchant for consuming chemically concocted food, always in a rush, fills me with guilt.

I push my cart up and down those overflowing aisles like a suburban mother. The more good-looking fruits and vegetables I pile in the cart, the more I feel like I'm caring for my family. I try to not think of how quickly they will wilt, how fast this excited optimism about change will probably fade. I buy a fillet of beef and some fingerling potatoes and string beans so fresh they snap like a mousetrap in my hand. I buy bread hot from the oven and a deep, smokey Merlot.

Caregiver is out when I get home and I stand in my kitchen, which is lightly coated with some greasy substance. We can never quite get to the status of clean in our house. That's okay, I think as I look around at the crayon marks on the wall and the edge of our cork flooring peeling upward. We're doing okay and I feel so hopeful. Speaking openly about our culture of risk and secrecy and invisible ceilings and playground behavior will be a really good thing.

I see a message from Henry in my in-box and I ignore it.

Like a four-armed person I marinate, chop, steam, and sauté. I uncork and decant the wine after pouring myself a plastic sippy cup–ful, which I gulp down. I pour boiling water into the sink and bend low to receive as close to a facial as I have time for these days. As I stand bent at the waist, two hands come from behind me and pull me close.

"You're home early." Bruce's voice sounds lower than usual.

"Yeah. Something overcame me today," I say with my face flush.

Bruce is making me feel girly, making me relieved to know I haven't hardened into some unmeltable Clarisse figure, some stoic Kathryn, or some sad Amy.

"That's not a béarnaise sauce I smell," he says, pushing his boyish hair out of his face. "I mean, whenever I smell something good coming up the elevator I just have to assume the smell belongs to the neighbors."

"Yeah, wish they'd invite us over sometime."

"Yeah, nobody invites us over. Why doesn't anyone invite us over?" He's laughing now.

"Would you invite us over?" I say, offering him the dregs of the sippy cup.

Bruce seems to actually think about this. "Maybe if Brigid would give the theatrics a rest."

"Or if Owen changed his own diapers," I add.

"Or Kevin stopped eating with his hands. And Woof Woof promised not to eat shoes. Yeah, we have promise as future dinner guests." Bruce pours more wine into the sippy cup and lets me have first dibs, all without letting one hand leave my waist.

"We've got to change that damn dog's name," I say.

"Woof Woof is a fine and telling name."

"Yeah, Woof Woof is the name that tells everyone his owners were too lazy to bother coming up with a real name."

"We were too tired to think of something, which is different than lazy. And besides, Kevin couldn't speak very well. He just kept saying 'Woof.'"

"But Kevin's seven now," I say wistfully.

And like that, we suddenly realize that five years have slipped by and we haven't gotten around to naming our beloved dog. We're pathetic.

"They say these years go fast," I tell Bruce.

"That's so damn corny. I can't believe I'm married to someone who speaks like that."

"I'm not your wife. Your wife doesn't talk like that. I talk like that and I cook. Your wife doesn't cook."

"Damn right she doesn't."

"I'm replacing your wife tonight, giving her a night off," I say in some June Cleaver tone. "Can I pour you a drink in a real glass? Get you your slippers?"

"Do we even own slippers?" Bruce asks while rubbing his non-wife's backside. I pretend to not enjoy my caveman husband. "No. We're slipperless."

"Did I tell you that your real wife can cook?" I grin and hold each of his shoulders with kitchen mitts that I've put on my hands.

"I know she can," he says, "but she doesn't."

"Poor you," I say. "That's got to be hard."

"You know what's hard?" he says, looking down at his pants. We laugh.

Something about the smell of meat raises the testosterone level in my husband and he lifts me as easily as he would a kid and takes me Neanderthal-style back to our perfectly-neat-and-without-one-toy-on-the-floor bedroom and I allow him to have his way with me. I fumble with the oven mitts still stupidly on my hands but he shakes his head no, as if this is some domestic fantasy of his, and I blissfully relax into letting him be in charge. Without thinking once about small feet and high voices that will come at any minute, we rock each other's world.

In the moments that follow, we're in that sweet spot where one is both vulnerable and able to listen well. This is also the moment before the meat will begin to burn so I have to talk fast. I inhale and let it rip:

"So about a dozen senior women at Feagin Dixon were invited to meet with B. Gruss," I say.

"B. Gruss? Haven't heard his name in a while. What the hell type of name is B anyway?"

"It's not a name. It's an initial."

"Like fill in the blank, like Brahmin or Barnacle Bob or Batman or—"

"Or Bruce. Yeah. So can we stay on topic here?"

Bruce shifts to his side and his shoulder is angled and bulging like that of a man in his twenties. He crinkles his face. "So a meeting. Will you do bong hits together and then figure out new ways to make money?"

"No, that's another bank that has the chairman pot smoker. This guy's addicted to caffeine and stuff you get a prescription for. Anyway, Gruss invited me to a lunch to discuss women's issues at the firm and this is big because he doesn't hold too many meetings and when he does, they matter. I'm thinking of speaking up and outing myself as a non–team player. I want your approval."

"My approval? Do you need the shoeshine guy's approval too? Lady, I'm the crushed bug. You don't need anything from me," he says.

I don't even begin to do the obvious, to tell him he isn't worthless and other responses too uncomfortable to get into. I just continue.

"I want to really illustrate to him the stuff that goes on, to explain what it's like for women who work there. He's been in an office and not on the trading floor for so long he can't fully understand it. I have suggestions for him too. I mean, he may not welcome them, but what if he does? Senior management adores him and they'll take his advice. What if it turns into a really fruitful meeting? I'm sticking my neck out here and, well, you know there'll be repercussions."

Bruce is silent for a moment. "Did you just use the word *fruitful*?"

"What? Oh yeah, I guess."

"That's so dorky." He smiles.

"It is. I'm a dork. The word *fruitful* suits me. I mean, look at me, I'm wearing oven mitts."

Bruce is quiet as he strokes my naked hip up and down, over and over. He seems fixated on a mole I have at the place where my leg dips toward the groin. After he tenderly removes my oven mitts, he pushes some hair from my face and speaks.

"Belle, there have been times recently where I don't know who I married anymore. In a sea of suits, you shone like some effervescent angel and I'm not some guy who believes in love at first sight but man, you were ethereal."

He hasn't spoken so gently to me in a very long time. I know I should say something equally flattering back but I don't. I also know that whatever is coming next won't be so nice. It's going to be something about how I've changed, something about how unhappy he is with me, or about how I stink as a mother and that if it weren't for him our kids would be in social services. As a rule of business, now would be the time to nip a conversation heading toward the negative and take it over. But I don't want to be Ms. Managing Director right now, I don't want to be Henry's virtual lover right now either, I want to be Bruce's wife.

"I cheered for you as you climbed the ladder in that mad place you work," Bruce said. "I listened to some of the stories and tried not to be judgmental. Baby, I'd be lying to you if I didn't admit you make our mortgage payments easy to swallow and our kids couldn't go to their great schools if we didn't have your income. The emasculation is one thing and I'm fine with that now."

Bruce is still looking at my freckled thigh, still stroking away at me. He suddenly smacks his fabulous six-pack abdominals and I notice everything is so solid there. My husband's been working out and dieting and I haven't even noticed.

"I can handle that, I'm a semi-solid guy," he says. "But the lifestyle?" He turns his deep-green eyes to look right into mine. "We aren't living large here, Belle. You never see the kids, you never see me—like this, that is." He pulls the covers down to reveal all of him, making his point funny, and yet not so funny. "You know I support you in whatever it is you're really about to do. Even if it costs us this lifestyle, 'cause honestly, babe, you can't tell me this is all that great. Whatever it is you want to say in that meeting, you say it."

I can't resist him. Even though I'm tired and my dinner is about to become undone. I cannot resist my husband in the late-afternoon sun on our big white bed with the almost clean sheets when I know his love for me is hanging by a thread and I know I still can turn so many things around. In his own Bruce-like way, he is saying, "Yes."

CHAPTER 25

Tribal Knowledge

THE ELEVATOR lifts me to the executive dining room and my calm grows with each passing floor. I've rehearsed what I want to say, so there's nothing left to do except play it through. To hold on to my resolve, I've left unopened every message from Henry and I've made Stone or Kathryn return every phone call to him. If Henry knew what I'm about to do, he'd talk me out of it.

I enter an intimate side room off the executive dining room. This room has a nasty reputation and another name, the BJ Ballroom, because it offers the perfect amount of discretion for afternoon delights that don't include food.

There's a round table with twelve silver place settings, starched white linens, and a simple flower arrangement in the middle. The windows are covered with a gauzy material that allows the presence of daylight to be hinted at. Gruss's place is set with a silver cigar cutter, a cigar, and an ashtray in the place where a soup spoon should be. I go to the seat next to his to ensure I get access to the guy.

A woman is already standing in the room, ready to greet Gruss's guests. It's Blythe Quidel, one of Feagin Dixon's legal counsel, and technically the last word on all things human re-sourcey. When she sees where I'm about to sit, she raises one bleached eyebrow in curiosity.

"Oh, is this assigned seating?" I say to the question on her face.

"Now, Ms. McElroy, of course not," Blythe says crisply, though I can tell my bullheaded move has surprised her.

I glance at the embedded microphones on the table. They're a permanent installation and there's no way to tell if they are on or off. I'm going to guess we're being recorded.

"Belle," Blythe gushes in her false southern tone, and comes around the table to shake my hand. Her accent is like Madonna's English affectation; it tells you where she wishes she were from. Blythe takes a moment to think about how to speak in a way that doesn't sound so defensive and goes forward with this person, altered from thirty seconds ago.

The top of her head only reaches my shoulder and I stoop a bit to shake her hand. It's hard for me to smile at someone I just don't like, but I do my best. Blythe is a fantastic lawyer and a complete sellout. Each time I took a maternity leave, she'd read me a speech that basically said Feagin owed me *a* job but legally didn't owe me the exact position I was leaving behind. Each time I had to sit there, my head lowered while I took a subconscious bashing for my audacious move of reproducing. Blythe's method of achieving success on Wall Street is to be one of the boys. It's as if she can't understand why any woman wants both motherhood and a great career. To her it should be one or the other and in nuanced, nonlitigious language, she will tell you that.

Other women now begin to enter the room exactly at noon and as a pack. They stand around air-kissing and admiring one another for a moment, but they aren't chitchatters so things quiet down fast. Most have never spent time with Gruss, so curiosity and an innate desire to please others makes everyone sit quickly and snap napkins to their laps and wait for something big to happen.

Blythe instructs everyone to begin eating even though B. Gruss II, the main event, hasn't arrived, and obedient picking of the salads begins. Stories of trades and deals, from Chicago, Boston, the West Coast, are swapped and a waiter fruitlessly tries to pour wine with no acceptor. I move colorful little legumes about my plate and feel my heartbeat pick up when I hear footsteps approach. It's one of the women who guard Gruss's office, followed by the man himself.

He seems taller than I remembered and more fit too. I'm told he now has a treadmill desk so he walks all day while manning his phone calls. The sheen off his head radiates some of the light in the room and he gives us a presidential wave and intense eye contact. His giant smile reveals expensive orthodontia yellowed slightly to appear real and I think to myself that BG could pass for any number of stereotypes: retired retail executive, 47th Street jewelry salesman, or sports celebrity handler, but the biggest deal maker at one of the world's largest investment banks? You wouldn't have guessed that one.

"So it's my girl partners and girl partner–lights," he crows. "All in the same room at the same time."

We titter because that's what we're supposed to do. He athletically moves himself to his designated spot at the round table. He settles into his seat and makes a few more jokes to make us feel important.

"I requested that the most senior women of the firm be gathered so we can talk about issues of concern to women," he says. "I see some memos running around here that I don't like and I thought a good place to start would be by discussing the glass ceiling." I blush and then hate that I'm blushing.

"However," he continues, "since you're all sitting here, it's obvious there is no glass ceiling at Feagin or you'd all be taking steno downstairs." He guffaws at his own humor and I scan the room thinking someone here must be too young to even know what steno is, but no, I at almost thirty-seven am close to the youngest. "So let me now throw the podium your way and let anyone discuss anything she'd like."

An uncomfortable pause follows, which he uses to pick up his cigar and inhale the contents deeply. His fingers roll it around with absentminded affection while we wait.

"I'd just like to say," pipes up the woman from corporate communications, "that Feagin has been such a wonderful experience for me and I'd like to tell other women how great it is here."

I take a hard look at this woman, whose job includes spinning everything and who doesn't work for a profit center of the bank. Her sprawling Upper East Side apartment is dependent on smooth relations everywhere and she will be of no help to me today and I start to wonder if she's been invited here for that very reason.

"And the meritocracy here," boasts a British banker. "I'd have never gotten this far had I stayed at my other bank."

I can't believe this. I've been dropped into the bleachers of a pep rally. I have to speak up. "Let's talk about why it's so difficult to attract female college recruits," I blurt out, shutting down the women trying to outpraise one another, women bowing to the purveyor of their golden ticket.

Blythe is ready. "We've been looking into this and think that our policy of a two-year program for investment banking is too short. When we have great prospects we'll keep them on longer and not force them to leave to get an MBA."

"So you think they don't take these jobs because our program is only two years long? All top investment banks offer only a two-year training program to an undergraduate, but many of ours don't even make it through the two years. They feel abused here. They don't see any women on the executive board so they don't see much future here for themselves."

"Nonsense." Gruss looks up from the cigar. With that single dismissive word he gets up and uses a phone on the sideboard to connect with someone presumably more interesting than us. The table conversation continues while I listen to him on the telephone, marveling at his rudeness. He seems to be trying to land some deal.

"Sweeten the bid by five hundred thousand," he says.

"Huh?" he retorts, looking like he's going to crush the cigar.

"Okay, okay, seven hundred thousand it is or they can shop their shitty deal downtown." He slams down the phone and turns back to the table.

"Where were we?" he interjects. "Someone has raised the issue of the 'girls down in the front of the building.' The women hired from the modeling agency to act as escorts. That's old news and that was a mistake according to some," he says. "Next."

Weird. None of us raised any issue about the downstairs girls. I wonder if he had to rehearse his answers before this and lost track of the questions in real life.

"Maybe we could form some version of a guidance team to help new women recruits find their way around here?" I suggest weakly.

"This is a meritocracy, as you've just heard," he storms. "You didn't have a pen pal when you came here and you survived."

"Yes, but women can be a little sensitive to the mosh pit downstairs," I say. "They get repulsed by the behavior around them. What if someone was to mentor her, tell her she could sue the firm if a guy told her to put Band-Aids on her breasts when she gets cold so he doesn't have to look at her nipples? Maybe then women would stick around longer if they felt they had support. Instead they quit and feel as though they did something wrong."

I'm trying to shock him. He must know how lucky Feagin is to not have our own class action suit to contend with. I'm threatening him in a subliminal way and he doesn't like it.

"But women like you don't quit," Gruss guffaws. "That's the sort of girl McPherson and I like around here. That's the sort of person we need. Let the quitters go home."

Someone comes to my rescue. It's Kathryn. The world's most perfect bond trader climbs out on this limb with me. "I'm uncomfortable having a partner who will only entertain our mutual clients at titty bars," she says quickly. *Titty bar* is not terminology I'd expect from Kathryn's mouth.

"Why does that make *you* uncomfortable?" Gruss asks.

"Because I don't want to go to topless bars, even though the partner on my accounts does. It's just more teamlike to entertain together. We should only entertain in ways suitable to a professional business."

I see a vein rising in her neck though she doesn't redden. Not one bit. I hadn't known she was assigned a partner. I wonder why she didn't tell me, until I remember that she doesn't tell anybody anything.

"That sounds to me like this is your issue," Gruss says. "Why are you uncomfortable? Whatever the client wants to do, that's what you should be doing. Yes, that's definitely your own problem."

A tiny grimace, like she's just tasted something surprising, creeps across the legal lady's face. Her ironed-on smile has an involuntary twitch to it.

"Maybe Feagin could at least take the higher road, and not reimburse expense accounts for entertaining at strip clubs?" I suggest, in a professional voice.

BG is ready. "People are going to go whether we reimburse or not. It's where men want to go to have a good time and it's mostly men who run these accounts. They don't want to go to the ballet. These are men who work hard all day, who are under pressure all the time. What's the harm in letting off steam? There's nothing more bonding than when we entertain our clients and when we do that, in either banking or trading, guess who bonds with our trading floor? Guess what you get to bond with? Your bank account. If some women are that sensitive, they'll never cut it in this business and don't belong here."

Seeing that this conversation is too narrow, a star currency trader named Caleigh Caruso shifts gears. "Tell me how I should deal with a situation like this: I have a major Boston account that I cover with a man. I'm the senior person on the account. One day I'm on the phone to the account and they say something to the effect that we've got a great day for the Feagin golf outing. I know nothing about this golf outing and I'm a scratch golfer. This was done behind my back because it was being held at an all-male club in Boston."

"Oh, yeah? What's your handicap?" Gruss laughs and then turns serious. "Look, ladies, all I'm saying is that we have to get along and be the most productive we can be. If that includes adjusting yourself so you work better with the person sitting next to you, so be it."

"Nobody should have to compromise their morals so that they can have a job," I retort.

"I haven't heard anything today that sounds remotely like a moral or ethical issue." He pushes back on his chair, making an expensive scraping sound on the floor, and continues. "My door is always open and I welcome the chance to chat individually."

With this he rises from his chair and, without touching his lunch, he leaves. The cigar/pacifier is still being fondled in his hand. He's leaving? This is just the beginning. I look at my list of items to cover and realize we've barely touched one of them.

His legal counsel is left there alone, awkwardly recleaning her red spectacles.

"How can you stand to defend that?" I burst out, motioning to the closing door.

Without responding, Blythe stands. "Look, every firm has issues normal to the course of their doing business. We are thriving here despite your criticisms. I too have an open door, and invite each of you to walk through it and visit me."

"Why visit you when we're all here now? When will all of us in the same room ever happen again?" I ask. "Look, some of you have come from California, Chicago, and even London to discuss this. There's been no discussion so let's have a discussion right now, with or without management!" I feel energized, like some community organizer. Defiance is suddenly the most liberating drug and it's surging through my system. I expect to hear a chorus of "Hell yah!"

Except I don't.

Nobody says anything and all eyes are staring at the microphone jacks on the table, the ones that are probably recording every bit of my rant. But I'm crazed and don't care.

"Ask Chungda what it feels like to be back at work when she gave birth four weeks ago," I beg. "That is not normal."

Chungda makes clear that she disowns me and wishes I would shut up.

"Ask Kiera why she still isn't a senior managing director after winning the *Institutional Investor* poll seven years in a row?"

I am referring to Kiera Goodfriend, a wiz accounting analyst who sits rigidly, staring into space.

I continue, "There isn't a person in this whole firm who has been so consistently recognized by the outside world as her, yet she still hasn't been promoted to partner."

Kiera twists her very styled hair and looks away, letting it be known that she too is separating herself from anything I say.

"And Kathryn, how is it that you're a director on the mortgage desk and have no say in the portfolio holdings in our subprime packages? There are no women on our risk committee, no women on the executive board. These bonds come with ratings we tell our clients are triple-A but the holdings look like crap. How are they getting these ratings? Who will take the fall for these when they crash? Do you know how much risk that puts all of us in?"

A few quiet seconds pass and I start to look around the room. Everyone is frozen. It's as if I'm at an intervention for a dysfunctional family, all squirming with pain but unable to find any words. Whatever sisterhood thing I was feeling is not being felt both ways. It's not just a lack of love that I'm picking up on, I'm feeling downright disowned. The individual shuffling, the electrical glances they exchange with each other say it all. Nobody wants to be associated with me. In just minutes I've switched from being a golden girl just like them to an ugly, ranting, contagious disease. I stuck my neck out for these women and I don't even like them.

"Look, when I was pregnant here," I start to softly explain, "I would cover my stomach when someone downstairs dropped too many f-bombs on me. I had to laugh with King when he mooed at the sight of my breast pump. I ignored the time someone taped torn panties on my screen when I came back from my honeymoon. I'm just depleted from all of this. I don't want to hear slut jokes all day long. I don't want to work in a frat house. I want to be paid equally. I want my input on abnormal rates of risk we take to be heard. I want this place to live up to its potential.

"This is the same environment your daughters will work in, getting her ass pinched like it's a 1960s advertising agency, unless we do something to fix our broken culture."

The women in the room aren't moving. They look like they're

desperate to hear more yet know they should leave. I can almost hear them trying to control themselves from speaking.

Keep going, I say to myself, so I do.

"Most of you came here from business school. You thought you'd run a division of this place or lead this bank in some meaningful way. I know women like you because I'm just like you. By now you get the joke. We aren't going anywhere. This is it for us. No women are in truly senior positions that matter. We all have fancy titles that are worth as much as Feagin Dixon stock is going to be worth once this mortgage façade cracks."

I can see Kathryn looking upset under all of that hair. I think she really wants to join in; she's obviously weighing the consequences.

"Look, you're all exceptional women who get paid to be creative and smart. Why are you able to turn that off, to act stupid and submissive when it comes to things that matter?" I ask.

They won't make eye contact with each other or me. They act like frightened children who've been yelled at. They can't wait for the adult to leave. Everything depends on the next move.

Everything.

A full minute passes. It's as if we've been told to freeze while someone paints a portrait of us to capture a significant moment before everything will change. But the change doesn't come.

A waiter walks into the room and stops abruptly, sensing that something has just happened. Someone sighs. Another looks at her watch, then rises slowly. Another clears her throat and walks over to Blythe to shake her hand good-bye. I look down at my plate while the rest start filtering gratefully toward the door. Nobody says anything as they all try to exit as quietly and fast as possible. I'm left alone in a room of amped-up microphones to record voices that don't speak.

CHAPTER 26

Golden Handcuffs

BACK IN 1996, when I was first hired here, I noticed a woman straining to keep her skirt zippers up and her belly sucked in. She didn't tell anyone she was pregnant until she had what appeared to be a watermelon under her dress. She returned from maternity leave to find her accounts ransacked, and because there was not much of a job left for her, she quit. When I anticipated the same happening to me with the birth of my first child, I got ready. I made myself as irreplaceable to my accounts as possible. I made promises to clients that I was coming back in a short amount of time and I did. I only lost two small accounts.

I paid attention as other banks were accused of this same practice along with the harassment-as-usual environment. I watched lawsuits filed against Smith Barney and their "boom-boom room," watched as a Citibank boss was accused of noting which women "liked to blow." When Nomura was sued after their traders apparently told female colleagues they belonged at home cleaning, I was sure something would come of it. The lawsuit was thrown out. Then a British bank, HBOS, was sued with X-rated details that I was sure would sound scarily familiar to Feagin Dixon and force a change, but again the suit was thrown out.

For years, allegations have been settled in arbitration and the quiet exodus of women in banking has remained hushed and steady. Merrill Lynch had fifty complainants that increased to almost nine hundred by the time their class-action suit was filed. An arbitration panel found there was a pattern of bias against female brokers. As the winning lawyer explained, "The essence of the finding is the standard operating procedure at Merrill was to discriminate against women." That cost them $39 million. Feeling emboldened that same year, some women from Morgan Stanley opted out of arbitration and filed for class action status. The members of the GCC all waited to hear if their details were similar to ours. The night before the story was to be told in a public courtroom, the women settled for $54 million and the details remained private.

A few months ago a prominent banker at another big bank was sued for relentlessly commenting on women's breast size. The female executive settled for $1.3 million. I have twelve years of boob comments under my bra, a relative treasure trove in current litigation dollars, but the idea of suing Feagin Dixon seems absurd to me. Dixon is my firm. I'd be suing myself.

The Glass Ceiling Club gave me a frosty reception after my unsuccessful performance at the Gruss lunch. Amanda, Amy, and Violette were in a private conference room when I got back downstairs so I joined them there to tell them everything.

"That's it?" Amy asked, thinking that I was kidding. "Nothing?"

"I would have crushed that damn cigar in his lettuce," Amanda ripped. She was walking in circles around the table.

"My guess is that Belle handled it like a reporter, like you presented it as thoughts that maybe other women had, maybe like they were thoughts that you didn't share," Violette said. "That way you managed to protect yourself as always."

"Why do you dislike me so much?" I asked Violette. "Those women sat like statues. Like they didn't even know how I got to the table. They acted like I was a freak."

My hands were shaking.

Amy stood. "This was such a stupid idea in the first place. I'm going back to work."

The other two followed close behind. I just sat staring into space, wondering how I should tell this story to Bruce. How could I have done anything differently?

Clarisse poked her twitchy face into the room. "Heard you're getting all antiestablishment on us?"

I rolled my eyes at her.

"Thanks for leaving more room at the top for me, Belle," she gushed, and she really meant it.

That afternoon what would be the final Metis memo arrived:

To: All Employees
From: Metis
Subject: White Flag

I'm done warning you people. You seem to want to continue on this miserable path. You don't ever want to move forward. You've made your beds so go sleep on them. Enjoy your unflippable mattress.

Stone left a yellow Post-it on my screen. "Did you get writer's cramp? Did you girls break up?"

I'd never met such an entitled empty suit in my life, a kid who just seems itching to be fired.

"Stone, very glad you signed this thing. It's going in my memory book. The one I use when your next employer calls for a recommendation."

He smirked and pulled up his Facebook page, posting something that undoubtedly pertains to me. I've heard he does this regularly.

When I tried to thank Lisa for allying herself with me at the Gruss lunch, she acted indifferent, as though she couldn't remember it ever happening, and when I relayed the details of the lunch to Bruce, he looked at me with something bordering on contempt. He's suddenly so removed again and I can't help but think that I've let him down too.

A few days after the lunch some of the attendees sent me emails that could almost be considered supportive. While they never apologized for not speaking up or adding anything at all to the conversation, they thanked me for saying what I did. As one put it, "Thanks for putting into words what we all think and experience, yet never say." She sent it from an untraceable IP address and I was too angry to respond.

I forwarded it to the GCC and it was finally Amy who replied all, "Enough with this stuff. It's time we all get back to our jobs. Take me off this email list." In just a few moments everyone else had done the same. The club I had been practically begged to join dumped me. I'm so exposed now and want to see this thing through. I'm fully out of ideas and very much alone.

CHAPTER 27

Standard Deviation

THIS AFTERNOON, the noise from the dais sounds like a World Cup soccer match, and it is distracting the whole trading floor. A young trader has returned from Europe bearing the spoils of a scavenger hunt. He had been given forty-eight hours to find the items on the list, many of which were found on another continent. From the noise level it seems he has been successful. He enters, victorious and dragging behind him a wheelie bag containing what promises to be a corpse, but is instead a collection of the world's most noted performance enhancers—not trading performance but vitality-in-the-sack performance. This trader they call New Guy gets a full standing ovation. He's all of twenty-two, blushing a scarlet hue but filled with bravado. The guys have a folding table snapped open right in front of the dais. A tablecloth is handed to New Guy, which he brandishes like a matador before carefully placing it on the table. The traders keep cheering as he unzips the bag.

I type an email to Amy with the exact wording from the Merrill Lynch lawsuit.

" 'Environment that is hostile and offensive.' Is this offensive enough for you?"

The young trader pulls a large feathered something from the big bag and the cheering turns to roars because the birthday boy, the person all this fuss was for, has entered the room. Monty. The fat, wheezing heffalump of a guy, the one who threatens to staple body parts together, has arrived.

They first sent New Guy to the British Isles to collect some phallic-looking wake-robin. Someone announces over the hoot 'n' holler that it's a root, taken from the ground only the day before. I search on the web to find it was used to stiffen Elizabethan neck ruffs among other things. New Guy then unwraps Greek orchid tubers, the name of which the master of ceremonies tells us derives from their resemblance to testicles. His trip then took him to Paris, where he got a French partridge, a live one. It's supposed to be fluttering about but from where I sit the poor bird sacrificed its life for a bunch of morons. The bird is dead. New Guy leaves it there, dark shimmering feathers hanging off the end of the table, while he sets out the rest of his bag's contents. There's a big tray of raw oysters from the Oyster Bar, a local restaurant, a bowl of artichokes FedEx'd from some organic farm in California. It keeps coming: asparagus, dark chocolate, and a Dixie cup full of little blue pills—Viagra. New Guy puts on plastic gloves and pokes at the poor bird's corpse until he gets blood to drip into a cup. Who knew that French partridge blood is supposed to make one virile? I feel sick yet have trouble looking away.

Monty's gift is explained to him: the guys are giving him the biggest boner. Ever. The festivities will be topped off by a happy ending. I'm not sure who will provide the final act or where that's happening. It seems Monty has been sharing his remorse about his diminishing sexual potency. In honor of his birthday, the guys decided to right this wrong in the form of a buffet lunch that would include remedies for impotence. I'm fixated on the fact that New Guy graduated last spring from Yale and now is sneaking through U.S. Customs with a dead bird.

The few women traders on Estrogen Row are not invited to Monty's lunch and they've been left to complete every trade that comes in while the boys play. It's a Friday afternoon and there's a meeting upstairs I have to get to so I decide to take the women with me.

I turn to one, a tiny, nunlike woman in her fifties named Marie.

"Come to a learning session upstairs. We're going to brainstorm about the volatile mortgage market," I say. She doesn't need to know much about them but needs to get out of here. She crinkles her forehead, about to tell me she doesn't trade mortgages, but instead throws her headset on her desk.

"Fuck them," she says.

She walks over to two other women, points to me, and I feel emboldened as they toss their headgear down too.

CHAPTER 28

It's Because You Fit Me

O N A winter morning that feels like spring, I find myself walking down Park Avenue with Henry. We haven't seen each other in a while and his emails have slowed to a trickle. Whatever weird blip in our lives that was, it's fading away.

We've both just left an uneventful preschool chapel where everyone behaved. I was walking toward the office when Henry had his driver pull the Escalade over.

"Ride for Ms. Belle?" he asked with incredible sweetness. "Maybe even go get a coffee?" His angled face tilted up to grab the sunlight. He had such a huge smile on his face, making his mood contagious. I knew there wasn't an overwhelming in-box pile to greet me at work this morning, and I didn't resemble a packhorse with bags of papers. I even had on nice shoes, so why not keep walking to work and maybe even walk with Henry? But a coffee date? No, that's off-limits.

"On this morning where the sun shines right on me?" I responded, referring to a song we'd just been singing in chapel.

"Days like this you should be walking, not riding your lazy carcass around town," I said, "and no coffee unless you have a cappuccino machine in that rig of yours."

"You're right," he said, hitting his head as if a lightbulb had exploded in his brain. He opened the door, causing some stepping platform to slide from beneath the POLO-mobile, and stepped out.

"It's good to walk rather than caffeinate," he said, "but maybe we can do both." With that he handed me a hot, foamy coffee in a porcelain cup.

"So you *do* have a cappuccino machine in there, of course."

"No, Bells. Don't be ridiculous. My driver picked these up when we were in chapel."

"And just where do they serve takeout coffee in porcelain?" I ask.

"It's a bring-your-own-porcelain kind of place. Can we just shut up and chug?"

Like we did with the vodka shots of our youth, we down the delicious drink and hand the glasses back to the nameless driver who never makes any eye contact.

"Do you have a dishwasher in there too?" I smirk as I walk away.

Henry grabbed his briefcase off the seat and caught up to me on the sidewalk. Walking in step on a morning that hints of spring, with happy God music still stuck in our heads and caffeine in our veins, we seem positively saved at this moment.

"Might I remind you," I say as I notice we are on East 65th Street, "I work on Park and Forty-Seventh Street while you're on Madison and Twenty-Third. This is a much bigger commitment for you."

"I'm still not afraid of commitments, or have you forgotten that?" he jokes, and puts his arm around me.

I blush. "I'm trying to forget that." I look straight ahead and try to navigate the parade of strollers that take over Park Avenue at this hour. Wait. Did I just sound flirtatious? I hadn't meant anything by it.

"Have you gotten my emails?" Henry asks, removing his arm from my shoulder.

Here we go. It's time to talk about the emails. The truth is, if they are flowery I sweep them into a special folder; if it's all business, I deal with it. I think of his last one, from three weeks ago, a message I've memorized:

Wanna be in that place along the roof of the sky, upside down along the horizon, someplace unreal where you could have everything you need.

What did that even mean?

Please, Henry, I think, *please don't make me respond to that. Please don't make me tell you to stop sending emails.* But right now Henry is scrunching up his face, truly concentrating on what he is saying and thinking about . . . the currency markets. We are two well-dressed geeks talking about money, not lovers thinking about when we can rip each other's clothes off. Now that I understand that, I can relax. It's business.

He smells so good this morning. I walk on his left side and the wind blows his smell toward me. He's never been one for artificial men's scents and aftershave, instead opting for the smell of soap and clean. I hate that he's making my heart pound.

"I think my partner, Stone, has been speaking with you," I say, "but last I checked I think you wanted to buy some Australian dollars?"

"Yes, Australia is one of the few countries that doesn't live in debt and has livable pension payments in its future, and by the way that Stone guy is appropriately named."

I ignore the dig at my partner. "So we're down with Australia?" I ask.

"We are down"—Henry stops as if he had cleats in mud—"with this dress!"

He points to a store window, a French atelier that sells gorgeous gowns that nobody can really have much use for. The dress he likes seems lit from the rays of the morning sun. It's a sea-foam color, not blue nor gray nor green, and it's fitted to just below the waist, puffing slightly as it dips lower. The front plunges. It's meant to be worn by someone with young or never-nursed-upon breasts that are large and springy enough to hold up ample gossamer frontage without slipping. The silk satin fabric is cut and sewn in overlapping diamonds. It's the perfect gown for a mannequin, or maybe Naked Girl.

"Looks like something a mermaid would wear," Henry says dreamily. He had once loved my fascination with water: my love of swimming, of being underwater or some version of soaking, in my past life. He loved that I left for work each morning with wet hair, or unshowered skin after a weekend at the beach. I hated washing the sea from myself. That was so long ago.

"No time for that life anymore," I say as we walk away. "You were mentioning Australia. I hear they have beaches there."

"Oh, really? Beaches in Australia? I didn't know."

Henry and I took a trip after college. We spent two months in New Zealand, three in Australia, and one in the Fijian Islands. Our money ran out in the fourth week and we worked mindless jobs, planting kiwi, picking apples, holding sheep about to be sheared for a rancher, and finally for a courier service. We started the trip as hotel guests, and eventually lived in a tent. We wanted to be married so badly then that it hurt. Love can be so perfect that it's painful. There were mornings I'd wake up next to him and not be able to tell where my skin ended and his began. We felt like one person. I remember wondering if anything would ever feel that good again, if maybe some of the hurt from love stems from the rest of your life being spent trying to re-create a time that has passed.

How we went from that couple to the one currently sauntering down Park Avenue talking about money, I can't explain. As I walk I wonder which was the real me and which was the real Henry?

Henry asks about work so I update him about the Glass Ceiling Club. He asks thoughtful, caring questions, and I tell him about the Gruss lunch, about being left twisting in the wind by the other women, about the GCC not believing I had really tried to speak up and how that made our little group fizzle out. I tell him how frustrated I am not being able to get any further in the firm, how few hours I spend with my kids. I tell him how gutting it was to go home to Bruce, who also reacted with nonreaction to the Gruss lunch, and then I am quiet.

"I forget what your husband does?" says Henry.

It isn't a sarcastic question. It's real. Can he really not know what Bruce does? Is that really all he cares about after all the stories I've just told him?

"He's a communications technician," I say, bracing myself for comments about my husband and my pretending he actually goes to a job every day. "How could you not know that?"

"How? Because I always think of you as mine and Bruce doesn't really exist for me."

Silence follows. Our heels on the sidewalk pavement seem noisy in this awkward moment. We have to stop for traffic and standing without moving is extraordinarily uncomfortable.

"Sorry," Henry says, and clears his throat. "Well, it sounds like he gets to be home more than you do," he continues truthfully. "I think you're still doing most of the kid work even though he's home most of the time."

"I wasn't talking much about my home life, Henry. I was speaking about work." And then, even though I knew what the answer was, I ask him the same thing: "What about *your* home life? Is Danielle working?"

I know his wife doesn't work, but it feels more respectful somehow to pretend to not know this. I choke down the idea that he thinks of me as his. "Because she exists for me."

Henry laughs. "No, she loves to play," he says, but there isn't scorn in his voice, it's admiration. "She knows exactly what she wants and what she wants is to not work a day in her life."

This makes sense to me. Of course Henry prides himself on taking care of a woman, kept by her father and then by him. He would never get the chance to do that with me and it is suddenly so clear how much he needs to be that sort of man. Henry lets her keep living the cared-for life she has always known. Danielle is the opposite of me.

"She must be very happy," I say, like a smarmy Hallmark card and feeling no jealousy at all. "Does she ever get a wifey bonus?"

"Two million a year and she accounts for every penny."

"No."

"Yes. She has one-third for fun, one-third for charity, and one-third for clothes and gifts."

"I imagine seven hundred fifty thousand dollars can buy a lot of fun."

"They take great trips."

"They?"

"Her girlfriends. I'm too busy."

"And she's able to squeak by on a seven-hundred-fifty-thousand-dollar clothes budget?"

"Well, she buys the boys' clothes too."

"That's tough," I say, and we both laugh and then are silent.

"Henry, about those emails—"

He interrupts, "Belle, baby, everything is okay." He turns and looks directly into my eyes. "Please don't make me stop. I need this. You don't have to read them. I'm asking you to not ask me to stop. It doesn't come from a place of disrespect. I've grown up since we knew each other. I don't cheat on my wife. I just . . . I just . . . need this."

"Henry, we slept in the same *bed* not that many weeks ago," I point out. "What was that? We both don't want that."

"It was close to something I want," he said, "but it wasn't cheating. I think that I should let you know that we didn't have sex, in case I'm that unmemorable." He laughs. "It's just that you fit me."

Henry steps away from me and there is an angle of sunlight hitting his dark eyes, which makes them come alive. If we were in a movie, this is the part where we would have gotten a room, but this is real life, our bizarre, real life.

Henry squeezes my hand and dashes across Madison Avenue, against traffic, disappearing in a crowd of boys with rolling backpacks and acne and their entire lives still before them.

CHAPTER 29

Short Squeeze

THE TRADING CLOCKS, LED lit with giant numbers, note the precise time a trade crosses a buyer with a seller. Each trade is clocked in every time zone in the world. We keep the clocks clean and lit here because time is money. When the clocks pass 5 p.m., my guilt grows in tandem with the flipping of the numbers.

It's easy for me to be happily settled at work when my kids are in school, but at noon, I imagine Brigid and Owen finishing preschool and I feel just a little bit worse. By 3 p.m., Kevin finishes big-kid school and my spirits sink lower. By 5 p.m., the sound of idle chitchat and banter in my workplace grates on my nerves. Conversations better have a point if they're to include me. When I begin to wonder what frozen food product is finding its way into our microwave oven, I feel positively ornery. From that time forward I'm continually calculating, how many more minutes until I can leave? Can I possibly make it home for story time or will I miss it again? Do the people I work with realize how much time they waste?

217

This evening, the clocks on the floor have all clicked to 5:15 p.m., leaving only a few minutes before I break for the door and get home to my small people. I combine stacks of paper accumulated during the day. I flip on screen savers and congratulate myself on what will be a successful early exit. Better than that, tonight I plan on being Supermom—I'm hosting Owen's playgroup.

Caregiver found a playgroup for me consisting of frazzled working mothers and their three-year-olds. A group of nannies that frequent the same playground in Central Park decided their bosses should get to know the kids their own children hang out with. In some sort of reverse-networking feat, babies who liked each other brought together their caregivers, who then brought together the moms. Tonight will be the fourth meeting of this group but the first one the McElroys have hosted and the first one I'll actually attend. Bruce has gone to the last two.

"Playdates at night?" a disbelieving Ballsbridge inquires as he sees me readying for the exit.

"Part of the working mom's guilt-reduction program."

"We have Home Depot night," he says. "I get home so late, the only place to bring my kids is home improvement centers. I run them up and down the aisles, we treasure-hunt for weird shit like posthole drills, lug nuts. You may want to try that instead of six p.m. playdates."

"Yeah, I'll keep that in mind."

"Seriously, Home Depot. Now open on Lexington Avenue. Check it out sometime."

This is what I love about Marcus. The guy makes a few million dollars each year and the high of his day is recreating at Home Depot. It's hard to believe he is or was trysting his nights away with Naked Girl.

"Where's Tiffany?" I ask. Naked Girl has missed a lot of work lately; it's quieter without her cloud of excitement hovering behind me.

"Belle, I do not know and I do not care," Marcus says in a way that makes me believe him.

"You can talk to me, Marcus," I say, surprising even myself. I want him to know that I'm on his side, that I really do understand.

"She is a complicated em-ploy-*ee*, Belle. Let us leave it at that." He smiles for the first time in what feels like forever and seems less jittery without her around. Maybe his marriage is safe for now.

As I stand to leave I notice gobs of dust bunnies clumped under my computer screens and they bother me. Before I can stop myself I pull some chemical cleaner from my drawer and am just finishing a quick wipe when Greene approaches the memo board. I freeze. *Please, God*, I think, *nothing today*. I just don't want an interruption tonight. I don't want anything to interfere with Owen's playdate and my chance to meet his three-year-old entourage. I want to make some mom friends.

I mutter to Marcus, "Should I run?"

Marcus mimics Greene's penmanship moves, trying to figure out what the guy is writing. Soon it's legible: "Mandatory meeting at 5:30 p.m. Auditorium. 23mm share IPO."

This means that we'll be the bankers selling 23 million shares of stock to the public. The men on either side of me pull out their HP-13s, the calculator of choice, and multiply the share amount by the cents per share, ranging from $0.50 to $0.95. The sum of this is the commission, or roughly $10–$20 million that will be up for grabs between only two firms. The numbers are heady and the whole floor buzzes.

"Marcus, grab me a set of handouts," I say as I head for the door. "I have to get my Goldfish snacks."

"Belle Bottom, you can't just skip it. It'd be one thing if you were out of town. Just dip in there for a minute, sweetheart. A little face time won't hurt the McElroy bank account."

"I have a partner. My partner can cover it for me." I nod toward Stone.

Marcus and I both glance at Stone, who is now peering into the limited reflection a dark screen provides. Whatever he sees on his turned-off monitor he seems to like. He smiles at himself as he adjusts some stray hairs around his forehead.

"Really?" Marcus says, nodding toward Stone.

"Argh," I say. "I'm giving this twenty minutes."

I call Caregiver and ask her to cover the Goldfish and string cheese purchase, buying myself an additional fifteen minutes while I feel the guilt rise in my chest. Dirk Milazzo, one of the heads of investment banking and a swarthy, balding figure, paces in the front of the room. He's talking too loud, moving too fast. He makes my heart race in a bad, anticipatory way.

"What's up with him?" I ask Marcus. "Is he on speed? He's making me nervous."

Marcus muses, "Well, there's that, but also the fact that he's got some twentysomething girlfriend who is hotttt."

"No way," I retort, "he's one of the happily marrieds. I met his fifty-something wife and she's lovely."

"I'm sure that's true," Marcus says. "One is lovely and one is hot."

Milazzo interrupts our conversation by flipping on his Power-Point presentation. The ten-foot screen at the front of the room fills with the initials PLC, Private Label Credit, the people who produce credit cards for individual stores and extend high-priced credit to the people least able to afford paying them back. They're taking their company public and I'm going to be late for a playdate.

The meeting goes on for seventy-five agonizing minutes and I watch each one of them slip by. The head of each division of PLC elaborates on their success and potential. They wrap it up and I am the first to rise, ready to charge the door, until I hear Milazzo say, "The road show starts tomorrow in the South."

"Sit down, Mama," Michael whispers, "you're in for a long night."

The South is my territory.

A road show is a marketing trip involving bankers, potential institutional investors, and the top management of the company coming public. These face-to-face meetings are more effective than conference calls. Investors are given time to question, and hopefully trust, the companies they will invest millions in. These shows are put together as soon as the Securities and Exchange Commission gives the thumbs-up to the reams of documentation each company supplies for its IPO. Sometimes there's only several hours' notice before the trips begin. In these instances, to speed thing up, the mode of travel is often private jet. I'm told to meet the Private Label Credit group at Teterboro Airport at 7 a.m. the next morning. We'll be gone for two days.

What this also means is that I have to actually set up the meetings for tomorrow. The clocks tell me it's 6:35 p.m. My playdate has begun. Money managers in Atlanta will be going home and I somehow must make them want to meet with us in the morning and I have to make this happen before they leave. My insides chug like a washing machine as I speed-dial all the southern numbers on my turret, hoping for an answer. My peripheral vision catches the sight of Stone tucking in his shirt, picking up nothing but his iPhone, and heading for the door.

It's after 7:12 p.m. when I've managed to wrangle a few meetings for the morning and I try to leave. The CEO of PLC, a short, rounded man in a double-breasted suit, asks me to join management for dinner as they are all from Cleveland and have nothing going on tonight. I suggest instead we take a ride through Midtown together. We can at least talk in the car and I'll walk home from whatever restaurant they're eating at.

"I have to pack," I say feebly, not mentioning the other human issues involved in my getting out of town by tomorrow morning.

I call Caregiver and relay my changed plan. In the background I hear squealing children.

"These kids are overtired and going nuts and I need to go home," she snips at me.

"Isn't Bruce there?"

"Yeah, he's like the wine sommelier to these mommies. He's gotten them all drunk and I'm the only one paying attention to their kids."

"Hey, you won't believe this," I start.

"It's hard for you to surprise me."

"I have a business trip. It starts tomorrow morning."

"And you're telling me now because you know I have no life?"

"We are both lifeless." I try to be funny. I'm not funny. "Seriously, I just found out."

Caregiver launches into a tirade about her not being able to drop everything when I need her to. She does this in a judgmental way and I can't deny her venting. I deserve every word but wish I had a partner to share the punishment with.

When she finishes, I give her more material for her examples of crappy mommy anecdotes. I let her know that I believe it's only a two-day trip but could be three. There's a moment of silence on the other end, a pause to reflect on yet another mind-blowing revelation about me.

Caregiver informs me that I can't rely on her to help any more nights after 6 p.m. I promise Bruce will be there, having no idea what he has scheduled for the week. I just know he will have to drop everything and do this for us.

"I understand," I tell her, conscious of my pounding heart.

For a moment I suspect she's going to quit. If she did, my life would fall to pieces in just one moment, instead of hanging tentatively together by thread that feels no sturdier than a fishing line. The one thing I have going for me is that my children have wormed their way into her heart and that I pay her very well. These are the only reasons she stays.

I call Bruce's cell and when I get no answer I text. I tell him about the trip and that I need to talk with the management of the company coming public for the next thirty minutes. I get no response and I imagine him topping off the wineglasses of the other working mothers, riddled with boredom and bristling with anger at me. He must appear to be the perfect husband to these strangers in my living room and maybe he is but right now he's on my nerves.

The stretch limo pulls to the curb at 58th and Lexington Avenue, where there's a rounded driveway into Le Cirque and people hanging outside the restaurant crane their necks looking for Reese Witherspoon or Matt Damon or anyone more interesting than some corporate guys from Cleveland and myself. The disappointment on their faces is evident and my disappointment in myself, about to help sell the stock of a company providing easy credit to poor people often unable to pay it back, is something I push far away. How many more companies who do this sort of thing can we take public?

We all shake hands as we agree to meet in the morning. These mostly graying men are trembling, on the brink of being very rich, and I'll be along for the ride, to hold their hand and make them look good. In just a few days they'll be celebrating. They'll never have an inkling of the anxiety I went through during our meetings and our breakneck travel. They'll never know about the play within a play going on here, the quest for the McElroy family to hold it together.

It's almost 8 p.m. when I begin walking up Madison Avenue, phoning home once again and going straight to voice mail. Bruce must be putting them to bed and I've missed it all. I should hail a taxi but instead let my feet slowly drag me home. I hate facing the drama I'm about to face so I walk, mostly for air, the almost-fresh kind you get in Manhattan. I don't really want to see a bitter husband with several drinks in him tonight, so I walk.

Soon I'm standing in front of the chic little dress shop and the mermaid dress I saw with Henry. It's still in the window looking somewhat alive at this hour, not from the early-morning sunlight as before, but from the streetlights.

Even though it's late, two salesladies are inside all dressed up and sitting erect on counter stools. I don't stop to consider why I'm doing what I'm doing before buzzing the door. I guess I just want to be transformed by a dress, to try it on and feel something resembling fun at the end of a very long day, or maybe I just don't want to go home.

"*Oui, madame.*" A young woman, chic with dark, flat-ironed hair and kohled eyes, answers the door. She needs to fill her twiggy body with baguettes, I think as she, with visible annoyance, stands at the door and considers whether I'm worthy to enter. Stores like this don't let just anyone in. I ignore her superior position as she places herself between the sidewalk and the store interior. She looks me up and down.

"I'd like to try that on," I say, pointing at the window and acting like I buy such dresses at the same rate I buy skim milk.

She pulls her face into a scowl when she sees my giant bag containing every document I need for my trip, my sensible walking shoes, and my corporate getup. It somehow insults her gestalt. I'm not her usual customer.

"Zat dress? Ooh-la-la." She laughs, gazing toward the window. "Eet won't fit. None. And ees so many dollars."

"Oh, okay," I say. "But I'd still like to try, and I have a job," I add pathetically.

I'm arguing with her, trying to convince her to let me potentially part with thousands of dollars, and I'm doing it from the sidewalk. This is absurd.

"*Non, non.* Maybe, how you say, maybe in the high school?"

She is cracking herself up. And for lack of something clever to say, I rip, "At least I *went* to high school."

She laughs again, not having a clue that I've just insulted her. She swings the door wide.

When she manages to wrestle the mermaid off the mannequin she walks me upstairs to a giant dressing room and lays it across a sofa. She is annoyed by all her efforts and stands in the doorway defying me to just try to get into the thing.

"Privacy?" I request.

I can already tell that she was right, that my high school body had a slim chance at wearing this, but my current body? I was delusional to even attempt it. Before leaving me alone to wrestle with the big fish dress she looks carefully at my giant bag, wondering if it's at all possible that I may be plotting to steal the thing. It takes her a minute to satisfy herself that I am low-risk. She sighs and waves, as if creating wind to blow my patheticness away. She clacks on down the stairs in high and red-soled shoes to converse some more with her friend.

Carefully, I step into the dress as if it were a bathtub of hot water. I had thought about an overhead entrance but saw myself drowning in all the tulle spread across the bottom. There are many hooks in the back but by turning the dress backward, I'm able to hook it pretty easily up to my shoulder height. I spin it again, cheered by the fact that I'm managing my body into this garment with no telltale size sewn into it. For this kind of money, this dress is whatever size a woman wants it to be.

Now things get harder. The bodice is very fitted and I can just get my arms through the holes with an extra push. While I admit this isn't the size for me, I can't picture myself admitting defeat to the French.

My arms are held tight now to my sides, as the gown is stiffly sculptured. This isn't a dress to cut a rug in. I stand back for a moment and despite my lack of mobility, I can see the magnificence. This isn't a dress. This is art. This dress is an elixir of the sort I've been too practical to drink, yet now seem to want. I decide that the people who buy dresses like this are either in love or angry and maybe I'm both.

I sidle up to my phone and can't even bring my arms together given the rigidity of the sleeves, but I get it to camera mode, set the timer, prop it on a handbag shelf, and stand back for the flash. The result is a small miracle. Perhaps the lighting is slimming or the fact that nobody can tell the dress can't fully close in the back. I've taken a photo worthy of the cover of *Allure*, and even though it's all an illusion, it's a great souvenir of this bizarre day.

I begin to reverse the process. With one hand swooped behind my back I carefully unhook the lower closures. But I've either gained a pound while standing in the dressing room or have begun to sweat and stick because the dress seems attached to my too-big body. I tug and inhale and hold my breath and anticipate some expensive ripping sound, but none comes. It's clear that I can't turn the dress around again without tearing it. I fuss with things for a full three minutes before feeling panic about to kick in. I know the signs of panic—the accelerated heartbeat, the shortness of breath, the sweat—and I also know how to stop it. I sit down and watch my reflection in three-sided absurdity. I inhale through my nose, hold my breath, and count to eight. I exhale through my mouth and I do this again and again until I feel my heart rate normalize. I may have bought a yearlong yoga studio membership that I've used three times, but it can't be said I came away from "my practice" with nothing.

"Calmly," I say out loud and tell myself that I simply need another pair of hands, and that those hands are just down the stairs. I can even hear the French voices that go with those hands. I call out to them in a humbled and embarrassed way. No answer. I turn the knob on the dressing room door, but it's locked. The bee-otch has locked me inside to prevent me from stealing? My heart picks up the pace again, forgetting every calm thing I've just told it. I yell.

Nothing.

The ladies are positively hysterical for some unknown reason, laughing and shrieking, and I presume it has nothing to do with me. I reach down for my phone in an attempt to call the store. I first call directory assistance to get the number and a computer voice asks the name of the business I'm inquiring about and I realize I have no idea what the name of this place is. I look at the $15K price tag, but no name is printed on it. I get switched to a human, a supervisor. Pathetically, I attempt to tell some sweet, unsuspecting operator my story, and tell him approximately where on Madison Avenue the store is.

"It's a dress shop," I say.

"Ma'am, I have several listings of dress shops on Madison," he says patiently.

"But it's in the East Seventies," I say. "Some French name."

"Ma'am, it's hard for me to find this place without a name or an address, and I don't speak French."

I'm starting to blubber when Directory Assistance Guy offers to call 911 for me. I say it's okay and hang up. Again, I sit and try to calm myself. I see that Henry has sent me an email and for lack of anything to do at the moment, I open it.

We cannot be what we promise to be, which is something, someone real, not just a beautiful idea in a secret place.

I'm not rational enough to stop myself, so this time I write back. With one finger I slowly type my metaphor-filled message, feeling anger well inside me.

Last time I checked I was real. It's you who are unreal and me who fell into your little fish fantasy for just a moment, me who got tangled in some mermaid dream disguised as a dress. Well, the dress doesn't fit, the dress is too small and now I'm locked and tangled with no way out.

I attach the photo from just seconds ago and let emotions get in the way of my carefulness. I hit the send button. It's the first personal email of his I've responded to.

After a few moments, I hoist myself up again and wiggle my way to the door and begin to pound. The French ladies are quieter now and I'm surprised they can't hear me, nor have they checked on me. I keep hitting the stupid door with the brunt of my palm. Tears that come from nowhere now roll down my face and feel so relieving.

"HEY!" I yell.

Instead of a response, I hear the buzzer that indicates the front door is opening. I'm terrified, thinking they may be leaving for the night, that they forgot the almost middle-aged hag upstairs trying on a dress for someone ten years younger. Finally I hear footsteps, pounding up the stairs, letting me know that at last someone, somewhere, has remembered me. Without so much as a knock, the lock clicks and the saleslady comes into the room, followed by Henry.

"Zees is your girlfriend?" Franco Lady asks as if it's incredible the gorgeous Henry would be caught with someone like me.

"This is her," he says, searching my splotchy face. "I can take it from here."

"Henry?" I frantically try to cover my back, which is exposed now in a three-way mirror. "You said I was your girlfriend?"

"She didn't understand that I was using the past tense."

"Look, Henry, I didn't mean to go all damsel on you. I . . . I . . . ," I sniff to him.

Taking charge, Henry turns me around and expertly begins unhooking me. "Belle, it was just fun to say the *girlfriend* word again. It's no big deal."

"Don't think I tried this on for you," I say as I grasp for composure.

"Oh, sure. I know that," he says. I see him grinning in the mirror. "Anyway, I was only five blocks away when I got your email."

"I probably could have done it myself . . . eventually," I say while thinking that Henry has taken off my clothes a hundred times. He must have been thinking the same thing.

"Yeah, but I know what I'm doing here," he says. "I'm familiar with the territory."

"There's more terrain now," I say.

"Slight changes in topography," he quips. "A real improvement, if you ask me."

Women who have children really like being told they still have a nice body. I feel a rush of happiness flow to my heart while Henry's hands linger for a moment at the nape of my neck.

When I look in the mirror, he looks like he's still in his twenties, like we're the couple who once went to Australia. The flush of exertion or embarrassment in my cheeks makes me look better too.

"I was just wondering if it fit," I say weakly, still sniffing a little.

"And did it?" he asks as he unhooks the last eye, releasing me from my bondage and letting me take a whole breath of air again. I tug myself out of the sleeves and hold the dress up in front of me, grasping for modesty.

"It did not," I finally answer.

"And"—Henry fake-coughs to hide the fact that he's now laughing—"what have we learned from this lesson?"

I don't know if I'm laughing or crying and breathing is a little hard again. I fall back onto the tulle-filled floor, my dress falls forward, and I sit there in my matching black lacy bra and panties that somehow found themselves on my body at the same moment of the same day and, in this trick lighting, make the person in the mirror look borderline stupendous. And there's Henry in this perfect light, pulling the dress from under me, holding it in front of him, hanging it carefully on the four-inch-wide hanger, holding his hand out to me, lifting me from the floor, holding my hands up, pulling my work skirt over my head, zipping it back onto me, buttoning my blouse up, kissing me deeply on the cheek, and leaving.

CHAPTER 30

The Misery Index

I GET HOME from my dresscapade to find that Bruce has left the place like a crime scene. His message seems to be, "I'm leaving every overturned sippy cup, every empty wine bottle in exactly the position it was left in. I want you to see what you missed and then I want you to clean it up."

I sit in the dark for a long time, trying hard to regulate my breath and to stop gasping. Something is smothering me with what feels like giant gobs of felt in my throat. I try some feeble form of meditation to calm myself and get this imagined gauzy film off my face and out of my nostrils. I need air. The only visual I can focus on, the only thing that my heart will listen to, is the scene where Henry's hands are on my neck, unhooking that fish dress, releasing it from my skin an hour before. His fingers were so manlike, he was so in charge and responsible when things didn't go as planned. With Henry I didn't have to be the only one doing everything, all the time. What would that be like with a family? It's the first time I think that I would be happier, that it would be easier to be with someone like him. It's the first time I have let my thoughts go to a dangerous place.

My heart starts to slow. I have to fix this. I have to reclaim control of the situation that is my life. The obvious place to start is the chaos in my living room. I have to kill this thing that threatens to smother me and I'm going to do it with Pine-Sol.

Fumbling in the low light, I remove my shoes and methodically begin picking up raisins, rice crackers, and bits of masticated apple. My stocking feet stick in some half-dried liquid and I raise the lights a bit and thrash and fluff at the pillows. I spray a vinegar/water combo on every wood surface and clean with an assured, angry energy. It's all I can do to not vacuum and wake everyone up. In ninety minutes the place sparkles and in the morning I hope Bruce will never even mention the lost night.

I unpack and then repack my bag for my trip and print out the schedule for everyone for the next two days. I put out cash for Caregiver and playdate notes for Brigid. I don gloves and sanitize the hamster cage that smells like the end car of the 6 train and I let the rodents run wild in their exercise balls the entire time. I lay out clothing for all three kids in three sections for school, play, and night. I chop up apples and raw carrots and bag them in fifteen little snack bags because I do not forget I am Healthy Snack Mom for Brigid's class tomorrow. I wake Woof Woof and shampoo him while he looks at me with questioning eyes. I do not forget anything. I just can't get to everything the exact moment the world says I have to.

By 1 a.m. I attack the last item on my mental list: I need to amp up my husband's happiness. He doesn't get to be angry with me for things I can't control. While he isn't exactly lighting my fire and what I really want is to sleep, I force myself to want the guy. I find a bottle of Victoria's Secret bubble bath, crusty and hard at the top but still usable. I pour the whole thing in the tub and take a bath that makes me smell like a French hooker. I shave my legs, my armpits, and put on some Italian lacy thing that still has the price tag on. Not bothering to snip it off, I jump on my angry husband's sleeping body. He smells like body odor and alcohol.

"What?" he asks, squinting at me and not being sure he likes what he sees.

"Queek, before za wife ees back in zee haus," I say, going with what I imagine works for Rudolph Gibbs, Eastern European.

His hair stands straight up and he has a fuzzy hangover face on. It isn't sexy but I force myself to think it is.

"Ugh, I have a headache," he says.

"Zas ees a line for dee ladies, not for real man," I return.

"C'mon, Belle."

"Eees impordant to know I also a doctor?" I say. "Specialty ees vee fix dee headache for free and also vee do, how you say, house calls. Eees your night of the luck." I keep kissing my way down his body.

"You think everything gets repaired by screwing. It doesn't work that way." Bruce speaks to the ceiling and makes no eye contact.

"Screwing fixes many sings," I chirp as I kiss him behind his knees. His body is getting ridiculously perfect from all his gym time. He appears to have no body fat left at all.

"Stop," he says, pushing me away from his shoulder. "Stop." He really means it.

I flop over next to him and try to tear the price tag that's digging into my side. Instead I manage to tear a huge hole in the corset.

"Dammit," I say, waiting and hoping for him to mimic one of our kids and say in a pretend baby voice that Mommy made a swearword, or anything that'll make this moment funny.

233

He rubs at his head like he's thinking of just the right thing to say. I don't want some heavy discussion right now and Bruce has never, ever refused sex. It's the one thing that hits our reset button every time and it's not working. I have no more remedies in my doctor bag. I look at the ceiling too.

"Don't you want to save this tenuous thing we have together?" I ask softly, surprising myself with what I just said. Mentioning a troubled relationship is a tough thought to put back in a drawer. This is the part where I expect him to say that we're fine, that he's just tired, that he needs a day to recover from hosting a bunch of strange ladies and their wild offspring. But he doesn't.

"I don't do guilt sex," he mutters, and turns away.

CHAPTER 31

Chasing Returns

G UESS YOU'RE not working today?" I had asked Bruce
gently, two days ago. He hasn't spoken to me since.
Bruce has mastered the silent treatment that's big with the four-
year-old set.

Regardless of Bruce's limited earnings power, he used to be
a man who got off the couch and rolled up his sleeves but now
seems like a boy to me, careless with responsibility and fixated on
his appearance. The search engine history on our home computer
lists all self-improvement sites, and he buys protein shakes by the
case. I don't mind the low-earning-working-guy thing, but the
deadbeat dad from a bad sitcom, who flexes his muscles in every
mirror he passes, does nothing for my libido. I desperately want
to know what's up with him but every word out of my mouth
is taken as an insult. We are roommates who barely tolerate each
other.

Before I left the apartment this morning, I came upon a scene
of mismatched pajamas, kid hair that seemed whipped in a wind

tunnel, and my husband doing a Sunday-morning-chef routine with no regard for time management. It was clear they'd all be late for school.

Eminem songs rapped in the background. Plates containing eggs and pancakes were placed around a vat of syrup that Owen was drinking from with a straw. Bacon, hash browns, and fresh-squeezed orange juice were spread about while Kevin lay sprawled across the banquet with his hands down his pants. Brigid dabbed syrup from Owen's hair with a wet paper towel and nobody was actually eating anything.

I think Bruce has made some decision to be at home, to be with the kids and maybe just let me earn the money. I'm fine with that but wish I had been consulted. Am I really fine with that? I'm not sure. I think I like telling people my husband has a job only because I also have a caregiver, a dog walker, and an occasional housekeeper, so I need to know what his role is. The stay-at-home-dad scene this morning should have warmed my somewhat frozen heart but lately I'm in a semipermanent state of anxiousness and Bruce isn't helping that at all.

Looking at that kitchen scene, I wanted to be the cool mom, a relaxed, fun lady who throws up her hands and shakes her booty along to repulsive lyrics no three-year-old has any business listening to. I wanted to be the hip-bumping wife who high-fives everyone, kisses their foreheads, and boogies on out the door. But instead I frothed over the immaturity of a husband pushing forty years old. It made my heart race and my mouth want to say things I'd regret. I swallowed my comments like acid and silently turned and walked out.

Henry has been distant ever since the night of the mermaid dress and I blame the slowing mortgage market. He owns a tremendous amount of inventory that has few buyers. He has sent me exactly zero flirty emails and dozens of business ones. I'd like to say this relieves me but mostly what I feel is loneliness. He seems troubled and aloof but I can't exactly reach out to him without crossing that zone of intimacy.

Over the past three weeks, I've met Henry four times at his office, a sleek forty-ninth-floor corner of a building built of glass and chrome. His personal office looks over Madison Square Park to the north and the Hudson River to the west through floor-to-ceiling glass. His two interior walls are made of cerused oak and have paintings hanging on them that even I, not a terribly cultured person, recognize. Henry's office has professional photographs of his children, all taken on beaches with everyone in the family wearing white and pale blue. Nothing is left to visual chance and everything is perfect. The sole photo of his wife stands tastefully on a low shelf. She's coyly looking away from the camera in her wedding dress, as if dreaming of her future life with Henry. She sits wrapped in silk and satin in some version of a fairy tale that I could never have pulled off.

Henry has a small wine cooler in his office, a private bathroom, and fresh flowers in the corner. Spending most of my day in trading chaos, I inhale the order here, the small stack of aligned papers on his desk and the three large screens that scream the details of markets overseas. When I peek at his holdings screen, it lists the symbols for CeeV-TV, Emergent Biosolutions, and so many names I've helped put in his portfolio. I feel grateful to Henry. Maybe he couldn't be faithful to me as a boyfriend, but as a client he seems to only trade with me.

We meet this morning so I can help him pare down his mortgage holdings. We painstakingly review his inventory the logical way, the way most investment banks don't bother to do in their efforts to move merchandise at sparking speed. We dissect the real humans on the other side of the trade and try to guess the probability of their paying a loan back, and the likelihood that Henry will or will not get screwed on his investments. Henry has given up on Standard & Poor's and Moody's, who have slapped triple-A ratings on bonds that appear to be junk. I've been leaving these meetings with plenty of sell orders and never a buy.

In the afternoon, I will bring the sell orders for unloved mortgages to my trading desk and the traders will try to find a buyer for them at any price. Most likely it will be our own desk that will buy them.

On this Wednesday morning, I've brushed past Henry's secretary, who never ceases to have a bitchy comment for me.

"Again?" she asked while rolling her eyes. She is a stick-thin, model-like woman with long black hair and skin that seems to have never met an ultraviolet ray. Her name is Opal and even though we've spoken almost daily, she always pauses in an attempt to recall who I am. I went right into Henry's office and sat in my usual seat, a tightly pulled crème chenille chair. In front of me hangs a real Roy Lichtenstein painting on the wall. Tim Boylan decorates Cheetah's walls with his personal art collection that he rotates from his home. The Lichtenstein wasn't here a week ago. Opal follows me in and asks in some affected way, "Might you enjoy some sparkling water?"

"No, but can you tell me when Henry will be here? I only have two hours this morning."

"Mr. Wilkins shall return in ten minutes." Opal places a hand on the small of her back, adjusts her hips forward, and catwalks back to her desk.

I snap open my laptop and place it on the far side of his sumptuous desk. Using a color-coded system, I begin to group Henry's inventory into three columns, based on worthiness. After a few meetings like this, the enormity of the problem, the futility of trying to make worthless, make-believe mortgages turn into something of value, is apparent. Henry and I seem to be in some

slow dance of doom. And because this is our job and because
we've inherited this problem together, we go through these motions together.

Henry comes up quietly behind me and I smell him before
I feel him look over my shoulder at the red splotches on his
screen. He sighs and pulls his French cuffs farther down his wrist,
twisting off each cuff link one by one and placing them next to
my screen. He folds back his starched sleeves, revealing greatly
defined forearms from years of sitting in front of a computer
while choking the life out of a squeezy ball.

"Belle," he says simply.

"Hmm. Hi," I say softly, getting right to the point. "Look at this
one." I show him a basket of mortgages I'm particularly troubled
by. I don't turn around. "A two-hundred-forty-thousand-dollar
vacation condo in Myrtle Beach. It's not on the beach but on what
appears to be a highway. Second home. B-minus rating. She's a
hairdresser."

"Put it in the trash," Henry sighs.

"Who wants a second home on the highway?"

"It's your American dream," Henry says softly. "You guys just
want to own a lot of stuff."

Sometimes when Henry isn't thinking, he assigns us to different socioeconomic classes. He seems to forget his own simple
roots, assuming the fancier childhood of his wife's as his own. He
leaves me behind in his calculation. I'm the beauty salon owner
with a second home on the side of the highway. And maybe I
am. The only difference between her and me was an education
that taught me what I can really afford. How was she supposed to
resist the offers from a slick mortgage broker selling her a dream
home? It's clear that the lenders preyed on the ignorant and the
misinformed. How had I become involved in this?

"It's a hundred-fifty-thousand-dollar home in Nowhere,

Nebraska," I continue. "Both owners unemployed. Five dependents. I can just see the sheriff taking some crying babies out of the house." My eyes well up and we sit there for a moment with something bordering wonder. I never saw things going this way. When I see Henry's face, I don't believe he thought this game all the way through. Or did he? To me, these mortgages were always lines on an Excel spreadsheet and I want to believe he saw it that way too. I want to believe he didn't know what he was buying when he filled his portfolio with baskets of greed and lies.

Henry gives up trying to lean over my shoulder to see what I see. He hikes up a pant leg and slips behind me, straddling me from behind and sharing the wide chair. It's so hard to defamiliarize ourselves.

"You have to separate yourself from this. It's not reality," he says matter-of-factly.

"But it *is* reality," I say. "The ride up was the unreality."

"Nobody thought it through, Belle. Everyone had so much faith in our rating agencies, in the banks writing the loans, and in a government that encourages cheap money so everyone can own a home."

He gently removes my hands from the keyboard and places them on my thighs. He lets his own hands ring the executioner's bell, quickly dragging and dropping loans into red baskets, as if he were picking berries, but only the rotten ones. I watch him place the soon-to-be-homeless family from Nebraska into the red basket but at least I see a pause, a show of some deference.

"How can you do that?" I ask softly. "How can we do this over and over?"

"I'm tearing the Band-Aid off fast, and yes, I hate how sad this makes you."

Henry thinks he has found happier news on the screen. "Triple-A, twenty-five-million-dollar Florida mansion that sold with three percent down."

He puts it in black and I lean over and swoop it to red.

"Read the details," I say. "A formerly rich guy in a desperate attempt to hang on to something. His personal credit rating sucks. Everyone knows Florida won't take your house in a Chapter Eleven. He's done and the loan is trash."

I pull up the next one. "Dental practice in Wenatchee, Washington state, became overextended on their dental equipment purchases. They cater to the indigent," I read.

"Excellent clientele to seek your fortune from," Henry says sarcastically, pulling it to red. "Maybe migrant farm workers really didn't want to purchase teeth laminates."

"You sound like an ass."

"I'm a humor-seeking ass. What we're trying to do here is find a plug for this flood. We aren't here to save humanity. We can't."

"I'm drowning in the debt of other people, Henry," I say. "I think of these people and this situation far into the night. These people who were just numbers on a spreadsheet now haunt me."

Henry puts his hand on my back and rubs the right spot between my shoulder blades. I really shouldn't let him do this, but it feels right to have human contact, possibly the only human not mad at me right now.

"Look at this one," I say. "Former librarian, has lived in the house for thirty-two years, refinanced to pay for medical care, now unemployed, no income." The human crisis on the other end of these trades is making it harder to hold it together. The staggering amount of debt that banks have drummed up sits with people who can't pay it back and why isn't anyone talking about this? It isn't possible to bring this stuff up at work without looking like a traitor. The newspapers barely mention it. Henry and Kathryn Peterson are my only outlets and she won't talk about it. That just leaves Henry.

He continues dragging and dropping with his outstretched arms alongside my own, like a father helping a kid steer an amusement park ride that dips and lifts and almost crashes but as of yet has not.

CHAPTER 32

Consumption

W HEN I RETURN to the office, I find even fewer buyers for CDOs and CMOs than even one week ago. The stock market has been having intraday swings that are abnormally large only to finish up close to where it started.

Back when I first started working, the Securities and Exchange Commission enforced something called an uptick rule, a rule that had been around since the 1930s. Any trader who was selling short, meaning taking a bet that a stock was going to fall, could only add to a short position after an uptick in the stock price, meaning the stock price moved slightly higher on the last trade. This severely lessened the chances of a stock collapsing. If a stock ticked up once, meaning there was a buyer out there, then someone else could sell that stock without owning it. Now stocks can be sold uncovered, nothing borrowed against the sale, all day long and I recall watching Muriel Siebert, the first woman to own a seat on the New York Stock Exchange, speak on a news show. She was railing against the possibility of this rule being taken away.

Less chaos in the market means fewer trades, but yes, a woman seemed to be the only one who could foresee that market order is more desirable than more money in her account. In just a few months the uptick rule would be tossed to the curb.

I notice the number of uncovered shorts we own, the stocks that are sold that nobody really owns, is ticking up quickly. The stock market seems poised to do something dramatic and not good.

To keep maintaining a somewhat active market, Feagin Dixon buys back the CDOs and CMOs that Henry and other institutional investors owned. Granted, we're giving him less than he wants but still, it's a lot of money and we're left with possibly worthless bonds. I try to calm myself, telling myself stories of these things having AAA ratings and insurance and backstops in the event of a calamity, but my mind can't still itself when I look at these screens.

With Henry's enormous trades, I'm earning commission both when they are bought and when they are sold and that should make me, Stone, and Kathryn happy. I think of the truckloads of returned inventory and how many other subprime players have the same issue. What about the really big banks, the Merrills, the Bear Stearns, and the Lehmans? What are they doing with their inventory? What if every pension fund and investor wanted to sell this stuff all at the same time and we had to return everyone's money simultaneously? Does Feagin have that sort of money in its account? Do any banks? Banks don't actually sit there with the cash in a vault. We sit with electronic notes and promises of an ability to tap cash when needed, but what if everyone demanded it at the same moment?

Kathryn Peterson isn't rattled by this turn of events. Whenever I go up to her land of make-believe money, the floor has the nervous hush of people waiting for their flight to be canceled.

Everyone wants words of assurance from someone in charge, but nobody's in charge. The traders on her floor are subdued and their moronic antics seem forced, almost melancholy. Monty's birthday party seemed to have happened years ago. Tension is making people jittery, with the exception of Kathryn, but when I try to meet with her, she claims to be busy.

When I review the McElroy escape account, the lack of liquidity we have is almost incomprehensible. I have Feagin Dixon stock I'm not allowed to sell. I have a CeeV-TV position in a deal that hasn't closed. My salary is paid by a bank with extreme risk on its balance sheet. If Feagin had to pay out cash to everyone trying to sell subprime back to us, what would that do to our own stock price?

All employees are supposed to pretend that it's business as usual. When a client calls and asks questions about our liquidity we have a party line about insurance and backstopping and repeat that there's nothing to worry about. The tension is tight like an overstretched guitar string.

I have a gripping need to speak to someone in the real world, someone in a job not related to this. I need a girlfriend who teaches or runs a bakery but I have none. The closest I have is Elizabeth, who works for a start-up where I don't understand what she does, but I'm desperate. She was my best friend from college, though she gave up on our getting together months ago. I ask her for another chance and hope she'll pick up the phone.

CHAPTER 33

Front Running

O N SATURDAY MORNING Elizabeth offers me a limited chunk of her time on neutral turf. She's not one to spend an endless afternoon in a germ-infested indoor gym or on a cold playground. We meet at a high-end brunch place filled with beautiful people who all seem to be experiencing some kind of postcoital *tristesse.* I'm bringing the only kids who will be in this place and as any parent of young kids can foresee, this is a commitment to failure.

I jam the stroller through a too-tight door and catch the mystified face of Owen. This is not Central Park, he seems to say. I can let myself feel a little set up by Elizabeth, and Owen maybe feels a little set up by me. His face is asking me what I'm thinking.

There's another tidbit that makes this plan an assured fail: meeting at 10 a.m. I mean, yes, Elizabeth is probably freshly rolled from her boyfriend's bed, but we McElroys ate breakfast three hours ago, had a midmorning snack, and are headed for a nap in an hour. We don't do brunch. We don't even know what that is.

Elizabeth is married to her work, a career that consists of cranking up social media interest for her clients' companies. She is paid handsomely for what really is her intuition and ability to notice trends. She's an expert on the human mind and its varied desires, and she's so good at this because she never stops studying men—her data are always virgin and her honesty makes her a valuable friend.

"Isabelle . . . It's been . . . like, a month!" she proclaims for all fellow diners to know. She leans forward to kiss my cheeks and the thinnest cashmere scarf brushes my neck. It feels like a thousand-dollar scarf.

"Or six months or whatever," I say, taking in her übercool yet classy look. She takes in my look too.

"What's that?" she asks, pointing to my little muffin belly. Yoga pants are slimming but when you toss a long white shirt over the show, it clings to the spandex. It's not my best look.

"These pants make me look fat so I wore them for you," I say dryly.

Elizabeth shakes my kids' hands, being clueless that they aren't twenty-one. She never brings them gifts or makes silly voices or fart noises on their bellies. She never even tells them they've gotten big. She's one of my best friends and probably doesn't know my kids' names. I love her for this because she really only cares about me. The surveys of human life she seems to constantly be conducting don't include children.

"What's his name?" I ask, reaching out my hands to imply that I've taken in her whole look. Her face is glowing with pheromones. She's tall like me but with some Polynesian Hawaiian thing in her genes. Her skin is just enough olive to be exotic, her teeth are vibrant and white, and she's always rocking some fabulous jewelry. She wears jeans on Saturdays that are the three-digit-price-tag kind. You don't know why they cost so much but they just look better and someone like Elizabeth knows how to wear them. When we were single and walking into rooms together, all heads turned toward our tallness and youth. Now when she stands to hug me, the room turns as expected but all eyes are for her. I'm not sad to give her a solo. I just take note of it.

"Felípe? He's, like, amazing."

"Is he 'like' amazing, or is he in fact amazing?"

She cocks her head. "*Like*, amazing." We both laugh.

Elizabeth pours the three kids bubbly water in real and breakable stemware. Owen is in my lap but not touching or banging anything. It's like she mesmerizes kids by ignoring them. I think about pulling out the bright red plastic sippy cups conveniently located on the back of the stroller and suggesting we veer toward the ingestion of BPAs, but I hesitate. The table looks too perfect. Everything is white and crisp. A single, perfect lily on a tall stem sits in the middle and no small hands grab for it. If I weren't wearing the yoga pants and maybe took the scrunchie out of my ponytail, we could even look like some two-mommy photo shoot.

I pass the basket of croissants around and, leaving no time for niceties, dive in and tell her about the mortgage market. She nods her head and asks if there's any part of me that's surprised by this. She acts like I should have seen this all coming. No. I'm boring her, and the fact that she doesn't care soothes me. If real people don't see this as a crisis, it probably isn't.

I move on to the Glass Ceiling Club. I can't let this chance pass for me to share all this with someone I trust. When I delve into the Gruss lunch she again looks bored.

"Belle," she interrupts, "you're describing the whole tech start-up scene in this town. We have options instead of real money, we're probably scruffier than your crew, but what's the news here? Men need to react to threats to their superiority so they misbehave. Businesses with big money at stake become arrogant and chauvinistic. Where's the news flash in that? Why are you so bothered?"

"I'm bothered because I work there. I have stock in the place and, well, I'm ashamed of it."

"What makes you think the finance industry is so different from the rest of America?" she responds. "What makes you think I don't see the same stuff just with younger guys? Am I ashamed of my company? Not really. I let the bullshit go."

"What other industry in America keeps this behavior so secret? I mean, our contracts ensure that you will never read about this in the newspaper."

"Maybe the paper doesn't want to print these stories. Maybe this is the oldest story ever written. Maybe it's boring. Look, I get that you Wall Street people lose good women because they can't handle the environment. We have the same thing, but guess what? The committed ones stay, the ones we want to stay, stay." She points a butter knife at me when she says the word *stay*.

"You sound like B. Gruss II."

"Is he still alive?"

I sigh. "Elizabeth, doesn't it bother you to be spoken to like that?"

"Like what? Nobody speaks to me any certain way 'cause I'm their boss. They're all, like, twenty-two. I'm the babysitter, the one the parents left in charge."

"So that's the difference. What if you weren't able to be the boss? What if you know you're better than people more senior than you but never get promoted?"

As we shoot back and forth, three little-kid heads turn in unison. What's making my kids suddenly intrigued by adult conversation? Why are they being so good?

"Here's how I see it." She pushes up the sleeves on her blazer and flips her hair from one side to the other. Two men at a nearby table have their mouths almost in panting position. One even drops his phone on the floor, right at her feet. I roll my eyes at him and even though it fell to her side it's me who snaps it up and puts it back on their table forcefully, ignoring his gracious thank-yous.

She's used the moment to contemplate what I've said. "We both work in really open environments. There's not so much as a cubicle wall in either of our lives, okay? People let their guard down when they operate like that and then they go tribal."

"Tribal?"

"Yeah, like those orphaned elephants in Africa who find a new family in the pack of other orphaned elephants. They get wild 'cause they have no parents."

"Elephants!" Owen squeals, and proceeds to move his head like he has the weight of a trunk swinging off his front.

"Orphaned elephants?" I repeat dully. "That's an excuse?"

"Can I get champagne?" she asks the waiter. "Does anyone else want one?" She looks at me in my yoga pants and my disheveled kids and doesn't bat an eye. "Anyone?" She's not even joking. This is whom I'm seeking advice from, someone offering champagne to minors.

"Look at it this way," I try again. "I have these MBA women, graduates from Duke and Harvard and Wharton, and they've got so much potential and we hire them, we train them, and then some dope does something and there we are watching her leave with a nice check in her hands, never to work on Wall Street again. I never get the upside of that woman. I spend the time to train her, I use up my very limited energy bucket to mentor her, and in a way it's *my* money spent to have her leave. Is it worth it to me to even hire someone like that? These women could be so useful to the firm, they could be a voice of reason on the risk commit-tee, and they could help raise the whole culture of the bank, but instead the men treat them like sex objects and they run."

"Wait, so your question is should you hire these types of lass-ies? You just answered yourself."

"So I should never hire women."

"Never."

"Liz, gimme a break."

"They frickin' whine, they reproduce, they're litigious. Stick to guys."

"You only hire guys?"

"I *mostly* hire guys. Guys and lesbians. I'm not going to lie. I just have less drama with those two groups. Maybe do your next recruiting trip to the LGBT office at one of those fancy uni-versities you visit. Minorities too. They work out well. They're hungry to move ahead and don't give a rat's behind about Johnnie thwacking someone's ass."

"Enough. You're saying gay women and minorities don't mind being harassed? Who the hell are you these days?"

"I'm saying they aren't so sensitive. They're above it, they're focused, and they're not analyzing every nuance of every com-ment, looking for some sort of harassment angle. I've always said the stuff you think but are afraid to say. Look at that description I just gave you of successful women. You're one of them. I'm one of them. You're even more of one of them 'cause you have the whole kid package too. You're like one of those women leaning in. Or is it leaning over?"

"You're hurting my ears."

"Belle. Reality check. We're ambitious and we aren't overly sensitive. Guys like us. They know how to work with us. The guys aren't going to change. It's too late for them. The women need to just deal with it. I get to move ahead 'cause I picked an industry where the average company has twenty employees and very few rules. You work in a big bank with lots of structure and rules that nobody pays attention to anyway. You're talking like you suddenly want to enforce stuff that's never been enforced. You want to be the headmistress of a bunch of cowboys wearing pinstripes and that's a loser's job. Any growth industry is too busy to adhere to lots of rules and manners. It's a wild landgrab for me and for you and so yes, a little ass pinching goes along with that."

I sit back on my faux-fur banquette and think about this while Elizabeth rants on. If I didn't love her, I'd hate her right about now. She still isn't done talking.

"Look, if you want to run something you have to go small and start it yourself, and speaking of small, I have a job for you."

Elizabeth proceeds to tell me about a group at her firm who created a high-speed technology that allows traders to see stock market orders coming in a millisecond before they trade. Elizabeth's group can then jump in and buy that stock before the trade is executed and before the order will make the price rise. They are essentially buying the stock for a smidgen less, a millisecond faster. Once the big order is done at the higher price, her group sells and takes their minimal profit. If you do this hundreds of times a day, it adds up. To me it sounds like front running, to me it sounds illegal. I can't believe her firm can do this and still have clearance as a broker/dealer. But they don't. They outsource this stuff as a service to a bank that does. This side business at her social media firm is now raking in cash at such a rate that what I call frontrunning is their largest profit center.

"I'm worried about the market," I tell her. "There are too many people finding loopholes like that. I have no interest in making someone's grandmother pay one-sixteenth of a dollar more than she should and pocketing the difference. There's so much credit and borrowing and people doing things they can't afford."

Finally one of my kids spills something. Brigid had pulled multiple flakes off her croissant and watched them float like flotsam to the bottom of the glass. But now her glass is sideways on the table. Kevin tries to be helpful by grabbing a fresh diaper from the stroller and dabbing at the mess. The result is something that looks horrifying and we need to roll on out of here.

As we assemble ourselves and rise from the table, I look back at my beautiful, ruthless friend. One of the guys at the next table makes all the body language clues that he's about to begin chatting her up. My tribe and I can't get out of there fast enough for him and I see the relief on his face as he figures Elizabeth is in fact mother to none. He's irritating me. She's irritating me. There's something I want to tell her.

"I'm covering Henry," I say, loving that I can shock her right back, loving that I can tell someone who knows.

"What? WHAT?" She turns her back on the lover man and gives me her full attention.

"Covering? Like with your body?"

I smirk and grab hold of my baby muffin top. "I probably could," I say wistfully.

"Tell me. Last I heard he has an anorexic wife and a roaming eye."

"I cover his account, you moron. He works for my biggest client. I have no idea what his personal life is like." I lie but it's just a smidge.

"So you two have real conversations?"

"Just about the market. Just business."

"No. I refuse to let this happen. No. There is just too much history here. Is he still gorgeous?" Elizabeth grabs her coat, preferring to rescue me than flirt with her neighbor.

I laugh, redden a little. "Well, he's held it together pretty well."

"But gorgeous?"

"Okay, yes, gorgeous," I admit.

"Has he gotten that thick middle thing that guys our age are starting to get?"

I laugh. "No, by all appearances, his middle is just fine."

"You're quitting tomorrow."

"What happened to all your tough talk about women who can take it? I can take it."

"Really?" She puts a hand on my shoulder but looks across the street in thought. For some reason I feel like I'm about to cry. It's a muscle memory reaction; it's being close to someone who knew me when I was close to Henry, back before she and I were wealthy and involved in incomprehensible businesses. I let just an inch of that hurt make contact with me again. To fight back tears I start to buckle things. One of the best talents a mom can have is being able to buckle baby carriers, stroller handles, and kids' coats with one hand. My fine motor skills have greatly improved with motherhood and buckling makes for great conversation filler. It's something to do when you need to look away.

She won't let go of my shoulder. Even though I'm bent forward and not looking at her, Elizabeth hangs on to me. My kids grab at different parts of my lower leg and I'm being touched everywhere that invites access. It's very loving and very suffocating all at the same time.

I think of my current life and how different and grown-up I've become since my time with Henry. Our life together was something I once saw in a movie. I think I liked the movie for the most part, but it's faded from memory, with only the highlights and lowlights still on the reel. The highs and lows have narrowed in their intensity so much, becoming less and less discernible, moving toward each other until the whole memory will mercifully flatline with the passage of time.

"I'm fine," I whisper to Elizabeth, "it's just a lot to hold together."

CHAPTER 34

How She Gets By

I ASK KATHRYN to meet for a drink after work, the third time I've asked her this week. Kathryn doesn't seem annoyed by my repeated requests, but just keeps saying no.

"It's just that I'd like to talk to you away from the office," I say. "I'm a little rattled."

"I don't drink," she replied pleasantly enough. "And I like to leave work at work."

Most people would feel offended or discouraged by her constant rebuffs, but the more I know Kathryn, the more I know not to be. I think of her desk, her clean, freakish life, and her perfection in all things. Losing any control is not her style. A request like mine is just a diversion from her original game plan. I need to reason with her, to show her the simplicity of the request, and when I do, she says no again.

"But why?"

"Is this about women's rights?" she sighs. "About you wanting me to join that group of complainers?"

"No, those women are pretty disappointed in me and we've disbanded. After the Gruss meeting it dissolved."

"Very anticlimactic," she says.

"Even Metis thinks I've failed 'cause the memos have stopped. I didn't exactly get anything done at that lunch, now, did I?"

"You did okay."

"I swear, Kathryn, this group of women seem to think I hardly opened my mouth. You were there. You saw how catatonic everyone was."

"You were right."

"I was right. I don't regret a thing."

"We all should have supported you. We were just in shock."

"Well, thanks for nothing," I say, "because in the end Metis was my only friend. Metis spoke up even if she did so while hiding behind an untraceable server. You know what's weird?" I ask Kathryn. "I miss her. I miss those spunky emails. I liked thinking there was some woman in a far-off office whom I could be friends with."

"Don't get weird on me."

"I'm only a little weird, but anyway, I want to talk to you about something else."

Kathryn shrugs. "I have to be at yoga at seven p.m."

"I'll walk you to yoga."

"I do yoga at home."

"I'll walk you home," I say, not bothering to check in with Bruce about the time.

There's a small pause while she considers this before answering.

"Okay," she says while sighing in a way that makes me think she feels sorry for me.

I'm not sure what type of comfort I think I'm going to get from Kathryn, but there's something wise about her and I want some of that to rub onto me.

Within minutes we're walking all the way down from Midtown to SoHo, giving us plenty of time to talk.

"So"—I cleared my throat—"When I spoke with Henry Wilkins today, um . . ."

"I know what you're going to say."

"What am I going to say?" I ask shakily.

"You're going to tell me he's freaked out about the market," she says coolly as she pulls up the collar of her cashmere coat. She looks regal while I look like her disorganized Sherpa.

"It's not just the stock market, Kathryn. It's the entire United States financial system, which is essentially the world financial system."

"Calm yourself," she practically hisses at me. Kathryn stops and glances around us as if she wants to see if anyone heard what I just said.

"What you meant to say is that Wilkins feels some banks may fail," she says evenly.

"It's possible, right?"

Kathryn takes a moment before responding. "The Fed will open the discount window and lend us money. They'd never let us fail because every hedge fund, every mutual fund, every granny in the land would put a run on the banks. Nobody wants a banking panic and that's what we'd have. Worst case is government intervention."

Kathryn acts casual but I can tell she's thought this through. Just like at work, she never looks my way, always forward, as if she's containing herself. All the way from our offices, with only the switching *walk* and *don't walk* signals slowing us, we talk through every possible scenario of doom.

"The discount window is for commercial banks, not investment banks, and I don't think the government is about to bail out a bunch of rich people," I say.

"That'll change if something terrible happens. It'll change in a nanosecond," Kathryn answers calmly.

"Still. Henry's pretty confident Feagin, Bear Stearns, and even Lehman Brothers are looking for someone to buy them. He thinks we aren't able to go it alone anymore, that we're getting so many requests for cash we're running out of money. He thinks Morgan Stanley could fail."

"That could be true," she says, adjusting her leather gloves just so, and then she is silent while she thinks. "By nature that Wilkins guy runs extremely hot and cold. Are you sure he isn't short the stock?" She stops to take a good look at me, as if she suspects something about him. "People are making a lot of money from our stock going down. It wouldn't surprise me if Henry is one of them."

I think about this. What if Henry had a short position in Feagin Dixon stock? What if he were actually helping to create this doom scenario by scaring people like me to sell into the panic, sending the stock down and making him even more money?

Kathryn has moved on in her thoughts. "Worst-case scenario is Feagin Dixon finds a buyer and life goes on," she says like she's convincing herself of this.

"But whether or not the rumors are true, our stock is crashing," I note.

"It's short sellers and dumb money that's selling into this. It's panic. Buy on the weakness."

"Yeah, but it doesn't *feel* dumb."

Dumb money is arrogant street lingo referring to the individual investor, the lemming, and the uneducated in all matters financial. If Average Joe is selling stocks, it's probably a good time to buy.

"But this feels smart. It's the hedge funds that are shorting the life out of the financial stocks. They can make this disaster happen by making the individual so frightened she'll run to liquidate her retirement account. This disaster can be self-fulfilling and could take all of us down with it."

"So how can this be something you control in any way? Why worry about it?" Kathryn asks in a mantralike voice, as if she's in a trance.

"Because, it's our firm, our country, my family, and lots of families. It's all our money and my job. Being complicit in this, whatever this is, bothers me. I used to think we were doing something good. Now it all feels dirty."

Kathryn looks at me again, this time raising one eyebrow into the most perfect question mark.

"You're such a complex creature," she says, and actually smiles.

What I haven't told Kathryn is that Henry told me to get out. That if I quit right away I could cash in some of my depreciating stock within two weeks, take my profit on CeeV-TV, and be gone. But I don't want to quit. I'm haunted by this thought of Henry possibly shorting my stock, of what a keen trading sense Henry has and how he's always one step ahead in the race. Henry thinks the common man and woman is about to get crushed but what if he's part of the crushing?

We've walked all the way down to loft-filled TriBeCa, where people look cool and arty and where fancy women like Kathryn appear lost. I did notice that we passed right through SoHo but didn't want to say anything.

"Come upstairs," she says while turning abruptly into a nondescript building with grating across the windows. A single digital keypad gives her access.

She lifts the gloves from each finger as if she is plucking flower petals. She touches the keypad and buzzes us in.

"You live here?" My voice squeaks a bit, embarrassing me, and I want my heart to stop racing. "I thought you said SoHo."

"Surprised? Don't tell anyone. I demand privacy. TriBeCa."

"I, um, I just had you pegged somewhere north of here."

"We all do that stereotyping thing. You may need to open your mind, Miss Isabelle. You may be enlightened."

I'm in an industrial elevator large enough to hold a Volkswagen with a woman who belongs in a mannequin catalog. The elevator opens into white space, large and mostly empty, with a few white couches, a single white orchid, and some white candles, mysteriously already lit. There is no obvious center to the place, no nucleus where one can imagine the kitchen sitting just to the left or the bedroom just behind a hallway. There isn't a magazine, a book, or a forgotten coffee mug. I feel as though I'm in an under-construction, minimalist spa.

Kathryn pushes something on the wall and a white door slides back to reveal white coat hangers and about ten pieces of clothing, all dark-colored. She mechanically removes her coat, places her hat on the one empty shelf, and offers to take my coat. As she hangs it she seems to sniff it for bedbugs or kid remnants. Yet whatever Kathryn does I find more intriguing than insulting. There's nobody like her. She removes her shoes and indicates that I do the same while handing me Asian-influenced slippers embroidered with white silk and I dare not refuse.

I wonder to myself, when was the last time I wore slippers? I believe it was in the hospital after having my last baby. Children make some things fall to the wayside, where they enter a black hole of distant memory. They're the incidentals, the side items. For me it was things like nice makeup, jewelry of some value, manicures, cashmere, and waxing. Those left my life one by one until the last slipper was lost and never really missed. For me wearing slippers was replaced with Owen's life. That was a good trade.

I want to say "Nice place" to Kathryn but it doesn't feel nice. It feels big.

"Big place" is what comes out of my mouth. "Did you just move here?"

"Bought this place six years ago when I got divorced," Kathryn says. "It's how I keep centered."

"Centered," I say simply, wondering if she has a hired candle lighter. Surely she doesn't let them burn all day.

"I had a life that didn't work, chaos, drama. I was always behind," she continues. "I always felt panicked and encumbered and confused." I listen as I hear Kathryn describe me. "Then I met someone who taught me to unfetter myself, to keep my eye on the prize."

"The prize being . . . um, becoming a managing director?"

"Aren't you proud of us?" she says, with some acknowledgment of sisterhood on her almost smiling face. This is the closest she's ever come to being human around me.

She steps behind a white screen and speaks from there. The slight exertion necessary when one changes clothes alters her cadence slightly.

"So how exactly did you unencumber?"

"Got a life coach and a yogi. Traded them for my needy husband and thoughts of having a family. I wasn't getting pregnant no matter how many drugs they pumped into me. The coach made me get laser sharp about the things I wanted, the yogi gave me my mind and body back. My shrink pointed out that I couldn't have it all, nobody can have it all, at least not at the same time. I made my choices about the things I needed to change to get what I wanted and it worked."

I thought about this. Was that why I was so unhappy with Bruce right now? Was I just trying to have it all at the same time and squeezing him in the middle of my own personal pressure dome?

Kathryn emerges now in yoga pants and an exercise bra. Her abdominals look like mine used to but I can't remember the decade. She comes and sits before me, cross-legged.

"What you should be concerned with is hanging out with those women. They're so non-contributing and they're not at your level. They're sucking energy from you and you should distance yourself. They're giving you a bad reputation and you're not like them."

I know Kathryn is referring to the Glass Ceiling Club and I have a déjà vu moment, where my mother is telling me to rid myself of my fourteen-year-old friend Abigail Acuna because she wore bright blue eye shadow and Miss Sixty jeans.

"We aren't exactly friends, Kathryn, we have a professional motive that unites us. We know we can change some things at Feagin. We never imagined these other firms getting brought to their knees like this, never foresaw where crummy loans and hedge fund rumors could get us. Seems like a bigger problem now than crappy treatment of women."

"Oh, Belle, we aren't some government agency, we aren't a team. Nobody can succeed in these jobs without some ice chips in her veins. Your emotional lovelies weigh on you. Be free of them and any other baggage and you'll find happiness."

I think about this insight for a moment and find myself liking Kathryn just a little bit less.

"There's nobody in my life I want to rid myself of," I say bluntly. "I mean, maybe there are a few who should hit the road," I say, sadly thinking of the two-faced Henry. "But I really like them all. So what if I'm spread a little thin?"

"Belle, look at you. You're a wonder in that you've gotten so far despite your parade of dependents. Those women are hangers-on and completely disposable. Do yourself a favor and cut the cord."

"Cut the cord with other women at work?"

"Cut the cord with everyone who isn't helping Belle get every-thing she wants every minute of every day."

I digest this odd thought for a moment. I review my list of de-pendents and codependents that I adore. I'm beginning to believe Kathryn is possibly the loneliest person I've ever met.

A door closes on the far side of the apartment and I hear the sound of barefooted steps. I turn to see a thirtysomething, dark-haired Adonis step forward. He's a goateed, tight-white-T-shirted-with-tight-black-shorts guy. He's carrying a green sludgy drink. Before he hands the drink to Kathryn he leans forward, never acknowledging me, and kisses her passionately, which flexes his sculpted thighs. As she holds the drink he rubs her shoulders and my own neck aches with sympathetic desire, not for Buffy Boy, but for touching of any kind. Kathryn does have a connection with another human! I'm relieved and happy for her all at the same time. Adonis moves behind her to get further down her back as she sips the slithering green muck.

"A visitor?" he inquires with a raised eyebrow tilted toward me. His tone is more accusing than inquisitive.

"This is Belle McElroy. We work together."

"Together?" he asks with soft deprecation. "Kathryn Peterson works with nobody. She works for Kathryn."

Kathryn seats herself on the couch, thoughtfully sipping. "Yes," she responds, as if hypnotized. "I don't know where that came from."

"It came from the old Kathryn, the gone-away-forever Kath-ryn," Adonis says.

"Yes," she says dreamily. "Forgive me, it's been so long since she was here."

"Let's make certain old Kathryn doesn't come back."

Quack-face comes around the couch to stand before me. He closes his eyes and does that yoga breathing thing, inhaling through his nose, holding it for several seconds, and exhaling through his mouth. He does this three painful times. I awkwardly extend my hand to a man who can't see it.

"He's testing your aura," Kathryn whispers. "His name is Apollo."

Apollo opens his eyes and shakes his head the way my father did when my brother took the car for a joyride at thirteen years old. There's disapproval and then there's that sigh that implies great disappointment in the person. It's too much for Kathryn. She immediately stands up and walks toward the door. Something in her manner tells me I should be following her, as I clearly haven't passed the Apollo sniff test. Kathryn pushes the closet door aside and we both enter to retrieve my coat.

"Well, you have a cute boyfriend," I say, that being the best thing I can come up with.

"Oh, I don't have a boyfriend," she says as if I have accused her of insider trading. "Apollo just services me. It's a mind-body connection that I pay for. I needed someone available by contract with no attachments and no drama. In fact, I believe he has a girlfriend or maybe she's his wife."

Again, I try to comprehend what she's saying. Didn't they just kiss? Is she saying she pays him to touch her?

"Well, I'm about to begin my practice," she says, and removes my coat from the hanger.

Apollo has put something in a bowl and I see him light a match and begin to burn it. As the elevator arrives my nostrils fill with a smell I know but have trouble naming. I focus on this, knowing I've cooked with this familiar herb. When the elevator reaches the ground floor again, it hits me: sage. He's burning sage to rid the bad energy of Belle McElroy from the white, perfectly ordered, and purchased world of Kathryn Peterson.

CHAPTER 35

Triple Witching Hour

W HEN MY family boards an airplane and the seating con-
figuration is two rows of three seats, there will be one
lone passenger stuck with the five of us. I always feel for that person, sitting there innocently, not knowing we're about to become
their living hell for the next few hours.

Today that person is an elderly woman, neat and prim. Except
for the visual groan on her face as we settled ourselves, she's
been ignoring us. We'll be in her turf for hours and my sense is
she already can't stand us. We do better with sullen teenagers or
Hispanic men. Not to categorize humanity, but I've come to learn
which bunches of people come installed with a gracious tolerance
for small children.

Bruce and I had one magnificent showdown, worthy of reality
television. It happened in the comfort of our home, in front of
our caregiver, in front of our kids. It was a textbook example of
everything you aren't supposed to do as a parent.

I had come home from a business dinner where I only stayed for the cocktail portion of the evening. Instead of my usual glass of white wine, I had not one but two dirty martinis and not one bite of food. Drinking my dinner turned me positively fearless. I walked into our apartment at 9 p.m. with some vision of a quiet house and possible husband romance. Instead I opened the door and was assaulted by the television blaring some sexy talk in front of three young faces. Caregiver and Bruce sat there, bookending the kids and both talking animatedly into their cell phones. The whimpering dog told me he hadn't been walked, and my peripheral vision caught sight of the dish-strewn kitchen table. The children weren't tuned in to *Handy Manny* but what seemed like an X-rated movie, *Mr. and Mrs. Smith.* This wasn't some cozy movie night at the McElroys, this was the television babysitting my kids long after bedtime because neither adult in the house could summon the energy to put them to bed.

"I've just finished my fourteen-hour work shift so I thought I'd skip dinner to come home early and help you two out," I said sarcastically.

Caregiver jumped up. "We thought you were coming home later," she muttered as she headed to the kitchen and started banging things around.

Moments like that parents expect young children to run with outstretched arms to their mother, but I was no match for Mrs. Smith—er, Angelina Jolie—who picked that moment to mount Brad Pitt's hip and keep my kids' eyes on her flawless thighs. While straddling Brad, her knife, which she kept tucked into her garter belt, revealed itself.

Bruce, whose finger was in the air—implying I should hold my fire—finished some sweet sign-off and ended the call.

"Who the hell were you talking to?"

"Belle, Jesus, my mother called."

"Your mother? You don't give your mother the time of day, never mind miss a movie for her. When the hell did you start being nice to her?"

"I'm always nice. I'm like a bag of niceness, all the frickin' time."

Jolie and Pitt then attacked someone, breaking stuff in their house, shooting at bad guys, destroying everything, implying the sex was inevitably great and by all appearances not having to clean up the mess they made. That was exactly what I wanted to do.

I made a dive for the television, trying to turn it off manually, but some plastic stacking rings on the floor got under my feet. I fell flat on my face.

"I want to break stuff too!" I yelled, grabbing some of the rings and furiously throwing them at Bruce. "I want to HIT someone." Even the rings disrespected me, being too light to get far and falling about three feet short of Bruce.

"Chill, Belle. This movie is, like, PG-13 and these kids are being parentally guided. What the hell is your problem?"

"My problem is you won't get off your fat ass to either work or turn into a dad who acknowledges he needs to do more of the mom stuff." The red plastic slide that's been sitting on its side was next on my hit list.

"Would it kill anyone in the house to do this?" I said as I turned the slide upright, letting little rubber balls spill everywhere. "Am I the only one who notices anything around here?"

"Oh, because having an orderly house where the slides are set upright would mean that I'm a better dad?"

"It would make you a better *partner*. Do you know what this here says?" I asked as I kicked the slide because, dammit, that's what Angelina would have done. "It says nobody cares at all. It says, let all this shit hang out till Mom comes home because she'll fix everything. She'll earn all the money! She'll order all the groceries and arrange for cleaning and cooking. She'll get the car fixed on weekends and walk the dog at midnight, so let's not get our fat asses off the couch EVER!"

"That's the second time you mentioned my ass being fat and it's not" was all that Bruce said before rising and walking out of the room.

The couch still held three, now sobbing, children. What had been a relatively calm room was then a disaster sight.

"Mom," Kevin sniffed. "The slide was like that 'cause it was our fort. We played Forts tonight and the balls were the ammo and Daddy had to make a phone call so he just put on the TV, like, a minute ago." Kevin stood up and stalked away.

"Oh," I said weakly to his retreating back. I felt a little stupider and turned to Brigid.

"Oh, Brig, please stop crying. Mommy didn't understand what she was looking at. I think I may have made a mistake."

Brigid stood and pointed at my feet in disgust. "You changed your shoes," she wailed, and threw her stuffed bunny down in protest. She too marched out of the room. Usually I remembered to just take my shoes off when I came home to keep the shoe deal between Brigid and me unquestioned. That night I had assumed she'd be asleep.

Several teary hours later, Bruce and I were speaking again. He can't take my having this job any longer; the hours are too long and our kids are too young and I'm too uptight about the state of the financial world. He's never said I'm a bad mother but I know he thinks that.

From my point of view, he's too lazy in his life, he doesn't share any financial worries, and never takes care of any family logistics. He gives our credit cards too much of a workout for an unemployed dad. I can hardly do more than glance at our state-ment of charges each month to spare myself from exploding over things like a $250 massage at a SoHo men's spa. A spa during the day? He got his chest waxed, he told me, and "maybe" a hot stone massage. The hypocrisy hurts my stomach.

His defense is that he's able to bench-press far more than his weight, he's skateboarding again, and he can stand on his head in his yoga class. Achieving these mighty aspirations makes me a lucky woman, according to him, and aren't I glad he's not some paunchy guy headed to his middle-aged Barcalounger? We've cranked up our mutual feelings of frustration to full relationship distress.

To end our repetitive discussion about why I should quit my seventy-hour-per-week slog, and our only paycheck, Bruce insisted on this trip—his quest for me to gain some clarity, to see things his way, while deep down I feel he's asking impossible things of me to justify his own immaturity. There, I said it. My husband hasn't aged a day since we met because he hasn't matured a day since then either. When I calmed down enough to reach for an olive branch, I would have agreed to anything to make our circular discussions stop and to find some common ground, so this trip seemed to be the solution and so here, on the runway, we sit.

My sister is married to a former member of the French ski team who now instructs three-year-olds to assume the pommes frites position with their baby skis. They moved to the small town of Argentière, in the French Alps, to rise above the sort of lunacy Bruce and I live within. They have four young girls, which should be just the happy ticket we seek: seven small children, two maritally challenged adults, and two other adults living out some scene from *Heidi*, all within the confines of a cabin and its wood-burning stove. We are calling this plan our vacation.

Frolicking in alpine beauty in spring or summer is for amateurs. We're going in March because it's spring break, which feels more like a winter break and promises to have the most delays.

It's snowing here at JFK Airport and that's why we're sitting and sitting on a runway in Queens. We've been sitting here for four hours.

Kevin's Nintendo DS has run out of power. I've changed Owen's diaper twice. He's three now and still in diapers because nobody is showing him the path to the toilet. Brigid has tired of drawing in her coloring book and has decided her forearms are a good canvas, coloring both of them solidly green. She tells me she looks like Little Pea. She says this over and over to my blank face until Bruce disgustedly tells me that Little Pea is the small vegetable boy on the Green Giant box, where all of our children's frozen vegetables come from. He shakes his head with disgust; his wife and Brigid's own mother does not know this rather crucial bit of information. It takes every ounce of self-control for me to not turn on him and say, "Dickface, the little green kid's name is Little Green Sprout, not frickin' Little Pea."

When Brigid's self-mutilation is complete she moves to my arms, and since I have no dignity anymore I let her. She gives me stripes of deep navy, angry vein lines all over my arms and somehow the graffiti suits me. I'm craving a hit of my office, just a simple phone call while the stock market is open and we're sitting on this runway, solidly within U.S. cell phone range. The markets have been trading wildly, a few hedge funds have failed, and here I am going on vacation. One of the vows Bruce insisted I make for this trip is that I live unconnected during the week of European frolic. I sit in my seat trying to rationalize that this moment cannot possibly be considered the start of my technology cutoff, can it? I'm afraid to ask him, afraid of his wrath, so instead I just sit, feeling the heat of the clear airplane Wi-Fi signal burn an imaginary hole through my ski jacket.

I glance across the aisle to look at Bruce, Owen, and the elderly woman now wearing radio headphones, circa 1989. Bruce is playing the good daddy by reading GQ magazine to himself. I watch him chuckle, blissfully unaware that Owen is standing and bouncing on his seat, and I pretend I'm not with those people.

I think about running to the toilet with my BlackBerry, to get a quick read on the currently open financial markets. Even though I could pull this off without Bruce knowing, the very act seems to symbolize so much more, something to further fray the wisps of dental floss holding my marriage together. When someone is looking for reasons to fight, reasons to justify their own lousy behavior, I'm not the one to give them any. Instead I force myself to sit in my seat, taking big gulps of stagnant air, and try to concentrate on my oration of *Stuart Little 2* for my other two children.

I had a terribly confusing day yesterday, the day before this journey began. I called over to Cheetah Global, to tell them I'd be out of town and that my assistant, Stone, was going to be their coverage for the next week. When this message got relayed to Henry, he called me right back.

"Where're you going?"

"To visit my sister, you remember, Carron?"

"Of course I know Carron but she lives overseas."

"You sound very genteel with that 'overseas' thing, Henry."

"You don't have to be snippy. You do have to meet me before you leave. There's something I have to show you."

Something about another man demanding things of me seemed way out of line. After my showdown with Bruce, my limited tolerance for drama was kaput. The only reason I'd have liked to see him was to ask how much money he made shorting Feagin Dixon stock.

"Henry, I can't be your Feagin Dixon blankie anymore." Henry was silent for a moment, so I continued.

"All this time, I'm listening to your so-called concern about my firm and I bet you're shorting our stock."

"That's not true."

"I bet it *is* true."

"Belle, I do some unusual things, but I don't lie to you."

"It doesn't matter. We're not going out of business."

"That I don't believe. I am short Bear Stearns. I am short Lehman. And I *would* short Feagin Dixon if you didn't work there. If I were you, I'd cash out now. I'd run."

"Look, Henry, it's not just that. I mean, this whole account relationship has come to be something more than just business for me. I don't completely understand this dance we still have going on after all these years, but it's one of the things coming between Bruce and me. I need to go away with my family and fix stuff and you need to talk to Stone."

"Who the hell names their kid Stone and what the hell is his job at that place?"

"You don't say the word *hell* enough."

"Seriously."

"Stone is that very expensive backup person you sometimes speak with."

"I don't want to talk to him."

"Stop whining."

"Come meet me."

"No."

"You have to."

"I don't have to do anything. You're going to shove bonds at me and ask me to find buyers where there are none and I can't sell stuff I don't believe in."

Henry isn't fazed. "You'll be glad you came, Belle. I promise. This will be so good for you." This time his tone is softer, even caring, something I respond to way better than a demand.

"What could possibly be good for me?" I asked. I started to consider what he meant. Maybe he had an exit plan for me, maybe a job offer or some strategy to salvage the risky bonds we owned. The more I thought about it, the more intrigued I got.

So I went.

Two hours later I stood on the street outside my office knowing I had no time to be there. It's one thing to talk business with Henry on the telephone, and it's another to see him. I watched his huge frame cast a shadow over everyone else on Park Avenue, as he walked like some superhuman—at a crushing pace that had him veering around the mortals in his path. Henry saw me and stared as he came close with the slightly googly-eyed face that admiring boys had when my teenaged breasts were surprisingly new and growing by the day. But from Henry that look really isn't for me, it's about the potential deals he's looking to do, or other trades he's thinking about executing. Maybe the reason he wanted to meet in person was to avoid speaking over taped phone lines about the grim future he foresaw in the financial system of 2008. I decided to start speaking first.

"It's March fourteenth and Feagin Dixon is still in business," I said in my best Pollyanna voice.

"So I hear." He pecked me on the cheek. I hated that I wanted to really grab hold of him, to have him hug some of the worry out of me.

"I don't know how to replicate this job in any way," I said. "I know you think I should be bailing out and selling my stock while it's still worth something, but I like my job."

"There are other jobs."

"We have a lot of expenses."

"Perhaps your husband could get a job."

I rolled my eyes at him as we walked purposefully toward something that only Henry seemed to know about.

273

"Do we have a train to catch?" I asked. "Because if we do, I have to be home by tomorrow."

"Do we ever," he said, and I saw a very un-Henry thing: he blushed. Farther north, around 60th Street, Henry went into one of those fancy luxury condo buildings, remodeled out of old buildings on Park Avenue, everything except the façade of the building ripped out and replaced by golden glitz. The doorman tipped his hat to Henry in a way that told me he knew him.

We got in the elevator and rose to the penthouse level, giving me the sudden clue that maybe we were going to visit Tim, the master of the hedge fund and Henry's boss. It was well known that Tim liked to go home and nap in the middle of the day. That's how big a deal Tim is—he gets to nap. I smoothed my hair while I thought of intelligent responses to what I imagined would be Tim's insisting we buy back the awful bonds I had sold them. Had Henry set me up again? Was I about to be ambushed by his boss?

When the elevator opened directly into the apartment, there was no Tim Boylan. The entire floor of the building was one apartment. The sight before me made my eyes widen the way Charlie's did when he entered the Chocolate Factory, the way Alice's did when she fell into Wonderland. It was that good. The windows made up the entire outside wall, with one thin seam every ten feet or so, and there wasn't a child's handprint on any of them. Gossamer-fine, sheer curtains puddled loosely on the floor like veils of golden protection from the outside world. The whole place made me think of the perfect movie set for the one about the rich, single banker. I couldn't help but walk from window to window, sucking in the view, touching the linen-colored couches so plush I had to push a cushion down just to feel what luxury can be when Froot Loops and Cheez-Its are outlawed. I gently put my bag down on a white ottoman, thought for a moment that it might leave a mark, and put it on the floor.

"I have to use the bathroom," I said as an excuse to see more, and in a voice that suggested that nothing here surprised me. I had no intention of letting Henry hear me be impressed. The bathroom was finished with Waterworks fixtures and glass tile in a muted sea-grass tone. Back when I was single, I tore photos from magazines depicting rooms I liked, and always, my bathroom choices had tile just like that. There was the smell of gardenia from somewhere, white gardenia, my favorite flower, and I could smell it but couldn't see it.

My head was pounding as I opened the medicine cabinet to find it full of all unopened women's toiletries, nice stuff from La Mer, La Prairie, the type of cosmetics I used in my old life, before my bathroom got taken over by Power Rangers. I wondered if this place was Henry's second home. Maybe this is where his wife freshens up after a day of being driven around in her Escalade or maybe it's where Henry gets to satisfy his insatiable appetite for women. It was so wrong for me to be here, and I closed the cabinet, letting the magnificent magnets suck it shut.

I brushed my hair and put on the makeup that had made it into my bag this morning but never onto my face. I brushed my teeth and felt the surge of confidence that comes with a nicely tailored suit and a decent haircut and a clear mind. It was time to leave.

When I came out, Henry was on the phone with a glass of champagne in his hand. I walked by him and waved good-bye to whatever the point of this visit was. Something about my being here now seemed a little dangerous. Was this a Henry love shack? Would he be capable of having such a thing? I thought of him dating his wife while engaged to me and answered my own question. He raised his finger in that "wait a minute" signal and I pushed the elevator button just as he got off the phone.

"So you have a pied-à-terre in Midtown to get away from the demands of your Upper East Side life?" I asked.

"It's not that."

"Is it the secret girlfriend Batcave?"

"Not exactly."

"You see, Henry? I knew this about you. I knew it the whole time and it's the only thing that kept me sane after you left me."

"Knew what?"

"Knew that you were capable of something like this. A trysting apartment? Please."

"What the hell?"

"I just knew you'd always fool around. You're too funny. You're too handsome. You're far too good in the sack. Women do absurd things for you. I couldn't have been married to you."

Henry looked genuinely hurt, which was oddly appealing in a man wearing a $3,000 suit. We were both quiet for a moment.

"I've missed you," he said.

"Stop it," I answer with a catch to my voice. It was unsettling to feel someone be sweet to me when everything else in my life felt mean. I felt too vulnerable. "You're about a hundred years late."

"I never stopped loving you."

"You need to cut it out," I said, drawing my hand across my neck like I meant it, because I meant it. "Really. We're better than this."

I imagined that conversation more times than I have brain pathways. I rehearsed what I would say, how clever I would be with my pithy one-liners about my life being better without him. But when that moment finally arrived, and that did appear to be that moment, it was just no good. We stared at each other, like we were stuck on the same packed subway with no comfortable place to rest our eyes.

"Too much has happened. We don't even really know one another. Maybe we never did," I said.

"I know you," Henry said. "I've never stopped knowing you."

We then had a staring contest. I blinked first.

"So what is this place, and why did I have to come here?"

"Don't you like it?" He looked hurt. "It's everything that screams your name to me. It's for your birthday next week."

Henry remembered my birthday was next week when even I didn't. Nobody thinks of my birthday. I looked around to see what he meant. What was for my birthday?

"The art, the fixtures, and the stuff from magazines you used to collect back when you cared about things like your clothes and how many threads were in your sheets. I just thought maybe you'd like to meet yourself again, the real you who takes charge and runs things, the woman who dresses like a hottie and is quirky and funny and completely sex-crazed."

I waited thirty seconds before answering him. I wanted to get this right, and wanted to say all the rational things I had rehearsed when my mind was clear and not full of the smell of champagne and gardenia. "There are other things to care about now, Henry." I swallowed hard. "I grew up, you know. I tossed the shit that didn't matter, like the thread count of my sheets, back into the proverbial bin."

"You didn't have to grow up." He took my hand in his giant, lovely hand.

I dutifully pulled it back, exactly like I should have. "What, like your wife? Staying a child her whole life because some sugar daddy takes care of her?" I knew I should stop. I was being mean and I'm not mean or maybe I'm becoming mean, but anyway, I had to stop.

"It gives me so much pleasure to take care of her," he said. "I can take care of you too. You could become you again if you'd let me help."

There was just enough daddy-ism in his tone to make me find him, for the first time ever, the tiniest bit creepy.

"What happens in this place anyway?" I asked again.

Henry looked crestfallen. "I told you. It's for you and I thought you'd just love it," he said softly. "Why don't you go see the closet?"

I knew I shouldn't, that I really had to get in that elevator, which by then had arrived. In the next awkward silence, the sound of an elevator leaving without me could be heard, swooshing with that noise of descent.

I walked back toward the one and only bedroom I could see, with its massive bed and eight pillows on the most delicate white duvet. The trim on the duvet was a pale blue gray that looked like—

"Sky before it snows," said Henry, coming up behind me.

I used to say that was my favorite sleep color, the color of the sky right before snow fell. To me it is the color of calm and happiness and being somewhere safe.

"Yes," I said. "Sky before the snow is what that color looks like when you're in love. Now I would call it blue-gray."

I walked over to the closet, full of cute dresses and sweaters and jeans too large for Henry's matchstick of a wife. There were two pairs of Louboutin shoes that looked like works of art. They still had their price tags on them.

"So who *lives* here, Henry?" I asked, letting a delicate cashmere wrap come close to my nose so I could feel what perfect feels like. "Because it doesn't look like a real human does."

It was then that I saw a ring on the dresser. Not just any ring but a small diamond engagement ring I'd worn ten years ago, back when Henry had no money. I had loved it so but returned it to him via the U.S. Postal Service, dropping it in the mail as casually as a postcard, mailed to his parents' home. I was never certain Henry had gotten the ring back. Now I knew.

"We do. We live here," he said softly.

"This"—I waved my hand, my throat catching—"makes no sense."

Henry whipped his hand through his thick hair and began. "Baby, I need you to sit down to tell you this. I promise, no funny business."

I sank into that perfect bed while he pulled up a delicate desk chair across from where I sat. I found myself looking into his eyes without blinking so I forced myself to instead look down, to not notice his giant forearms. I determinedly hung on to my friend named Control.

He sighed. "A few years ago, before you called me about that nursery school application for your son, I was in some mad depression. I worked seventy hours a week, had these fabulous sons and a wife who really loved me. I had everything, and yet I was so sad. I hated myself for giving in to depression, like it was a character flaw I couldn't toss. In my head I constantly lectured myself about the audacity of letting myself get to that state."

I didn't say a word.

"When I met my wife . . ."

"You mean when you were screwing a woman while you were engaged to me? You mean that time?"

He sighed. "Yes. When I did that, I was distracted by something temporary, which in retrospect was a terrible human weakness of mine that I believe I've fixed. I never cheated again."

I chose to not point out the bed we shared in Florida. It seemed we both decided to not label that as cheating. "We were so imma-ture," I said. "We had bad timing but that was a long time ago and we've both moved on with our happy lives." I searched his face, trying to see if he knew I was being ironic, but he didn't seem to.

He continued, "Danielle was already pregnant then."

"No kidding. I'm still pretty good with math, you know. We date for almost eight years; you suddenly have a new girlfriend and have a baby four months later." My voice sounded like someone on one of those angry-person talk shows so I told myself to stop talking.

"So I did the right thing, became totally focused on being a great dad and nailing my job instead of women."

"How poetic you are."

"Anyway, I read a lot, tried to consider what was the gaping hole in my life, and the hole was my unfinished business with you. I imagined going back, building a life with you, and just started doing that. Being with you was the happiest time in my life. I wanted to feel that again."

"So you feel that again how?"

"By buying this place, imagining us being together here."

There it is. "Oh, you mean you bought an apartment for us to screw in because we were really good at that and by taking it up again, like an old sport, we would both revisit the dewy glow of our youth?" I said this in a flat monotone. "Like we could really go back to . . ."

"Australia." We said this at the same time.

The pause in the room was long, filled only with a siren noise from the street and a curtain catching the breeze of the forced air heating system. We were both thinking.

Henry spoke first. "I bought this place a few years ago and fixed it up with a designer I knew you'd like. I thought we could have our life together again without ruining our other lives. We could have those intense times again . . . so funny, so carefree."

"Henry, I want to tell you I know exactly what you mean but

it wouldn't work the way you think. We are different people now. We are . . . married people."

He ignored me. "When I started this project I felt excited again, felt closer to being me again and the cloud in my head cleared up. When I'm in this place that connects us it feels like we live together again, like you are about to walk in. I send you emails from here. I buy you things that I leave here. I got everything ready."

"Ready for what?" I asked softly.

"Just ready."

"And then what?"

"And then I've just been thinking about how to, you know, respectfully ask you to start meeting here."

"Meeting here to start everything up again? You did notice that I ignored your non-work emails? That they went unanswered? You noticed that, right?" I whispered.

"Yes, it was perfect. We both had a piece of each other again without destroying the lives we have with our families. I knew you wouldn't answer those emails because I knew you'd be great at being married. That's one of the reasons I asked you to marry me. You're so loyal."

"Henry, your reasoning is like nothing I can even follow. And that insane performance of yours at the Four Seasons? Where you pretended we never met? That was to make me want you again? 'Cause if that's true, it didn't work."

"It killed me to be so mean to you. But I had to be. I had gotten this apartment all ready but on that day, I freaked out. On the way to the restaurant I still hadn't told Tim I knew you and then it seemed too awkward to mention so I just acted like we never met. I confessed to him later but that day my head was spinning. I was thinking about us doing business together, about this apartment, how you had turned into such a big shot that you had probably changed and what if you weren't the Belle I remembered? But then you dropped your earring on your plate and your hose was torn and you seemed so clumsy and adorable and it reminded me that you're so capable and so vulnerable all at the same time. It let me know you were still you and that this"—he swept his arm around the room—"that this was possible again."

"Henry, I'm not going to say I saw this coming"—I choked for a second—"but don't you think we're a little old to play make-believe?" I asked this gently because Henry seemed unrecognizably shaky and vulnerable. While I wondered many times about his character, I had never once considered him to be mentally ill.

"Belle, you're right. I've been having this pretend life without you. You know, *you.*" Henry said this with both hands outstretched.

I was trying to follow his gorgeous mouth and the words coming out of it, but this whole thing made me woozy. "Look, I'm not exactly riding on the same train track as you. Um, if you think I'm dumping my life for this beautiful room? Henry." I shook my head. "I'm speechless."

"I bought you those clothes, had a moment of Christmas with you right here for the past few years. I gave you these earrings two years ago," Henry said as he pulled out some shiny earrings with rubies surrounding them from a nearby drawer. Casually he tossed them toward me like they were something he'd bought on the sidewalk. "Can I put them in your ears?" he asked like a little boy.

"No," I said, though I did take a second to really look at those beautiful stones.

"I bought you underwear I imagined you wearing for me. I filled your bookshelves with your favorite books," he said.

"You should be committed," I sighed, feeling overwhelmed that someone could care for me so much, someone I had loved so completely. "Henry, you went from being super-supportive of my career to hating that I even worked to being a cheerleader for me, all in one lifetime. You start dating your wife while I'm in Atlanta, and then there's the Four Seasons, and interrupting me at the media conference, and how about not sticking up for me when my son yanked your wife's underwear?" I smiled. I wanted him to smile, to see how silly this was. To prove to me that he wasn't crazy.

"Belle, baby, how else could I keep you at a distance? How else could I have you in my life but not destroy my own life? This apartment is the solution. What if we had an understanding? A place that always stayed in 1998, and the moment we cross that doorway we get to care for one another the way we used to, where we could be free to be twenty-seven and fully alive again?"

I thought about this, about how I loved his body, and his brain that was always firing new ideas. I thought of how he liked to whip my milk for my morning cappuccino and put peppermint oil in my bathwater before climbing in the tub with me. I thought of how he loved to pick out my panties and brush my hair. It had all been so lovely. It had all been so long ago.

Somewhere deep down I felt the resolve I had looked for but could never completely find when I thought about making the emails stop. It wasn't a firm thing at that moment, but it felt just a little bit clearer. Henry was good at taking care of people and sometimes I wanted to be taken care of, but I certainly didn't need to be saved. I just needed to become strong again, the way I was before I worked in a place that made me feel battered.

He went on. "Do you think it was an accident I ended up working where I work? Taking a job at one of your clients? A place I knew you had to call every single day so we'd get to speak again? I had a few job offers and the only reason I chose Cheetah was because I chose you."

"You chose me? You didn't choose me, Henry. You chose something else. I thought we chose each other and then you unchose what we chose."

"It was a horny, three-month decision. I'm not asking you to leave your family, Belle, and I'm not leaving my own family. I'm just a guy who loves you, who has always and will always love you, fiercely, and wants to be able to express that again."

"You've said that to me before," I said.

"I didn't."

"You did. That's what you said when you proposed to me. I remember 'cause I didn't want to get married before thirty and then you said that and I thought if someone will always love me fiercely, then nothing in my life can ever go wrong and it shouldn't matter when I get married."

Henry put the defeated champagne glass onto a bureau, stopped for a second to put a piece of linen under it, and turned away from me.

"I need you. I need us."

There it was again, Henry talking about Henry and what works for him. I felt a wave of calm at both the clarity and unattractiveness of this; sometimes it's nice to know that something that is over is really over. Henry's shoulders caved forward and he could even have been crying.

I came behind him and hugged him tightly. I had loved this man so much and with everything I had but we had split and grown and formed new branches and we had to nurture those now, not something we gave up on long ago. I spoke into his back.

"The problem with us, Henry, is that we never broke up. We never had the crying scene, the one where we sadly admit it isn't going to work. Instead, we had this thing that began in college that was great. We traveled, we started careers, we moved in together, and our lives kicked in. I left New York City for three short months when my dad was in the hospital and even though I came back to see you every other weekend, and even though we were having nonstop, mind-blowing sex at that very same time, when I moved back to New York I find that not only have you been seeing someone else, you're expecting a kid with her.

"Losing my dad and you all in a few months—" My voice caught, I wiped my face on the back of his shirt but was determined to finish saying what I had to say. "You and I never even had what humans call a conversation, an admission that it wasn't going to work out. We never had the scene where we ask who gets the toaster or where I accuse you of stealing my tennis racquet." I was sniffling into his back but wouldn't let him turn toward me. I didn't want this to lead to kissing. I wanted to just speak.

Henry leaned forward and put his head in his hands. His back started heaving. In all our time together, I never once saw Henry Wilkins cry. "It was too painful to break up with you because I wasn't sure it was what I wanted."

"So let's say that today." I snort-laughed. "Let's break up, ten years after we stopped seeing each other. We've got six kids between us with other people, it's hot time we ditched this thing!" This thought was suddenly hilarious to me, so freeing that I couldn't stop talking. I'd made a giant soggy spot on the back of his shirt. I started to pat it, to clean up my mess. I suddenly found everything to be funny. "Let's break up because you never shut up when I drive or because you dress like a golfer from Nantucket or because I hate the way you sing Beatles songs," I gurgled.

But Henry wasn't laughing. He just looked sad. He hadn't taken his head from his hands. Trysting away at odd moments in this beautiful place would be so fun until it wasn't. Then it would have done irreparable damage to everyone else in our lives, and relationships aren't inert. It would have to go somewhere and any scenario I thought of ended in tears and broken promises. There was nothing I could do to help him with whatever it was he really wanted. I wasn't his.

I held on to his giant body, inhaling every bit of his tight form and following his waves of sadness. It was my last time to hold him, to know what he felt like and know why I was letting it go. It felt good that this was my choice. Henry could never have saved me. It would be up to me to do that.

We are now first in line for takeoff. Stuart Little has driven off in his shiny little sports car to find Margalo, the bird. Henry is taking the family to their ski house in Jackson Hole on their Gulfstream IV and Bruce is sleeping with his mouth open in coach and snoring very softly. Owen has removed the old woman's headphones and she's actually playing with him. I begin to talk to her and find she's a sweet French grandmother who doesn't laugh at my terrible French. I feel an overpowering love at that moment for United Airlines and their ability to finally get things moving, for my kids, who still seem to like me despite myself, for my imperfect situation, and for my imperfect family that somehow suits me very well.

CHAPTER 36

Crash

A LARGE BLOCK of snow has found its way into the top of my boot. I feel it melting, sliding down over my ankle and surprising my foot. Why am I wearing bulky, suede, and impractical UGGs on a tiny portion of the majestic Mont Blanc? I'm the equivalent of the North Dakota tourist showing up in Times Square wearing five-inch stilettos to fit in with the presumed natives, only to discover that New York is a walking city and that her shoes start squinching her toes five blocks into walking and nobody is noticing her fabulously chic footwear. Not a soul admires my fat boots, not even the ladies in their fur-trimmed ski jackets, making their way toward the Aiguille du Midi, the main ski lift, wearing gold-rimmed sunglasses and speaking Russian. Only Russian women get away with walking uphill in thousand-dollar ski outfits while puffing on a cigarette.

I'm currently the helmswoman on a handmade toboggan that looks like it belongs in a sledding museum. My focus is solely on victory. My team consists of Brigid, Kevin, and myself and we've been having trouble steering this alpine artifact. My sister's kids are regular lugers and we city people have been eating their snow all afternoon. Repeatedly they whiz by us and some sibling competitive feeling that exists between Carron and me roars, and I'm answering the call.

I need a strategy to win and I need a team behind me. I turn to my now eight-year-old.

"Kev, I'm the heaviest and I should be in the back," I say. He's wearing a ski helmet that Bruce made him put on.

"But I need to be in the back," he says, hovering between earnestness and whining.

"Why do you need to be in the back?"

"It makes me feel safe to hold on to you," he whispers.

"No. I need to be in the back," I respond firmly. "We can't let these pseudo-French dropouts beat us."

Kevin looks puzzled and tries to understand whatever it is that I've just said. I turn to Brigid, who is now off the sled, making snow angels and really burning my rubber.

"Come on, Brig, I want to beat them just once."

"Mommy is whining," she says, and points her finger to an imaginary friend in the sky, making certain that supreme beings know this about her mother.

"Get on the sled," I say firmly. "And stop that dreaming stuff."

My sister rolls her eyes at me and points to Kevin, who seems to have adhered his backside to the last seat in the toboggan, also known as my seat. His snow pants are sodden and heavy and his lips appear bruised, having turned a purplish shade of blue. We're riding that thin line between having fun and not having any fun.

"Don't you want to win?" I practically beg of my kid while wondering to myself, what sort of a kid doesn't want to win?

Kevin also looks upward toward the crystal-blue sky with

round, thoughtful eyes. He appears to really consider the question before turning his gaze toward me to say, "No."

"What do you mean 'no'?" I've never met anyone who didn't want to win, have I?

"Isn't he his father's son?" My sister laughs as she straddles herself onto the last seat of their extended Flexible Flyer, pulling her long legs in with the ease of a teenager. Their team shoves off and showers us with shredded shards of snow.

For the past three days this form of transportation has consumed my children. Bruce usually opts to stay indoors doing planks and watching Owen nap while my sister and I take the six other children out on the mountain. I love seeing their cheeks get red and their bodies winded, something that doesn't happen often in New York.

Last night we did something we haven't done since we were all on this earth together. We slept as if we had no fear. There were eight solid hours where neither child nor adult made a disruptive sound, no boogeyman came to visit Owen, and no financial markets melted my dreams. When I woke up, Bruce joked that I had gotten a face-lift during the night. A simple compliment to me and I filled with hope again, hope that our marital train wreck was just hitting track bumps, that maybe it was all just job stress that was making me so mad at him.

After the sledding Carron and I drive into Chamonix, a town torn from a page of a fairy tale. Weathered farmers have set up stalls in the main square where we go to shop for food. With so many growing bodies, the hunt for sustenance is constant and my kids' newfound appetite for these slowly cooked and lovingly prepared meals is notable.

My sister is a younger, hipper version of me: prettier, more fun, and always bouncing on the front of her feet while she tells you about the next big adventure she's going to have. Her career has always involved skis, first as a champion racer and then as a product promoter for certain brands. Sprung from Bronx apartment dwellers, champion skier was a less predictable career path than even mine. Carron never got the capitalistic itch the way I did. Her existence has always been about living her life, rather than planning her life. But I see her in this town with her healthy tribe of girls and her marriage that seems solid enough and I'm wondering, what's she faking? I've never seen such an uncomplicated life.

As we walk amid the stalls, men lift their tankards of beer to us asking "*Êtes-vous des jumeaux*?" or, "Are you twins?" I feel the glow that only the French can reflect. Carron flits around as if she's in the place she's meant to be and I wonder what that feels like. She showers petals of compliments on each shopkeeper and they appear to swoon over this "Anglais," as they keep calling her.

"American," she keeps correcting them in her lilting, beautiful French and they all wave and wink as if to imply she is far too cool to be from anyplace real.

Carron is the only human I can share the bizarre Henry saga with. I feel like my chest will implode if I don't tell someone what happened.

I take a deep breath. "So I cover Henry," I say simply enough, but Carron stops moving. She's holding a bag of clementines.

"Cover? Like, you have his account?" she asks.

"Yes."

"You mean Henry, right? Like, from . . . our life?" She puts down the bag and gives me her full attention.

"Henry is dead to us," Carron says, drawing her hand across her throat. "Do you hear me?"

"Yeah. Except he works for my biggest client, therefore he *is* my biggest client."

"Rather . . . inconvenient," she says.

"Well, it's not a problem," I say. "I mean, we get along fine."
I'm speaking so stiffly that she turns toward me.

"Define 'fine'?"

"I mean, we do a lot of business together." I feel my face redden
and she stares, waiting for me to say more.

"What sort of business?"

"Not that sort of business."

"How can you and Henry be in the same room without fire-
works?"

"Easy. We grew up."

"Very hard to believe."

"Look. Some of us need a job that pays something," I say a
tad defensively and off-subject. I did not mean to imply that my
sister lives hand to mouth and saves nothing but that's what she
has heard.

"Oh, right. You have to keep that fabulous Manhattan lifestyle going. Yes. Got to get a board of directors seat at the Met.
I forgot."

When she seems to be done ranting I say, "It's just been really
hard with Bruce. Like, crazy-hard, and I think the Henry reentry
program . . ." My voice trails off. "It was just nice to see him again,
that's all."

She remains quiet for a moment before replying.

"Yeah. Does he remember what he did? That filthy dippy-do?"

"We all don't have to hate him forever. I think nine years of
abhorrence is about the correct penalty time."

Carron softens her tone. "Belle, you loved him so much. When
he heart-slammed you, right before Daddy died? You just never
recovered. That girl we all loved? She left. Went right out the door
with Henry. Henry made me lose part of my sister."

Carron's eyes are misting. "Henry made you all hard and busi-
nesslike. All you do is worry and plan and push yourself."

I feel some vile thing rising in my throat, some animal I should swallow back down but instead let it sneak out. "So easy for you to say. Have you ever had to work for anything? Just smile, swivel your genetically blessed hips, and doors open."

I want her to get mad at me, for us to have some sort of confrontation, but that's not what we've ever done in our family, we just sort of take it. We were raised to be stoic; we'd rather swallow the acid of fight than let it out but I've been swallowing so much, it's getting harder to breathe.

"What?" she says. "I worked my ass off to get what I have. It may not look like much, Belle, but it's enough for us. You never seemed to think anything was enough after Henry took off. He changed you. He made you want things you didn't need to want. He put some desire in you to own things, to run things, to be the top, to win. And that makes you miserable and you can't escape from it. I blame Henry for you becoming someone you really don't like and so, no, I certainly don't want to know about him or his stupid life."

"I didn't change after Henry. People don't really ever change," I say softly. "You completely forget that I was always ambitious, that I always wanted big things. Henry just taught me how to get laser-focused."

"I would describe you as getting all man on us." Carron flexes her muscles under her ski jacket, which just looks stupid.

"I got man on you because I'm with a guy who isn't so man, and I work in a place where you only get ahead by manning up. Someone has to be the responsible one."

"Bruce is responsible."

I sigh. "He is. It's just at a different level."

"You just want more than him," she says simply.

"It's not more as in more stuff, it's a more equal sharing of responsibility. It's me bringing home ninety-nine percent of our income and still having to do eighty percent of the non-caregiver kid stuff. It's not the Aston Martin, the driver, or diamonds that I want. I just want real partnership. And yes, I want more from work too because I've followed all the rules for more. And if Bruce were following the husband/father rules he would know that he has to do more than work out and be a decent companion. He should be out there dragging that sled up the hill or helping buy the groceries."

"So you, Isabelle McElroy, are saying that you need help?"

"I don't need help. I need *partnership*. A helper is someone who does favors for you, someone you have to thank all the time. A partner is someone who's in it with you."

Carron interrupts me. "Because if you say you don't need help, why would anyone help you? If help *is* what you need and you ask Bruce for it and he doesn't help, then you have the right to be mad but not before you ask and he says no. 'Cause if you asked, he'd probably say yes."

I roll my eyes at her and move on to the bean section of this produce bonanza, wondering why even my sister doesn't get it.

"So is Henry cheating on that Barbie doll wife of his yet?" Carron asks.

There's nothing like a protective little sister. Her sarcasm makes me feel loved.

"How should I know?" I say, thinking there is no way I'm telling her about the secret apartment. Now it's Carron's turn to roll her eyes at me.

Across the square I notice the glowing lights of an Internet café and for a moment have a pang to check in with Stone. I've given my phone to Bruce to prove my commitment to this vacation endeavor.

Like a junkie seeing her dealer across the square I allow myself to look but not touch. I remind myself I'm in recovery and that

I don't want to have to lie to Bruce should he ask if I've talked to my office. I tell Carron how jumpy it makes me to see those glowing computer screens from outside the café's frosty window. Like a moth to light, I let myself walk over to the doorway and take in the sight of the familiar blue screens, each a potential portal to the financial markets everywhere. I let the shakes of withdrawal wave through me.

Carron reaches for my arm. "We have a connection at home," she says. "Bruce has been using it all day while you ski. I'm pretty sure he's looking for a job, Belle. I think he wants to get something going and then surprise you."

"He's looking for a job?"

"I mean, he's online all the time, so I asked, and that's what he says he's up to. Wants it to be a secret but I thought if you knew, you wouldn't be so mad at him."

I feel something swell in me, something hopeful.

"Anyway, why didn't you just ask to use our computer if you miss work so much? You have to *ask* for what you need."

"Can't, not allowed," I sigh.

"Okay, that's weird."

"It's not weird, it's just that Bruce doesn't think I can do it, thinks I'll spend this week on the phone once I reattach the cord so I'm in some sort of banking detox here and seeing those computers makes me jittery."

"Well, I just think it's weird that the U.S. markets are falling apart and Bruce isn't allowing you to take care of your business. Aren't you the breadwinner? Doesn't that make it his business too?"

"The markets aren't really falling apart. They're just weak."

"I don't really get what you do, but with your company in the *poubelle*, it sounded like you were out of business."

I've had one year of high school French, which is just enough vocabulary to know that *poubelle* means "garbage." Feagin is in the garbage?

"What do you mean about Feagin?" I ask. Who is she to be telling me this?

"Something about them being sold for a buck or something. I don't know. I wasn't really paying attention but I thought you knew. Anyway, you can always get a job with us being a ski guide." She laughs. "You're really pretty good."

"Feagin didn't fall apart. We just have problems with some of the products we've been selling and our stock price is getting slammed."

"No, I meant that thing that happened yesterday."

"Nothing happened yesterday," I say, feeling panicked. "I can't do this mountain girl act for another second." I hand Carron my sack of produce and positively gallop into the café, almost pushing aside a teenager about to sit down.

"*Excusez-moi*," I say.

"American," the kid says, and rolls his eyes.

My fingers tremble as I bring up my work screen in this place that smells like wet wool and smoky coffee. First I see my email in-box containing 2,303 messages. There are alerts for every stock I follow, meaning they've moved at least 5 percent in price and they've all been downward moves. There are countless requests to be present on a company conference call held this morning; it's already over.

I don't even need to find the U.S. financial headlines, because those are the headlines everywhere. I learn that Bear Stearns was saved from bankruptcy by a $2-per-share offer from JPMorgan Chase, down from the $159 they traded at a year ago. They will be sold for less than the value of their worldwide office buildings.

Morgan Stanley and Lehman Brothers stock both closed down 70 percent on the week. Both are rumored to be seeking either buyers or government intervention. Feagin Dixon has stopped trading and is rumored to be purchased by a midwestern bank. My $145-per-share stock looks to open at five dollars.

Banks all over the world are considering the implications for themselves with the inevitable tighter lending and the slowing of growth that will follow. It seems that the time I was so afraid of, that time when everyone came calling at the same time, is right now.

My chest heaves, my fingers shake, and besides the whir of an espresso machine and the clicking of keys, the world around me falls so very silent.

At first my sell orders have limits on them, meaning I will only sell at a certain price. But as thirty minutes of finding no buyers becomes forty-five, I'm crazed to sell at any price. Selling seems the only way to regain control. Nothing in my life is certain anymore and I need to feel something solid like cash in our account. The McElroy account loses columns of numbers with the speed of a spinning roulette wheel. I sell and sell.

My final trade is the sale of a small lot of EBS, that same stock that had rocketed upward for me so many months ago. I sold it below my purchase price despite how promising their cancer therapies appeared. I sell and sell like I'm ridding myself of toxins and washing myself clean.

Carron went home to make dinner for the crew. The moon rose over the picture-perfect mountains. The café fills with beautiful, athletic people who seem to have no worries. Seeing them reminds me of that time in my life, back when I was the more confident me that Carron had been speaking of.

I hope Bruce will understand what I've just done, that I've sold everything because I needed to know we still have something solid in our accounts. Then I'll tell him we have to make *us* solid again too.

Hours later I walk back to my sister's cabin on a winding road, ice and shale crunching under my feet. The stars are so bright I can't take my eyes from them. Maybe it is the clean air or the fact I know my children are happy and safe somewhere, but an odd calm that closely shoulders the feeling of happiness comes upon me. Being fearful that a terrible thing is about to happen can be worse than when it actually happens. I like having a solid number in the bank, even though it is less than I thought it would be, and I like having three healthy kids and a semidecent husband who, while not perfect, loves their little souls as much as I do. Yes, tonight I feel hopeful.

Bruce spent the rest of the vacation broody and silent. He became the one who watched the panic in U.S. markets. When I tried to calm him by saying the government would probably backstop bad loans in some of these banks, making them easier to sell and calming investors, he would spit things at me such as:

"My United States will not throw taxpayer money to help out a bunch of rich people."

So I stayed away from his anger by keeping quiet and avoiding the news. Bruce begged me to call into Feagin Dixon and touch base with my clients but I had nothing to say. Any news was on television and I didn't need to call in to gossip. I was mad at a small band of men who destroyed the place with greed, bad behavior, and testosterone-fueled decisions but that bank wasn't mine anymore. I stayed on the sidelines of a different continent and felt remarkably unafraid.

Ten days later as we waited to board our plane back to New York, it was Bruce who told me that Bear had sold to JPMorgan Chase for $10 per share and that Feagin was rumored to be taking a similarly low bid. Instead of my stock being worth $145/share, Manchester Bancorp offered us $7 and Gruss, who had apparently been difficult to locate in the days of this disaster, would be forced to accept.

I felt dizzy walking down the jetway, overwhelmed by the fortune change and yet slightly excited to be getting home. I was carrying Owen, who smelled like the sunshine he'd been playing in. Kevin was proudly wheeling a bag of books, blankets, and sippy cups and leading us in a way I hadn't witnessed before. Brigid had one loving hand in the back pocket of my jeans and I was starting to think about all the things I could do, the possibilities that come along with change. We had everything good ahead of us if only Bruce could see that.

CHAPTER 37

Trade This

I T'S BEEN three months since our trip to France and everything has changed. I'm married to a guy in search of six-pack
abdominals and social media recognition. Bruce occupies himself
with many hours at a gym, followed by checking in with his new
Central Park mommy friends, who now seem to include him in
everything. While his buff factor continues to grow, any moves he
was making toward getting a job seem to be shelved while he trolls
online to reconnect to people he remembers from high school.
Countless times he mentions to me that people he thought were
less than him—less smart, less connected, less athletic—now inexplicably run some part of a company. I refrain from telling him
that's what happens. People take the low-rung job, they stay with
it, they sometimes find success as they get older. That's what can
happen when people get a job. But to him, seeing his happy, successful former peer group now on Facebook has made him wave
some white flag of surrender on the career front. Fitness and good
looks are the field where he can eat their proverbial lunch. Ac-

cording to him, everyone's looking old and fat. His saggy sweats of six months ago have been traded for slim-cut straight pants, tailored blazers, and Chuck Taylors on his feet. He showed up once for breakfast wearing black Lycra and I told him I'm drawing the line for soon-to-be-middle-aged men everywhere: no Lycra. But overall he seems almost euphoric. Maybe he's happier that rich people finally had it handed to them.

While his 9 p.m. yoga sessions continue to ensure we've embraced the celibate life, neither of us addresses this. Instead, I suggested he become a trainer or find a way to link his fitness enthusiasm to gainful employment, but he smirked. He was fine hiring a trainer but becoming one was not for him, and oh, can I please use his phone to take a photo of him flexing?

He's also using his ample free time trying to make our kids smarter. He's been subjecting them to bizarre and trendy education methods that one of the moms told him about. In the last months, he has purchased crates of stuff that promise to create superhumans. He sets up intricate living room obstacle courses to elevate the McElroy gross motor skills to Olympic levels, and has some flash card system that promises to get Owen to miraculously read. All I've witnessed from this endeavor is Owen folding up the cards or drawing on them. I'm no expert but I'd bet that reading before a kid knows his letters is unlikely and that my husband has purchased snake oil, but I dare not whisper this to anyone. Bruce has so little going on that a patronizing comment from me won't help. I keep my thoughts to myself and soothe myself with the knowledge that my husband is at least spending time with his kids.

I find myself relaying this state of affairs on a warm July day to what's left of the former GCC. The few management strategy meetings I was included in have stopped, so we're all directionless. Still, we work as we wait for more shoes to fall and for more of us to get fired. There are only a few people from my row left: Amy,

Amanda, Marcus, and myself, while Violette, Alice, Stone, and most others have been let go. There's so little banking business that Manchester Bank has cut about 60 percent of our employees since April. Violette is looking for a job, and Alice is trying to start a family. I'd been thinking about our GCC conversations about fairness, but they now seem beside the point and I mention this to the people I'm sitting with.

"Boy, were we strategizing about the wrong stuff," Amanda says.

"Not really," I say. I still believe a few women on the risk committee and we never would have had so many worthless bonds in our portfolio. Gruss just wouldn't listen."

"He was just responding to shareholders," says Ballsbridge. "If our growth rate is less than other banks our stock gets hammered."

"Yeah, it's not like that happened." I laugh, thinking of the $7/share price. "After that meeting with Gruss you ladies left me twisting in the wind," I mention.

"It was like we all gave up at once," Amy says.

"I didn't give up. I was just starting," I say. "And you tossed me under the bus after my meeting with Gruss."

"We should apologize," Amanda says. "It wasn't some organized group decision to disband like that. It was just our frustration, realizing nothing will ever change here."

"Except everything," Marcus says, looking at the few people on the trading floor. He loves that we include him when we chat. "Not to sound like an obnoxious oaf, but is it possible that some careers are just not compatible with a balanced life?"

I'd been thinking the same thing and wondering if Kathryn Peterson was the only one who had this figured out all along. Still, I don't believe it. Feagin would never have gone out of business if women were at the top. We just don't have testosterone helping us along the path of decisions. We are happy with base hits and don't need to swing for the fences if it's too risky.

We toast Amy's recent promotion to managing director at Manchester with some apple juice from the vending machine. I'm thrilled that she's going to join me at director meetings and yet I'm surprised that she's succeeded in doing this at such a tough time. With the meltdown of the stock market and everyone's business being in the tank, no one is thinking about things like promotions. Any thoughts I used to have of being made partner are gone. If it didn't happen after my stellar year of production last year, it would never happen, and while I'm happy for Amy, I'm also very curious. I think about her largest accounts and biggest trades and the minimum amount of revenue one has to bring in to move upward. I know Amy's accounts and I can't figure how she did it.

Amy asks me how Bruce's work is going and I tell her that he's primarily employed in childcare, yoga, and cycling, so we still need both my income and a nanny. I tell her Bruce and Caregiver make a good team and she leans forward, concerned.

"How good a team?" she asks, turning her lightly lined face toward me. Today she is wearing some short, funky dress, plunging at the neckline and ending mid-thigh, an expensive-looking vision that fell off a high-end fashion runway, not something I'd pick for a woman usually in tailored suits. I wonder if our change in fortune is making us all a little less inhibited.

"Not like that," I sigh to her. "Bruce is not like the men we work with."

"What does she look like?" she continues.

"Caregiver? Um, petite, dark, cute, sort of Hispanic-looking. She's taking a break from college."

"Hasn't she been with you for years?"

"Yeah, um, three."

"That's quite a college break," Amy says, not believing for a moment that a man can be left alone with a young woman without things heading below the waist. Her wandering spouse has scarred her. I still can't make these women believe that Bruce just doesn't stray. The women of the GCC don't have men like my man and for a moment I have a twang of love for him even though nothing between us feels right.

"So, the dress?" I ask, nodding to the sexy thing she has going on today.

"Catching a Jitney," she says, referring to the bus service that runs between New York City and the Hamptons. "No private car service out there for me. Spending five hundred dollars a weekend is something I don't do anymore."

"That dress was more than five hundred dollars."

"Four hundred twenty dollars on sale. It's like take a bus instead of a car service? Get a free dress."

"But you're a managing director!" Amanda said. "Why should you care if you buy your clothes on sale? Why not take the dress *and* the car service?"

"Not sure how long this market will last." Amy smirked. "You seem to forget that I'm the last girl at this party and everything's been picked over, but yeah, happy to be a managing director."

I knew Amy had lost her Hamptons house in the divorce but she doesn't seem too bothered. She's just happy for some recognition.

"You bought a new house?" I ask her.

"Rental. Sort of," she says. "Like a house share."

"House share?" I ask, thinking of the boisterous party houses of our youth. "Aren't you, like, thirty-five or something?"

"Yes, er, thirty-six. And most of my housemates are in their forties. So fun to be the young kid again. We're having a party this weekend and you should come. No kids." She smirks. "Kids, ewww."

"Yeah. Maybe. I'll just drop them on the beach and hope for the best," I say sarcastically.

"She'll never come," Amanda says.

"It's complicated for us," I say, thinking of the logistics and also thinking it could be fun. "It's hard to find a sitter in the Hamptons. Ours is not an easy gig, three young kids all whining at the same moment. There's no employment line outside my door."

I'm surprised again by my openness; I never speak of my domestic situation in front of colleagues.

"Please try," Amy says, positively glowing at me. "I really want you to come."

And for some reason I agree to try.

That night, I mention Amy's party to Bruce. There's no atmosphere my party-loving husband adores more than kegs of beer on tap, great music, and tanned ladies in cotton hoodies over short shorts. There's nothing he likes less than the life he grew up with: overprocessed hair, Lilly Pulitzer clothes, real jewelry at the beach, and champagne with rose petals in it. I have no idea which end of the spectrum Amy's party will be on and I tell him it's probably somewhere in the middle but still, he says we should go.

I wrangle two high school students to watch our kids for a few hours on Saturday night. I promise myself to be as perfect to Bruce as possible, as close to the person who fell in love with Bruce years ago as I can be. I want to feel something tonight. I will laugh at his jokes, not mention kids, not allude to work or how much money I'm not bringing home anymore.

For the past seven years we've been renting an older, aluminum-sided house on the side of the highway away from the ocean. We're pretty distant from the happening parts of Southampton and live among year-round residents. We have a yard that rolls down to a freshwater lake so we have no need for a swimming pool. Our lawn is brown for most of the summer and the few flowers that manage to bloom get eaten by deer the very day they do. When summers get rainy, moss creeps into the kitchen and up the walls and the place takes on an earthy smell, the smell of nuts and life and something that reminds me of tea. We call our house the Tea Bag.

As the people I worked with became rich, the Tea Bag House no longer felt like a place to invite them to. Many of them purchased palatial places on the other side of the highway, shingled, classic homes with quickly assembled interiors of wood and stone, soaring ceilings, and powerful air-conditioning systems that assure a constant seventy-two degrees. Their homes have names, painted on quaint wooden boards, posted on their automatic gate systems, names like Swann's Way, Aspen East, or Meadowmere. We could have afforded the same if we hadn't been saving for the suburban escape hatch. Anyway, we liked our old Tea Bag House.

As we drive over to Amy's house share, I again get that almost-feeling of happy, the same feeling I got after selling most of our stock at that French Internet café.

We turn in to the estate section where the homes hug the ocean. Several of their owners are people I've either worked with or been on deals for IPOs with. I challenge myself to see if I remember who lives where and I point the homes out to Bruce. "Linda Wachner from Warnaco, the clothing company. Calvin Klein, designer, what a gorgeous house. John Paulson in that one, he's a hedge fund manager, was short the market in this latest crash and made a billion with a *b*. George Soros, who is George Soros, Howard Stern, that radio guy, Bob 'SFX Entertainment' Sillerman, Lloyd Blankfein, CEO of Goldman Sachs. Tory Burch designs clothes, and King McPherson is somewhere along here too." I was pretty pleased with myself for being able to speak as fast as Bruce was driving.

"You should man a tour bus" was all Bruce said.

I glance at the even number of Amy's address, which surprises me. The evens are the ocean side, not the bay. No house sells for less than $25 million on the ocean side. What sort of multi-gazillionaire rents his house out to be shared? We turn in to a graveled drive and a valet parker takes our car from us. Embarrassed, I chuck the Happy Meal toys stuck between the front seats into the back before I hand him my keys. I glance at poor Bruce in his surfer hoodie and Quiksilver shorts and compare his dress code to the white-jacketed waiters with trays of drinks standing at attention beside golf carts, ready to whisk us up the hundred yards to the starkly modern estate we can see from the bottom of the driveway. I sigh for Bruce. I married a regular guy who unstuck himself from the pretentious family he grew up with only to find himself in that world again. I think he just wants to have some fun and look where I've brought him.

"Well, you look nice," he says generously as he smirks.

I'm wearing a simple cotton shift with a belt so tight I think it belongs to Kevin. At least it's colorful.

"We don't have to go," I say.

"I don't give a shit if your friend doesn't know how to have fun. I'm happy to drink her beer." He laughs in a crazy, unattractive way.

I look over at him, standing in his self-righteous, smirking slouch, and see something in Bruce I have never seen before. Bruce thinks he is better than all of us. The entitled way he was raised is still in his DNA. He thinks he is doing me a favor by even being here. All this time I was worried about hurting his confidence when really, he was quite certain that working for anyone was beneath him, that maybe even having kids with me was beneath him. It is the first time I feel something bordering hatred for him.

Our golf cart pulls up close and the driver indicates for us to get in. I need to let Bruce's words simmer to not get mad and ruin the night.

"I'm as surprised as you, Bruce. Maybe it's the people she shares this house with. Maybe one of them is really wealthy and just likes having people around." My voice is steady.

"Let's give this ten minutes, tops," he says, and I nod because that's what I need to do to keep from punching him. I'll do whatever it takes for us to make it through this evening, but my new realization is shaking my world. My husband is an arrogant, self-involved ass.

When we get to the golf cart, a uniformed waiter comes over to make sure we don't get too thirsty from the bottom of the driveway to the house. He offers us some rosé champagne. I take one and, still standing, empty the contents in two suffocating gulps. Bruce passes on his so I take his and gulp that too. I put both empty glasses back on the tray. The waiter looks impressed with me as I turn back to the cart.

"Let's go," I say to the driver, jumping in the seat next to him and not beside Bruce.

Bruce sees him cradling a walkie-talkie. "I need you to pre-order me a cold one, man," he says like some demanding toddler in the backseat. "Tell them you have a desperate guest." He does this while he texts on his phone, as if he has something important to take care of.

The driver doesn't even crack a smile. He lifts the walkie-talkie, eyes on the road, and inquires about the type of beer being served. A voice on the other end relays the fact that while it's a top-shelf bar, Mr. McPherson isn't serving beer tonight. Bruce digests the beer part of this answer while I digest the name part. McPherson? King? Amy is in a house share with King and his family? Kevin's belt seems to be strangling my middle.

The cart stops at the perfect place to inhale the ocean's magnificence and the modern art sculptures. The statue on the front lawn appears to be a bodacious woman holding a giant earth on her head. She's made of shiny metal.

"Looks like you," says Bruce, and I can't answer him nor pull my eyes away from Amy. My world is upside down and I'm being sliced in two by a belt I borrowed from my eight-year-old. Boy.

Amy stands in a floor-length maxi dress that makes her look like some dewy-eyed trophy wife instead of the smart, brash managing director she is. King stands next to her, hand on her ass, greeting a guy I recognize as the latest Internet bazillionaire in caveman fashion. They chest-bump. Two middle-aged white men chest-bumping just looks stupid and I hear Bruce snort under his breath. Amy sees me and waves and I can't figure out how to get myself out of the cart and up those few steps. I hate being bulldozed. I never saw this coming.

Amy breaks from King's grip and comes over to Bruce and me. We appear to be two random people removed from the beach and placed here as a joke. She plants a kiss on my cheek and giggles through her whisper.

"There are several ways to get ahead, girlfriend. Welcome to our coming-out party."

CHAPTER 38

Better Offer

B Y SEPTEMBER, Amy is living with King and he has left his family behind, like a shoe style he tired of. Amy has no intention of marrying him; she's just enjoying the elevation of her career, the changed status of her social life, and King's intense attraction to a woman with no domestic ambition. She will not be begging him for babies. Marcus informs me that Amy is capable of pole dance–worthy gymnastics in the bedroom and though King is almost twelve years her senior, he manages to keep up with her through pharmaceutical encouragement. There may be fewer of us but still we have no secrets.

I remember the holiday party, nine months ago, when Amy was appalled by the women flirting at bonus time in the hopes of a bigger paycheck. It's hard to recognize her at the moment.

I mention this vignette to Marcus, who shrugs and says, "She wasn't beating them so she joined them. Where's the surprise in that?" He seems defeated these days. Besides taking a terrible financial hit from the markets, he's also contending with a harassment charge launched by Naked Girl. She was going to be one of the fired employees, one that Manchester realized they didn't need, so she beat them to it by plopping harassment charges into the human resources in-box and leaving. Naked Girl maintains she was not promoted because she was having sex with him, that Marcus held her non-career back in order to maintain control over her as his girlfriend. My stomach churns when I hear of women like Tiffany who never had much career ambition yet opportunistically yank the inequity card.

The purchase of Bear Stearns by JPMorgan Chase closed in June but it will be early 2010 before their trading platforms are fully merged. Manchester will take a full year to merge with us. Like the Bear employees, we too sit in isolation where remnants of fired employees—family photos, deal mementos, and the bulletin board of chopped Hermès ties (whenever a huge trade was executed, the trader would be tackled, held down while someone chopped his tie off before pinning it to the board) now look like roadside grave markers. What happened to my career is a question that jumps out at me each day when I lean against or sit at the desk of someone who used to work here but has since vaporized.

Without the anxiety of selling mortgages, my job has gotten easier. I look at balance sheets with real numbers on them of companies I believe in. The clients I have left are nice to me, and our trades are more long-term ideas we both want to see grow. Cheetah Global has begun trading with me as a Manchester Bank employee but at a fraction of the volume we once created. Henry has promoted a woman named Ariane Thanik to do much of his work and she has negated the need for Henry and me to speak. He called me once, just to tell me that he would no longer be the daily contact for investment banks, that Ariane would be that person who made more of the trading decisions for Cheetah. He told me that because of our Glass Ceiling Club discussions he specifically wanted a woman for the job. It wasn't because he felt an inequity he wanted to address, but rather because he agreed a woman could be more levelheaded, risk-averse, and representative of fifty percent of the population. Henry was being groomed to take over for Tim and would eventually run all of Cheetah. He never mentioned our terrible time in that apartment.

I felt a thrill for Henry, a genuine happiness for someone I used to care about. I missed the mental challenge of him forcing me to learn new things but I would find that somewhere else. Whenever I feel a wave of sadness about our really not knowing each other for the rest of our lives, I smack it down and wait for the healing power of time to wipe it away. A few times I wanted to reach for the phone just to update him on everything: the end of Feagin Dixon as we knew it, the evaporating markets, the scattering of GCC—but it just isn't possible. We had been something else that existed in a different place and time.

My only real professional friendship, if one could call it that, is with Kathryn Peterson. Kathryn was made a partner at Manchester Bank. These days she is Kathryn's version of happy, which looks a lot like Kathryn's version of unhappy, but I have a sense of her now, and there's a sincerity about her that I like.

Visiting with her is like a trip to the could-have-been-me museum. Kathryn is wealthier than me in the bank account but empty in everything else. I visit her at her trading turret almost daily, to get a sense of which toxic positions are left and what we're doing to get ourselves out of them. Nobody wants to buy the bonds we hold in inventory. Each night we mark the stuff to market, meaning we pick a shot-in-the-dark value of what it's worth and every day, with no buyers in sight, it becomes worth less. Manchester stock trades down accordingly, day after day. The McElroy net worth is less than it was three years ago and I sometimes imagine all the time I could have been with my children, been with Bruce, instead of my sleep-deprived, overeating, overdrinking, almost celibate lifestyle. To end up with this much in the bank, I could've done real things and still had a job, just a regular type of job.

On September 10 I went upstairs to speak with Kathryn when CNN announced that Lehman reported a $3.9 billion loss and was selling a majority stake in their investment management business. I sighed with relief, expecting the stock to rebound. It slid 7 percent. I wondered when this thing would find a bottom. The former CFO of the bank, Erin Callan, possibly the most senior woman on Wall Street, was asked to step down in June and she did. Now every discussion about the company comes from the CEO himself, Dick Fuld.

On September 13 I sat with Kathryn to listen to Tim Geithner, the president of the Federal Reserve Bank of New York, make a televised announcement. Tim admitted we were looking at a possible emergency liquidation of Lehman assets. All the financial stocks traded off again, lower than I ever thought possible. On September 15, before the market opened, Dick Fuld told the world that Lehman Brothers was filing for bankruptcy protection. Chapter 11. The market dropped over five hundred points, the most since September 11, 2001. It dropped like the world had lost its floor and I filled sell orders like a concession stand attendant filling orders for French fries.

My daily visits to Kathryn become therapy sessions, knowing that as long as one of us doesn't crack, we both are okay. On September 20, there are rumors now of Korean buyers willing to buy portions of the ailing banks, there are southern banks rumored to be stepping up too. The discount window is open from the Fed, meaning investment banks can now borrow money from the government. Feagin Dixon wouldn't have fallen had we been allowed to do this but even with this change of law, nothing seems to calm the markets.

On September 29, the market is plunging and I visit Kathryn because she isn't as rattled as the other people on my floor. She isn't throwing phones or punching screens or swearing about horses' backsides. She is staring at her screen and watching everything turn red, and the only thing turning green is the price of gold. Investors are running for anything safe, safer than stocks or bonds or the U.S. dollar, and that's why only gold is trading up.

I notice Australian currencies swing higher and I smile and think of Henry and how he was buying everything Aussie six months ago. Henry is so sad and so rich.

Without looking at me Kathryn keeps typing and starts talking.

"I like you well enough, Isabelle," she says. "And you know I'm not interested in being part of movements or change or anything like that and I'm sorry I didn't help you and your friends out."

I let out a short laugh. "Yes, well that didn't go as planned," I say. "You know those venture capital firms are the same; the technology start-ups are the same. Anywhere the culture is loose and lucrative, the same thing exists. Maybe our mistake was thinking Wall Street was unique when it comes to the advancement of women." I can't believe I've quoted the things Elizabeth said to me at brunch eight months ago.

She doesn't seem to hear me. "And I like you well enough to not allow you to be made a fool of."

"Kathryn. It's not a problem. The guys don't bother me and I'm done with thinking I'm going to be a partner here. I see things for what they are now. Don't you worry about me." I wink.

Kathryn lifts an eyebrow and turns back to her turret. "You see, that's what's so maddening to me. You're too nice. You just don't see people for who they are. People like you get taken advantage of."

"I don't feel taken advantage of, I just wanted a fair shake, but a lot of life is luck. Maybe at a different bank, things would have been different for me," I say with no enthusiasm.

Kathryn seems glazed, like she isn't even listening.

"You aren't hearing me. This isn't about Feagin Dixon, it's about your husband, Bruce. He's no good."

I watch her expertly manicured, not pink, not beige, not white fingernails stop tapping on her keyboard. I watch as she takes one of those hands that the fingers are on and she places it on my thigh. I stare at the hand like it's some repulsive insect.

"You have no right to speak of someone you don't know like that," I say crisply. She's never even met Bruce.

Then she places both hands on either arm of my chair and swings me to look right at her. I don't think I've ever made full-on eye contact with her. It's unnerving.

"He cheats on you, does yoga with someone I know and has sex with her."

When I look at her it's as if some ugly reptile has attached itself to her tongue. Everything I thought about her was wrong. Kathryn is certifiable.

"You do not know my husband. He may not have a great job and maybe your yogi friend sees him at the gym, but he is not a cheater. And besides, I'm your only real friend. Bitch."

She looks startled. I look startled. Whose words are coming out of my mouth?

Kathryn wants to try again.

"How do I put this? He's into tantric. Some of my yoga associates practice this with a partner, and the extended sexual revelation is intense. He's partnered with a friend of mine, someone he met at a baby playdate at your apartment. He spends money on her, little stuff—bicycles, hotel rooms, and private coaching. But I'm bothered by this for you because I wasn't sure you knew and you seem like the kind of person who wants the full picture. You're the one making the money. You've been all in at this place, and all in with your family. I just thought you should know."

"Tantric what? Don't you think if my husband were into anything beyond laundry and chicken nuggets I'd know about it? It's not like he's going to an office every day. He's home."

"Not at nine p.m. he's not."

"Because it's a yoga relaxation class. It helps him sleep."

"But my friend—"

"What friend of yours? You don't have friends. You have people you pay to be nice to you, to try and keep you on this side of sane. I had no idea you were such a calculating bullshitter to say something so hurtful to me. Do I intimidate you? Is this some psycho head game of yours? Are you worried Manchester Bank will assign Cheetah to just me? Is that what this is about?" I say, while a part of my brain begins listing the clues; Bruce's constant texting, his new love of social media, him being online during vacation, and his obsession with his body. He checked every cliché box, and I never even noticed.

Kathryn is silent and puts her hands to her sides. "People who enjoy tantric sex as part of their yoga practice don't always consider it cheating. They justify it because of the revealing nature of the practice. To truly achieve enlightenment and extended sexual pleasure the mind has to be so centered and yet adrift. It's like tripping on drugs except there are no drugs save for the limits of your own mind."

I let this garbled woo woo language swirl around for a full ten seconds before I respond, "What the WHAT???"

Nothing I can say right now will make sense and I feel jittery and sick to my stomach, like one of those ticker symbols in front of me, blinking around in value, not knowing which direction to trade. I'm living in a world where everything and everybody in it is make-believe.

CHAPTER 39

Dead Cat Bounce

T HE CHINESE consider the number 7 to be lucky. I'm
staring at my illuminated screen, black background, everything else red, like spilt blood. My screen is full of 7s and
none of them are lucky. The Dow has lost 777 points, or over 7
percent of its value in one day, one terrible day, this terrible day.
Bruce and I have been married for nine years and my husband
evidently has a seven-year itch.

I search the Internet for tantric yoga enlightenment and I learn
that it's wonderful for channeling the mind/body/spirit connection and leads to improved sexual health. With the sex Bruce
and I haven't been having he certainly isn't getting much home-
tutoring. My mind whirls and I read on. Tantric yoga is great
for people who have lost their soul connection in the mundane
world. What the hell? Belle McElroy is apparently the mundane
world that my husband suffers within.

I imagine Bruce being stretched into fantastic positions by
what I picture to be a lithe, tattooed young mom he met in my

living room, the living room that I paid for, that came with the apartment that I bought.

I know that the first step of grief is denial. Why am I not denying this news? How do I know that Kathryn is right? Maybe the denial stage was the constant throb I've had in the back of my head for months. Maybe it started in that golf cart in Southampton where it was apparent that everything between us was wrong. Why have I always defended Bruce and his non-contributing life?

I think about how easy it's been for Bruce to sit back and justify his low efforts while getting to point a finger at the wife who does everything for him, who enables each new idea that pops into his head, and who gives him the chance to navel-gaze and decide he isn't being sexually fulfilled. How simplistic for him to get to pretend I'm a bad person because I work on what he considers the evil Wall Street.

People began packing to leave for the day, wiped out by the markets. I want to plead to any of them, these Dicks of the Dais, women of Glass Ceilings, to stay with me, to please, please stay and hold me close in this terrible time. Don't leave me alone on this giant floor of this broken-down company.

I've been watching people file out one by one, to be with their own families, to be comforted by someone else, people willing to love them, flaws and all. I wonder how welcome they'll all be now that they're worth so much less money? I think of how Bruce enjoyed dropping $20 tips for $5 beers with the wink of "plenty more where that came from" to assorted waitresses. I thought he was just generous. Part of me had applauded Bruce and the way he acted, but really, he was mocking me. Maybe when he acted supportive of me on a big trade, he was also clapping himself on the back for his choice of mate and her ability to sow and reap while he performed sun salutations.

By 11 p.m. there are only three humans left on the trading

floor, three men I hardly know who work in the risk arbitration department.

I should call a friend right now, a Carron or an Elizabeth. What do regular people do at times like this? I've had bad things happen to me before but I always fixed things on my own. I'm a fixer, I remind myself, and I need to resolve this. But I don't know where to start and I catch myself for one weak moment wishing I could call Henry.

I want to see my kids right now but I'm not going home. I'm afraid of what I'll say. I have to be sure of the outcome I want before I enter a room with Bruce in it. If I get sidetracked with drama and tears and rebuttals, I'll lose the resolve that has brought me to the decision that I have already made. It's interesting that Bruce hasn't called once today. He doesn't miss anything about me.

The three "arb" guys stand, ashen-faced. I guess the weak markets made them go long, buy stocks on weakness, expecting them to rebound quickly for a profit. Had they done that in recent days, their clocks would have been cleaned. There are no buyers out there at any price, so they watched their positions sink, Titanic-like, while they smashed things on their desks. Their faces tell me that entire story.

The last one of them to leave looks across at me. I pretend to be engrossed in my screen of 7s.

"Isabelle?" he asks.

I used to love when coworkers, men I didn't know at all, knew of me just by reputation, but not tonight. He's a midsized, athletic man, gray at the temples, and I don't remember ever seeing him.

"Yes?" I answer with a frog noise blocking the usual sound of my voice.

He walks over to me and stands behind my screen, looking over my shoulder at the nothingness in front of me.

"Belle," he says again, "you look like you need a drink. Want to get a drink?"

He appears to need one terribly, and I know I should try to be friendly. If I had a drink with him I might possibly tell him, this stranger, everything.

"Thanks," I say gratefully. "But no. Need to be getting home."

"Maybe we should both go home and face the music," he says.

He believes my problem is the worst stock market since the Great Depression. People recovered from that.

"Need to go make a home," I say, knowing it will mean nothing to him, but oddly it gives me some comfort.

CHAPTER 40

Yield

M Y LAST DAY at Feagin ended in a blue-collar town in New Jersey in the arms of a large Hispanic man.

I was on a business trip, seeing clients in Trenton and Princeton and then, in a crazed attempt to make it home in time for dinner, I took the New Jersey Turnpike. Like some teenager in her rich-girl convertible, I wove in and out of HOV lanes I didn't belong in, desperate to pick the kids up from Bruce's new one-bedroom apartment, a place of glass and chrome that screams bachelor to all who enter. Bruce took none of the trappings of little kids with him. Besides some nice pieces of furniture he took nothing except half my money and a sizeable portion of my gut. We're all new to this split-custody lifestyle and to me it feels like an unending game of make-believe, as if we're playacting in someone else's uncomfortable drama. Nothing feels routine or natural yet.

The markets have rebounded some, but loans to businesses

and individuals have dried up. The only trades I was having were sells and some value buyers tucking blue-chip names into young investors' accounts, people who would see this thing through for the long haul.

Since Bruce and I separated, I've had a vicious need to be with my children. World markets imploding and deals being canceled make no impression on me. I just need the people who need me. The apartment seemed suffocating in Bruce's absence and I have taken to leaving windows open all the time, exorcising some virus that infected our world. I put the thing up for sale in the weakest real estate market in a decade and haven't gotten the slightest sniff of interest from anyone. The playground and the Tea Bag House in Southampton are the only places where things feel right to me and I keep wondering about the public school system out there on Long Island and how my kids would fare in a world not artificially partitioned by money.

Each night I scan my children's faces for some sign of distress. I've oversensitized myself to the point where I consider every instance of lethargy or aggression to be some fallout from our lousy parenting. I never stay at work past 6 p.m. and I no longer entertain. Work has become simply a means to a paycheck and the paycheck is just to cover the day-to-day expenses for this unhappy existence. That evening in New Jersey where everything changed yet again, I was just a harried worker, needing to get home to her kids.

I was about halfway home when I stopped in Rutherford, New Jersey. I needed a bathroom so badly and couldn't make it all the way home. I took an exit and entered a town of old brick buildings where the businesses had names like Luigi's and Carmine's though everyone appeared to be Hispanic. I saw a Burger King, home of the easily accessible toilet. I jumped out of my rented

Ford Taurus, locked the doors, and went into the stall with toilet water chemically coaxed to purple. I placed the keys on top of the toilet paper holder, that shelf too small to hold a purse but large enough to be in the way of getting to the paper. But in a rushed attempt to get out of the stall and back to the turnpike, I swung to hit the flusher with my foot. My size-10½ pointy-toed boot caught the Hertz key ring in just the right place and knocked the keys into the toilet, where they splashed the second I pushed my foot against the flusher. While I tried to tell myself that I hadn't actually done what I did, I waited in vain for them to appear at the bottom of the toilet as the water settled. I pleaded with invisible forces to reverse the actions of those last two seconds while I suppose the swirling vortex of keys headed speedily on their way to some wastewater treatment plant in New Jersey. I was instantly a transportationless, frantic, pathetic mother who couldn't manage to get home to pick her children up from their father's one-bedroom sex pad because she flushed her Ford Taurus keys down the toilet.

I stood motionless in the locked stall, and I begged for a do-over. In fact I demanded a big do-over, a many-years, many-choices do-over and I wanted it to begin right away. I had always been the good girl, the cooperative one, the girl who didn't party too much or get facial tattoos or sleep with strangers. I was the one who answered the teacher's questions, who did her homework, who opted to rise early and work late after everyone else left. Shouldn't it be guaranteed for that girl to not have her life turn out like this? Isn't there a pact with some sacred being, a deal with the angels? I didn't realize I was actually pounding on the metal wall that separated my stall from the one next to me. I didn't realize I was moaning in some guttural, frightening way that would send little girls running for their mommies. I also don't know how long it went on.

Some man was sent in to save me from myself though I could hardly see him through my tears. I caught sight of something paper and golden on his head that appeared to be some sort of crown. I think he was the King of Burgers, and somehow he got assigned to the lunatic in the ladies' room. He was a nice man, large and Spanish-speaking. I know enough Spanish to understand the word *loca*, spoken into a radio receiver. He was telling people this white lady in an expensive suit was nuts. He put his large, brown arms around me in an effort to contain me but I interpreted this as his desire to hug me. I hugged him right back, with a force that I'm sure surprised him. I couldn't hold tightly enough to his thick middle that smelled like French fries. My ferocious grip caused his crown to fall into the toilet but I didn't let go, wouldn't let go of this adult-sized human who felt strong and supportive and in charge of something, even if it was security at the Rutherford Burger King.

Eventually my heart, which had been racing, slowed. I heard people come and go, turning on water, pushing on hand dryers, sighing at us just standing there in our open second stall. Another man came to the door to ask if he was okay and he said, "*No problema.*"

I pushed back enough to read the name tag on the man's shirt. "Leonardo," it read. He winced and adjusted the tag and only then did I realize it had opened and I'd been stabbing him with the pin. He even had droplets of blood forming on his mustard-yellow shirt.

"*Lo siento,*" I said, reaching for toilet paper to dab at his wound.

He shook his head and squeezed my shoulders and said, "You're okay." It wasn't a question. It was a statement.

I thought about my next move, about how I should call Hertz

or call a locksmith. I thought of the fact it was now 6 p.m. and that Friday evening at 6 p.m. in New Jersey is probably a time that all locksmiths and all Hertz car rental agents have universally agreed to go home. It's the time that no human should ever do something stupid.

I went into the dining area and sat in a Formica booth watching some soccer team scarf down food and grab fries from each other's pile, chattering over each other's words. I could see Leonardo playing some sort of Simon Says game with a group of kids inside a glassed-in room. It seemed everyone around me was speaking but I couldn't understand anyone's words.

I rose and went outside to find the wind had picked up on this early spring evening. I peered in the car window and took inventory of what was inside: my work computer, packets of deal material for an IPO, an HP calculator, and a cold cup of coffee. Then I looked at what I had with me outside the car: my wallet and my phone. Really I had everything I needed. A police car pulled into the parking lot and I thought about asking them to jimmy open the door but everything in my car appeared to be so bulky, so heavy, my car was full of quicksand. Instead I asked them if there was a bus to New York City.

The young officers looked curiously at my suit and boots not designed for walking, but they pointed and said it's about three miles from there and that was good enough for me. The road rose about one hundred yards away from that Burger King and I stopped for a moment to look back at the car and all I was leaving behind. The hill offered just enough pitch for me to catch the final moment of daylight reflecting off the darkened Taurus's window. It was there I said good-bye to the Glass Ceiling Club, which, while well-meaning, represented nothing in the end, good-bye to obsessing about Bruce screwing his flexible friend, good-bye to that white car with its load of papers and the suck of the money inside it. I said good-bye to it all on a hill in New Jersey as a last flash of sunlight hit the driver's window at just the right angle. For a moment I could have sworn I saw that car wink right back at me.

CHAPTER 41

Rational Exuberance

September 2015

THE GLASS DOORS of our offices at Arbella Financial are propped open, letting the spring ocean breeze fill the trading room. If it weren't littered with LCD screens, the place would look like some trendy downtown showroom, rather than a boutique investment bank. Colorful boxes, all framed in white plastic, contain the few papers we deal with each day. Amy designed and Bruce built out the trading turrets. As a single man he's become a fantastically talented carpenter and the result is stunningly beautiful.

Once you grab your egg crate of possessions each morning, you pick your favorite colored cushion and go find yourself a seat—not unlike a preschool class where each kid chooses her circle spot. We make ourselves sit next to someone different each day, to help us share ideas and to avoid planting the seeds of clique-gossip that exists in most offices. Our mission is far too important to play the games of the past years.

We have a Ping-Pong room, which makes us look like a hip technology start-up, which we are not. We aren't very cool and we haven't overextended our adolescence; we have a playroom because we have kids. We are a boutique investment firm, predominately run by women. While we have a tiny office in Manhattan to make us seem more legitimate, our headquarters are here in Hampton Bays, New York, about two miles from the Atlantic Ocean and ninety miles from New York City. It's a town with simple ranch houses and no celebrity visits. A yellow school bus stops outside our door each afternoon and deposits five of my employees' children, plus my three, whom I now get to see while a bit of sunlight still is present. I like just about everything going on in my life right now, here in September 2015.

We started this place with settlement money the GCC received. Manchester Bank set aside money for pending Feagin Dixon lawsuits. Once they got to know the firm they bought, they foresaw litigation raining from the sky regarding shady mortgages, extreme financial instruments, and, where the GCC came in, harassment and unfair pay practices.

An accrual or reserve was set up to hash this stuff out before the banks became one. For a brief while, the management of Feagin Dixon still ran the firm and settled these smaller issues before the deal closed. While a small rounding error in the face of the mortgage crisis numbers was to come, the GCC was handed $27 million. It was a lot of money with not one cent for me. I was too puzzled to sue and was unclear what exactly I was suing for. But my friends, yes friends, from the GCC were rich. They combined their settlement money to start this firm, and they chose me as their leader at a nice salary, which rocked my pride button more than any promotion I've ever received. We manage our own money and provide seed money to small, promising companies. We help them to grow and one of them has even come public. We aren't making millions but we're doing really well.

Why didn't I sue? That night I was racing from a Burger King in New Jersey to New York City, desperate to pick up the kids on time, I was supposed to have swung by a law office to join the other women in their complaint. I took the glass elevator up to Bruce's sex pad. Instead of him being mad, he fixated puppy eyes on me and acted like he was in mourning.

"So run and do your thing and leave the kids here tonight," Bruce had said in a tone far too nice for me to trust. He sounded so giving and borderline loving. He sounded like someone I used to know.

"Yes, but I'm late, and what if you use that against me?"

"Against you?"

"With the judge and all."

"Belle, we aren't living out some episode of *Kramer vs. Kramer.*"

"We're not?" I hated that Bruce was looking so well. I thought he'd get scruffy and fat. I had heard he broke up with his young girlfriend and hadn't dated since and was working. Some part of me wanted him eating Fritos on the couch and bankrupting himself.

"We're in this thing together," he went on, "and you got stuck in traffic or whatever, so no biggie."

"Yeah, traffic, or lost my rental car keys, actually," I said.

"You lost them? You don't lose stuff."

I remember thinking that even though I was still wearing the spiky boots and a nice suit, I was anything but hot-looking. I looked more like what I was, the bedraggled soon-to-be divorcée. I sat on his bottom step and Bruce instinctively bent over and pulled each boot off. They made a sucking sound as they detached from each foot and he laughed while we looked at each other awkwardly.

"Sorry," he said. "I forget who we are now."

"Yeah," I said, trying to change the subject fast. "Well, all I know about the keys is that they're still in New Jersey. Maybe underground."

Bruce lifted his eyebrows, making his face look adorable. "Underground? So how did you get to the city with no car keys?"

"I took a bus," I said. "Like on Buses of New Jersey or something. They offer very slow service."

When he gave me a slight smile, I suddenly remembered how I once loved this man. It all came back to me.

"Well, I think that subliminally you didn't want to be on time. You didn't want to sign on to any lawsuit," he said.

"Not true."

"You were treated poorly and you were treated great," he said, nailing exactly what I was thinking. Despite the sometimes insane working conditions, that place gave me a shot to move so far, so fast, at least for the first bunch of years. This was what I loved about Bruce. He could see through everyone and everything and then could tell me what I already knew about myself. I forgot he could do this. I forgot that once, Bruce had been my friend.

"I just didn't think that my getting money out of this was going to help change anything about Wall Street. I mean, how is paying *me* going to help the women coming behind me? Besides, I do like to move on."

"Yeah," Bruce said. "You move on fast." His eyes misted up.

I couldn't believe it. While this whole gut-throbbing, anxiety-plagued, crappy separation managed to bring me to my knees, and sometimes had me walking around teary and terrified, Bruce had shown as much emotion as the guy who collects toll money on the George Washington Bridge. I was starting to think he should date Kathryn Peterson just to see who could exhibit less feeling. But that night something was changing about him, or some feeling was returning to him. There we stood, on child-defying slate floors, with bad modern art canvases hung at finger-painting level, and he went gooey on me. I could tell the guy still loved me and I wanted to figure out a way to love him back. But I couldn't. Not then.

That was the night that Bruce and I became friends and he started growing up. He supported my decision to go live in the Tea Bag House, and to put the kids into a public school. Within three months he missed our joyful chaos far too much, so he gave up his bachelor pad and, I believe, his tantric yoga practice. He rented a quaint, tiny house in Southampton and planted a vegetable garden with the kids and got a job. He has a young, single, next-door-neighbor lady, who hits on him, leaves him cutesy notes and (gag me) casseroles. Really. A frickin' casserole with condensed soup as an ingredient, which I asked him to not serve the kids, as canned foods are a known carcinogen. That was my own way of saying, "Please don't take your neighbor's bait. Please. We may just still have a chance."

His job is designing and building furniture, mostly in fancy homes, and he even worked in King's house, which is no longer Amy's house, because Amy is in love with a really good man and going to be a mother. Bruce and I also never bothered to get divorced after this five-year pseudo-separation. Neither of us is dating anyone seriously, we just sort of work out a lot, run one-hundred-yard dashes on the beach together with the kids planted at the fifty-yard line. We don't have a caregiver. We look better than we did a few years ago, we're better parents, and we're good to each other. We flirt like crazy and we remember how to be kind. We're boring as hell, but aren't bored at all.

The few women heroines the Glass Ceiling Club had have all been taken down. Ina Drew, one of the top executives at JPMorgan, was responsible for a group that managed a $6 billion loss and became a very public casualty for women everywhere. Sallie Krawcheck got promoted to run the two wealth management divisions of Bank of America/Merrill Lynch and was touted as the most powerful woman on Wall Street, at least for a few months, and then got fired in what the company described, in original terms, as "delayering."

"Delayer my fucking wedding cake," Amanda had shouted at the television when the announcement was made, hurling a box of pencil erasers at it for good measure. Just last month, Bank of America was ordered to pay fines to the federal government of close to $17 billion for their role in the mortgage crisis. They never saw it coming but, as I think to myself sometimes, I did, and so, I believe, did Sallie.

The report continued, "According to Bank of America, Sallie Krawcheck has no immediate plans for the future."

"Get her on the phone!" shouted Violette, who, in the quiet of our own firm, has certainly found her voice. She is our largest producer. Who knew?

"She doesn't want to work with us," said Amy.

"She wants the fight," said Amanda. "She hasn't figured out the only truly successful women on Wall Street are at the small firms, where we can hold on to control."

"It's the Slaughter Rule," I said, referring to the most emailed story of 2012. Anne-Marie Slaughter wrote an article for the *Atlantic*, talking about why women still can't have it all, that they have to make compromises the men in their lives don't have to make. When she mentioned that having control of your own schedule was the only way to make it work, it suddenly made sense to me. Of course my not knowing how each day would unfold was the basis of so much anxiety. And when you start every day in some anxious state, you spread it like a toxic odor. Everyone in your zone can smell it—your spouse, your kids, the cabdriver getting you to the meeting too late. Who would want to be around that?

By the time that story was printed, I was long gone, already running this firm and still wondering about the Feagin Dixon days, wondering what happened to me and who, for those years, was that unrecognizable woman I had become, changing so many things I believed in, all to pursue some belief that I was getting my family ahead. I never did end up with that fat pot of money that was going to allow me to retire young, but life now isn't nearly as difficult. We don't worry about money and I also don't think I need a magical number in any savings account. We don't splurge much, but we also don't worry much, and living at the corner of No Splurge and No Worry is fine.

I'm looking through the glass walls into our boardroom, where Amy, in her seventh month of pregnancy, is leading a meeting with two marketing guys who'll be representing our firm overseas and raising some capital for us. Elizabeth is in there too. She coded some of the trading screens for us and they're spectacular even without the ability to front-run a trade. We use her as our consultant and she will soon join us permanently. She's still dating the guy from that brunch restaurant, the one she hadn't actually met at the time. He does have a name. It's Matt.

Clarisse is divorced now and has tried her hand at some other large New York firms. She has never gotten back to the director level at any major bank. Alice came back to work in our New York office and so did Kathryn Peterson. I rarely see Kathryn, as she mostly works from home, but that's what she needs. She continues to be exceptional at what she does. She invests our fixed-income money the old-fashioned way: she looks for value and yield and she buys and holds the bonds. I imagine her sitting cross-legged on her wooden floor, surrounded by candles, and knowing she is centered lets me know she's also doing the best job she's capable of. It's just how she works.

When I called Kathryn, trying to hire her, I told her secretary I was trying to reach Ms. Metis. The secretary told me nobody with that name worked there.

"Then can you please ask Kathryn where she's gone?" I asked.

Kathryn came on the phone quickly.

"How long have you known?" she asked, the closest to rattled I'd ever heard her.

"Since our walk," I said.

"What walk?"

"Our walk to your apartment when you said something about tribal knowledge. I knew I had read that term only once before, in one of the Metis memos."

Kathryn was silent.

"You were brilliant," I reassured her. "Very gutsy."

"I was brilliant." She laughed. She actually laughed. "That club thing wasn't for me, but you ladies sure did have a point."

"We did have a point," I agreed.

"Did you hear about Stone?" she asked.

"Stone? I mean, yeah, he got fired, but so did most people."

"Stone is Bob Dennis's grandson, you know, the CEO and owner of Monaghan Multimedia, the guy who gave Feagin millions in banking fees each year. That kid's gonna inherit a cool billion. No wonder he wasn't too motivated on your accounts. He was hired as a favor and knew it and anyway, Belle, he actually called yesterday."

"Stone called you?"

"Yeah, he wanted your phone number. Think he's looking to give a chunk of his fortune for you to manage."

"The little f-worder," I marvel. "How did I not figure that

one out?" For a second I think of how it'd be great to get a billion dollars under management at Arbella Financial, and then I reconsider.

"I don't want his fortune. I don't ever want to talk to him again. I'm listening more to my instincts these days, Kath. Some money costs too much."

She laughed again. "Isn't that the truth."

As for the leftover people from the younger crowd, most, like New Guy, went to start-ups, while people like Monty and King retired early. I see Naked Girl on Taxi TV, advertising a gym in New Jersey that she undoubtedly used her Marcus settlement money to launch. Her body appears to only have gotten better.

I'm not in touch with Henry. He is CEO of Cheetah and is often on television, providing pithy quotes and market insights. When Henry is on the television, the room becomes a corral of insults.

"Could your lips be any thinner?"

"Maybe you could adjust your hair one more time."

"How about those mortgages you shoved back in Feagin's face?"

And when I hear that, I make people shut up before we sound like we're back in the barnyard we formerly worked in. I used to wonder what happened to the apartment Henry imagined being ours, but now do not.

I still think about why I didn't pursue the lawsuit. The case was open-and-shut and the money was there for the taking. Sometimes, like a tired old lady, reliving her glory years, I raise the subject to whoever will listen. It's an ongoing joke. Last night I did it while Bruce drove our minivan to the beach for what he pleasantly called our "broken family workout." A shining, souped-up Land Rover cut in front of him and peeled through a red light, the driver's aggression palpable.

"Damn, I shoulda sued," I said, referring to the hotness of the car and the absurdity of the driver. "I could have been as cool as that guy if I drove a car like that."

"Here we go again," Bruce said, looking adorably at me. He flirts with me constantly. It's like one-way flirting because I'm holding on to my resolve to not screw anything up by screwing. I love our days together, love that he cooks dinner, love that he's respecting me again while the respect I lost for him grows by the day.

We really should be sleeping together, I thought as I looked at his beautiful hands on the steering wheel, but not until we know we're never parting again. I couldn't put my kids through that one again. I couldn't get through that one again myself, and besides, there is something delicious about the wait.

"You know why I didn't sue?" I asked.

"I know why you didn't sue, you lunatic," Bruce said.

"Tell me why," I said. "'Cause I don't think we've talked about this enough."

"You didn't sue because you didn't want to sign a non-disclosure agreement."

Kevin leaned forward, putting his head between the front seats, always looking for some sort of action from his parents. He's fourteen now and thinks he's a kid detective.

"What's a non-discloser agreement?" he asked.

"Noniscloserweeeement," says another little voice from the back, for no obvious reason. Owen still has an unusual way of speaking.

"A non-disclosure means you won't disclose, you won't tell any bad stories about someone or something. Usually you accept money to sign something like that," I said to Kevin, "and then you have to keep your promise and not tell any bad stories."

"And your mom," said Bruce. "Your mom didn't want to sign something like that."

"Because Mom wanted to tell the story?" Kevin asked, looking very much like he just figured something out.

"Yes, Kevin," I said. "Because I want to tell the story."

ACKNOWLEDGMENTS

Numerous times this manuscript was set aside and each time Steve Klinsky encouraged me to reopen the file. For hounding me with your love, all the way to the finish line, I'm very grateful.

To my mother, Kathleen Sherry, who could never have a conversation without asking, "How's that book coming along?" Dementia was a deadline that gave no extension and I truly regret not finishing this in time for you. Ditto for my father, James Sherry, who raised his girls on the north side of strong.

I thank William Klinsky and Hugh Boylan, who love to talk shop with me, and to Aunt Alice, who has spent her life dropping everything to pick up others, including small children and despairing adults. There's nobody like you.

To the women in my life with strong backbones, work ethic, and indefatigable humor: there has never been a problem we couldn't solve by walking or swimming it out. I include Nancy Hébert, Amy Goodfriend, Adele Malpass, Michele Lindsay, Cathy Price, Lisa Arnold, Vicky Elanowitz, Roxann Couloucoundis, Susan Dunne, Denise Hurley, Sara Hawes, Brenda Earl, Maryann Marston, Cynthia Remec, Kim White, Jane Pollock, Laurie Mandelbaum, Elizabeth McElroy, Colleen Surlis, Patricia Meehan, Hilary Polk, Shari Gluckman, Jill Lloyd, Monique Dana, Kathy Sherry, Laura Freeman, Katie Shah,

Acknowledgments

Maebh Brennan, Amber Turner, Kim Griffiths, Jennifer Hatch, and Jeanine Oburchay. Elements of you are within these pages. Thank you for allowing me in.

To the more open-minded bosses and coworkers I've had who wondered aloud about keeping working mothers on track: Mitch Jennings, Ricky Greenfield, Jolyne Caruso, Ace Greenberg, Jay Mandelbaum, Chris Lenzo, and Larry Kudlow.

I'm so proud to be with Simon & Schuster and thrilled to have the direction of my editor, Trish Todd, who with her sharp pencil and natural storytelling ability always had me feeling encouraged. For the editorial assistance of Kaitlin Olson and the fabulous production assistance of Ciara Robinson—thank you! To my agent, Melanie Jackson, who gave me the thrill of my life when she said, "Send me that manuscript." I thank you for your time and insight. Thanks to David Vise for encouraging me to make that phone call, and to Sandy Climan for his Hollywood insights. Another shout-out to Reese Witherspoon and Bruna Papandrea and the crew at Pacific Standard. Thank you for taking an early chance on me. You're all fabulous women who can somehow raise a family and move the world at the same time and I loved seeing toys in your office.

To the original Glass Ceiling Clubbers from Morgan Stanley, Goldman Sachs, and Bear Stearns: Your names are tucked away here and your secrets are safe, but your stories helped this book take flight.

To Rich Hogan, whose knowledge of derivative financial devices and work-life balance is astounding: I thank you for the tutorials on both.

I'm grateful for the help of Aripcy and Kevin Salazar, whose support made work possible. I thank Nicole Milazzo for being upbeat and beyond helpful about this project. Your insights as a decades-younger woman were invaluable and you always make me laugh.

For patient reading and suggestions I thank Matthew Klam and the Southampton Writers Conference. I'm also grateful to my earliest readers, including Carron Sherry, Lily Hogan, Kiera Klinsky, and especially Elizabeth Dennis, who thinks this is the story of her life, which it is not.

ABOUT THE AUTHOR

After twelve years at an investment bank, **Maureen Sherry**, a managing director, switched gears to earn her MFA, and then to write mysteries for middle school audiences (including *Walls Within Walls*). For many years she has tutored at inner-city schools. She is an active board member for several charities dedicated to public school transformation, and is passionate about educating women about money and working for environmental sustainability. Her biggest project to date is raising, together with her husband, four children and their assorted pets, which never feels like a job at all. She lives in New York City.